The
Storms
of Eddie Greer

MARY PERRINE

Water's Edge
Publishing, LLC

2023 Water's Edge Publishing, LLC
Copyright © 2023 by Mary Perrine
Cover design by TC Designs
Published in the United States
by Water's Edge Publishing, LLC, Cologne, MN

PRINTED IN THE UNITED STATES OF AMERICA

DEDICATION

To the people of McGregor, Minnesota.
*Where everyone knows your name
and loves you anyway.*

When I was in the hospital,
you drove 150 miles roundtrip to visit.

After my dad died,
you attended Father-Daughter events in his place.

When I cried, you held me.
When I fell, you picked me up.
Whether I lost or won, you cheered for me.

You modeled caring and compassion.
I learned those characteristics from you.

There was no better place to grow up.
You will always be my family.

The
Storms
of Eddie Greer

MARY PERRINE

PROLOGUE

Eddie

Cloud-to-ground lightning ripped the September sky in two, tugging the hairs on the back of Eddie's neck to attention and shredding his confidence in getting the hay off the field. Thunder instantly erupted, reverberating inside his chest and sending his heartbeat askew. Smaller flashes electrified the darkening sky. Tilting his chin upward, he shouted, "Screw you." He shook his fist toward the heavens. Eddie did not have time for Mother Nature's fury—not today, not ever.

The door of the nearly fifty-year-old tractor flew open. Missing a hinge pin, it hung slightly off-kilter. Cade jumped from the top deck. On the grace scale, the landing was nothing more than a two. He stumbled toward the decaying hay wagon and grabbed the edge. Beneath his hand, a piece of rotting wood gave way and was swept away in the wind. "Grandpa! We need to head in. The storm's getting too…"

"Are you scared?" Angrily, Eddie hoisted a hay bale onto the stack at the front of the decades-old wagon. "Get your ass back in that tractor, boy." Muscles bulged across the front of his denim shirt as he tossed another fifty-pound bale onto the growing stack. It did not faze him that his grandson had spoken his first words to him in more than five years. "You don't see anybody else runnin' like a little girl, do ya?" He jerked his head toward the battered tractor and glared at Cade. "Now stop being such a little chicken shit and do as you're…"

A second bolt zigzagged across the sky, slicing through the mid-morning murkiness. The pressure sucked Eddie's feet from beneath him and catapulted him off the wagon. His breath was snatched from him as he hit the ground, chest-first. He struggled for air, but his effort was hopeless. Black spots swirled before his eyes, slowly seizing his ability to see. But the last thing he saw before his world turned black was his grandson's lifeless body.

1

Eddie

Thirty minutes before the funeral, the small log church overflowed with locals. Shoulders were pressed together; some turned slightly sideways, making room for latecomers. Eddie could have named every person. Most he had known his entire life; others he had met through farming or the gossip grapevine. Like him, many had been born and raised in the tiny town of Holland Crossing. The majority had likely never ventured farther than Minneapolis. Most would spend eternity planted in the ground out back. The ever-expanding cemetery behind the church was a testament to that.

Eddie was confident he could not walk five steps through the graveyard without locating a schoolmate, a neighbor, or a townsperson. He would wager a bet he could find more than a handful of his past teachers on the grounds as well. But then again, that was only a guess. Unlike the rest of the town, church was not his thing. Oh, he believed in God, but the gathering to share in the community of religion angered him. Then again, it was not just church causing that reaction in Eddie—it was people in general. As far as he was concerned, they could all go to hell. But that would not happen because no one ever left Holland Crossing.

People did not stay in the area because of their deep affection for the town, the breathtaking lakes, or the unwavering sense of community. Instead, they put down roots because they did not know what else to do with their lives. They had no plans, no dreams bigger than those of their parents or grandparents. However, there *were* a few who wanted something better for the town, filling a need that could only otherwise be achieved through a day trip to the county seat of Ashton, the nearest city with a population of just under two thousand people. But that was nearly an hour away—time the farmers, business owners, and hourly employees could not spare. Others felt the pull of the small community: a friendly smile, a wave, a greeting, gatherings at the local bars, and school events. Staying answered the need for familiarity and a longing to be seen. Comfort was what held them there.

None of those reasons enticed Eddie to stay. He had never planned to spend one day longer than necessary in the remote town. Sometime during his junior year of high school, he began collecting boxes. As seasons and events passed, he packed. He planned to escape before anyone noticed. But things change, and plans and wishes are often overruled by those who have more authority, speak with the loudest voice, or carry the biggest stick. So, when the time came to walk, Eddie failed to launch. Not that he was incapable, but out of obligation to his mother. While he loved her immensely, he felt powerless to drive away. Every day since, Eddie woke to the pain of salt being rubbed into a gaping wound of regret and anger.

The unusually warm fall necessitated the back doors of the church to be propped open. He watched for a moment, but soon escaped the mourners cloaked in black. They all had tales to share about his grandson, but he wanted to hear none of them, so he turned away, rounded the corner of the church, and disappeared. There was no one he wanted to chat with; small talk was a knife to his heart. Growing up on the farm, rarely leaving, he had never been schooled in the art of socialization. But that did not stop him from knowing everyone in town. For Eddie, knowing people and liking them were on the far ends of the spectrum.

Contrary to what anyone else thought about him, Eddie missed nothing. He likely knew more about them than they knew about themselves—like *Joe Grayson let go of secrets halfway through his second drink. Jolene Clayborn was not only cheating on her husband, but she was also stepping out on her consort. And the Happy Bookers book club never read a single book. Instead, they spent meetings discussing the best gossip of the month and drinking wine.* Pleasantries were a waste of time for Eddie. He did not give a rat's ass about anyone here.

Eddie's hands were clammy. Searching for a place to wipe them, he pulled open his suitcoat and ran them down the lining. Multiple times, he whisked a hand through his hair, combing the lengthy mop of graying hair away from his face. Since before they married, Jules had been the only one to cut it, but she was barely speaking to him these days. Eddie knew enough not to trust angry people with scissors near his throat.

Foreboding music drifted through the propped doors. Eddie checked his phone for the time. He shoved it back into his pocket before crossing the threshold. He froze in the entry. Stepping through the next set of doors put him inside the church. Days ago, he had tempted fate…and lost on the hayfield. Had God been gunning for him but accidentally took his grandson? Was it possible a lightning bolt *inside* the church had *his* name on it? Eddie knew God would not miss twice. The first was a warning; the second was the real deal. But then again, Eddie was not even sure God knew who he was. For sixty years, he had hidden in the shadows and avoided anything remotely religious. If God truly knew him, He would not have missed the first time.

Scanning the pews, he recognized every person by the back of their head and the company they kept. The population sign at the entrance to Holland Crossing read *384*, but that number did not tell the whole story. The community stretched for miles in every direction, far beyond the signs: into other small villages, countless lakes, and massive farms. In the summer, the population swelled to nearly ten times that number, keeping businesses afloat with an influx of cash they depended on in the lean months after snowmobiling and ice fishing, but before cabin time—and again in the fall, between the end of summer and winter's burst of cold and snow.

This was the beginning of autumn. Those who summered in Holland Crossing had left, and the pulse of the town had slowed. Nearly every car that passed was a local. They were referred to as *friends*—even if they were not. In a small town, your life was an open book, and like the dead deer who met their demise on the narrow country roads, your privacy was picked clean by the gossipers. You were fodder for tales and lies by those so-called friends. As a kid, if you did something wrong, your folks knew about it before you stepped foot in your yard. As an adult, you were judged by prying eyes. It was for that reason Eddie kept his distance.

The people who filled the church were Eddie's *acquaintances*. There was no need for friends. Friends required a commitment he was not willing to give.

In Holland Crossing, funerals and weddings were a call to gather. The town virtually shut down so the locals could pay their respects—joy or regret. Nearly everyone came—just not Eddie. He could count on one hand the number of times he had stepped foot in the church since his eighteenth birthday: on his wedding day, his parents' funerals, and the day they laid their

28-year-old daughter to rest. When he exited the narthex, it would be the fifth. He would not have come had his estranged wife not guilted him into going.

He plunged his hands into his jacket pockets and cautiously stepped into the nave. Judging eyes followed him down the aisle as he trekked to the front of the church. Hands over mouths kept whispers corralled. But what difference did it make? They may as well have shouted it from the altar because, in seconds, they would repeat those exact words to the person on the other side, behind them, and in front. Eddie was the only one they would not tell. By the time he reached the casket, he speculated every tongue was thick with criticism.

The maple coffin housing his grandson's body was an overindulgence. Why would anyone waste money on something so intricate that would be hidden beneath twenty-five hundred pounds of dirt? The overpriced *box* had led to words between him and Jules. He stared at his 22-year-old grandson. Instead of apologizing, Eddie wondered how long he was supposed to stand at the casket before he could crawl into his pew and hide. Too long, and the self-proclaimed saints behind him would think he was making it about himself rather than honoring the boy. Too short, and they would question his disrespect for the deceased. Being on display made him extremely uncomfortable. He placed a finger inside the collar of his shirt and pulled, but its refusal to grant him breathing room annoyed him. Everything about the day irritated him.

After Cade's death, it took no more than a heartbeat for word to spread that *he* had forced his crew to work during the storm. Who but his men could have spread that message? Evidently, he was not paying enough for their loyalty. In the same breath of the telling of Cade's demise, someone let the rumormongers know his grandson had begged him to head in before the next bolt of lightning struck. He saw it in their eyes, the look of disgust. As far as they were concerned, the sole responsibility for Cade's death fell squarely on his shoulders.

As in any small town, judgment was a beloved pastime. And it was no different in Holland Crossing. The townsfolk turned it into a hobby, refining and polishing it until it shone—each one-upping the other with a flashier story of stupidity. Clearly, it was a talent to whisper about someone behind their back and show concern to their face.

As a lifelong resident of Holland Crossing, Eddie knew which people started the whispers and who fanned the flames to keep the rumors burning. Cellphones continuously pinged off cell towers as they kneaded the gossip into rising lies and innuendos. Eddie knew. This was not his first condemnation by the locals, and it likely would not be his last. Thirteen years before, it was another death for which people vilified him. And more than two dozen years ago, he had been blamed for the accident that paralyzed Mayor Thorp's son. He was not claiming responsibility for either of those. But defending himself against the fault-finding hypocrites who chose not to come to his rescue when he was a child was not a game he wanted to play. They could think whatever they wanted. At 60, sympathy or understanding was not something he needed.

His hand shook as he touched his grandson's cheek. He could not recall touching the boy—not even as a child. There had been no need. The responsibility for the boy's upbringing belonged to his mother and grandmother. The women had mollycoddled him, turned him into a softie, a whiny pantywaist. Until recently, Cade had been worthless on the farm. All those years, Eddie saw him as nothing more than another mouth to feed, a body to clothe. It was not about the money; there was plenty of that. Eddie did not like wasting it on something that would not give him a return.

Suddenly, his knees trembled. He clung to the side of the

casket. Before he fell into the pricey box with his grandson, he needed to sit. But if he was honest with himself, what he needed was a drink. Nearly every morning started with a shot glass and a bottle of whiskey. But this morning, he had opted for vodka. It still took the edge off, but Jules would not give him *that look* for smelling like a distillery at their grandson's funeral.

As he had suspected, all eyes were on him when he turned around. With one eyebrow arched, Eddie nodded at the congregation. After the blame game, it was more than they deserved. Stumbling, he grabbed the wooden panel at the end of the pew and stepped inside. He dropped onto the creaky bench next to his estranged wife. Jules slid away, leaving room for her anger between them. A side glance told him everything he already knew. Like everyone else in the community, she blamed him for the boy's death. But then again, there was not much she did not blame him for since they took their vows.

Jules daubed her eyes and blotchy face with a twisted tissue. Tiny pieces of white peppered her black dress. Eddie tried to tell her, but she slid away again. *So be it.* He folded his arms tightly across his chest and stared straight ahead.

He never thought to grab a handkerchief. Honestly, there was no need. Long ago, he had learned that internal and natural storms often blew up out of nowhere. Eddie had dealt with enough squalls in his lifetime to develop a hard shell. When they passed, as they always did, he would pick up the pieces and move on. Because if he did not, if he let them muscle their way inside to meddle with his emotions, they would never let him forget. Caring was something he could not afford to do. It would destroy him.

2

Eddie

Twilight faded from the morning sky as the sun crept above the horizon. Hank, Eddie's three-year-old yellow lab, was never farther than a step behind him as he wandered the kitchen in search of a notepad. Lists made sense. They were specific and attainable. Every item could be checked off, progress could be made. They did not allow for overthinking.

"Where in the hell would a guy find a piece of paper?" he grumbled.

Hank turned his head to one side and then to the other as if considering the question. Eddie rubbed the top of the yellow lab's head. "At least you don't want much from me, do you, buddy?"

Continuing to search, he jerked one drawer after another open but found nothing. *For the love of God, had Jules taken every scrap of paper in the entire house when she walked out on me?* With his hands on his hips, Eddie scanned the kitchen. The house had the earmarks of a ransacking, yet he did not notice. The opened drawers blended into the chaos of Eddie's life—since the day his wife abandoned him. Angrily, he unwound a sheet of paper towel and tugged. The corner let loose and took residency on the filthy floor. Eddie tore another section before grabbing a black marker from a cup of odds and ends.

Hank sprang onto the chair opposite Eddie. Tilting his head, he studied Eddie. From the moment the two met, they were inseparable. Except on rare occasions, the dog was never more than a step or two behind his master. Since Jules left, Hank slept on her half of the bed, keeping drool to a minimum. He was the ideal companion. Eddie, on the other hand, was not quite as flawless. But unlike Jules, the dog wanted nothing. Hank did not hold a grudge. Judgment, condemnation, and bitterness about the past were not entrenched in his character. He loved unconditionally. But then again, Hank was not old enough to have witnessed Eddie's decline into assholery.

With Hank still monitoring his every move, Eddie wrote *TO DO* at the top of the towel. The ink bled through onto the old oak tabletop. He lifted the towel and studied the words. For all he cared, he could have skipped the paper towel altogether and made the list on the scratched surface. Slumping against the chairback, he pondered what needed to get done before winter. But instead of focusing on the farm, his mind took side trips— traipsing through the past, stirring up troubling memories. Time and again, Eddie pulled himself from the black hole of despair, only to backslide seconds later. The marker spun in his fingers. It was a childhood habit that annoyed his teachers. After several deep breaths and a dozen or more starts and stops, he sent the towel and the uncapped pen flying.

The silence made his skin crawl. Since he had married, the house had never been without noise: the din of Jules whipping up breakfast, the driving beat of 70s rock and roll, or the hum of the washing machine. But all that ended six weeks ago—a month before their grandson's death. What felt odd to Eddie was that before Jules had anything significant to complain about, she walked away. No fight or negative word ever occurred. There had not been any words that day at all—until she walked into the living room with her suitcase. Calmly, she told him it was time. He asked if she was going on a trip. After scowling at him, she ended their marriage. Then, she picked up her bag and was gone.

Eddie had not gone after her; he had not even gotten off the couch until he heard the rev of her engine. Even then, he felt little as he watched her taillights through the kitchen window. When they vanished into the night, he went to milk the cows.

But even after her departure, there was still noise. Cade cooked meals—if you could call them that. They watched television in the same room, and the washing machine ran. Now the washer was broken, the door propped open, emitting a stench—much like his life.

Eddie worked the cork from the whiskey bottle. With one finger, he snagged the dirty glass from the other side of the table and blew into it before pouring the caramel-colored liquid. One drink was rarely enough. Two pushed the limits of a morning pick-me-up, but he indulged anyway.

Recorking the bottle, he grabbed his keys from the dish near the door and headed for his truck. Hank followed. There was work to be done. Eddie did not have a list, but he would figure it out. Except for his grandson being dead and his wife abandoning him for God knows what reason—the day was no different than any other of the forty-two years of running the farm.

Like a kitten, the truck purred to life. That is—if the kitten were fifty years old and had a smoker's hack. The old truck cut deep ruts into the saturated and neglected lawn as Eddie turned around before heading down the gravel driveway. When he came to the T, he stopped. Sweat beaded on his forehead beneath the filthy navy baseball cap. A left led him past the cornfields and out onto the highway. Right took him to the hay field. Too wet to work, he gave his crew the day off. Without them looking over his shoulder, he planned to go to town to pick up some chicken feed and drive to Ashton for a liquid lunch. As he pressed the gas, he meant to turn left, but instead, he jerked the wheel to the right, making a sharp off-road turn toward the hayfield. Halfway to the field, he passed the River House. Memories stirred, but there was no time for that bullshit right now.

At the hayfield, he slammed on the brakes. Hank lurched forward. The weight of the storm's memories beleaguered him, creating an upheaval of emotions. Eddie lifted his hat and wiped his forehead with the back of his hand. Being here weighed on him. He had not let himself care about much of anything for over forty years. He intended to pick up the last of the hay bales, but as he surveyed the field, he could not. This was where Cade had taken his last breath, where bits and pieces of memories rattled the cages of his locked-away feelings.

The old truck door returned a chunk of rust to the earth when Eddie slammed it, but he did not notice. His eyes were locked ahead of him on the decrepit wagon, the place the boy had met his maker.

A jagged breath cut through him; a horrible noise accompanied it. Anxiously, he glanced around to ensure there had been no witnesses. Like a geode, the fissures forming in his vile, tough-guy demeanor threatened to crack open and reveal the beautiful, soft heart he veiled years before. At 60, physical pain was undeniable. A throbbing back, a pair of achy knees, and sore muscles were part of a farmer's life. He was used to that. It was the emotional pain weaving through every thread of his being he couldn't handle. There wasn't an iota of his body that did not ache with anger, fear, longing, and disgust—or a tightly knotted combination of all four.

Cautiously, Eddie stepped onto the field. Hank leaned

against his leg. Not since his grandson's death had either set foot on the field. When he came to, he promised himself that this incident, like the other sixty years' worth, would be locked away deep inside. There would be no dwelling on it, no thinking about it—ever. Forward was the only way out. Looking back settled nothing. Except, that plan was not working. Since the funeral, his vault had been compromised, and his resolve undermined. Like the oil from the old truck, his emotions oozed out, and Eddie could not contain them. So he hid—from everyone.

Trudging across the field with Hank by his side, he stumbled. His feet were concrete blocks. The closer he drew to the wagon, the heavier they became. A ferning pattern cut across the ground, not where Cade had been hit, but where the first strike sent a warning.

Questions roiled inside him. *How had he not known another strike was imminent? But then again, even if he had, what could he have done?* It was too late by the time the lightning made itself known. They would have been lightning rods crossing the field. More people could have died.

"Son of a bitch," he muttered, shaking his head, disagreeing with himself. *Maybe people were right. Perhaps he was to blame for Cade's death. No. There was no maybe about it.*

Eddie and Hank slowly returned to the truck. Retrieving a rickety lawn chair from the bed, Eddie carried it onto the field. With a flick of his wrist, the chair fell open, and he dropped into it, completely unaware of the fraying webbing. And like Eddie, the chair would only hold so much before it gave way.

Emotions swirled around him—continuing to soften his protective shell. As much as Eddie did not want to admit it, they were winning. Maybe it *was* time he faced the ghosts of his past.

3

Eddie – 1966

The front yard captured Eddie's attention one hot summer afternoon. A balsa wood airplane, sans the rubber band, was attached to his hand for the better part of an hour. Eddie raced through the grass, blowing air between his lips to mimic the sputtering sounds of a small plane's engine. The lightweight toy rapidly dove up and down, necessitating imaginary airsick bags for the make-believe passengers.

Suddenly, Eddie froze. Pressing a hand to his brow, he gazed into the sky. The sun settled near the spot indicating his father's long-awaited arrival. Eddie tipped his head toward the driveway and cupped a hand behind his ear, listening for the old green farm truck bouncing down the gravel driveway.

The truck had been a secondhand purchase when his dad inherited the farm from his father in the late 1950s. Eddie prided himself on knowing it was a *1948 Chevy 2-ton*. Of course, knowing that and understanding it meant nothing to Eddie, but it always made his father smile when he announced the make and model to anyone who asked. There was nothing Eddie liked more than bringing joy to his father.

Once white, the scarred wooden platform and the slatted sides of the old truck were now gray, weather-won and rotting.

The grinding sounds of the engine, and the dents and gouges peppered with red and yellow flecks from old paint, told Eddie the truck was on its last legs. These days, it was only used for hauling cattle to and from auctions in Edgerton, eighty miles southwest of Holland Crossing. The rest of the time, it lived next to the barn.

"That truck's held together with hope and a prayer," his mother used to tell him. "One of these days, it's gonna hit a bump and crumble into a million pieces." Then, she laughed. "I don't know what your daddy's gonna do then."

On that day, they did not have to find out. Eddie heard the old truck turn off the highway nearly a mile from the house, gears grinding as it picked up speed, shifting from second to third.

"Daddy's coming!" He danced around the yard. "Daddy's coming, Mom!"

His mother wiped her hands on the front of her apron and pushed the creaky screen door open. "Listen, Eddie, you stay back until we see what kind of a mood your daddy's in. He's had a string of bad luck lately. I don't want you getting in his way and having him take his anger out on you. Do you hear me?"

Eddie nodded, but he did not heed her warning. As the truck approached, he ran through the grass at the edge of the drive, hoping his father would stop and let him climb onboard. But when his dad did not slow, Eddie made a U-turn and trailed it, struggling for breath amid the cloud of dust the tires kicked up. Finally, the truck came to a stop. Eddie leaped onto the running board and gave his dad his best smile. His old man grunted and shoved the door open, hitting him square in the face and hurling him to the ground. Caught off-guard, Eddie howled in pain. Tears mixed with blood from his nose, and he sobbed louder at the sight of the red drips. He swiped at the sticky mess with his shirt sleeve. A violent sob racked his little body, followed by a howl.

"Shut up, boy!" his father hollered. "You ain't nothin' but a big ole damn baby." Then, grabbing the front of Eddie's shirt, he jerked him from the ground. "You better grow up right quick, or ya ain't gonna be nothin' but some bully's punchin' bag."

"George," his mother clucked, "he's four. Let him be."

His dad glared at his wife. Eddie wrapped his arms around his mom and snuggled against her apron. "Shh," she softly uttered as she rubbed his back. "You're going to be just fine, Eddie."

"Oh, for God's sake, Elizabeth, you're making that boy soft. You're turning him into a baby." He tugged a chunk of Eddie's hair with his thumb and index finger, jerking his head backward and staring into his upside-down face. The awkward angle was painful. Eddie tightened his arms around his mom's waist to keep from falling.

"Daddy, you're hurting me," he whined.

George spit in his son's face. "Ain't nobody likes a wuss, boy. Nobody."

Eddie's face landed hard against his mother's hip when his father let go. He cried out in pain.

"I told you to shut up, boy." Angrily stomping up the front steps, George slammed the screen door as he passed through, only to return seconds later. Pressing his forehead against the already stretched screen, he grumbled, "Where the hell's my dinner, woman? When a man works all damn day, he should be treated like a king." He summoned Eddie's mother with his index finger. "Now get in here and make your king happy."

Quickly assessing the situation, Elizabeth bent down and whispered in Eddie's ear. "You go wash up and don't say one word at the dinner table unless your daddy asks you a question. Okay? And change your shirt before we eat. We don't need any reminders of what happened out here."

Eddie glanced at his shirt and nodded. This time, he was too afraid to disobey.

As they climbed the porch stairs and entered the house, he clung to the back of his mom's dress, hiding from the man he had happily thought of as *daddy* just minutes before. Once inside, he sidestepped around his mother and raced to the bathroom, hugging the side of the hallway like a frightened animal.

Scrubbing his face, taking great care not to relaunch the fountain of blood, Eddie replayed the scene with his dad. What had he done to anger him? He loved his father—maybe a little less now than before, but he was his dad. You could not hate your father, could you? Surely he would forgive Eddie for whatever crime he committed. Eddie had never seen him like that before, and he knew he did not want to see it again. Being loved was the only thing that mattered to him. And until today, he believed he was loved. Whatever he had done, he never wanted to do it again. If only he knew what that was.

His plate's blue and white pattern hid beneath the beef, carrots, and potatoes—swimming in a lake of gravy. The flood wasn't Eddie's doing; it was his father's. *No! No! No!* he silently screamed when his dad doused his plate with the thick brown liquid. Touching food set off panic bells—complete with a racing heart and wild eyes. His chest grew tight, and he held his eyes wide to keep his tears from falling, drawing unwanted attention. Finally, a whimper, held at bay by his clenched jaw, broke free. He froze; his father did not.

"Eat, dammit!" his father ordered. "Eat it all, or you can go to bed hungry. I'm sick and tired of your stupid issues."

His father poured some red juice into a glass with one long

leg. Eddie got a whiff. The smell was sharp and smelled like his father's breath when he had jumped on the truck's running board.

His mom rested her hand on his dad's and leaned toward him, drawing his attention away from Eddie. "How was the auction today, George? Did you get the price you wanted for the cattle?"

His father rammed a forkful of food into his mouth and shook his head before turning again toward his son.

"Dammit, boy! I told you to eat!" The table jumped under the weight of his father's heavy fist. Gravy sprang from his plate and splashed Eddie's face, but he dared not reach for his napkin.

Trenching his fork through Eddie's plate, his father thrust it toward his son's mouth. Eddie tightened his lips, and the food dribbled down the front of his shirt. Cowering, he held his breath. Waiting. Fearing for what was to come.

His dad's chair crashed to the floor, and he sprang to his feet. "I said EAT!" Again, he slammed his fist on the scarred table, and again the thick brown liquid leaped from the plate.

"George, leave the boy…"

"Shut up, woman." He poked a finger toward his wife. "Don't you be tellin' me how to raise *my* kid. You sure as hell ain't done a very good job so far. Look at him." His father circled behind him and bent low, pressing his face against Eddie's. "You're a pussy, boy. A namby-pamby. Ya ain't gonna amount to a hill of beans in this world."

Again, George plowed his fork through his son's plate and tilted the boy's head back. He squeezed Eddie's cheeks open and thrust the fork inside. Eddie squirmed as his father pressed his hand over his mouth.

"Swallow, boy!"

Tears trickled down Eddie's cheeks as he tried to get free. Finally, he grabbed his fork and plunged it into his father's hand before twisting out of his chair and escaping. He raced from the room and crouched behind a small partition so he could keep an eye on his mother.

She clicked her tongue. "Just because you had a bad day, you don't have to bring it home to the rest of us." She picked up Eddie's plate. "He's just a little boy. He'll have plenty of time to realize how cruel this world can be." She scowled at her husband. "I'm sure he'll learn that from you soon enough. For now, he just needs you to love him."

George daubed the blood off his hand with his napkin. "Love him? It's hard to even like that little a-hole. You've ruined him, Elizabeth. Don't you see that? You don't even call him by his God-given name—Edward. It's a manly name, a name any father would be proud to call his son. But you don't. You keep calling him that bullshit baby name, for God's sake."

His mother's jaw clenched. "Why do you care, George?" Her eyes hardened as she stared at him. "I've never once heard you call him Edward, Ed, *or* Eddie. You always call him *boy*."

His dad reached over and snatched a handful of his wife's auburn, chin-length hair. Eddie could see the pain on her face, but she never looked away. Finally, he let go. "Don't you correct me, woman—not ever." He pulled his hand across his body, threatening a backhand to his wife's face. "You've coddled that boy so damn much, he don't even know how to eat proper." He grabbed his son's plate from his wife. "Well, then, he can just go hungry."

Like a frisbee, the plate sailed toward the sink, spewing gravy across the kitchen before it smashed against the cupboard door and shattered. A permanent scar branded the wooden panel.

His father sneered at his mother before calmly righting his chair and settling in to finish his dinner. He shook out his cloth napkin and casually laid it across his lap before grabbing her upper arm and pressing his filthy nails into her soft skin. "Now, clean up this mess while I enjoy my dinner in peace. *Peace*," he warned.

The first of George Greer's rages reared its ugly head. Unfortunately, there would be many more to come. Eddie knew he would have to shoulder the responsibility of keeping his mother safe for the rest of his life.

4

Eddie

With the toe of his boot, Eddie hooked the chair leg, slid it out, and dropped into it. The whiskey bottle, the same fingerprinted glass with a modicum of liquor in the bottom, and Hank's bowl were the only items on the table—the necessities of Eddie's world. He grabbed the open bottle and held it over the glass. But instead, he swiped a hand across the table and sent the tumbler flying. Upending the bottle, he took a long draw—then, a second and a third—wiping his mouth on the back of his hand between each drink.

As usual, Hank occupied the chair across from him. Eddie snorted. "Et tu, Brute." He chuckled, recalling the line from *Julius Caesar*. Like Caesar, everyone was against Eddie. Other than the basics, that was one of the few things he remembered from high school. Somehow, he had tucked that particular line away for forty-plus years. But what a waste. When the opportunity to finally proclaim it, Hank was the recipient—a dog who cared only about a handful of things: eating and crapping, but not necessarily in that order.

"Stop judging me, boy." He scowled at the dog and took another swig, draining the last of the bottle. "I didn't think you were like the rest of them." He swung the container from left to right and back again, indicating the entire world.

Hank rested his chin on the table and let out a soft sigh. His mouth curved down. "Sorry, boy. I shoulda known better. You're not like the rest of them arseholes."

Eddie pressed the empty bottle to his lips and tilted his head back. Not a drop gave way. "Dammit!" He poked his tongue inside the narrow opening. Then, in the same way the glass met its end, he hurled the bottle across the room. It crashed against the cupboard door before landing upright. He grinned at the feat. Surely, it was worthy of praise.

"Did you see that, Hank? Did you see that?" The unimpressed dog didn't even lift his chin from the table.

From the previous morning, the words TO DO were visible on the table; they grabbed his attention. Eddie poked a finger into the air. There was something he could add. With his grandson gone, Eddie needed to hire another farmhand. Spying the black marker, he leaned out of his chair and snatched it from the floor. Below the title, directly on the table, he attempted to write—*Hire a new Cade*. But the tip was dried out, so Eddie scratched the words onto the tabletop. To Eddie, his grandson, like everyone else in his life, was expendable.

For survival's sake, Eddie viewed everything as a job—something he had to do to keep the wheels on the bus turning: farming, shopping for supplies, driving. Even his marriage was just a task—something Eddie could now check off as completed. He gouged a large checkmark into the table below the only item on his list. *Done.*

Slamming the marker on the table, he thought about Jules and his marriage. *Who the hell set the rules for marriage anyway? Who decided it should be full of mushy-ass shit all the time?* As far as he was concerned, marriage was about doing your damn job. The woman cared for the house and the kid, and the man did everything else. If no one deviated from their role, there would not be a problem. Rules were cut and dried.

The world would be better if people ran their lives like a business, if they thought with their brains instead of their hearts. Deciding anything with your heart was a big mistake. To survive, you had to use your head. As with a fire, stirring the pot caused more sparks, expanding flames, and creating the possibility of spiraling out of control. And once that happened, it left scars, memories into the soul. On the hayfield the day before, that was where Eddie landed—in the middle of a fire, surrounded by embers which kept igniting memory after memory.

After his emotional breakdown the day before, with Hank as his witness, he promised himself he would lock everything back up again, stuff it so far down, it would never see the light of day. But that was then. Because this morning, the more times the clock ticked, the more his feelings began to override his pledge. He could not shake them. And Hank was not helping the situation with his mournful face and judgmental eyes. If Hank had fingers, Eddie was positive he would point one toward him—and there was little doubt which it would be.

The heat of the booze initially warmed his stomach and was slowly meandering into the rest of his body. The tightness of anger he felt earlier turned to a numbness, erasing his ability to focus on anything longer than a few seconds. Plucking a second nearly empty bottle of whiskey from the counter, he headed toward Cade's room. The big dog lumbered up the dangerously steep stairs behind him. Eddie clung to the handrail, clutching it tightly to avoid tumbling backward.

Sliding along one wall of the narrow hallway, Eddie came face to face with the white door that once bore a sign claiming his ownership. Two nail holes were the only memories of the wooden sign his mother had painted. Shoving the door open, Eddie sniffed the air. The room was nearly the same as when he was a child. It had the same damp and musty odor mingled with a third unknown stench that had existed since the beginning of time. Rotting wood? Animal crap? Dead vermin? Whatever it was, it was there to stay.

Eddie slammed his hand against the slanted ceiling. Mice skittered behind the wall. Nothing had changed. The mice, bats, and most likely garter snakes shared meals of insects behind the protection of the lath and plaster walls of the late 1800s farmhouse. From his childhood, he knew they visited the house at night when the moonlight filtering through the curtains allowed them to hide in the shadows. There were signs.

A cockroach skittered out from beneath the bed. Eddie lifted his foot and smashed it. The crunch was so loud, Hank let out a small bark.

"Anybody else?" he grumbled. He stamped the floor and waited for additional scurrying noises to pass. "I didn't think so."

With the toe of his boot, he launched the remainder of the cockroach beneath the bed. Then, he wiped the sole of his boot on a brown and gold braided rug before dropping onto the edge of the bed. The bed creaked beneath his hundred and eighty pounds. A puffy multicolored quilt covered the twin mattress and metal spring frame. It was another piece of nostalgia, a feeling Eddie fought to keep at bay. The quilt was so old, dust mites had ensconced in it before he inherited it from the previous resident—his father. Who knew what lived in it now? Had his grandson not died from the lightning strike, he would probably have perished from the filth that moved in.

According to family lore, his Grandma Hazel made the quilt from her old silk stockings and pieces of his Grandfather Walt's work shirts, all of which had seen better days. By the time a piece of clothing made it to the quilt pile, it was damn near threadbare. It appeared either his mother or Jules had hand stitched the holes closed dozens of times over the years. The thread did not always match, and there were odd-shaped patches over some of the bigger holes, some of which he recognized as his old shirts. The recycled pieces intermingled with his grandfather's and his father's—three generations of Greer men tied together with bits of thread and yarn—and generations of anger. Rage welled inside of him. The last thing he ever wanted was to be tied to his father. But then again, the entire farm shackled him to the very thing he hated.

Eddie jumped up and jerked the comforter from the bed. He balled it up and shoved it into one end of the closet. He understood why Jules kept it, but just the thought of it disgusted him. According to his wife, you did not discard perfectly usable items. Like everything else that was part of the original farm, Jules was not about to say goodbye to any of it. She had said more than enough goodbyes in her lifetime.

After sniffing around the room, Hank collapsed in the doorway. He rested his head on his front paws and stared at Eddie.

"That's the way I feel, Hank. Your mom never wanted to get rid of anything. Well, except for me." Once again, he sat on the old bed. It bounced under his weight.

Eddie twisted the cork from the bottle, helping himself to another swig of *trying to forget*. Wiping his mouth on his sleeve, he glanced around the room. A framed photo of Cade's girlfriend held center stage on the nightstand. He jerked the top drawer open and swept the picture and several mouse turds inside. She was just another reminder of the bad decision-making Eddie was capable of.

Narrowing his eyes, he tried to recall seeing Amber at the funeral. She must have been there, but he could not place her at the church or gravesite. But then again, it was not like he was paying much attention to anything except getting home to his old friend—Jack Daniels.

"Ed?" a gravelly voice floated up the stairs. "You in here?"

After gulping the last swallow of whiskey, he shoved the bottle under the bed. "Yeah. I'll be down in a minute."

Swiping a piece of gum from Cade's desk, he shoved it in his mouth and chewed it for a few seconds before spitting it into the brown woven trash can. He held his hand in front of his mouth and blew into it. Sniffing the air, Eddie cringed. What made him think a piece of gum would cover the smell that never seemed to disappear? If he had to guess, he would say he sweated whiskey.

Half drunk, standing at the top of the stairs, Eddie realized how narrow they were. Like maggots on rancid meat, the stairs moved in front of him. The house was built long before building codes, long before people considered safety over space. There were a lot of things that would no longer fly with the county. Most likely, the farmhouse and the outbuildings could all be condemned.

Nearing the middle of the long staircase, Eddie stumbled when the black rubber tread slipped from the step. He skidded down the stairs, feeling the heel of one untied boot skip along the edge of every step on the way down. Snagging the banister, Eddie regained control—until it broke free from the wall, sending him bouncing down the last of the steps on his keister. Mortified, he sprang up and kicked the newel post, faulting it for his embarrassing descent.

"Geez, Ed. You okay?" Buzz asked, moving toward him.

"This damn house is falling apart." Again, he took a shot at the post. "It's nothin' but a piece of crap."

His farm manager snorted softly. "Well, the farm ain't doin' a whole lot better, Ed. Your old man never replaced anything unless it was with something nearly as old and was only hanging on by one more thread than the last one." He looked his boss directly in the eyes. "And I wouldn't say you've done much better."

Eddie ignored the dig. He was more focused on the monumental charley horse attacking his backside and controlling the pitch of his voice. Cautiously, he turned away from his right-hand man.

He released the breath he was holding as the cramp faintly released its grip. Eddie turned toward Hank, tentatively stepping in the dog's direction, hoping for the best but preparing for the worst. Stepping was easier than walking. Composing himself, he shifted his weight to his good leg and faced Buzz.

Eddie slapped him on the shoulder. "It's not my job. You're the one who's supposed to be keeping this place running. I just write the checks and touch base when I see fit."

Buzz nodded. "I get that, but you can only patch things for so long, boss." He scanned the house. "It might be time to quit patching and start replacing."

Ignoring him, Eddie and Hank headed toward the kitchen. "So, what'da ya want?"

"Just wanted to give you a heads-up that I'll be gone for a bit. I'm heading into town. Need fuel and grain for the chickens." He smirked. "Kinda thought you were gonna take care of that yesterday."

Finally, Buzz held a bowl of eggs for his boss to see. He opened the fridge and frowned. "Not eatin' much, are you? You gotta do something with all these eggs, Ed. They're gonna go bad. If you want, the girls could sell 'em out by the highway this weekend."

"Whatever. For your information, I cooked breakfast for Hank just this morning."

Buzz nodded toward the filthy kitchen. His mouth opened, but Eddie shot him a warning glare, so he closed it again. "Need anything from town?"

"Naw." Eddie grabbed the coffee pot. His hand trembled too much to pour a cup without question, so he returned it to the burner. "On second thought, yeah. Pick me up a loaf of cinnamon bread from the bakery. And, ah, grab me a bottle of whiskey from Matt's."

Buzz laughed. "I'll get the bread, but Matt's don't open 'til noon. And I ain't hangin' around that long."

Eddie nodded. "Well, just the bread, then."

Hank unleashed a yip, pitchy enough to make Buzz jump.

Eddie looked at his dog. "Right. Pick up a bag of dog food while you're at the feedstore."

Buzz studied Hank. "You got that from his bark?"

"Yeah. That, and the dog food bag's been empty for a good week." He folded his arms across his chest. "Course, I don't think he cares. He got a half dozen eggs and a slab of ham yesterday." His shoulders rose and dropped. "But then again, today's breakfast was a bowl of Wheaties and a handful of rotten strawberries."

Buzz rubbed Hank's snout. "Don't worry, boy. I got you covered."

Eddie paged through the stack of mail Buzz set on the table.

"What's on your agenda for the day?" Buzz asked gently.

"Headin' out to the hayfield."

Buzz's eyebrows pressed together. Two deep lines appeared, one near each brow. "I don't know, Ed. A little time away from there might be good for you. It's not…"

Eddie's nostrils flared. "Shut the hell up. I didn't ask for your opinion, did I?" He jerked the heavy wooden door open, grabbed Buzz's arm, and shoved him toward the opening. "I'm not payin' you to stand around and piss me off. Now, get back to work."

The door slammed shut behind Buzz.

Eddie pulled a metal flask from his inside jacket pocket. He opened his beverage cupboard and retrieved the last full bottle. With unsteady hands, he poured some into the flask. Not a drop missed the container. Whiskey was the one thing he would never waste.

After slipping into his coat, he slid the flask back into his pocket. Its mere presence gave him a sense of security he found nowhere else. Maybe he was a drunk. Maybe he used alcohol to survive. Or maybe he used it to dull the pain of the past— pain that seeped through every generation, trickling down to his grandson.

"Thanks, Grandpa Walt." In acknowledgment, he lifted his chin toward the ceiling and winked. "You turned the Greer men into some pretty pathetic humans, but at least we inherited the ability to find bliss in a bottle of whiskey."

He jerked the door open. "Come on, Hank. We've got things to do."

Between the fall down the stairs and the drive to the hayfield, Eddie's stomach sloshed and threatened to erupt. He had barely opened the door before his gut exploded. It was all liquid.

"Damn! What a waste." Eddie stared at the ground. "What a frickin' waste of a few Hamilton's and good liquor."

By the time Eddie settled on the hayfield, his stomach had calmed, but his mind had not.

5

Eddie – 1970

What good was math, anyway? It was not like Eddie would need it for anything he wanted to be when he grew up. At eight years old, his entire life was planned: a few years in the major leagues and then off to college to become a psychologist. He had learned about that job from the confidential meetings his teacher made him attend with Mr. Janki—sessions he was not allowed to mention to anyone. Eddie liked the older gentleman with big ears and a wart on his cheek the size of an M&M. It was the first time Eddie had ever felt seen by someone other than his mother.

Eddie knew his family needed help. The demons pervading his dad and causing his mom to allow the man to belittle and abuse her needed to be expelled. If his parents refused to get help, Eddie would bring it to them. He sighed loudly. Intervention was required, but math was not—at least not for his career goals, not for the perfect woman he would marry when he turned twenty-five. He already named his one-day wife *Becca*. And she may or may not be a real person, sitting two chairs in front of him in Mrs. Aase's class.

Eddie spun a ten-problem math worksheet in a circle on the table. When he grew tired of that, he rolled the paper around his pencil enough times for the page to form a tiny telescope. Then, pressing one end to his eye, he watched his mom finish the last of the dinner dishes.

He sighed loudly, begging for assistance without words. But none came, so he tried again—still nothing. Problem-solving was the worst. No one cared that Fred bought thirty-five oranges, Rick purchased forty-eight, and Polly picked up four more than the other two together. And no one gave two hoots how many people each got half an orange when Donna cut and shared them at her birthday party. It was ridiculous to believe anyone bought that many oranges. Besides, no store in Holland Crossing would even have that many for sale, proving his point that math was stupid.

Unrolling the paper, he flipped it over and rolled it in the opposite direction, attempting to flatten it. Even if Eddie finished all ten questions, he would be docked points for messy work. He rolled his eyes before reading the third problem, searching for one he could solve without short-circuiting his brain. The pencil, scarred with dozens of teeth marks, twirled like a baton in his fingers, and he pondered the work ahead of him.

The drain gurgled as the water escaped from the sink. His mother dried her hands on the dish towel and leaned against the cabinet, pressing her fists into the small of her back, massaging the knots with her knuckles. A smile lit Eddie's face. Inside her protruding stomach was his baby brother or sister. Finally, there would be someone to play with. Then, just as quickly as the joy appeared, his mouth straight-lined. That meant there would also be someone to commiserate with. Eddie felt terrible for the new Greer kid. He dropped his pencil and climbed off his chair to hug his mother. He knew she was equally concerned; he saw it in her frown lines. Carefully, he rested his head against her stomach and whispered his loyalty and protection.

The screen door shot open, and his father appeared. "Get up, boy. What's wrong with you anyway? You're contaminating the new kid. I'll bet you a dollar to a donut the kid comes out a whole hell of a lot better'n you." He grabbed Eddie's chin, jerking it upward. "Know why? 'Cause I ain't gonna let your ma ruin this one. Unlike you, this one'll be worthy of the Greer name one day." He shoved Eddie's face to the side. "I can't even look at you, boy. You disgust me."

Neither Eddie nor his mom spoke. In the four years since his dad lost his battle with the bottle, they knew when to keep quiet and when to speak. Eddie tightly squeezed his eyes shut and willed himself not to cry. His mom touched his cheek and nodded toward the stairs. Clutching his homework and the battered pencil, he made a beeline from his father's sight. Over the years, he learned the best way to protect his mother was to make himself scarce. If he were not around, there would be little to disagree about. Eddie often wondered if disappearing forever would make his father happy.

"And don't come back down 'til you got your work all done, boy."

The bedroom door closed harder than he intended, and he flinched. There was little chance his father missed the bang. Preparing to be whipped, he pressed his ear to the door expecting heavy footsteps. Instead, what filtered through the thick panel with the wide crack in the middle was his father once again cussing out his mother. After listening for a minute or two, Eddie moved to the far corner of his room and slid down the wall. Pressing his hands over his ears, he rocked back and forth until only moonlight lit the room. Eventually, he pulled a hand away but heard nothing. Quietly, he opened his door. His mother's quiet sobs floated across the hall.

His heart banged in his chest as he crossed the narrow space. "Mom?" The door creaked when he pushed it open to peer inside. The room was dark, too dark to see anything. Was his father hiding somewhere, ready to pounce? Eddie needed to be brave for his mom, even if it meant fighting his dad. It took him a few moments to find her on the bed. No matter how exhausted she was, his mother never rested lying down.

Eddie crawled onto the bed and whispered, "Mom? Mom, what's wrong?"

The downstairs door opened, and Eddie jumped from the bed and dashed across the hall. He was chicken-shit, a pussy, as his father called him. Standing up to his dad was something he only dreamed of. Today, that dream would not come true.

He turned the knob gently and closed his door without a sound before pressing his ear against it. The footsteps were light. He let out a sigh of relief.

"Elizabeth?"

Mona Woods, their nearest neighbor, tiptoed into his mother's room. Soft voices seeped across the hall but were too faint to decipher. Finally, there was a gentle tap on his door. Eddie jumped backward before it swung open.

"Eddie, honey, your mom's sick. I need to take her to the hospital."

High-pitched static filled his ears. Alarm bells rang inside. "W-what's wrong with her?" His heart raced, and he rubbed his clammy hands together. "I-I need to see her." He took off toward his parents' bedroom, but Mona caught him by the arm before he passed through the door.

"Honey, your mom needs to rest. You don't want her to worry about you, do you?" Her voice grew soft. "Listen to me. Right now, the best way to help her is to be brave. Can you do that?" Eddie nodded. "I need you to pack a suitcase. Dan's on his way to get you. Think of it as a fun sleepover." He peered around Mona toward his mom's room. "Eddie, do you understand?"

An internal vibration raced through him. "Y-yes, ma'am."

"Pack quickly. Dan'll be here any minute."

Tears threatened to explode. "I-I don't have a suitcase. I've never stayed away from home before," he whimpered.

Mona opened his closet. She grabbed a paper bag and flipped it upside down. Pinecones, rocks, feathers, and other treasures Eddie had taken great care to collect dropped onto the floor.

"Use this for now. I'll sew you a new treasure bag."

Eddie's lip quivered. "W-where's my dad?" he asked as he peeked down the stairs.

"Don't worry about him, honey. He's... Well, he's...busy."

Minutes later, Eddie shared the backseat of Dan's car with a torn paper bag brimming with clothes and Winston, his brown teddy bear. Kneeling on the seat, with his chin pressed on the rear deck, he watched Mona come out of the house with his mom. Something was seriously wrong, but no one was brave enough to tell him. This was a story problem, not unlike the ones on the sheet he had forgotten in his bedroom. *If your mom got sick, and it was a long way to the hospital but even farther from the neighbors where you are staying, how far are you from her?* The answer was simple. *Too far.*

When Mona drove him home several days later, his mom was there. Excitement erupted inside of him—until he saw her face. He barely recognized her. Her eyes were empty—like she did not live inside anymore. It made him want to cry.

Eddie wrapped his arms tightly around her waist, but she did not respond. Instead, her arms hung at her sides. Mona told him the baby was living in heaven, but he did not believe it until now. His mom's stomach was smaller and spongier than before she got sick, and he no longer felt his brother or sister greet him with a foot or elbow to his cheek. He squeezed tighter, willing her to hug him, but she did not.

He began to cry. A tightness in his throat made it nearly impossible to swallow. If he lost his mom, there would be no one to protect him from his father. For the first time, Eddie seriously considered making himself go to heaven. He did not know there was a name for it until he was older—*suicide*. But the longer his mother ignored him, the greater the desire became.

6

Eddie – 2 Weeks Later

A heaviness pressed down on Eddie. He often wandered the farm imagining ways he could die and end this stranglehold that made him feel everything, yet nothing at all.

Like the sound of humming into a fan, everything in his life was distorted. Instead of soft music from the old radio in the kitchen, the house was eerily silent. He swallowed his words rather than chance being ignored when he wanted to talk. Since his mom's return, she had not uttered a single word. Pain twisted her face, aging her far beyond her thirty-three years. She was so thin, she looked as fragile as a butterfly's wings. Her shoulders scooped forward, and her eyes rarely tracked anywhere but down. Once, they had sparkled, but now they were rimmed in a deep shade of brownish purple. And on the rare occasion she faced Eddie, she looked right through him. He wondered if she would ever see, hold, or love him again. His heart ached, and a lump permanently lived in his throat. At times, he could barely breathe. Often, he did not want to.

However, even in this state, her work was never left undone. The house was spotless, and their clothes were always clean. Meals hit the table on time but were shrouded in complete silence because he was the only one who sat. Eddie never ate enough to warrant the time she spent cooking.

Several days passed before Eddie's father's sudden reappearance. By then, rumors swirled through the schoolyard. Frank, the school bully, called his dad a baby killer. Eddie did not want to fight—not because Frank was a head taller and had arms as thick as oak trees—but because his father was not worth defending. But, when Frank threw the first punch, all the anger Eddie harbored inside rushed out as he whaled on the tyrant. Words that would have embarrassed his mother landed between his punches, and he tucked his head down and drove all fifty-three pounds of Eddie Greer into the bully's stomach. By the time the playground supervisor and principal pried them apart, Eddie was covered in his own blood and had a missing tooth and the beginnings of a shiner. Frank, on the other hand, was not even breathing hard. That was the moment he decided his dad had been right all along. He was worthless.

The school called his house multiple times before finally contacting Mona. She arrived in her 1969 Cutlass to chauffeur him home for his three-day suspension. It was the fanciest car he had ever ridden in, but he was too ashamed to enjoy it.

His mom did not even venture downstairs when Mona dropped him off. For three days, he tiptoed around the house, unsure if she knew he was home.

A second week passed before his father returned. He was dressed in the same clothes he was in the day his mom went to the hospital. The smell of booze had faded, but his malevolent remarks were still plentiful. Day in and day out, Eddie suffered the brunt of his hostility. His stomach churned with fear, afraid that if there were any truth in Frank's words, he could be his father's next victim. Eddie wavered between never wanting to face another day without his mother and fearing a fate he could not control. That night, and almost every night, he cried himself to sleep, not caring how much of a baby that made him.

When he arrived home from school the following day, his mom was lying face-down on the sofa. He called her name and poked her shoulder, but she did not respond. Shaking her elicited no response either. He pressed his face next to her ear and whispered he loved her, but she did not move.

"Mom," he begged. "Mom, wake up. Please wake up," When he heard her draw a breath, the tightest morsel of relief washed over him. At least she was not dead; she had not left him with his miserable father. His mother's possible death was a new scenario he now felt compelled to worry about. Not wanting to leave her alone, he lay on the floor next to the couch and held her hand. That was where his dad found them an hour later.

"Oh, for God's sake, woman, where the hell's my dinner?" he bellowed when he walked through the empty kitchen and into the living room. He shook his head and stared at his wife's back. "How the hell long's she been like this?"

Eddie shrugged.

"For God's sake, use your words, boy." He shoved his boot under his son's hip and pushed him away from the couch. "And get off the floor, you nitwit. You weren't born in a barn."

His father grumbled as he poked and prodded his wife to no avail. Finally, he traipsed upstairs and returned ten minutes later with a small green, hard-sided suitcase. He thrust it at his son.

"Get your ass in the car, boy, and take this with you."

His dad pulled her into a sitting position and struggled to punch her limp arms through the sleeves of her coat. She looked like a life-size ragdoll. Her bones appeared to have turned to rubber.

"Where're we going?" Eddie asked softly.

"Where're we going?" his father mimicked in a high-pitched voice. "Shut your trap for once, will ya?"

Eddie's father bent forward and rested his wife's waist on

his shoulder. He hoisted her off the couch and carried her to the door. By the time his father got her into the front seat and folded her legs inside, his breathing was loud and labored.

The car ride lasted nearly as long as an episode of *Gunsmoke*. Other than on the school bus, Eddie had never ridden in a vehicle for longer than ten minutes. He barely stepped foot off the farm. Several minutes later, they passed through the tiny town of Tilden. Eddie wondered where they kept the ninety-seven people the city limits sign laid claim to. Moments later, on the highway headed to who knew where, he stretched out on the bench seat and closed his eyes. The hum of the car lulled him into a deep sleep. Dreams of his mother cooing at a baby made him laugh. He did not wake until his father slammed his door, returning him to his reality.

The name on the sign was long, but Eddie had always been good at reading. *Milford Creek State Hospital*. Hospital? Was his mom sick again? Was that why she would not wake up? Maybe the doctor could give her a pill to fix whatever was wrong with her. He let out a long breath. Maybe by the time they left, she would see him, hug him, and love him again. He could only hope.

Eddie attempted to crawl out of the car, but his father roughly plunked a hand on his head, shoved him back inside, and slammed the door. He quickly rolled down the window. A cold wind blew into the car, but he refused to close it.

His dad pulled his mom out the same way he put her in. "One crazy in the family is enough, boy, don'tcha think? If they see you, they'll wanna keep you, and I ain't paying for that. Lord knows you're both nuts, but I can only deal with one of you crazies at a time."

Eddie's heart sank. He clung to the window as he watched his dad usher his mother away. Her feet touched the ground, but she did not take a step unless she was forced to. In one hand, his father carried her suitcase. The other he pressed into the middle of her back, pushing her toward the door.

"Bye, Mom!" he shouted. "I'll be waiting in the car when you get back."

His father turned around. "Shut up! You'll be lucky if this lunatic ever comes back."

Minutes later, his dad returned to the car alone. Eddie started shaking. His stomach ached—for food, for a morsel of normalcy, and for his mom. Thanks to his father, he missed the opportunity to hug her. Maybe his goodbye was the last thing he would ever say to her. He honestly was not sure he would ever see her again.

Days strung together into weeks, but his mother remained absent. More fearful of his dad than his teacher, and to the detriment of his grades, Eddie played housekeeper instead of focusing on his schoolwork. He took on the roles his mom left vacant. Day after day, he raced home from school to cook and clean and wash a load of clothes in the old wringer washer. Giving his father nothing to complain about ranked right up there with ensuring he always wore clean underwear. In the mornings, he set out breakfast cereal. And at night, he made grilled cheese for dinner—not because he liked it, but because there were several bags of homemade bread in the freezer and a large tan box of cheese in the fridge, and he did not know what else to make. Eddie had never been allowed to use the stove, but he did not see another option in his mother's absence.

Often, Eddie spent his nights in an empty house. He ate and washed the dishes. When night moved in, he shut off all the lights in the house and listened for noises outside. Under the cover of an old quilt, Eddie huddled on the floor in front of the black and white television with the antenna ears; a piece of twisted foil protruded from one of the thin rods. Afraid someone was outside watching him through the curtainless windows, he lay perfectly still with only his eyes exposed.

By the time his father stumbled in smelling of alcohol and burger grease, Eddie was almost always in his room—on his knees praying for his mom to return like she once was and for his father not to kill him as he had done to the baby. Most nights, Eddie would never see his dad. Other times, they would have a wordless encounter, marked by passing in the hallway or an evil look. Periodically, he dealt with his father's wrath and rants about the local drunks. "If that isn't calling the kettle black," his mom used to say when his dad went on similar tirades with her. It was not a phrase Eddie understood, but it must be true if his mother said it.

Mona continued to find ways to care for him. She was the only one who seemed to care about Eddie's drunken father and his crazy mother. One of her daughters secretly dropped a bag lunch in his bus seat every morning. Those sandwiches, chips, and small dessert tasted better than anything he had eaten since the night the baby died. A couple of times each week, Mona would drop off meals that needed nothing more than heating. Eddie was grateful for his neighbor's kindness.

Christmas arrived with no fanfare—no tree, decorations, or presents. Before winter break, the other kids exchanged gifts. The teacher's rule stated—*Bring and Receive*. Eddie did neither. He watched as his classmates drew numbers that matched random gifts. Dolls, toy cars, boxes of hard candies, games, and mood rings went home in paper sacks that day. Other than a purple sucker with the twisted paper handle his teacher gave him, Eddie got nothing. He hated everything grape.

One cold January afternoon after Eddie returned to school, his father surprisingly came home before dinner. Eddie raced into the kitchen and started preparing dinner while his old man helped himself to a glass of whiskey before burying himself behind the newspaper. With both hands, Eddie lifted a heavy ice cream bucket of soup from the top shelf of the fridge. It banged against his knees as he lugged it toward the stove. But as he hoisted it onto the counter, the metal handle let loose, flooding the kitchen floor and spraying soup up the fronts of the lower cabinets.

Tears of fear and exhaustion streamed down Eddie's cheeks. He frantically sopped up the mess with a pile of dirty dish towels he pulled from the kitchen hamper. Terror clutched at his chest. "I'll clean it up. I'll clean it up," he anxiously assured his dad. "I've got it."

He corralled the orangish liquid before it escaped beneath the stove by building a wall. Suddenly, he felt a hand grab the back of his shirt. His body instinctively curled forward, anticipating a whack across the head—or worse. But it did not come.

"Get up. This crap's gone on long enough. No son of mine should be cookin' like a woman. That's your mom's job." His dad punted the bucket across the kitchen, adding to the mess. "Get in the car, boy. This ends now."

Eddie did not think twice. He grabbed his coat and raced into the Minnesota snow with his toes crammed into his shoes and the backs folded under his heels. Fearing his dad would leave him if he was not where he was told to be, Eddie dove into the back seat before his dad opened the front door. There was no way to know where they were going. Maybe it was to the Hearthside Inn, the Roadside, or even the Dairy Barn. He doubted he would get ice cream, but anything was better than another bowl of soup. Regardless of where they went, he could eat a horse.

The car bounced down the driveway and out onto the

highway. When his dad hooked a left before town, Eddie knew food was the last thing on his father's mind. A bar, a Quonset hut-shaped theater, and a small post office were the only things he knew of in the direction they were headed.

Once again, they passed through the village of Tilden and turned left onto the highway. Eddie's hope rose. Was it possible they were going to see his mom? Was she fixed? His stomach growled loudly. Eddie faked a cough and wrapped his arms around himself. If his father heard the noise, there was a very real possibility he would turn the car around. It was not an idle threat; he had done it before. This was one time Eddie could not take that chance.

Once again, his dad abandoned the car in front of the Milford State Hospital. The vehicle was not in a lot or between lines. Eddie wasn't sure he had put it into *park* before he opened his door and climbed out. After checking the gearshift indicator, he collapsed against the backseat. He didn't attempt to follow his dad. If for no other reason, he was a fast learner with a long memory. After the last time, he knew better.

"Get the hell out of the car, boy. Can't you think for yourself? Good Lord," his father muttered as he climbed the front steps.

Eddie crawled out of the car, slammed the door, and raced up the steps toward the brick building. His dad opened the heavy door but did not hold it for his son. It slammed into the side of Eddie's face. He puffed out his cheeks and held his breath. The side of his face throbbed, and tears threatened to fall. Eddie wanted to cry, but more than that, he did not want to be called a namby-pamby, a pussy, or a wimp in front of people he did not know. He was uncertain if his dad had been teasing him about the hospital keeping him the last time they were there. Maybe because of what happened with the soup, his dad decided to leave him too.

When his father went to the desk, Eddie held back, cautiously sitting on a hard blue plastic chair near the door. He pulled the zipper on his coat to his neck and pressed his face inside. A few tears dripped down his shirt before he got control of his emotions.

"What do you mean, she ain't ready?" his dad bellowed. Eddie lowered the zipper. "I brought her here so you people could fix her. Ain't my fault you ain't good at your job." His dad's eyes narrowed, and his fists tightened into tight balls, denoting the beginnings of a meltdown. His voice took on a deep growl. "Listen, woman. She's *my* wife. I brought her, so I can take her home any time I damn well please."

"Mr. Greer," the woman said calmly, "rest assured your wife is getting the best care…"

"That care's costin' me an arm and a leg for every day she's here." One eyebrow raised as he tipped his head slightly to one side. "And I say she's been here long enough. That's what my wallet's screamin' too." He slammed a fist on the counter. "Hell, I coulda built an entire house in the time you've had her." Leaning toward the woman, he yelled in her face. "So, tell me, just how long does it take to fix a crazy person anyway?" He looked at Eddie before turning back to the desk. "Because if it's money you need, I got another one I could trade with you." His dad hooked a thumb in Eddie's direction. "Crazy seems to run in my family."

"Mr. Greer," the woman warned, "keep your voice down."

His father looked around the empty waiting room. "Who the hell am I gonna disturb? There ain't nobody in here."

A man burst through a door that led down a long hall. He wore a white coat and looked like the photos of doctors in Eddie's health book; he had never seen one in real life. That would have been a waste of money, and according to his father, he was not worth another penny; the wide, jagged scar on his leg proved that.

The man put his hand on his dad's back and pushed him away from the counter. At first, the two spoke quietly. Eddie was relieved the doctor came to help. Periodically, his father would raise his voice and spit out an angry phrase or two, but it was nothing compared to how he spoke to the woman.

Finally, the man unlocked the door and disappeared to the other side. His dad snatched a *Popular Mechanics* magazine from a table and dropped onto a seat across from Eddie. Eddie stared at the cover. The family looked so happy. A tent was perched on the top of their car. His heart sank. The last thing his father would ever do was take him and his mom on vacation. Heck, Eddie had not seen him smile since he was four.

Eddie jumped when the woman from behind the counter touched his shoulder. Like a mirage, a slice of banana bread appeared before him. He reached for it but jerked his hand back and looked toward his father. His elbows rested on the arms of the chair, and the magazine covered his face. For all Eddie knew, his dad was asleep.

"Go ahead, honey," the woman said softly. "Have you eaten dinner yet?" Eddie shook his head. "Then you must be starving. One slice won't hurt you."

Whispering *thank you*, he helped himself to the slice. He broke the bread into eight pieces. He shoved the first into his mouth and closed his eyes. The generous slathering of butter helped the dry bread slide down his throat. After the second piece, he scanned the room for a water fountain but found none. A red and white vending machine sat in the far corner of the room, but Eddie knew that was off limits. His dad was too cheap to give him a dime for a soda.

Suddenly, the door to the long hallway opened, and his mom stepped through. The man in the long white coat held her suitcase. Eddie's heart thudded in his chest, but he did not dare move. His father's wrath scared him motionless. But even more, he feared his mother's rejection—again.

His mom was almost unrecognizable. If he did not know it was her, he could have walked right past her. She was rail thin. But there was something different about her than the weeks before they dropped her off. Her eyes were no longer blank. There was a glimmer, a spark of life again. Tears welled in his eyes, and his lower lip quivered. The corners of his mouth ached as they tilted downward. He held his breath and waited. Finally, she held her arms out toward him. Eddie raced across the room and fell into them.

George picked up the suitcase and headed toward the door. A hollow whistle cut through the room. "Bus is leaving. Let's go. It's already way past my dinner time, and you got yourself one hell of a mess to clean up when you get home, woman."

Eddie took his mom's hand, and they walked to the car together.

For months, her smile was non-existent. But when Eddie finally heard her soft laugh, he believed things would be alright. Once again, he and his mother were a team. Eventually, his father would lose. One of them would make sure of it.

7

Eddie

Eddie palmed the top of the dented antique aluminum canister from the counter. For as long as he could remember, the *Coffee* and the *Tea* containers sat side-by-side adjacent to the oversized gas range with the double oven. Jules referred to them as "charming." But then again, she saw everything older than the hills that way. Nothing on the farm was important to Eddie—not the furniture, the equipment, or the canisters. When he looked at them, they evoked memories of events, none of which his wife was privy to. Eddie opened and closed his right hand, recalling his thirteenth birthday. Had Jules known about the boiling water incident, she would have tossed the canisters immediately. But Eddie never told her. Some things left scars too deep to share.

Frankly, nothing on the four hundred acres brought happy memories—nothing. Everything was woven with dreadful reminders of his father, including the town and its residents. He could only deal with it by drowning it in a bottle of whiskey.

As much as he hated everything, he understood Jules's attachment to the nostalgia of the farm. Eddie could have burned it down without a speck of guilt or sorrow. A few times, he came close. All he needed was a bottle of lighter fluid and a match; making it look like an accident was easy. The farm was remote, and the fire station was too far away to save the pile of kindling when the wheel fell off the grill, tipped, and sent it all up in flames. A couple of T-bones thrown in for good measure, and no one would be any the wiser. More than once, he played that scenario out in his head.

But he would not. He could not. While every item on the farm stirred horrible memories of his past, Jules had been left with nothing. After their wedding, the pair of spinster aunts who raised her after her parents' deaths burned, tossed, or sold everything. Not a dish, piece of clothing, or the box of memorabilia Jules cherished remained after they were done. Even the homemade quilt her mom gave her for her fifteenth birthday went up in flames. As guardians, they felt it was within their rights to make decisions for their niece—not asking, not telling, just doing. And in the eyes of the law, even though they were married, she was still a minor.

To make matters worse, before Jules's eighteenth birthday, her aunts sold the house and pocketed every dime. They emptied her parents' bank account and pocketed the insurance money. Their defense was simple: the little money they received had gone to pay for two years of babysitting, providing them each with a salary for giving up their jobs to take care of their ungrateful niece. The sixty thousand dollars from the house was payment for the pain and suffering of living in a podunk town like Holland Crossing—an area with a limited supply of unmarried men and the nightlife they were accustomed to in the city. But Jules knew better. They were not clubbers. In their mid-fifties, they drank sherry, dressed like a couple of eighty-year-olds, and fell into bed by 8:30 every night. Their self-centered behavior reopened the deep wound of her parents' deaths. But no local lawyer would go against their big-city attorney.

Jules clung to everything and everyone. Abandonment frightened her immensely. But clearly, she was okay with being the *abandoner*. That was abundantly obvious.

At times, Eddie feared she bordered on hoarding. Not because she brought things into the house, but because she would not get rid of anything. There were no keepsakes from her past, so she zeroed in on his. That was why the house had not changed in forty-two years of marriage. If it was there the day his mother moved to the River House, it was still there, in the same place, no matter how it affected Eddie.

Cussing, Eddie tugged on the lid of the coffee canister. Jules knew the trick to remove the cover, but he had not mastered it. Suddenly, it popped off and launched toward the sink, landing in the middle of a mound of dirty dishes accumulated in the six weeks since Jules left.

"Dammit!" he yelled.

A few errant grounds escaped from the can and dropped to the floor. Eddie tossed the canister into the sink and moved to the cupboard door with the long narrow dent. Coffee grounds crunched beneath his feet as he ran his finger across the scarred panel. Hank bent low and sniffed at the brown crystals before walking away.

Eddie could still remember the day his father threw that first plate. After the first one, each became less significant, not as frightening, not as attention-commanding. Only the moment of impact startled him. After that, it became just one more plate that met its demise in another of George Greer's rages. When his father passed, dishes were sparse. Deformed plastic lids, contorted by the heat of meals, served as dinner plates for his mother and himself. She dared not serve food to his father on anything other than an actual plate. On the day he died, only one plate remained. The timing could not have been more perfect.

Once again, Eddie fingered the mark. That was the start of his father's downfall. The first time he had spun out of control. It was just one in a never-ending list of reminders of why he detested his dad so much and why Eddie felt nothing but relief when he died.

Nearly two decades passed before Eddie knew what happened in the hours before his father returned in such a foul mood that late summer afternoon. His old man was not a bookkeeper, nor was he a saver. Honestly, money was not his father's forte—period. He was terrific at spending it; he just did not have the capability to manage it. It had taken Eddie seven years to make sense of all the old papers and receipts his father stuffed into boxes, drawers, and paper bags. Organizing it was like assembling a ten-thousand-piece puzzle without having the cover as a guide.

Beneath the last drawer in an old wooden filing cabinet, Eddie finally discovered the cause of his father's ugliness: notes from the bank and a foreclosure letter. Additional digging showed him the big picture. His father had not gone to sell cattle that morning; he sold the farm. Not all of it. Two hundred acres on the far side of the hayfield changed hands that day. Harvey Mayer's farm grew while Greer land shrank.

At some point, his dad took out a loan against the farm, but he had not kept up with the payments. It finally got paid back the day life went to hell. Until Eddie's discovery, his mother knew nothing about the loan or the loss of acreage. As for the land, his father lied to her. He could not manage it all, so he leased four large fields to the Mayers. His mother kept her head low and asked nothing. Questions led to fights, and fights led to the eruption of George Greer.

In Eddie's search, he could never account for the difference in the amount his father received for the land and what went to the bank. If he were to wager a bet, he would guess it was most likely wasted on loose women, gambling, and booze—the only three things his father loved more than himself.

As the memory faded, Eddie angrily yanked the cabinet door open, looking for a backup can of coffee. The black handle with the short screws came loose in his hand. "Son of a bitch," he mumbled, tossing it into the sink. Hank yelped when it bounced out and conked him on the snout.

"Not my fault. You could have moved." Eddie pointed to his forehead. "Think, Hank. Why do you think people call you dumb dogs?" Hank tipped his head, trying to understand Eddie.

Pressing his hands to the edge of the cupboard, Eddie leaned forward, closed his eyes, and drew a deep breath. Slowly, he scanned the room. If he did not know better, he would have sworn a bomb had been detonated in the kitchen. Even with all the *charm* Jules held on to, the one thing it never was, was messy—until now.

Orange juice from a glass Eddie launched across the room a week before left a sticky residue on the tiled floor. Because of the glass shards, Hank refused to clean it up. The dried liquid gripped the soles of his boots as he crossed the room. Rage billowed inside him as he listened to the ripping sound as he lifted each foot. He snatched the whiskey bottle from the table, but it, too, was empty. Reminiscent of his father's outbursts, he flung it across the room, where it cracked the hard plaster before bouncing off the wall. Shards of glass pinged off the floor and cabinet doors before joining the castoffs from weeks of not giving a damn.

Hank barked twice. Fear or reprimand? Since everyone judged him lately, Eddie assumed the latter.

"Don't start with me, Hank. Nobody walked out on you. I stayed. You get fed and taken care of, thanks to me." Eddie glared at his only companion. "You got yourself a dog's life. That's a hell of a lot easier than trying to deal with all the crap in my life," he growled.

Even though he would not admit it to her, he was furious Jules had deserted him. He stayed—through all of her complaining about every damn thing: the way he treated the boy, what she called his abuse of alcohol, and that he never *saw* her anymore. What did that even mean? It was not like she wanted anything she didn't get. Not once had he stood in her way of buying anything. Unlike when his father managed the farm, he was making money—a lot of money. The problem arose because she started wanting things *his* money could not buy. What she wanted was her daughter—*and Eddie*. Somehow, she had forgotten *he* was there—every damn day. He was not out carousing or picking up women. Secret loans and losing money to poker sharks were not part of his life either. And not once had he touched her the way his father grabbed his mother. As far as he was concerned, he was a damn near perfect husband. What else could she possibly need or want from him?

As for their daughter, that was an impossibility. Dead was dead. That was where they differed. Eddie did not live in the past. He did not engage in the *what if* game his wife played from sunup until sundown. That is not to say he did not visit occasionally, but he escaped before it sucked him under, wrestled him into a full nelson, and took him down for the count. Dwelling there was a losing match. He told her as much on the day their daughter died, fifteen years before. *Leave well enough alone. If you can't change it, forget it.* She disliked it then, and he knew she still did not agree today.

Now it was their grandson she wanted. And, like before, there was nothing he could do about it. But Jules could not see it that way. She would want to beat the issue to death until he stormed from the room. Talking was her thing. Walking out was his. She needed to stop blaming him for generations and generations of inherited issues. Did she honestly expect him to act any differently than the Greer cavemen had?

Still, like the rest of the community, he was a pariah to her—the reason their grandson died. It mattered not that he provided for them every day since they married—a week after his father's accident. She may have only been seventeen, but he was an adult. And he had been forced to give up his dreams, take over the farm, and care for his mom. Her only dream was to be a mother. They agreed to wait seven years to have kids. She told him getting pregnant at seventeen was an accident. He told her he believed her then, but now he was not so sure. So, by nineteen, he was responsible for feeding an extra mouth. It was not his fault that was not enough for her.

Hank jumped onto a chair, carefully avoiding the large pieces of glass scattered across the kitchen. He watched Eddie. As with the stickiness of the orange juice, the crunch of the newly added glass beneath his boots angered him. Rather than using a broom, he swept the large pieces under the cabinets with the edge of his boot.

Suddenly, he stopped. A thought poked at him as he spun around and stared at the cracked wall. Perhaps the melee with his emotions on the hayfield was caused by the alcohol. Maybe it made him soft. Drinking used to dull the pain. Lately, it made him feel things that were never intended to surface.

With an empty thermos tucked under his arm, Eddie and Hank headed toward the truck. By normal standards, it was still early, but Holland Crossing rose with the roosters. Stores and cafes opened at the break of day and closed in time to head home to put dinner on the table. This morning, he was counting on all the other customers to sleep in.

8

Eddie

Ear-piercing sounds of metal against metal radiated from the old truck as it bobbed along the rough driveway. They had grown louder recently, but Eddie was not about to waste money on a vehicle built in some foreign country or at all when this one got him everywhere he needed to be. Hank flopped onto the seat and laid his paws by his ears, adding to the noise with his own high-pitched whine.

"Oh, for crying out loud, Hank. Give it up, will you? It'll stop once we get off this damnable road." He laid a hand on the dog's head. "One mile, buddy. That's it."

The recent storms increased the precariousness of the potholes. An increase in size and depth, hidden beneath murky pools of rainwater, not only made them nearly impossible to miss but could take out an axel or tie rod. Potholes were the reason Minnesota was known for its ten thousand lakes. A divot became a hole, and the hole became a pond. Add another storm or two, and it grew into a lake, complete with a lifeguard.

Because the ground was too saturated to support the equipment, Eddie shut the farm down for several days. Work had finally started again in the last two days. Seed corn harvesting had gotten underway, but that did not give them much time. It needed to be done before the first frost. In central Minnesota, it was a battle between God and the devil, whether it would happen or not.

Finally reaching the highway, he hooked a right and headed north toward the Perk Up Coffee Shop. Thankfully, the screeching faded, and Eddie and Hank relaxed for the short trip.

A bell jingled when Eddie tugged the Perk Up door open. Hank scooted around him. Soft 80's pop filled the room. He winced. *Nobody should have to listen to that cheerful crap.*

"Good morning," Darcey called as she backed out of the kitchen with a massive tray of freshly baked cinnamon rolls.

Eddie cringed at the cheerfulness of her voice. Backing through the door with the immense pan proved to be challenging, but she had obviously accomplished it before. Her face was still blocked by the tilted pan when she turned around. Lowering the rolls, her smile melted.

"Hi, Ed," she said flatly. Hank barked loudly. The short-lived life of the rolls nearly came to a tragic end at Darcey's feet, but she saved them before they hit the floor. "You know we don't allow dogs in here."

Eddie looked around the empty room. "It's not like you got a crowd. Far as I can see, it's just you, me, and Hank."

"That's not the point. If the…" Darcey's voice trailed off. "What do you need, Ed?"

He shoved the ribbed thermos with the cracked cap toward her. "Coffee. Fill 'er up." Eddie studied the fresh pastries she set on the counter. "And pack up a couple of those rolls to go."

Darcey reached for the battered thermos. "This looks like it's seen better days." Eddie ignored her. She tried to engage him again. "Have any plans for the weekend?"

Frustration lines cut across his forehead. "In case you forgot, I'm a farmer. Weekends are the same as every other day."

He tossed a twenty-dollar bill on the counter and left the café with a white foam container in one hand and his thermos in the other. With the turn of the key, the truck sputtered once before springing to life. Eddie drove between the potholes as he cut across the lot to the grocery next door.

Shaw's was a staple of the area, run by four generations. Eddie was confident the fifth was in training. Opened in the 1930s, the store outgrew the original building. The need for a one-stop shop necessitated the move across the highway into an industrial-looking structure. Besides groceries, locals could purchase anything from toys to clothing to housewares. They catered to fishermen and hunters as well as the locals. After the Perk Up went in next door, the lunch and coffee counter closed, providing room for additional groceries. Today, the store carried a little of everything—things you wanted and items you did not know you needed. A shopper could buy groceries and lumber on the same trip. Eddie had done his fair share of hardware shopping at the other end of the building, but he could count on two fingers the number of times he had entered the grocery side.

A man with bristled reddish-blond hair peppered with gray pulled the door open. Eddie jumped. Standing side by side, they were the same height, but because the man was so thin, he appeared much taller—basketball tall—a sport Eddie never played.

"Ed." The man nodded to his first customer since unlocking the front door. He threw the keys back in the till and shoved it closed with his hip.

"Clark." Eddie focused on the floor rather than on his former classmate.

Clark sighed when Hank squeezed through the door. "Can't have that dog in the store, Ed."

"Like I told your wife next door, it's not like you're

swimming in customers this early."

"Still…" Clark sighed loudly. "Just be quick."

In high school, better at sports than many of their teammates, the two had been best friends, But that was back when Eddie saw a future beyond following in his father's footsteps when he imagined trading the sleepiness of the small town for the city's hustle and bustle. Back then, Eddie daydreamed of leaving Holland Crossing in his rearview mirror, but because of the farm, the closest he had ever gotten was a day trip to Duluth or Minneapolis.

The long reach of his father's death pulled him down. It kept him at the farm. Each day that passed was one day further from his dream. Almost faded beyond recognition, it no longer felt like it ever belonged to him. Frankly, he did not know if he was capable of aspirations. All his dreams had brought were pain. He was still branded with the embarrassment of facing a town that believed he would make it—when, in his mind, the only thing he succeeded at was failing.

In untied boots, with Hank at his side, Eddie clomped down one aisle and up the next in search of coffee. Jules always did the shopping. He silently cursed her for leaving him and making everything more difficult for him than it needed to be.

Finally, locating the coffee, he moaned. His shoulders fell as he stared at multiple shelves of coffee. There were bags and plastic containers. For crying out loud, where were the cans— the great big ones that lasted a couple weeks? Where were the ones his mother used to buy? After a minute or two, he settled on a red plastic jug with an indent for the handle.

"Wussy-ass container," he muttered as he made his way to the front of the store and dropped it on the counter.

"Sounds like we're in for a decent fall. It'll sure help you farmers." Clark rang up the coffee while Eddie fished his wallet from his back pocket. Throwing a five and a ten on the counter, he picked up the plastic can and left without a word or his change.

The truck door groaned when Eddie slammed it. He tossed the plastic container on the floor and looked up as he turned the key, hoping for divine intervention. Hank knew the drill. He tilted his head upward, barked once, and placed a paw on the dashboard. The truck whined for several seconds before the engine kicked over. He gently tapped the dashboard twice, his sign of appreciation to the man upstairs, before shifting into reverse and backing away from the store.

Like Jules, the truck was temperamental. It was not the first or second start of the day he fought with; it was the third, fourth, and beyond. Somehow the old girl wanted a little more loving once she proved herself to him. He snorted. Maybe his wife needed the same.

Eddie hit the gas and cranked the truck to the right at his driveway. He did not slow for the turn because some snot-nosed kid who had not mastered the finer points of braking was on his tail. The truck bounced onto the gravel and through the grass before returning to the road. He took a deep breath and blew it out between his pursed lips. Whether the run-down truck had enough solid metal left to protect him from a rear-ending was debatable.

There were pros and cons to the long driveway. The best part was it kept people away from him. *People?* Eddie was not a fan. The biggest issue was that it spelled trouble in the long Minnesota winters. But then again, he was not the one who plowed. That was Buzz's responsibility.

With a full thermos, a couple of rolls, and a crappy plastic jug of coffee, Eddie could keep himself from seeing people for a week or so—except for his crew and those he ran into on his unavoidable bar trips.

His men were out in the east field by the time he returned.

He held his foot on the brake, rolled down his window, and watched the harvest. Buzz wandered over.

"How's it goin', Ed?"

Eddie grunted. "About as good as it gets, I s'pose."

Buzz hooked his hands over the window frame. "Need to talk to you. We got us a problem out on the back eighty. That storm…" He awkwardly looked at the ground and unearthed an imaginary rock with the toe of his boot. "Well, you know the one." He shrugged. "Anyway, it took down a bunch of trees. Twisted 'em up real good and threw 'em into the cornfield back there."

Even though it was well out of his sightline, Eddie looked in that direction. "Too many to handle ourselves?"

"There's a lot of 'em. Not likely we've got time to take care of the trees and get the corn outta the fields before frost."

Eddie nodded. "Okay, then. Get Jerry and the boys to come out and deal with 'em. Try to get him to do it today or tomorrow so we can get this harvest done."

"Will do." Buzz twisted his mouth to one side. "You planning to…"

"Got no plans." Eddie shot a warning look toward his farm manager. "Headin' out to the hayfield for a while. I'll be back later."

Buzz nodded. "Sure thing, boss. Take your time. Nothin' we can't handle here." He patted the door as Eddie pulled away without another word.

For the third day in a row, Eddie parked his truck next to the field and grabbed the treacherous lawn chair from the back. He tucked his thermos under one arm and the white container under the other, oblivious that this move would likely make the rolls look like they had been pitched into the container from a dozen feet away rather than neatly boxed.

The ferning pattern from the lightning strike had not faded.

If anything, it was more noticeable. With the hay baled around it, the lines rose where the dirt fused to the smattering of clay just below the surface.

Eddie flipped his chair open. His elbow pressed into the box, smashing the rolls even more than they already were. He set the thermos on the ground and looked up.

"What the hell do you want from me?" he hollered into the brilliant blue sky.

Hank's eyes followed, and he let out a deep growl. Eddie looked at the dog. "He don't expect nothin' from you, boy. You're just a dog."

Suddenly, Eddie froze. Only his eyes moved as he examined the edge of the woods. The leaves were as still as could be. Again, he heard something. A voice drifted onto the field. He spun around, searching for the trespasser who dared come within a hundred yards of his land. But he saw no one. It was too easy to hide in the undergrowth. If he were smart, he would clear the space between him and Mayer. That way, he could keep an eye on the bastard.

A jagged sigh escaped. *Was he hearing things? Was he going crazy?* Wait! There it was again. The voice was muffled, but he was positive he heard his name. After a few seconds, he released a long breath. There was no doubt in his mind it was Ben Mayer trying to spook him into believing the hayfield was haunted after his grandson's death. The Mayer family had wanted the farm since they landed in Holland Crossing in the 1800s—weeks after the Greers. And because of his dad's ineptness, Ben's grandpa already snagged a big chunk of it. They were not about to get one more acre. As long as he lived, they would not get even an inch more.

"Go home, Mayer!" he bellowed. "Get the hell off my land, or the last thing you're gonna see is the barrel of my shotgun."

Eddie glanced at Hank, but the dog looked undisturbed.

"Some watchdog you are." He nodded toward the woods. "There's somebody out there, and you didn't even bark."

The chair moaned beneath Eddie's weight. Opening the foam container, he laughed. The rolls looked like they had been run over by a train. He grabbed the one with the least amount of frosting and tossed it in front of Hank. "It's your lucky day, boy."

The pair ate their pastries in silence as Eddie slunk into the past.

9

Eddie – 1974-1977

Eddie wanted a dog more than anything. With no siblings, he was lonely. The kids he knew in school and on his little league team were acquaintances, but on the farm, there was no one. Because of chores, he was not allowed to spend the night anywhere else. That was one of his father's many rules established solely out of spite. The animals who lived there were not exactly pets. The cows would not play, and the chickens pecked rather than licked. He spent more time trying to escape the wrath of the evil roosters than he did feeding them.

For years, he begged his mother for a puppy, hoping she would finally give in. He had not breathed a word of it in front of his dad. Eddie knew the fastest way to shut down anything he wanted was to let his father get wind of it. His old man took great joy in destroying his dreams.

"It's a lot of responsibility, Eddie. Are you sure you're up for it?" His mother held his chin in one hand and looked into his big brown eyes.

"I'm twelve, Mom. It's not like I'm a little kid anymore."

She shrugged. "Okay, then. Let's go get us a dog."

Eddie stepped back. "You mean now?" He pointed in front of him. "Like right now?"

His mom smiled. "Can you think of a better time?"

Pumping his hands into the air, Eddie trailed his mom to their turquoise 1962 Bel Air. He slammed the door and dove across the bench seat, wrapping his arms around her waist.

"Thank you! Thank you! Thank you!" he crowed as he squeezed her tighter.

"You work hard, son. You deserve to have something of your own."

Eddie pulled away. "But what's Dad going to say when he sees the dog?"

His mom patted his leg. "You let me worry about that, Eddie. If I were to guess, I think your father will fall in love with the dog too."

His mom drove to a farm on the outskirts of the village of Loganville. Nelson's had a litter of male black labs ready to go. Unbeknownst to Eddie, she made a phone call to let them know they were coming.

The car was still moving when Eddie jumped out near the small pen. He climbed over the fence and settled on the flattened grass. The dogs knocked one another over, vying for his attention. Eddie giggled at the affection the pups lavished on him. Slobber covered every inch of his face and arms, but he did not care. The runt of the litter kept his distance. He poked Eddie's ankle with his nose, but he did not move closer.

"Come here, buddy," Eddie called. He held his hand out, trying to coax the pup to him.

Finally, the dog approached. He flopped down next to Eddie and rested his chin on his leg. That was the moment Eddie fell in love. If you asked him what love felt like, he would have described that moment. Nothing could take his eyes from the pup—until Holly wandered into the yard.

"Oh, he's my favorite," Holly said, looking at the puppy in Eddie's arms. "Not because he's so small, but because he's so calm compared to these wild mutts." She frowned at her mom, then whispered, "I'm not supposed to get attached to them, but I secretly named him Tiny."

Eddie's mouth opened, but his tongue felt thick, and his throat tightened. He climbed out of the pen with his new dog and stood slightly behind his mom.

His mother winked at Mrs. Nelson and tipped her head toward her daughter. "I think maybe Eddie has a couple of favorites." The two women laughed.

His cheeks warmed, and he elbowed his mom in the side. He hoped Holly did not notice his embarrassment.

Holly moved toward him and scratched the pup under the chin. "I sure will miss this little guy. What are *you* gonna name him? You don't have to pick Tiny just because I like it."

Eddie nervously cleared his throat, hoping words would find their way out. "I-I was thinking of Zeppelin."

"After Led Zeppelin?" Eddie nodded. "I like that. That's a cool name. Way better than Tiny." Holly pressed her face against the dog's side. "What do you think, Zeppelin?"

The dog licked her nose, and she giggled. "I think he likes it."

With the pup snuggled in his arms, Eddie could not stop smiling. On the way home, Holly and Zeppelin traipsed through his thoughts.

When they returned, his father was waiting; Eddie saw his truck from the last turn in the road. He felt his body stiffen as they approached. Sitting on the front porch with a shot glass in his hand and a nearly empty bottle of rum in the other, he could already tell his father was anything but happy. Before his mom brought the car to a stop, his dad stormed toward them.

"Where in the hell have you two been?" he growled.

"George!" his mother warned. "You do remember it's Eddie's birthday. *We* got him a dog. Every boy deserves to have a pet."

His dad finally noticed the pup. Eddie stepped closer to his father, hoping his mom had been right about him melting his dad's heart. The dog, too young to judge character, licked his dad's arm. For a split second, Eddie thought his dad might smile. But he was wrong.

"Oh, for crying out loud. That's just what we need—another damn mouth to feed." His brow furrowed. "If that dog even thinks about taking a crap in my yard, he'll be dead. Got it?"

"Yes, sir." Eddie stepped away. "I understand."

Between chores and baseball, Eddie trained Zep to be the perfect dog: where to go to the bathroom, not to bark, and to ring a bell to go in and out of the house. As far as he was concerned, there was not a better-behaved dog than his.

Zep followed Eddie everywhere he went. The two were inseparable. When Eddie left for school, the dog moped around until he returned. They were best friends for three years—until that late May afternoon.

Eddie was at his last game of the season. At fifteen, he was the starting pitcher for the Holland Crossing Hawks— something unheard of. They had beaten their biggest rival 4-2, and he was anxious to get home to Zep and to tell his mom they made the playoffs. As usual, his coach dropped him off.

Eddie watched Coach Salo disappear before he headed toward the house. The last thing he wanted was for his coach to have any interaction with his dad. As he neared the front porch, he heard a gunshot behind the barn. It was not unusual for his dad or one of the crew to kill a fox who made his way into the hen house. But when his mother screamed, he took off at a dead run. As he rounded the corner, his knees buckled. Zeppelin was on his side, not moving.

"What did you do?" he screamed at his dad. He stumbled toward Zep. "You shot him?" He laid a hand on the dog's side but felt no movement. "You killed him? You bastard. How could you?"

"What'd you call me, boy?" Anger clouded his dad's face, and he raised the gun again and aimed at his son.

"George!" His mother grabbed the gun barrel, but he threw her to the ground and aimed it at his son again.

Eddie pressed his face against Zep's and sobbed. When he heard the bolt of the rifle, he stood. "Go ahead. Shoot me. I don't care!" Eddie hollered. "H-he was a dog. He didn't d-do nobody no harm." He dropped to his knees. "He was just a dog."

Finally, his dad dropped the butt of the rifle to the ground and wrapped his hand around the metal tubing.

"Maybe if you'd been home to feed him on time, he wouldn't have been drinking out of the milk bucket." He shrugged. "But since you weren't, he had to go. I told you even one mistake, and he'd be gone." He picked up the gun, shot into the woods, and started toward the house. "You can't have everything you want, boy. This looks like one of those lessons you had to learn the hard way. Ain't nobody's fault but your own."

His mother laid a hand on Eddie's back, but he shoved an elbow in her direction.

"Don't!" he screamed, shrinking away from her. "You could have stopped him, but you didn't. You let him kill Zep. You've never stood up to that son of a bitch a day in your whole life."

He saw her tears through his own but did not care that he hurt her. Zep was more than a dog; he was his best friend. Eddie had confided in him things he could tell no one else.

As darkness rolled in, Eddie finally got off the ground and went to the barn for a shovel and an old quilt. His arms trembled as he carried Zep's lifeless body into the woods and dug a grave. Reverently, he wrapped the dog's body in the quilt and laid him to rest. The first shovel full of dirt ripped Eddie's heart in two again. The lump in his throat was so large he could barely breathe, let alone swallow. Tears fell so fast that his saturated lashes blocked his vision. Still, he continued to fill Zep's grave. Finally, he rolled a stone over the top of the mound. Eddie leaned against the rock, bawling until the moon gave way to the morning light. He had no tears left—not just for the new day, but forever.

10

Eddie

Like the pungent stench of sweat, the memory of Zeppelin's death clung to Eddie. The thought of it still made his skin crawl. Anger surged inside of him. No matter how many chores he threw himself into after leaving the hayfield, it was impossible to drive away the video that looped through his thoughts. By 4:30 p.m., he returned to the house for several swigs of liquid painkiller, but as always, the bottle held less than he needed to bury the hurt. And, of course, the cupboard was empty.

He stepped over Hank and gently poked him in the side with the tip of his boot. "Come on, boy. We gotta go to town."

Hank stretched. With his hindquarters high in the air, he pressed his front legs in front of him and arched his back. By the time he was fully awake, Eddie was halfway down the stairs. Hank pushed the screen door open and raced toward the truck, arriving before Eddie. The dog hated to be left behind. Whether fear of being left alone or trepidation over Eddie finding trouble if left to his own devices, Hank was never far behind.

Sitting on his haunches on the worn seat, Hank battled the unpredictable convulsions of the nearly shock-less truck as Eddie maneuvered it over the neglected driveway. Like a bobblehead, his noggin jostled in all directions, but that did not keep the dog from staring at Eddie. One ear lifted, and his head to the right in question.

"Need some whiskey," Eddie finally explained.

A woeful whine escaped from Hank, and he plopped onto his belly.

Time and again, Eddie coaxed the truck back onto the rutted road and out of the still-muddy potholes.

"Listen, boy. *You* don't have memories tryin' to crush you. Worst thing that's ever happened to you is leavin' your mom when you came to live with me." He reached over and laid a hand on Hank's head. "And I'm guessin' you probably don't even remember her. Trust me, boy. Women aren't all that sugar and spice crap they try to sell you." Eddie winked at the dog. "Nah, they're naggy and can hold a grudge well past that *death-do-us-part* bullshit."

Forgetting to check for traffic, he pulled out on the highway. A small red car zoomed around the old truck, giving the one-finger wave. Eddie returned it with several choice words.

He looked at Hank. "And Jules is the worst. No matter what I do, say, or think, it's wrong." He gunned the truck and cut around a white Suburban that pulled out of Whalen's Marine. "Stupid drivers!" he grumbled. "Get your head out of your ass and pay attention. Might be time to hang up your license if you can't drive," he said. Yanking the wheel to the right, he narrowly missed a small car heading toward him. He sighed angrily, clueless of *his* hazardous driving. "I don't know, boy, but it might be a good thing she left us."

Hank repositioned himself to rest his chin on Eddie's leg. He raised his paw and laid it on Eddie's arm. The comforting gesture caused Eddie's shoulders to roll forward and his breathing to slow in the silence of the last few miles.

Matt's Bar was situated near the intersection of Highways 75 and 120. Over the years, a few shops left the sleepy downtown and joined a handful of other businesses out on the main drag. However, no other establishment had the long history of Matt's. The log-sided bar was deeply rooted in the community for nearly a century.

In 1933, within minutes after prohibition ended, Matt's opened. An old trolley car had been fashioned into the first local dispenser of hard alcohol. Almost instantly, the makeshift building outgrew the community's need to distract themselves from the Depression raging on around them. So, with the assistance of some down-on-their-luck carpenters, additions were built, and the bar continued to grow. At fifteen cents a drink, most patrons nursed their libation while shooting the breeze with friends, trying to forget their empty pocketbooks and cupboards. Others practically lived at the bar, drinking rather than eating meals.

After the war, when locals began trading home-cooked meals for an occasional splurge, Matt's began to offer food. Every resident of Holland Crossing had found themselves stuffed to the gills with a broasted chicken dinner or a black and bleu burger at one point or another.

Eddie cut left into the crudely paved lot. The truck creaked as it bounced twenty yards to where he parked it—not between any lines—just randomly in the lot along with the other twenty or so cars. Hank climbed out and followed Eddie inside.

"Ed," Jack called from behind the bar. "You can't have that dog in here. You can stay, but he's gotta go." The bartender hooked a thumb toward the door. "Now."

Eddie ignored the order and chose a seat in the corner near the old stone fireplace that once served as the only heat for the bar. As always, Hank leaped onto the chair opposite Eddie.

Jack stormed across the room. "Ed, you know damn well

you can't have that dog in here. You heard me. He's gotta go. Take him outside."

"Just want a couple of burgers and a whiskey. That's all. Not gonna be here that long."

"I mean it! Get that dog out of here!" Jack grabbed the dog's collar and tried to pull him off the chair. Hank bared his teeth and let out a low growl.

Eddie sprang up; his chair slammed against the table next to him. He towered over the man giving him orders.

Teeth clenched, Eddie snapped, "Look, I said I want two burgers and a whiskey. That's it." He stepped closer to the bartender and looked down at him. "If you got a problem with that, we can settle it outside." He glared at Jack.

"Settle down, Ed," someone across the room called. "Nobody wants that mangy mutt in here."

Eddie scowled across the room. "Shut up, Jansen. This don't got nothin' to do with you."

The bartender stepped back, clutching the back of a chair at the next table. He lifted it slightly off the ground, ready to weaponize it if needed. "You can order anything you want, Ed, but until that dog is out of here, you ain't gettin' nothin'."

Without warning, Eddie grabbed the front of Jack's shirt in one hand and pulled his right fist back, ready to drive it into the bartender's face.

"Hit him, and you're headed to jail, Ed." Sheriff Mick Tate entered the bar with his wife. Short but scrappy, the sheriff squared his shoulders and stretched his chin upward before stepping toward the pair. "Let him go."

Eddie locked eyes with Mick. He held the stare for several seconds before roughly releasing Jack, shoving him against another table.

"Now, wanna tell me what the hell's going on?" Mick's light-colored bushy eyebrows knit together, and his jaw tightened.

Jack smoothed the front of his shirt. "I told him he couldn't have that mutt in here, and he lost it." He nodded toward Hank, who was still sitting at the table.

Sheriff Tate nodded several times. "Seems pretty cut and dried, Ed. You can stay, but Hank can't. He's gotta go."

The sheriff knew Eddie well. They played baseball together back in high school. In recent years, he had been out to the Greer farm several times. Fistfights between him and his crew accounted for many of the sheriff's visits. And Mick was the one to deliver the news of his daughter's accident.

"Ed, you heard me," Sheriff Tate said firmly. "Take Hank out to your truck."

Eddie weighed his options. He and Hank could leave, or he could have his whiskey. It was not even a choice. The latter always won out.

"Come on, boy," Eddie grumbled angrily.

Hank jumped down and followed him to the truck. Eddie rolled down the passenger side window and slammed the door. "I'll be back in a while. Stay here."

The dog did not take his eyes off Eddie until he disappeared inside.

Malevolent applause attacked him when he stepped through the door. "You always gotta push everything, don'tcha, Greer?" Bruce Martin watched Eddie over his shoulder. "You never think rules pertain to you. And the rest of us just put up with your crap out of respect for your wife. But I think we've had about enough of it." He laughed softly. "Rumor is, she has." His laughter escalated to a roar.

"Shut up, Bruce," Sheriff Tate said, giving him a warning look. "Let's just move on with the evening, folks. The dog's gone, so get back to enjoyin' the evening."

With hands squeezed into tight balls at his side, Eddie

returned to his table. He was aware of the prying eyes, the whispers, and the judgment. Bruce's comment about Jules pissed him off more than being told to banish Hank to the truck. It also was not lost on him that the couple who sat at the table next to him had moved to the other side of the room.

Jen Crossley, a middle-aged waitress, trying to appear much younger than her fifty-odd years, with her heavily painted make-up and fuchsia hair, scooted between tables. She delivered food and took orders at a speed that made Eddie dizzy. Her forced laughter and ingenuine smile were a transparent bid to play on the generosity of patrons when they added her tip to the total. But the entire time he was there, she never approached him. It was obvious she had been told to keep her distance.

"Burgers are on." Jack reached across the table and set a glass of whiskey in front of Eddie. "Anything else you need while you wait?"

Eddie shook his head.

"Okay, then. It shouldn't be too long."

While he waited, Eddie watched the bar. Jack frequently ducked his contemptuous stare, fearing the return of the wrath he was subjected to minutes before. But Eddie did not give a rat's ass if he made Jack uncomfortable. Truthfully, he was not even looking at him; he was more interested in the wall behind the bar. The bartender's uneasiness just happened to be an added bonus.

A long shelf, now encased in glass, hung behind the log bar. Inside was an array of whiskey bottles from the 1940s. Nearly a dozen, both clear and amber, lined the narrow shelf. Like the unopened bottles, the people who purchased them had been different shapes and sizes. Except for claiming residency in Holland Crossing and joining the military during the second world war, the men likely had little in common on the day they left the small town.

Taped to the front of each bottle was a yellowed strip of paper no longer than Eddie's little finger. A name, written in the soldier's own hand, claimed ownership of each. The fourth from the left sent butterflies through Eddie's gut. It read *Bertram Walter Greer*. Eddie clenched his jaw and closed his eyes.

Bert was Eddie's uncle—his dad's only brother. Eddie never met him, and his father barely remembered him. Twelve years and three dead siblings, none of whom lived past the age of two, separated Bert and George. Because of their age difference, Bert refused to have anything to do with his little brother. But that did not stop George from idolizing him.

The younger Greer followed his brother from sunup to sundown whenever possible. He rode with his mom to the bus stop and waited on the porch for Bert to return at the end of the day. Day after day, Bert's animosity toward his brother grew. Except for his dislike of George, Bert was the perfect son—a son any father and a mother would be proud of. And Walt and Hazel could not have been more in love with anyone.

On the other hand, George had been a disappointment from the get-go. He was an oops baby, never meant to see daylight. Walt was more than a little disappointed at the possibility of another child. No one could blame him; he had already lost three children. And he watched his wife withdraw after each death. He was positive another death would break her. So, while his wife coddled George, trying to protect him from everything that could possibly take him away, Walt grew distant. He never bonded with the boy and barely claimed him as his son. By the time George turned four, it was too late. Walt was not interested in a sissy boy who would leave the farm in a dozen or so years anyway. His sights were set on Bert—the perfect child, the one who would take over the farm and carry on the Greer name with honor.

But a week after Bert's eighteenth birthday and two weeks post-graduation, he enlisted in the Army—six months after Japan bombed Pearl Harbor. Congress had declared war on Japan the following day. And the U.S. joined the Allies in a fight for freedom. The United States instituted the draft in 1940, requiring twenty-one-year-olds to register. Bert would not wait. Knowing the U.S. needed able-bodied men to join in the fight to take down the Axis Powers—Germany, Italy, and Japan— Bert enlisted. The Depression nearly bankrupted the farm. He hoped the fifty dollars he would send home monthly would help keep it running until he returned.

Smart as a whip, strong as a horse, a head taller than most of his friends, and stubborn as a mule, Bert saw himself as invincible. But he knew his parents would not share his enthusiasm for war *or* his desire to save the farm. By the time he confessed what he had done, there were less than twenty-four hours until he and two of his buddies needed to report.

His parents were shocked. At first, they were silent; then, his mother's emotions exploded. From disbelief to anger, from tears to acceptance—it was a whirlwind of ups and downs. Walt, on the other hand, could not have been more proud.

The night before he left, while his mother cried from her broken heart, Bert's father took the three boys into town for a last hurrah before they shipped out. Like every other Holland Crossing draftee, the four men bellied up to the bar at Matt's. Each of the soon-to-be soldiers purchased a bottle of their favorite whiskey. The bottles were placed on the high shelf behind the bar with the intent of celebrating when they returned. Three years later, two returned. Bert did not. The celebration, marred by the loss of their friend, sent both men packing. Neither returned to Holland Crossing again.

That was eighty years ago. Bert's bottle remained on the shelf with the others who said goodbye for the last time.

Eddie's father, George, was only four when his brother shipped out for boot camp. When the telegram arrived informing the Greers of Bert's death, George had not celebrated his fifth birthday. Ten minutes after the message arrived, his father hauled George to the barn and told him he "had damn well better learn to work the farm" since he was the only choice left—not the best choice, not even a good option—the *only*.

Like Eddie, George wanted to leave the farm; he had bigger aspirations that did not involve milking cows and planting corn. But *unlike* Eddie, George, with barely an eighth-grade education, did not have the aptitude to make the farm the success that golden boy Bert would have. That always stayed with George: comments from his father, the digs, the reminders of how Bert would have done it so much better, and the lack of belief in him. Walt always pointed to the heavens and reminded his son, "I guarantee you'll be the end of the line, boy. I'll watch you fail from up there. You ain't got the smarts God gave a turkey." Then he walked away, muttering, "All this work I've put into this place—running my pa's farm…for what? To watch you destroy it?"

George never felt worthy. It angered and frustrated him, yet, he had done the same to his son.

Eddie did not know about any of it until the night his father died. That evening, his mother opened a Swedish bible that had belonged to his Great Grandma Hazel's mother. Tucked inside, with a host of artifacts and photos, was a folded piece of paper telling the story of Bert and George in Hazel's handwriting. She explained the unfair expectations placed on the boys by their father. Knowing the past did not make Eddie appreciate his father more, but it did help him understand the mounds of anger his dad fertilized and dumped on him.

From the minute Eddie had taken the reins of the farm, he felt as if he were swimming upstream—fully dressed, wearing his heavy work boots. Had his dad felt the same way? It was possible, but there was one huge difference. When Eddie was thrown into farming, he was eighteen and had a wife and a kid on the way. His parents waited years to have him.

The surprise of learning he would be a father sent Eddie into a spiral. The squeeze of responsibility around his chest crushed his insides and traipsed through his brain day and night. He loved Jules, but at eighteen, he was not ready for a wife, let alone a kid. Regret turned to anxiety, anxiety to anger, and anger to rage. For those first few years, he could not like himself, let alone love a wife and kid.

Day after day, Eddie spent hours locked inside his head—fighting a war of dark thoughts. Suicide, disappearing, and even murder stomped through from time to time. He became a punching bag for unwanted feelings. And he was losing the battle. In those early days, he lay awake at night and watched Jules sleep, stared at her growing stomach, and wondered if she felt the same—trapped in desperation and misery. He wanted to like this baby, but he only saw the kid as a burden. At least, if it was a boy, there was hope.

Three hours and three whiskeys later, Eddie left Matt's Bar. The extra burger was cold, but Hank could not have cared less. He opened the side door of the truck and tossed the unwrapped sandwich toward his dog. The truck door rattled when he slammed it before heading toward the off-sale side of the bar. Sheriff Tate was standing next to his truck when he returned with two bottles in a plain brown paper bag,

"You okay to drive, Ed?" He eyed him carefully. "I wasn't keepin' tabs of how much you were drinking, but…" His voice trailed off.

"I'm good," Eddie grumbled.

The sheriff nodded toward a narrow yellow line near the truck. "Walk that line for me, and you can be on your way."

Eddie snorted. If anyone could handle their liquor, it was him. *Drunk Eddie* was not the person people needed to worry about. It was when he was sober that things went to hell. That was when his mouth got the better of him, and his fists developed a mind of their own. No, *drunk Eddie* was a patient man, gentle even. By the time he got that far in, he did not care who said what. Sober Ed had no time for the crap people shoved his way.

He raised his eyebrows and moved to the line. "What do you want, Mick? Skip? Hop? Dance? I can do 'em all."

"Walking'll be fine. Just put one foot in front of the other."

Eddie walked the line, spun around, and returned without so much as a misstep. He threw his arms out to his sides, palms up. "Happy?"

Sheriff Tate nodded. "I'd be a lot happier if you weren't wound so tight all the time." He watched Eddie's face. "You gotta learn to let things go, Ed. Nobody in this town hates Ed Greer as much as you hate yourself. You're a good man. At least that's how I remember you." He clapped Eddie on the shoulder. "I sure would like to have dinner with *that* Ed one day."

Eddie took a step toward Mick and leaned close. "He disappeared years ago. I don't think he's likely to return." As he stepped back, he caught the heel of his boot on a hole in the pavement. Mick grabbed his arm to keep him from falling.

"Not drunk," Eddie said. "Just lousy blacktop." Eddie pointed toward his truck. "Can I go now?"

"Yeah, you're good." Mick lifted his chin in dismissal. "Have a good night and drive careful. And from now on, maybe leave Hank at home when you come to town."

Eddie started toward his truck but stopped; he spun around.

"Just curious. Do you check everybody who comes out of the bar when you're here—or just me?"

Mick shrugged. "I just wanted to make sure you were good to drive, Ed. We go back a long way. Just trying to keep you safe." The sheriff headed toward the front door.

"Bullshit," Eddie said.

Tate turned around and scowled at him. "Ed, you can walk away, or you can keep this going. But I have a feeling if this continues, you won't like how or *where* it ends."

Eddie's jaw tightened. Finally, he nodded at his one-time friend, climbed into his truck, and drove out of the lot.

11

Eddie

After completing his lone morning task, the rooster quickly disappeared from under Eddie's window. But Eddie had not heard the beady-eyed little monster. Still rankled over the events at Matt's Bar, he came home and numbed his feelings with one of the bottles he had purchased. The old barnyard fowl could have crowed a dozen times, and Eddie still would not have woken.

Hank planted himself in front of the couch and waited for Eddie to wake. Periodically, he nuzzled Eddie's hand, but Eddie never moved. The sun was high in the sky when he awoke on the olive-green vinyl sofa. An empty whiskey bottle dropped to the floor, narrowly missing Hank. The dog jumped onto the couch, landing on Eddie's groin.

"Oh, balls," he groaned as he rolled onto his side and held his manhood for several moments. Last night's grog and grub almost made a reappearance—in the worst possible form. "What the hell, Hank! Are you trying to kill me?" He pushed the dog to one end of the couch and slowly sat upright.

Eddie pressed his elbows onto his knees and dropped his head into his hands. Which hurt worse—his head or his nuts—was debatable. But he could not recall a morning that left him feeling like he'd been beaten with a two-by-four and then stomped on for good measure. Truthfully, it was nearly impossible to remember much of the last dozen or so hours. The events of the previous night swam through a sea of fog. Flashes of memories exploded and faded quickly, making him nauseous. He accidentally kicked the bottle under the couch. The clink indicated it found a mate.

A soft thud came from the kitchen. Eddie jumped. "Who the…" What started as a bellow quickly disappeared because of his pounding headache.

Jules stepped through the doorway with a cup of coffee. "What happened here?" She looked around the living room. "The house looks like a tornado hit it, circled back, and took a second shot."

She put the cup in his shaking hands and sat on the arm of the sofa next to Hank. Wrapping an arm around the dog's thick neck, she glared at her estranged husband. "Seriously, Eddie. What happened?"

He scanned the room, taking it all in for the first time since Jules left—scattered papers, garbage, dirty dishes, and broken glass. Eddie could explain none of it—not the trash, broken chair, or overturned end table. The cops might have viewed it as ransacking, but even though Eddie could not piece together all the details; he was smart enough to keep his mouth shut. The mess paralleled his life. His shoulders fell, and his eyes dropped to the floor, hiding behind an invisible wall of shame.

Jules finally returned to the kitchen. Hank followed. Eddie attempted to roll his eyes at the dog's sudden disloyalty, but the pain was too great even to blink. He raised himself off the couch. The room spun; he waited for it to slow before staggering into the kitchen.

"Why are you here?" he asked. "You left because you didn't want to be here anymore." He cleared his throat. "So, why'd you come back?"

"I thought you might need groceries by now." She frowned after scanning the kitchen. "I knew you'd fall apart. I just didn't think it would be this bad."

"Fall apart?" Eddie's cheeks burned. "You knew I'd fall apart? That's a pretty shitty thing to think about your husband."

Jules did not respond. She cracked three eggs into a bowl, added water, and whipped them until they were a pale yellow. The pinging against the metal made Eddie's brain hurt. He covered his ears and gently lowered himself onto a kitchen chair. Hank joined him at the table.

"Are you staying?"

"Huh," Jules harrumphed. "How can you even ask that? Until you get your crap together and stop drinking your life away..." She shrugged. "There's nothing left of us, Eddie. And I sure don't want to live with you looking and acting like death warmed over."

Eddie grunted. "I don't have a drinking problem."

"Says the man who woke up with a whiskey bottle stuck to his face."

The pan sizzled when Jules poured the eggs into it. She worked in silence. Finally, she set a plate of toast and eggs on the table and pushed them toward Eddie.

"When was the last time you ate a real meal?"

"Last night..."

"Bar food doesn't count." She arched an eyebrow. "I heard about your run-in at Matt's last night. Honestly, Eddie. When are you going to learn that alcohol only makes things worse?"

He lifted his cup into the air. "Here's to the woman who thinks she knows me better than I know myself. To Jules, *The Perfect*."

Once again, Jules disregarded his snarky remarks. "So, when *was* the last time you cooked a meal for yourself?" Eddie did not answer. "That's what I thought."

Nausea swam through Eddie's stomach. He could choke down no more than three forkfuls. He pushed the plate across the table; Hank took it as his invitation to eat.

"Don't feed him at the table." Jules removed the plate and scraped it into the dog's bowl. "That's disgusting."

Eddie snorted. "What the hell difference does it make? You already said you're not comin' back."

Jules scowled at him. "Is that what you want?" Eddie knew no matter what he said, it would bite him in the ass. "Because if it is, then I'm done imagining the possibility of a reunion." Still, he said nothing.

While Eddie drained the pot of coffee, Jules washed the dishes and swept and mopped the floor. She fixed the washing machine and started a load of laundry before attacking the bathrooms.

Eddie was still seated at the table when she stowed the cleaning products beneath the kitchen sink. Except to lift his feet so she could mop, he had not moved for the better part of two hours. Courtesy of his wife, a bottle of aspirin and a pitcher of cold water replaced the coffee.

She sat in the chair next to him. "The shower's clean, by the way. You might want to try using it sometime." Jules flapped her hand in front of her nose.

"Screw you," he grumbled. He reached toward Hank, hiding his attempt to smell his armpit. His eyes widened in surprise.

"Is drinking worth how you feel right now? I'm hurting too, Eddie. I lost everyone I love. So many people have walked out of my life and never returned." She took a sip of coffee. "Even you."

"Where the hell did *I* go?" Eddie gawked at his wife. "I'm sitting right here, dammit. You're the one who left."

Jules swirled a finger through the air near him. "This is not

the man who used to be here—not the one I fell in love with."
She shook her head. "You can't pull all this crap and think I'm
just going to keep taking it—that I'm always going to be here
no matter how you treat me." She laid her hand on his. "You're
blowing up your life, Eddie. And for what? Do you think I
want..." She shrugged and held her palms out. "This?"

Eddie gazed into his empty cup but remained silent.

She wiped her hands on the front of her jeans and stood.
"You're wasting everything we ever dreamed of. I'm tired of
waiting for you to remember how to dream."

Eddie snorted silently. "Those dreams were a lifetime ago.
It's too late to pick up where we stopped."

Jules shrugged into her jacket. "Is it?" She pulled her blonde
ponytail from beneath the coat collar. "I'm still dreaming. As a
matter of fact, I've started painting again. It's helped me
connect with myself again." She touched his shoulder. "What's
something you always wanted to do but didn't? What's your
dream."

Eddie slammed a fist against the table. "Did you not hear
me? I already told you. I'm too damn old for dreams."

Jules watched him. "Maybe, but the day *I* stop dreaming is
the day I take my last breath." She rinsed her coffee cup and left
it in the sink. She stared out the window toward the cow pen.
"Do I blame you for giving up on us? Hell, yes. Am I angry?
So damn angry. You have no idea." Turning around, she leaned
against the sink. "But, Eddie, even with all that anger, I still love
you. You're my husband." She chewed on a hangnail. "Well,
not at this moment. Right now, I don't know who you are. And
I don't know what happened to the man I married forty-two
years ago—the one who told me he'd spend the rest of his life
trying to make me happy. The man who told me he'd bring me
flowers every week." She sighed loudly and shoved her chair
beneath the table. "I've never gotten a flower from you—not

once." Jules stepped toward the door and grabbed a cardboard box she had loaded with her old paint supplies. "I take that back. I do know who you are. I know *exactly* who you are. You're your father."

Eddie sucked in a sharp breath. Those were fighting words. Yet she was not wrong. To the entire town, he was a bitter man with a chip on his shoulder and ice in his veins.

"It seems pretty hypocritical for you to hate your father for destroying your life, yet you don't want me to be angry with you for ruining mine—*ours*."

The door quietly clicked shut behind Jules. Hank stood on his hind legs and watched through the small window. After she drove away, he returned to Eddie and laid his head in his lap.

Eddie ignored the dog. Instead, he stared at his filthy, callused hands. Farm soil was caked beneath fingernails that should have been cut weeks ago. But somewhere along the line, he had lost the ambition to care. He could not remember the last time he showered or combed his hair.

Wobbling when he rose, he retreated to the bathroom. Hank followed him, but Eddie closed the door before he could join him in the small room. The dog lay outside the door for the next hour with one ear tilted upward, ready to rescue Eddie from himself.

Ninety minutes later, in the warmest part of the day, Eddie and Hank found themselves on the hayfield, once again staring into the past. Eddie smelled of soap, which had not happened since Jules walked out. Even on his grandson's funeral day, he had not had the energy to shower.

A thermos of coffee and a plastic bag with two gooey caramel rolls, courtesy of his wife, sat in Eddie's lap. He tossed one to Hank before he bit into his. As he chewed, he heard the voice again. He glanced at Hank, but the dog's only interest was dessert.

Minutes passed before he heard the voice again. The sound was so close, Eddie was positive the culprit was hiding in the woods just beyond the hayfield. *Trespassing.* This parcel of land belonged to the Greer family since shortly after the Civil War. In those early years, his great, great-grandfather and his great-grandfather both purchased land from farmers who had failed to make a go of it. There was no way someone would take his land—not the state, not the bank, and sure as hell not the Mayer family who bordered them on the north and west. They were gravely mistaken if they thought they could scare him into selling.

Eddie picked up a small rock and hurled it across the field in the direction of the voice. At sixty, he still had a pitcher's arm. The rock landed a good sixty yards away. Silence meant Eddie missed whoever was playing these stupid games.

Thanks to his mother, Eddie participated in little league and high school baseball. George Greer saw no point in play—period. Work was what he deemed valuable. Since he was five, Eddie worked—hauling wood into the house. If he forgot, he did not eat. So, baseball was a point of contention. His dad hurled a slew of hateful words toward Eddie and his mother about what a waste of time it was. His mother fought for him as long as she could, but by the end of his sophomore year, she gave up. They both had. Absently touching the scar on his cheek, that memory washed over him with the same intensity as it had that night.

After it all went to hell, Coach Salo encouraged him to talk to his dad, but he would not; he could not. Words meant nothing to his old man. Instead, Eddie steered clear of him every day of George Greer's life. Begging and pleading only gave his dad power and joy—so much joy. Winning made his dad happy, and his father won *that* day.

Eddie could never talk to his dad about anything ever again.

The man was as pigheaded as they came. If his dad said no once, you did not ask again. If you asked a second time, you learned why you never mentioned it again—at the end of a willow switch. So Eddie gave it all up: the likelihood of a full scholarship and the dream of playing in the majors. In his heart of hearts, Eddie knew he could have been somebody. Instead, he ended up exactly as the community saw all Greer men: losers, misogynistic, disgruntled farmers, and carbon copies of the head of each generation. And while most of that rang true, Eddie knew the one thing *he* was not was misogynistic. He hated everyone equally. That was another thing he had learned from the old bastard.

12

Eddie – 1979

"Are you sure?" Eddie's eyes were wide in question. "If he finds out, he'll kill both of us."

His mom kissed her son's cheek. "Then we can't let him find out." She pointed to the table. "Sit down. I have a foolproof plan."

By the end of the week, Eddie was the owner of a white 1960 Volkswagen Beetle. It was more rust than metal. The rough driveway stole pieces of the car daily. But even though it was not pretty, the engine sounded better than his dad's old truck. The car gave him a sense of freedom and independence he had never known. On his way to school each morning, he imagined the junior high kids calling out *slug bug* and pummeling each other as he drove past.

Eddie's mom worked a miracle. Between the car and her plan, he finally felt his father's hold on him loosen. The DX Gas Station was a safe location to falsely claim as Eddie's employer. His dad would never step foot in the lot, let alone speak to anyone who collected a paycheck from the owner. George Greer cursed the station, even told his wife and son he wished for it to burn to the ground after a bet with the owner went south.

It was fifty dollars George never intended to lose. With Tarkenton back as their quarterback, there was no way the Minnesota Vikings could lose to the Packers at home. But he was wrong.

On the evening of December 11th, Carl not only came looking for George to collect, but he made it clear he wanted to rub his face in the loss. An argument came to blows inside the Buckthorn Bar in downtown Holland Crossing, but Gene and a few sober patrons forced the pair outside into the icy parking lot. During the brawl, one of Carl's employees five-fingered Eddie's old man's wallet and collected some of the money he owed before tossing the wallet toward the road. George never forgave Carl—for *stealing* his money and getting him permanently booted from the bar. Everyone knew you were a forever enemy once you stepped on George Greer's toes. As for Carl, he only collected twenty-three dollars of the bet, but he still came out on the good end. Unlike George, he had not been banned from the bar. It was worth losing out on the rest of the money not to have to run into George Greer while he was enjoying a drink, or several.

Out of sheer contempt for Carl, George agreed to let his son work there seven years later. In his eyes, Eddie and Carl were equal simpletons—a pair of losers who deserved one another. He even said as much to his family. If the DX wanted to hire his bumbling idiot son, then Carl was as dumb as George believed—and it gave him even more reason to stay away.

But the DX was not what captured Eddie's time every evening; it was baseball. Elizabeth spoke with Carl—just in case George came snooping around. Carl was all about pulling a fast one on his most hated adversary. Besides, it did not hurt that he had an eye for Elizabeth in high school. For her, he would do almost anything.

Except for the farmhands who were sworn to secrecy, his

self-absorbed father associated with no one in the community. He began buying farm supplies and his much-needed alcohol well beyond the borders of Holland Crossing from the bigger towns surrounding them. Many days, George disappeared in the afternoon and did not return until well after Eddie and his mom turned in for the night. That meant the chance of catching wind of his son's success on the field was virtually nil. It *was* the perfect plan—until it was not.

Eddie's athleticism and cunning ability to deliver the perfect pitch led the Holland Crossing Hawks to the conference championship game against the second-seeded Cantrell Cardinals. That mid-May night was when Eddie's world fell apart.

The manual scoreboard read 3-2. The Hawks' lead was too meager to let their guard down. A pair of junior high boys, Jason and Mickey, sat on the ledge of the wooden structure. Their feet dangled in the air as they cheered on the Hawks, waiting to change the score, but in eight innings, there had been little opportunity. Jason's job was scorekeeper, and Mickey took pictures. With the strap around his neck, he held the new school camera in one hand. His brother was the editor and cameraman for the school paper—*Hawk Talk*—but he also played first base, making it impossible to photograph games. He gave Mickey a crash course on the three-hundred-dollar camera.

Batting was not what kept the Hawks at the top of the conference. They did not have a strong offense. What caused them to triumph over their opponents was Eddie's pitching. But the Cardinals had a pitcher who was a close match to Eddie. That knowledge gave the coach and the team pause. *Nothing* could go wrong if they wanted to win.

The top of the ninth saw the Cardinals at bat. Runners on first and third sent a wave of anxiety through Eddie. The count was two and one. Those numbers buzzed through his mind as he contemplated his next pitch. Two or three pitches stood between the Hawks and the title. With any luck, he would throw two more pitches and end the game early. Eddie blocked the roar of the crowd; he did not even hear the noise fade. Shaking his head at Dennis Wagner, the catcher, he waited for another signal. He bobbed his head in agreement. Eddie stepped onto the rubber and glared at the batter. Suddenly, his hands came together, and he lifted his knee as he let go of a perfect curveball. It happened so fast that Mickey missed capturing it on film. The baseball crossed the outer corner of the plate. The batter did not even swing.

"Strike two!" The umpire's deep voice resonated through the stadium.

"Ed-die! Ed-die! Ed-die!" The crowd chanted his name while he contemplated his next pitch. The Cardinals taunted Eddie with insults.

Again, Eddie shook his head at Dennis and waited for an alternate signal. The catcher and pitcher were a winning pair. The town knew how lucky it was to have such an incredible young team.

Eddie was ready to pitch when he heard a panicked uproar. He stepped back and looked around. The boys on the scoreboard caught his attention first. The camera was pressed to Mickey's eye, but Jason waved one arm and pointed toward the end of the dugout with the other. Suddenly, the crowd was on their feet, and his coach and assistant stepped onto the field. It took Eddie several seconds for the events to register. Even then, they did not make sense.

With a baseball bat in one hand and a freshly lit cigarette hanging from the corner of his mouth, Eddie's father stumbled onto the field. He jerked the bat from the batter's hands and threw it over his shoulder. He pitched forward as he clumsily raced toward his son.

"You son-of-a-bitch! You lyin'. Son. Of. A. Bitch!" he screamed. "You ain't nothin' but a worthless piece of crap!"

Eddie ducked as the first of many swings narrowly missed his head. He heard the wind whistle as the bat passed a second time. Trying to grab it as it came around again, Clyde Monson, the assistant coach, took a lesser blow to the side of his head. Blood instantly oozed from a small gash, and he dropped to his knees.

"Stop!" Eddie hollered as he dodged a pair of back-and-forth swipes. "What are you doing?"

"Teaching you a lesson, boy. I t-told you no baseball, and you didn't listen, you little bastard."

Breathing heavily from his repeated swipes at his son, George dropped the end of the bat onto the ground and leaned heavily on the knob. Sneaking up behind him, Coach Salo grabbed the barrel of the bat and pulled it away, nearly toppling his father. Instinctually, Eddie grabbed him to keep him from falling. His dad reached up, put a hand behind Eddie's neck, and pulled him close. He pressed his forehead to his son's. The pair stood that way for several seconds. They stared at one another. For the first time, Eddie thought his dad saw him, really saw him. Casually, George withdrew the cigarette from his mouth and took a long puff. The ashes burned orange. After studying it, he pressed it into his son's cheek. His skin sizzled as he jumped backward and swiped at the hot ashes, trying to brush them from his face.

"What the hell?" Eddie knocked the cigarette from his father's hand.

George spat in his son's face. "I branded you, boy. That means you belong to me." He swung an arm at the crowd. "Y-you don't belong to them. You listen to only m-me. And I want you the hell off this field."

Deputy Almer grabbed one of George's arms, twisted it

behind his back, and escorted him off the field.

"Greer, what the hell was that?" The crowd cheered as he put more pressure on George's arm. "That's your son, for God's sake."

Once his dad was out of view, the spectators grew quiet. The deafening silence echoed loudly. Everyone waited while the coach cleaned Eddie's burn. The team stood in a half circle, encouraging Eddie to find strength to keep going. His dad was an idiot, not Eddie. But he knew better.

The other team's patience grew thin. Every minute or so, someone would yell, "Let's play already!" Finally, their coach crossed over into enemy territory. "Jay, are we playing this game, or are you forfeiting? 'Cause…"

Dennis Wagner stepped in front of the other team's coach. His voice was low and firm. "You know what? You're a dick. You're a big fat asshole dick."

Assistant Coach Monson stepped between them. Yet unpatched after connecting with George Greer's bat, blood dripped down the side of his face and off his chin. "Dennis, back away," he told his player as he pressed his hands against the catcher's chest.

Dennis stared at the Cardinals' coach. "Have a little compassion, man. It's not Eddie's fault his dad's a piece of shit."

"Dennis!" Coach Monson warned.

The Cardinals' coach sighed heavily. "Five minutes. If we don't get this game underway in five, you're forfeiting."

Dennis smirked. "You'd like that, wouldn't you? 'Cause that's the only way you're gonna win."

A Cardinal player appeared next to his coach. He stepped toward the catcher. "You better shut the hell up before I…"

"Tony!" The Cardinals' coach pulled the boy toward their dugout. Still holding on to his player's arm, suddenly, their coach spun around. "Dennis, is it? You might want to reel in that attitude of yours," he said. "One day, you're going to mouth off to the wrong person, and there won't be anyone there to save you."

Dennis arched his back and puffed out his chest. "One day, you might wanna learn not to be a DICK!" The catcher waited for a response, but the opposing team's coach turned and walked back to their dugout without further comment.

Four minutes later, Eddie stood on the mound with his hand behind his back and a patch on his cheek. He shuffled the ball through several different holds as he watched the catcher's signals. Glaring at Eddie from outside the batter's box, the Cardinal player tried to rattle Eddie by swinging the bat as Eddie's father had—over his head and back and forth. By the time number five stepped into the batter's box, Eddie was ready. The count was two and two, exactly as before his father's appearance. One more strike, and the game was over. Seconds ticked by, but Eddie did not pitch. The crowd watched in silence. No one called *Delay of Game*, yet Eddie knew more than twelve seconds had passed since he placed his foot on the rubber. Finally, the ball fell from his hand, bounced several times, and rolled off the mound. Head hanging low, Eddie raced off the field toward the school. Eyes followed, but no one dared intervene.

In the locker room, Eddie changed into his tennis shoes and shoved his street clothes into his bag. He dropped his spikes in the garbage can before exiting the gym. In the hallway, he slid the unlocked gate to the side and headed to locker 313. He emptied it of his personal belongings before racing to his car.

The old Beetle shook as he pushed the speed limit. Eddie pressed the pedal to the floorboard. Still, he did not catch up to the car in front of him. He had to get home before his father returned. His mother would pay the price of his betrayal.

George would know she helped him. More than anything, Eddie needed to convince her to leave the bastard, to walk away and never return. As he turned into his driveway, he knew he was too late because Almer's squad car pulled out—empty. Instead of taking his father to jail, he brought him home. His heart thudded in his chest as he sped down the road, the loose gravel taunting the small car.

Taking the stairs two at a time, he raced into the house. His mother's forehead was bleeding. Blood dripped between her eyes and from her nose. Her head was tilted to one side, and her hands were pressed over George's as he repeatedly yanked her hair.

"Leave her alone, George!" Eddie screamed. He would no longer claim him as his dad. Eddie dove at his old man and tried to free his mom.

"What did you call me? Don't ever use my name again. I don't want it sullied by you." He looked from his wife to his son. "Came to save your mom, did ya? Well, you ain't nothing more than a lyin' little bastard raised by a lyin' bitch."

"I said let her go."

George finally shoved his wife aside. "Do you want to fight, boy? Come on. I can take a little girl like you. You wouldn't have stood a chance on that field today if your friends hadn't rescued you."

Something broke inside of Eddie, and he charged at his father, knocking him to the ground. He punched him twice in the face. George's eyes rolled back, and he stopped moving. Eddie did not care if he killed him; the son of a bitch deserved it. There were at least a hundred witnesses who saw what happened in town. No one would fault Eddie if George died— no one. They would believe it was self-defense. Almer was there; he would believe him. But then again, the deputy was stupid enough to return his drunken father to the farm. He should be sitting in jail for assault. But, like always, George Greer got off scot-free once again.

"Help me get him in bed, Eddie." His mom pulled on one of her husband's arms. "By morning, he won't remember what happened tonight." She dropped George's arm and cupped Eddie's chin in one hand. "I'm proud of you, son. I'm proud of the man you're becoming. You aren't going to be anything like your father. I raised you right."

Once they got George in bed, Eddie and his mom went to town to retrieve his truck. It was almost ten by the time Eddie showered and fell into bed.

Just after 8:00 a.m., Eddie showed up for breakfast. George was long gone. "Did he say anything?"

"Not a word. Of course, I went out and broke one of his headlights and dented the front of his truck last night." She pointed to the bandage on her forehead. "Then I told him we'd been in an accident."

His mother set a plate of scrambled eggs on the table and smiled. "Your father's not the only one who can swing a bat." She winked.

Eddie did not return to school until the fall.

13

Eddie

The days were growing shorter. Morning and night crept closer together by a few minutes each day, but Eddie barely noticed. Unless he got wasted the night before, his internal clock woke him before sunrise nearly every morning. The rooster, who often looked worse for wear than Eddie, was useless most of the time. Today, he had risen a good hour before the little beady-eyed monster arrived for duty.

Hank lumbered into the kitchen shortly after Eddie. He pushed the screen door open and let himself outside to do his business before returning to take his place at the table. Eddie fried up a half-dozen eggs and a hunk of ham. He held the pan sideways over his plate but did not dump it. His stomach surged. Instead of splitting their breakfast, he scraped all of it into Hank's bowl and tossed the last caramel roll on top. Instead of food, Eddie settled on a pot of coffee. He brewed a second pot and emptied it into his thermos.

The house was quiet—too quiet. The second hand of the fern-green clock was like a drum beating inside Eddie's head. The ticking reminded him just how alone he was. Yes, he had Hank, but the best he got from the dog was the occasional whine or judgmental bark. He could not hold a conversation, not the way Eddie needed. Honestly, no one spoke to him anymore. Buzz and the crew tiptoed around him, the bar patrons eyeballed him from a distance—rightly so—and Jules had just walked out for the second time in two months. He would be lucky if she ever spoke to him again.

Eddie leaned against the counter. Jules's absence weighed on him. Once, they were inseparable, but over the years, their life had become a science experiment—fighting to press the like poles of two magnets together.

Multiple times each night, he opened his eyes, hoping it was all a nightmare, but his wife was always gone, and he was in the one place he never wanted to be. Disappointment clung to him—with himself, his wife for walking out, and even his mother for not going eye to eye with his father years before. As for his father? Well, the man was a complete and utter craphole. The best thing about his dad was that he had the decency to die while Eddie was still a teenager. George Greer was not worth a moment of his thoughts, yet, he was stuck in Eddie's head.

Eddie set his cup in the sink and headed toward the door. "Come on, boy." The dog's chin lay on the table; one ear rested on the edge of his empty bowl. It was clear he was suffering the ill effects of the huge breakfast. Eddie whistled. "Let's go. I got some thinking to do."

The dog took his time getting to the truck. Ten minutes later, Eddie and Hank were settled on the hayfield in their usual place. Hank was asleep within seconds of dropping to the ground. Eddie's mood rapidly oscillated as memories flooded through him—those he wanted and those he could not stop from elbowing their way in.

In the fall of his senior year, he fell in love with the girl with the blonde ponytail—a cheerleader who jumped a little higher, yelled a little louder, and smiled a little brighter than her teammates. Eddie was not sure any of that was true, but to him, it was. Living under his father's thumb, Eddie was always cautious of getting too close to anyone. Yet something about Juliette Weston pulled him out of the protective shell he built around himself.

Like all Greer men, Eddie was good-looking. Thick sandy-blonde hair and near perfect features were passed from one generation to the next. But Eddie had nothing else going for him. Sure, he was reasonably intelligent, and he had been a good baseball player, but that was about it. He did not even have a car any longer. His Volkswagen was parked next to the shed, completely defunct, thanks to his father. He was penniless—except for the few bucks his mom passed him periodically. According to his dad, he was allowed to sleep and eat at the farm. That was payment for the work he did. Embarrassed, Eddie kept to himself. But there was something about the Weston girl that made that impossible.

By the end of September, Jules and Eddie held hands between classes. He carried her books, and they kissed in the shadows of the doorways of storage closets. By mid-October, they declared their teenage love for one another. Jules said the words first, but Eddie instantly repeated them. In November, they found a handful of locations to take their relationship to the next level—not the farm or Jules's house, but in the backseat of an older car Jules's dad gave her before he died, at an abandoned cabin off Lily Avenue, and at the Freedom Pines Resort where Jules cleaned rooms.

For Christmas, Eddie bought her a promise ring—a pledge of their future together. He selected it from a tray of colorful gemstone rings at Poppy's Drug Store. It looked like a diamond but was as fake as a three-dollar bill. The metal turned her finger black and easily dented whenever she bumped it, but that did not matter because she would be his *always and forever. Mrs.*

Edward Greer and *Jules Greer* were scribbled across her notebooks and on signs inside her locker. Somehow, it just felt right.

Moving, going to school, and raising a family of their own—unlike the one Eddie experienced—snuck into every conversation. A discussion on Jimmy Carter, China, or anything else always led to one of them bringing up their wedding and the perfect family they would have—far away from Holland Crossing.

During the summer, Jules's aunts secretly sold the house. But it would not have mattered because they were both leaving Holland Crossing. Then she got sick. Day after day, she consumed nothing more than soup broth or a few crackers. Except to use the bathroom or empty her puke bucket, she never left her room. She did not have the energy.

When Eddie was not working on the farm, he sat beside her, rubbed her back, and listened to her soft cries. He assured her she would get better soon, but silently, he worried. *What ifs?* stomped through his head, battling with his hope for a positive outcome.

After two weeks of waiting and watching, he could no longer sit around and do nothing. He scooped her off the bed, hauled Jules to her car, and loaded her into the backseat to find answers.

Weak from days of inactivity, Jules clung to Eddie. After one look at her pale face and greasy hair, the receptionist immediately settled her into a wheelchair and swept her through the double doors of the clinic, leaving Eddie with nothing but worst-case scenarios. Everything inside screamed of a horrific disease—cancer or another ailment that had yet to be discovered. He began bartering with God, promising everything from attending church to an entire personality overhaul. There was nothing he would not do for the woman he loved.

The small waiting room overflowed with people of all ages. Uncomfortable plastic chairs were placed side-by-side in long rows. An older man with a cane chose the chair next to Eddie. To keep from having to make small talk, he grabbed a magazine from a side table. Eddie pretended to be engrossed in the articles, but he could not say if they were about cars or women's underwear. He checked his watch every few seconds. The more time passed, the more certain he was he would lose her.

Finally, after an hour, three minutes, and twelve seconds, Jules walked through the doors that separated knowing from not knowing. Her eyes were wide, and her face was even more pale than when they arrived. She grabbed his hand and led him through the lobby and out of the clinic door. Eddie's legs were rubber. No one gave bad news where others could hear; he knew that. The door closed behind them, and he barely made it to the bench on the corner before he collapsed.

It was on that bench, in front of the clinic, while cars cruised up and down the four blocks of stores that sold a limited supply of nearly everything, Eddie learned their new reality. She took his trembling hands in hers. Her smile was faint. Tiny beads of sweat soaked her hairline, matching his damp forehead.

"J-just tell me. What's going on?"

She released a long breath and blurted the news of their impending parenthood. Shocked, a gush of air rushed from his lungs as if he had been socked in the stomach. He bent over and dropped his head into his hands. The words *Oh God* attacked him repeatedly, and his heartbeat pounded in his ears, drowning out anything Jules was trying to say.

Children were always part of their long-range plan, just not so soon. Finally, he heard her crying, felt her shudder as she drew a breath.

"E-Eddie. I'm so sorry. I-I'll get an abortion. I should have done something to make sure I didn't g-get…" A woman carrying a baby passed in front of them and walked into the clinic. "Pregnant," she whispered. A sob shuddered through her. "This is all my fault. I'll take care of it. You don't even have to think about it. I'm so, so sorry."

Her words swelled inside Eddie. *It was her fault. She should have done something. She would take care of it.* It took two people to make a baby, and he had been a willing participant.

Blindly reaching toward her, he took her hand and squeezed. "*We* will deal with this. This isn't your fault. I'm just as much to blame." He turned sideways and looked at her. "I'll always be there for you. I promise." He spun the ring on her finger. "I told you I would."

Jules wiped her face on the sleeve of her sweatshirt. "W-what are we going to do?"

Eddie bit his lip and considered their options. He was the man; it was his job to be strong enough for both of them. Resolutely, he stood, grabbed her around the waist, and swung her in a half-circle.

"It looks like we're going to be parents." Pressing his face to hers, he smiled. "And I'm going to be your husband." He ran a thumb over her lips.

"You-you want to get married?"

He nodded. "Soon. Very soon. I want our baby to be born into a family that will never be torn apart. I want him or her to have a father and a mother who are head over heels in love."

Jules wrapped her arms around Eddie's neck. "I love you, Eddie. I always will."

At that moment, all he saw was *happily ever after*. That was his promise. But all he had given Jules was misery. He should have given her so much better. She deserved someone to bring her flowers, to make her happy. Instead, she ended up with Eddie—a cranky asshole who blamed the world for everything and never took responsibility for anything.

He slumped into the lawn chair, righting it when it dove to the side. Of all the things he could have been, his father was not on the list. But Jules was right; that was exactly who he had become—George Greer, a bitter drunk who spent most of his kid's life clutching a whiskey bottle or a willow switch. Suddenly, the realization frightened him. A deep sigh parted his lips, and he crumbled deeper into the chair.

Eddie's memories ran rampant. To hold them at bay, he poured a cup of coffee into the cracked thermos lid, squeezing it tightly to keep it from leaking. Butterflies fluttered inside his stomach. Every inch of Eddie felt jittery. Was it from the entire pot of coffee he drank earlier or the lack of alcohol? He did not like the feeling. A full-fledged battle erupted inside his stomach, and he was sure the entire pot would reappear at his feet if he took even one more sip.

Eddie turned the cup upside down and watched it seep into the ground. The dark liquid on the golden hay took him back to his father's last day—the day his mother finally reached her breaking point. Eddie always wondered if she killed his dad. If she did, he would not blame her. The same thought plagued him daily.

The morning of his death had started with a pan of caramel rolls, not unlike the ones Jules left before she walked out this last time.

14

Eddie – 1980

Eddie had just broken the news to his mother when he heard the truck door slam. His heart thudded against his ribs as he crossed the kitchen, putting distance between himself and the door. It was never safe to have your back to George Greer. His mother tried to shoo him upstairs, but there was no way he would leave her alone with his dad. He did not trust him. No one trusted him. This was Eddie's mess, but like always, he knew his old man would somehow make it his mom's fault.

George Greer's footsteps were a good indicator of his current anger level when he arrived home—the heavier they were, the more dangerous his mood. Today, they sounded explosive. The old man could not have stomped harder had he been wearing army boots encased in cement.

His mother's face sent a warning. "Not now," she whispered in her son's direction. "We'll tell him later."

The screen door flew open, and his father locked on Eddie.

"Well, well, well." He took a step toward his son. "You screwed yourself this time, didn't ya, boy?" An evil grin crossed his face. "Or should I say, you screwed that little trampy girlfriend of yours?" His eyes looked almost red in the afternoon sunlight that bled through the kitchen window.

No matter how frightened Eddie was of his father, he was more afraid to look away. Vigilance was the only way to save himself and his mother from the man who took immense joy in belittling him for screwing up again.

"Looks like I'm gonna be a grandpa. Now that's something I never wanted to be." He glanced at his wife with a quizzical expression. "You're awful quiet, Elizabeth." With his go-to move, he grabbed a handful of her hair and yanked her head sideways. "You don't seem too surprised by what I just told you about our dumbass son. Did you already know he knocked up that slut?"

Elizabeth leaned into him as he pulled harder. Like always, his mother wrapped her hands over her husband's but did not utter a sound. "Have you two been keeping secrets like a couple of schoolgirls?" He dragged Eddie's mother across the kitchen, closer to their son. "That's right. You're a little sissy-ass, aren't you? One who can't keep his pants zipped up."

"Let go of her," Eddie hissed. "She just found out. And she's got nothing to do with this." Eddie angrily stepped toward his dad, ready to defend his mom.

Menacing laughter filled the kitchen as his father shoved his wife's head upright, readjusting his grip. "Well, I suppose a man *can* have sex without his mother knowing. Ain't that right, boy?" He snorted. "But I said a *man*—not a *boy*." Anger lines deepened across his forehead. "Oh, wait. You're not a boy either. You're a pussy—a great big wimp." Still holding his mother's hair in one hand, he squeezed her face between his thumb and index finger. She winced. "And that's your mother's fault. She made you that way."

After releasing his wife, he swung an open hand across her face. The thwack echoed in the kitchen. Elizabeth dropped to the floor. Eddie stepped toward her.

"Don't! Don't you dare! Take one more step, and you'll be

down there with her." His father poked a finger toward Eddie. George shot daggers at his wife and then his son.

With both hands pressed against her cheek, Elizabeth crouched in the corner of the kitchen.

"If she hadn't coddled you for the last eighteen damn years, maybe things would've been different. Maybe you wouldn't have become an impregnator with no money and no prospects for a job—except the one your daddy gave you."

George picked up a chair and launched it at his son. Eddie stepped to the left as the chair sailed past, slamming into the wall behind him. His father poked a finger into his own chest. "I-I made you, you little son of a bitch. And don't you ever forget it." He stepped toward Eddie. "If your mom had listened to me, you could have become a decent human being."

Eddie curled his fingers into tight fists. "You mean like you?" He stepped closer to the man he hated more than anyone. Lording his six-foot-two height over his father's five-eight, Eddie pulled his shoulders back and slammed a fist twice into his open hand.

George's jaw tightened as he looked up at his son. "What'd you say, boy?"

"Go, Eddie. Get out of here." His mother got to her feet and moved between them.

"You're nothing but a bully. Does that make you feel big, *Dad*? Do you like hurting Mom?"

George pinned his wife against the counter with his hip. He reached behind her, grabbed a butcher knife, and pointed it toward his son.

"Eddie! Go now!" She squirmed from her husband's hold and raced through the living room and out the back door. "Go!" she screamed as she ran.

After the back door slammed, Eddie bolted from the house in the opposite direction of his mother. George chased him, swinging the long knife and spewing a string of indecipherable phrases between gasps. There was no way his father would ever catch him. The old man had twenty-five years and a good three dozen pounds of fat hanging over his belt—not to mention a fifth of whiskey he had sucked down since sunrise.

Attempting to baffle his drunken and out-of-control father, Eddie raced around the barn and stopped. His sudden appearance near the hen house created a deafening alert. Contemplating which direction to run, Eddie finally settled on the back forty. He crouched slightly and tiptoed toward the corner. Just as he was going to run toward the woods, his father stepped in front of him, still wielding the knife.

"Outsmarted you again." His dad lunged toward him with the knife. Eddie leaned back just in time.

"What do you think you're doing?" Eddie took several steps backward. "What's this going to prove?"

George hocked a loogie and spit it at his son. "Prove? That you're a loser. Kind of makes me laugh to think you're going to have a loser of your own soon." With dark eyes and flaring nostrils, his father pointed the knife at the front of his son's pants. "I should have castrated you years ago when I tied off the balls of the herd. That would have kept you from adding more idiots to this town."

His father jumped toward Eddie with the knife. Eddie swung, connecting with his father's forearm and knocking the blade to the ground. Spinning around, he headed down the driveway before veering into the thicket and through the trees. His dad followed. Even with his heart thudding inside his chest, he could hear the heavy footsteps behind him. Twenty feet or so into the woods, Eddie crouched behind the thick branches of an evergreen. Eddie carefully watched his father between the branches, refusing to look away. His old man was almost folded in half, struggling to catch his breath.

Finally, George righted himself. "It ain't just that you're bringing an imbecile into the world, boy. It's that you're gonna make one piss-poor father! If you're gonna run from your problems, you ain't nothing but a deadbeat." His dad drew a deep breath. "You don't see me running from you, do you? So, get back out here and face me like a man, you little girl."

George angrily kicked at a gopher mound that should have been taken care of by his crew. "Then again, you must've thought you were a man a couple months back when you screwed that floozy, didn't you? Well, you weren't. 'Cause wussy-ass little boys don't grow into men." His dad guffawed. "Mark my words. That bitch'll ruin your life. Once you put that ring on her finger, she'll have it wrapped around your balls before you know what happened."

Not wanting to give away his location, Eddie cupped his hands around his mouth and yelled to his left. "Must be what Mom did to you, huh?"

His dad turned in the direction of the sound. "Your mom don't control me. Nobody controls George Greer. You got that, boy? If you even think that again, you'll be in the same hole as that old dog of yours. Making you disappear would not take much." His dad scowled in the direction he last heard his son. *"No, Sheriff, ain't nobody seen Eddie for weeks. I'm guessin' he knocked up that girl and ran away 'cause he was scared shitless to be a dad. Couldn't face his responsibilities."* He laughed. "Nobody'd come looking for you. Nobody'd give a shit."

Eddie whispered, "Everybody in the whole town would thank me if I put you six feet under, you son of a bitch."

Minutes later, he watched his dad trudge back to the house. Hanging from the edge of the double doors in the barn loft, Eddie saw the old white towel. It was their symbol—how he and his mom let each other know they were safe.

The screen door slammed, and Eddie knew his dad would dive into another fifth of whiskey. With any luck, he would drink himself to death before daylight. Eddie chided himself for running. But it was likely for the best. If his dad had so much as touched him, he would have killed the bastard on the spot.

Staying in the woods, Eddie circled the farm before making it to his safe spot. Years ago, he had left a lawn chair and a blanket buried beneath an old green tarp. He covered the canvas with branches and leaves. It was his mother's idea—a place to wait out the storm. Today, he needed it.

It was nearly milking time when Eddie made his way out of the woods and into the barn. Most likely, the bottle of whiskey would be empty, and his dad would have gone limp. The fight in him would have faded, and the events of the day would be nothing more than a distant memory—one his old man would not be able to piece together no matter how hard he tried.

Because of George's incompetence in handling money, the farm that had once been a massive cattle ranch made the shift to crop farming. Often too drunk to care for the herd, many of them died. When his dad disappeared for a month, Elizabeth instructed the farm manager to sell off the rest. Since then, they only kept four cows: two dairy and a pair of males for yearly butchering.

Eddie patted the black and white Holstein on the side as he prepared for milking. Suddenly, the hairs on the back of his neck rose. The shuffle of feet told him someone was in the barn. Based on the huffing and puffing, he knew who. Silently, he picked up the three-legged stool, hunched down behind the wall, and waited to defend himself.

George stumbled into the stall. "Well, now, if it ain't my baby-making son." He clutched the doorframe to steady himself.

Grabbing a pitchfork with a broken handle from outside the stall, he poked the sharp prongs in Eddie's direction. He laughed when he saw his son raise the stool.

"Boy, you brought a chair to a gunfight." He poked the pitchfork toward his son again, hitting the old wooden stool. "Dumbass." A sideways grin lifted one corner of his mouth. "That's just like you. Once a loser, always a loser. You wet the bed until you were six, for God's sake. That makes you a failure in my book."

Enraged, Eddie swung the stool at his dad. The seat caught him in the side of the head, and he went down hard. Fighting the booze and the strike, his dad attempted to right himself while Eddie raced from the barn. Until his father passed out, the cows would have to wait. They would be uncomfortable—but it was him or them. He returned to the woods and kept watch on the barn. Worry exploded inside him as he waited for his father to appear in the farmyard. Because the house was on the other side of the barn, he could not see or hear his mother. She could trust he would be in his safe space, but she had not moved the towel to the opposite side of the loft yet. So, he had no idea if she was safe. All he could do was pray.

As twilight settled on the farm, Eddie heard the thin threads of sirens in the distance. The whirring drew closer, and shards of light splashed across the fields and eventually up the driveway. Cautiously, he moved from the woods and into the opening. His heart raced as he made his way toward the barn. Had his father killed his mother? If so, he would never forgive himself.

As he reached the double doors, his mom stepped out. She grabbed her son's arm and held it tightly. "You don't want to go in there, Eddie. Your father's had an accident." She swallowed hard. "It's bad. Real bad."

Sheriff Ray Porter shouldered past her and into the barn. His deputy was on his heels.

"What happened?" Eddie whispered.

His mother watched him for several seconds. Finally, her shoulders fell forward, and a look of relief crossed her face. "It looks like he fell from the loft."

"Is he…" Eddie's voice trailed off.

A head bob and a shrug told him everything he needed to know.

"Are you okay?" Eddie reached for her hand. "Did he hurt you?"

She nodded slightly. "I'm fine." Leaning toward him, she whispered. "And now you'll be too." She ran her hands down the front of her jeans. "We both will."

"I have to see him for myself." Eddie pushed past her and through the door. Seconds later, he returned. His face paled, and he struggled to breathe.

His mom wrapped her arms around him. "I told you not to go."

The sheriff exited the barn as the ambulance backed toward them.

"Elizabeth, I have some questions for you—if you're okay to talk."

Eddie watched his mom's face shift from relief to grief.

"I don't know much, Ray. I came out to call him and Eddie for supper. He didn't answer, so I came looking for him. That's when I found him—like…like that." A tear rolled down her cheek, and she wiped her face on her sleeve.

"It's okay, Elizabeth. Take your time."

The sheriff looked at Eddie. "Where were you during this time?"

"He was on the phone with his girlfriend most of the afternoon." She looked down. "It's so sad. We just learned we're going to be grandparents." His mother shook her head. "George was so excited."

"I'm so sorry, Elizabeth. What a terrible accident. He must have impaled himself on that pitchfork in the fall." He shook his head. "I've never seen anything like it."

Just before 10:00 p.m., everyone was gone, and Eddie and his mother were finally alone. He needed to know, yet he did not want to hear the answers. He wanted nothing more than to believe his mother was not responsible for his dad's death. Greers were good at burying their heads in the sand. It was a trait Eddie fell back on often.

An hour later, he crawled into bed and turned off his lamp. The moon streamed into his bedroom. The shadow of a tree hit the far wall. He watched the leaves dance in the night breeze— celebrating his father's demise. Eddie closed his eyes. For the first time in fourteen years, since that first plate hit that kitchen cupboard door, he could breathe.

15

Jules

Jules was all too familiar with the hospital, morgue, and cemetery. Since her parents' death, she had spent more time there than she ever cared to admit. The smell of each was burned into her memory.

At the hospital, she knew the location of the coffee machine and most private bathrooms. It was one hundred forty-one steps from the waiting room to the chapel. One and four were her unlucky numbers. Whenever possible, she avoided them—BINGO cards, highway numbers, prices, and gas pumps.

She could practically drive to the morgue with her eyes closed. If they were lucky, most people were never called to identify a body—but not Jules. She knew the entire process—including the shock of the thirty-eight-degree room where the bodies were kept.

Then there was planning the funeral versus attending. They were completely different. The first was business, accomplished out of need. The latter took everything out of her. It was the first time in the entire process that she allowed herself to feel, to grieve for all she lost. She had been through it too many times: her parents, her best friend, Elizabeth, and her daughter. The two trips to the morgue had been soul-crushing.

They left memories rooted so deeply, they were impossible to forget.

The one-way grassy driveway wound around the church, splitting the cemetery in half before exiting the far side. Any headstone could be located from the road. But Jules did not need to search. She knew where she needed to go. Almost weekly, she visited a handful of relatives and friends. Sometimes she would ask questions she knew she would never get the answers to. Other times, she shared stories. Sometimes she would laugh, but usually, she cried.

Jules parked her Explorer on a grassy pull-off, allowing others to pass on the narrow drive. Climbing out of her vehicle, she stepped into a small hole—leading to a slow-motion *America's Funniest Video* moment for anyone watching, but not for Jules. She grabbed for the inside door handle but missed. Her ankle twisted, and she toppled to the side, slamming her head into the flexible metal of the back door. Trying to save herself, she turned, but her forehead made direct contact with the running board, throwing her onto her back, directly at the base of the grave of Lottie Carlson, her best friend.

Unsure of putting pressure on the side or the front of her head, she opted for both. She pulled her knees up and tipped her forehead into them.

"Shut up, Charlotte Jean," she said to the headstone. "I know you're up there laughing, but it hurts like hell."

She pulled her hand away from the side of her face. A trickle of blood ran down her hand, and she exhaled deeply. "Great. When it rains, it pours," she said. "I just want one thing to go right—just one."

Pulling the sleeve of her sweatshirt past her hand, she used the cuff to put pressure against the cut.

Footsteps pounded the ground, growing louder. *Oh, great.* It was bad enough that she fell, but someone else saw her clumsy move. Some days, it was hard to believe she had ever been coordinated enough to be a cheerleader—to stand at the top of three-person pyramids and straddle jump off. These days, she could not even walk a straight line sober.

"Oh my gosh, Jules, are you okay? That was one heck of a fall you took." Karol Lehn squatted next to her. "I saw you fall from the office." She pulled Jules's hand away from her face and smiled. "Not only did you cut your forehead, but you also have the indent of the running board. It's going to be real pretty in a few hours."

"Yeah, I was just telling Lottie to stop laughing, because you know she is."

Karol turned toward the headstone and smirked. "She laughed at everything. There isn't a day that I don't think about her. I miss her."

"Me too." Jules's eyes burned. If she needed anybody right now, it was Lottie.

Her head throbbed when she stood. Momentarily, everything weaved before her, and she grabbed the car for balance.

Karol took her arm. "Can you walk?"

"Well, I couldn't even get out of the car without falling." She laughed softly. "So…"

Her first step was tenuous. A tightness pulled across her ankle, but there was no pain.

"I think I'm okay. I was just a little lightheaded for a second when I got up. I think I may have been a little too ambitious."

"Come with me. I'll have Pastor Grace patch you up and decide if you need to see a doctor." Karol held Jules's arm, taking part of her weight as they navigated the uneven ground. The pair slowly made their way toward the church, often stopping so Jules could rest.

"Did you know Pastor Grace used to be a paramedic?"

Jules looked at Karol. "Really?" She shrugged awkwardly. "Well, there's not much use for a paramedic in a cemetery, I suppose."

Karol giggled. "Do you want me to call…" She exhaled softly. "I can take you home or to the ER if Grace thinks you should go."

Jules did not respond.

"I heard about the accident. Grace called me when I was at my sister's. I'm so sorry, honey. I should have called you, but I… You've been through so much."

"It's fine. Your sister needed you."

Karol opened the backdoor to the church and ushered Jules inside.

"Yes, but two months is a long time to be away. A lot can happen in that time." She stopped walking and looked at Jules. "Some friends get married, and others break up in that many days."

"You heard?"

Karol nodded. "I did. I know things have always been rough, honey, but I guess I didn't realize how bad it was. You're so good at smiling through the pain."

Jules started moving again. "That's me. If you ignore it long enough, it's not real." She winced. "There's been a lot I've ignored over the years."

"I just want you to be happy, Jules."

"Me too."

A cup of black coffee, a couple of butterfly strips across the cut, a heavy dose of ibuprofen, two ice packs, and a little laughter made Jules feel better. Grace checked on her every ten minutes for almost two hours before she declared her *most likely* concussion free.

"It wouldn't hurt you to see your doctor, though. It's been a while since I've used my paramedic skills."

"I trust you. Other than a small headache, I feel okay." Jules raised her eyebrows. "You've got an in with the man upstairs. Say a prayer and render me good."

Pastor Grace laughed. "I've been on that for a while now."

The hole no longer existed when Jules returned to her car. It had been filled with black dirt and grass seed. The likelihood of anyone committing that same faux pas in the exact location was pretty slim. But then again, Jules was not exactly living her best life.

Opening the back of the SUV, she removed one of a handful of brightly colored bouquets and leaned it next to Lottie's headstone.

"You must have gotten a good laugh today. Glad I could make that happen for you." She smiled. "Oh, Lottie, I've missed you so much." She chewed on her bottom lip. "I have so much to tell you."

Very aware of her stiff ankle, Jules awkwardly lowered herself to the ground, questioning whether she could get up again. She waited to speak until her thoughts settled.

"Remember that cute boy you hooked me up with back in high school, the one you thought was perfect for me? Well, I walked out on him a while back—and so much has happened since then." An acorn bounced off her leg and dropped onto the ground. Startled, Jules looked up, expecting to see a squirrel stockpiling food for winter. But she saw nothing.

One eye narrowed in question as she glanced at the gravestone. "Was that you? Are you trying to tell me I'm nuts?" She shook her head. "If you only knew, you'd understand."

A second acorn struck her. "Alright, already. I get it. You know." She sighed. "Eddie's not who he once was, Lottie. He's not that sweet boy who held my hand and left love letters in my locker." Jules blinked back tears. "I didn't marry his father, but that's who he became." Her nose burned, and tears fell. "I miss the man I fell in love with. But with everything that's happened, I'm not sure how much longer I can love *this* Eddie."

16

Jules – 1978

Moving to Holland Crossing was not on Jules's bucket list. She had never heard of the small town. Vacations were spent in New York, California, or Disney—not in the boonies. Their idea of roughing it meant staying in a hotel without room service. But when the opportunity arose for her dad to help build a company from the ground up, she and her mom hid their disappointment in leaving the city behind fake enthusiasm.

A group of investors selected the name, location, and Doug Weston as the CEO of Venta, a unique vending machine company. For her dad, it was a huge step up from being the manager of an auto dealership.

The small town had been home to the Weston family for four years, four months, and fourteen days. In her head, Jules always added *one hour and forty-four minutes*, the *exact* length of time her parents lived in Holland Crossing before the accident.

Her dad was big on celebrations. He announced the time they passed the city limits sign—the minute they became citizens of the small town. The police report stated *10:04 p.m.* as the time of their deaths. It was the precise moment Jules became the only Holland Crossing Weston. In the days that followed, she calculated it multiple times. It was a series of numbers that haunted her.

The school bus returned to school just before nine thirty on the Friday night of the accident. The game had been postponed halfway through due to power issues at the rival school. When they returned, Jules made her usual collect call from the school pay phone. As always, her mother rejected the charges. That call was her parents' way of knowing they had returned, and she and Lottie needed a ride home. Her family thought they were so clever to be able to bilk the phone company out of ten cents once or twice a week. It was not about the money but rather the joy of pulling one over on Ma Bell.

Jules and Lottie were the only sophomores to make the varsity cheerleading squad that year. In Minneapolis, her mom enrolled her in gymnastics as soon as she could walk, and her dad insisted she take swimming lessons. Both activities taught her grace and agility and prepared her for cheerleading. Lottie, on the other hand, was simply a natural.

After hanging up the old black payphone with the stiff silver cord, Jules grinned. She had no way of knowing—*No. I won't accept the charges*—would be her mother's last words. Those six little words turned her world upside down. She listened to them in her head whenever she needed her mom. It kept the sound of her voice alive.

Repeatedly, the front door opened and closed as friends disappeared into the night. It was not long before they were the only two left.

Jules called again. "I'm sorry, ma'am. No one is answering." She was unsure which irritated her more: the operator's voice or her parents taking their sweet time picking them up.

Lottie knew better than to say anything that would upset Jules. So, while Jules sat on the floor, tearing a sheet of paper into tiny pieces, Lottie wandered the halls, studying the graduation pictures from years past. Periodically, the janitor pushed a trashcan past them between the boiler room and classrooms. Had it not been for him, they would have been sitting outside in the cold.

Suddenly, there was a rap on the locked door. Lottie skipped down the hall, expecting to see Mr. Weston. But instead, it was Sheriff Porter on the other side of the glass. She shrank back and glanced toward Jules before opening the door.

"Is Jules here?" he asked softly. "Jules Weston?"

"Jules," Lottie whispered, pointing toward her friend.

The officer's shoes squeaked as he approached her. She saw the bottom of his dark blue pants and black shoes but refused to make eye contact. Looking at him made what she already knew real. Her heart thudded in her ears, and she missed every word he said. It was not until he helped her to her feet and out to the squad car that it truly hit her.

A halo of fog surrounded every light, adding to the trancelike feel as they drove through the town. Lottie slid next to her and held her hand. Jules leaned on the door handle and stared up at the moon. Ten minutes from town, emergency lights lit the sky. She pressed closer to the window, trying to catch a glimpse of her mom and dad, their car, or something that told her it was a huge mistake. But she saw nothing more than a blur as the sheriff raced past.

Rose Baker met them outside Lottie's house. She wrapped her arms around both girls and held them tightly. Jules was empty; on the ride to Lottie's, she had flipped a switch and turned her emotions off. The following morning, when she woke up next to Lottie, she finally began to feel. Never again would she watch a scary movie with her mom or plan vacations with her dad. She would never feel their arms around her or hear them tell her how much they loved her. Her dad would not walk her down the aisle when she got married, and her mom could not give her baby advice when she became a wife and mother. Jules Weston was an orphan.

At breakfast, she pushed the food around on her plate but never took a bite. She was more focused on what happened and who destroyed her life. Mrs. Baker held her hands and explained. A truck driver had fallen asleep at the wheel, hitting her dad's Honda Accord head-on. She supposed she should be grateful the driver and a passerby pulled their broken bodies from the wreckage before the car burst into flames, but it changed nothing. They were dead.

Later that morning, Jules accompanied Lottie's mom to the morgue. Neither her mother nor father had ID on them, so someone had to identify them. Jules begged to go. Afraid Mrs. Baker would say no, she ran to the car, crawled into the front seat, and refused to get out. The entire trip, she wavered between anger at her dad for refusing to sit on his wallet when he drove and relief she would see them one last time.

A blast of cold air attacked her when she stepped into the room. Lottie's mom wrapped an arm tightly over her shoulder. Whether for support or warmth did not matter; Jules was grateful for either. When the woman or man, she couldn't recall which, pulled the sheet back and exposed her mom, she pressed her face into Mrs. Baker's shoulder and sobbed, grateful to have someone she knew at her side.

"That's Millie," Rose said tenderly. She turned Jules toward the door, but she refused to move.

"I-I have to see my dad too. I can't leave without seeing him."

Rose stood in front of her. "Are you sure, Jules? You don't have to do this. They were in the car together…"

"I n-need to know, or I'll always w-wonder." Her teeth chattered.

"Okay." Mrs. Baker nodded to the person and walked Jules toward the second table.

When the sheet was lifted, Jules froze. She was daddy's little girl—until now. Today, she belonged to no one. The man lying before her was not her father. Except for his skin's bluish tinge and pale purple lips, he looked like Doug Weston. But it was not—not anymore.

A ragged sob escaped as she nodded. "Yes, that *was* my dad," she whispered. She pointed toward the other table. "And that was m-my mom."

For weeks, Jules had a recurring dream. While she watched their lifeless bodies, they sat up and called out *April Fools*. While it would have been the cruelest of jokes, she would have given anything to hear those two words when she woke to her new life.

Jules stayed with Lottie's family for almost two months. Then one spring day, a fancy black car pulled into the driveway. Two women who looked much older than her mom came to collect their niece. Jules did not know them; she had never met them or heard their names. But for the next two years, Gloria and Evelyn Hanley, a pair of spinster aunts with a fondness for the *Price is Right*, soap operas, and the national news, lived in her house, spent her parents' money, and rarely spoke more than a few words to her each day.

Even after their arrival, Jules spent more time at Lottie's house than at home. It was during one of their long Saturday night gab sessions at the beginning of their senior year Lottie launched the idea of hooking Jules up with Eddie Greer, the hottest boy in school. All they needed to do was to get Eddie's attention.

Lottie carefully orchestrated the *accident* that led to Eddie carrying Jules to the nurse's office. It was uncomfortable and completely out of character for Jules, but she played along anyway. When she left the office on a pair of wooden crutches, Eddie waited for her in the hallway. That night, he called her, and they talked for an hour. A romance burgeoned that day, and life was never the same. For the first time since her parents' death, Jules was happy.

17

Eddie

Instead of going directly to the hayfield, Eddie pulled into the neglected driveway at the River House. Once lush and green, the yard had been taken over by creeping Charlie and other undesirable vegetation. A few hardy flowers and bushes survived being ignored for twenty years. Branches, pine needles, and seedlings littered the lawn.

Although he drove past the tiny house almost daily, Eddie had not stepped foot on the property since a few weeks before his mother fell, landing her at the Avia Nursing Home in Ashton. A month later, she was gone. Jules emptied the house, discarding food and personal supplies that would go bad before she locked it up. Since then, he had not given it another thought—until today.

When Eddie opened the truck door, Hank hopped over him and raced onto the porch. Eddie was not as eager. There were memories inside he did not want to poke. He dropped one foot onto the running board but could not make himself leave the truck. Hank sat in front of the door and barked. *Stupid dog. Who did he think would open it?*

From inside the truck, it was nearly impossible to tell if the weathered steps had ever seen a paintbrush, but Eddie knew better. As punishment, his father forced him to paint them, making him repeat the process if needed. By Eddie's calculation, the paint must be a good inch thick. "If you can't do what your mom tells you, then, by God, you'll do what *I* tell you." There were always other words thrown in for good measure: pussy, sissy, dumbass, little shit. Over time, Eddie became immune to his father's words. He would take them over the belt, willow switch, or the occasional whiskey bottle any day.

Compared to the farmhouse, the River House was tiny. It was built in 1884 for his great, great-grandmother after the death of her husband. Greer men died long before the women—most likely from listening to countless hours of nagging. Each widow, forced to leave the farmhouse as the next generation staked claim, had lived there. With Cade's death, that tradition was over. The house would never see another Greer. Family ownership would end with him—most likely becoming Mayer land once he died. While Jules failed to give him the son she promised, the Mayers produced boys at breakneck speed. Ben, the most recent owner in a long line of Mayers, already had bases loaded. And, if his wife's current shape was any indication, it looked like they were going for a grand slam.

A wave of jealousy sucker-punched Eddie. It was one more dream in a long list of things that had been taken from him.

Finally ready to face the ghosts of the past, Eddie climbed out of the truck. Each of the four narrow steps groaned as he ascended. He wondered how long it would be before a leg was sucked into the world of the animals, insects, and weeds that most certainly had taken refuge beneath the rotting porch.

Hank head-butted Eddie in the groin when he reached the top of the stairs. "What the hell, Hank?" Eddie held himself and breathed through his mouth for almost a minute. "I would have expected that from your mom, but not you."

At some point, the screen door parted ways with itself. One half lay on the porch; the other leaned to the right and hung by one rusty hinge. What was once a fan design was just a few sticks. It was no longer a screen door; it was less mesh and more hole. What remained was rusted.

A long crack ran across the single pane of glass of the living room window. Eddie wondered how much pressure it would take to push it inward. He was surprised the wind had not pushed it in already.

Still uncertain whether he wanted to face whatever was on the other side, Eddie stared at the door. If he knocked, was he as dumb as Hank? Finally, he tapped twice on the thick wood panel. He knew no one would answer, but he wanted the ghosts of his past to have fair warning before he barged inside. He pressed his shoulder against the heavy wood. The out-of-square frame refused to let the door go. Eddie's muscles bulged as he battled the warped piece of wood. In the end, two hinges gave up, and the exhausted door tipped sideways and rested on the rippled floor inside the house.

Cautiously, Eddie stepped over the threshold. Time stood still. Elizabeth Eleanor Greer had died in her sleep nearly two decades before—not in the River House, but at the nursing home. Eddie would never forget that day. He was planting the east cornfield when Jules's car bounced into sight. Somehow, Eddie knew before she even turned off the ignition. He felt his mother, heard her soft voice telling him he would be okay without her. Waving Jules away, he turned the tractor in the opposite direction and headed out for another pass.

His mom was his everything, but he never let that loss inside. Instead, he drowned it in whiskey and strangled it when it tried to resurface. He had lost her before—when the baby died, when she refused to speak for six weeks, when she would not stand up to his father before he killed his dog, but eventually, she returned to him. This was different; it was permanent. Still, Eddie never cried. His tears dried up years before when he finally realized he had no control over his life. It was in the hands of his father—and fate. It was worthless to think you could control your destiny. Like everyone else, he made the best of the cards he was dealt. But, as a Greer, he had prepared himself to lose.

Hank wandered around the four tiny rooms, pushing his nose along the floor, collecting information. Eddie could smell more than enough without bending over. The scent of mold, dirt, and rotting animals filled the air. Everything was covered in a thick layer of dust, giving even the ornate pine table an antique appearance—but then again, it was. The small icebox door was propped open but still held a strong stale odor. There was evidence mice were frequent visitors. An inch-wide trail cut through the dust on the floor. It was unlikely the mice hung around once the snake appeared.

Eddie pushed the back door open and stepped onto the porch. The swing hung by one rusted chain, and the cushion was black with mold. About a hundred feet from the porch, the river flowed slowly toward the east—a stark contrast to the wild waters of spring. Birds fluttered the leaves on the trees near the river. A rabbit sprang from the underbrush to the left of the cabin, and a deer stepped into what had been the yard years before. For the first time, Eddie understood why his mother loved it here. He finally felt the call to calm.

In the past, seeing deer would have made him anxious for the season to open. A deadeye, Eddie would not have missed, even from this distance. The small buck would have been an easy target, but he had no desire to do anything but watch. There was something different about seeing him behind the River House. Here, he was nature—not food or sport. After the buck disappeared into the coppice, he reentered the house.

A sepia-tone 1800s photograph of the farm hung on the wall dividing the living room from the bedroom. Organized by generation, photos in elaborate frames were set around the room and on the highboy dresser in the bedroom. Eddie held the image of his father as a teen. He could not remember ever seeing his father with a genuine smile. Once his dad started drinking, the only emotion he ever exhibited was anger. Eddie whipped the picture across the room. The corner of the frame poked a hole through the plaster before crashing to the floor. Hank sniffed the photo before squatting and defecating on the picture.

"Hank!" Eddie scolded. But a grin slowly curled the corners of his mouth. "I guess he deserved that."

A crystal-cut perfume bottle with an opulent plug held a place of honor on top of a couple of old books. The liquid inside had oxidized and was a dark amber color. He lifted the lid and leaned in. A metallic scent escaped from the bottle. Eddie's lips curled inward, and his eyes narrowed, nearly closing. It smelled of old people and rusted iron. He quickly recapped the container, but the scent clung to the hairs inside his nostrils and would not let go, even when he wiped his nose with his sleeve.

A pair of round wire reading glasses lay on top of a book on the nightstand. He recalled his grandmother wearing them. The leather-bound book was significantly worn. Sliding the spectacles to the side, he picked it up and rubbed a thumb across the cover several times. It was his mother's bible. She started and ended her day with that book. Jules must have returned it to the house after his mom passed.

His mother lived by the word of God. Daily, she quoted verses to him—words to live by. Eddie chewed on his bottom lip. How could a God-loving, God-fearing woman have killed his father? Maybe he was wrong, or maybe, like the place in hell he hoped his father was suffering, there was a place in heaven for putting up with all his dad's abuse. Would God eventually forgive her? If she had taken her husband's life, she had saved Eddie from an eternity of damnation.

The old bed creaked when he sat down. He drew a deep breath before opening the book. His mother's tiny script handwriting filled the margins. The dog-eared pages indicated it was well-read. Eddie ran his thumb across the edge of the pages. The book fell open to a folded sheet of paper with his name on the outside. Every muscle tightened, and he held his breath. Tracing his name with the tip of his finger, he tried to imagine what his mother felt compelled to tell him. Was it a confession?

He glanced at the old windup alarm clock, which had stopped years before. Since his grandson died, time no longer mattered. The hours blended into a train of relentless thoughts, never giving him a moment's peace. Finally, he grabbed the paper, folded it with one hand, and shoved it inside his front pocket. Nothing his mother wanted him to know twenty years ago had any bearing on his life today. If it truly was a declaration of guilt, he did not want to know.

"Come on, Hank. Let's go."

Less than ten minutes later, the pair were sitting on the hayfield. Hank worked on his afternoon nap. His feet moved as he chased rabbits in his dream. Eddie wished he could be as carefree as the dog.

Eddie reached into his pocket and touched the paper. He could not decide if he should read it or burn it.

18

Eddie - 1980

There was nothing Eddie wanted less than to own the farm. Had he not felt obligated, he would have run. But that was impossible. Juggling the farm, a wife, a kid, and his mom was a burden he would carry until he could devise a better plan. At least the farm gave him an income until he figured it out. He convinced himself it would be a year—*tops*.

The handful of men who worked for him were almost three times his age. He had known them since childhood, yet it made him uncomfortable to be called *boss* by the crew. That name was for someone who knew the ins and outs of running the farm. That was not Eddie—at least not yet. So, he leaned on his farm manager to keep the place running until he got up to speed.

"Someday, you'll pass the land over to your son." His mother signed the last paper, transferring the farm to him. After laying the pen on the table before him, she patted his cheek. "Be proud, Eddie. You are one of a long line of Greer farmers." Then she removed her wedding band from her finger and dropped it in her purse. "Maybe you'll be the one to conquer the curse of the Greer men." She stared at him. It was the profound message buried within that look he did not completely understand.

Eddie eyed her bag. His mother slipped off her wedding ring and removed George Greer from her life. Was it really that easy? He opened his mouth to tell her he would sell the farm when he discovered a path out of Holland Crossing, but he could not. His courage had been beaten down by years of abuse. He heard his father call him a pussy. This was the one time he would have agreed with his old man. Even though his mom never stood up to his father, she was always there to pick up the pieces when his life fell apart. So, he smiled at her, grabbed the pen, and silently signed the contract in front of John Lintner, the only lawyer in town.

How could his mom hang this anvil around his neck, knowing it was not what he wanted, knowing how it broke his father? Eddie loved Jules, but none of this was part of his immediate plan—not the farm, not what felt like a forced marriage, and definitely not an unplanned kid. Weedkiller soaked into his dreams and destroyed them before the roots could take hold.

Two days later, he and Jules helped his mother move into the River House. Several boards on the porch needed to be replaced, and the inside walls needed to be painted. But more than anything, it required a lot of elbow grease to make it livable. Eddie suggested she live with them until the house was inhabitable, but she refused. She did not want to be the third wheel in the honeymoon stage of their marriage. What honeymoon stage? They said their *I do*'s in front of a dozen people, came home, and changed clothes for a long day of work. Their honeymoon was over by 11:12 a.m.

Elbow deep in cleaning supplies, Jules scoured bird poop from windows and swept rodent droppings from cupboards. The women bonded over mops and scrub buckets while he shored up the porch and hung the back swing.

By evening, his pregnant wife was too exhausted to

consummate their marriage. It did not matter to Eddie that she fell asleep holding Doctor Spock's *Baby and Child Care* book or that her hair was a mess, and she wore a ragged t-shirt and a pair of knit shorts instead of a negligée. When she drifted off, he took her book, snapped off the light, and rolled away from her. Eddie loved Jules, but this marriage was beginning to feel like a rope around his neck as much as the farm did.

19

Eddie

It was nearly 7:30 a.m. when Eddie sauntered into the kitchen. His hair was damp, and for the first time in weeks, he had not chosen his clothes from the bedroom floor by sniffing them to determine which were the least offensive.

The morning sun filtered through the stained-glass panel in the living room. A deep red color stretched across the tile of the kitchen. Eddie purchased the window hanging as a wedding gift for Jules. His mother was given a similar one when he was young. But the picture window and the colorful hanging met their demise in a single shotgun blast. Eddie was unsure if he bought it for his new wife or as a middle finger to his father.

With his dad gone, and money tight, Eddie had all he could do to keep the farm afloat back then. Now, money was plentiful, but his *wife* was gone. In the weeks since she walked out, spiders had spun an elaborate display of delicate white threads between the ceiling and the bottom of the window casing. The silk lines crossed in front of the stained glass, making the stained glass appear cracked. Eddie added spiders to the list of inhabitants of the old house. At least they were not alone.

He studied the kitchen. Thanks to his wife's visit, the sink was not heaped with dishes, and his feet did not stick to the floor when he crossed to the stove. The crumbs beneath his boots did not crunch, and his dog no longer wove through the obstacle course of broken glass.

Hank jumped onto the chair at the table and waited for breakfast. Eddie's eyebrows raised as he poured kibble into the dog's dish and set it on the floor.

"We're gonna try something new today, boy." He held Hank's chin in one hand and pointed to the dish on the floor. "You're gonna eat dog food like a dog." Eddie grinned. "I know you're not gonna like it, but…"

Hank looked at the bowl and jerked his nose upward, making it known he wanted it moved back to the table.

After an intense stare-down, Eddie gave in. "Oh, what the hell." He set the silver bowl in front of Hank. "If God didn't build the whole world in one day, I shouldn't have to change everything today."

Eddie turned the stove on and put the coffee pot on the burner. He stared out the window while he waited. In his mind, he saw Jules's taillights as she drove away that August night. With a proverbial pat on the back, he congratulated himself on not being the first to leave. He could have walked away so many times, but unlike his wife, he stayed. No matter how bad it got, he was there for the long haul. Didn't that make him the better person?

In their twelve-minute wedding, Jules promised to love him in sickness and in health, for richer, for poorer, and for better or worse. He could not deny they had lived through the *worst* part of the promise. Sure, they suffered their share of verbal knock-down-drag-out fights. They often slept in separate beds and didn't speak for days. And over time, Eddie had thrown enough dinnerware to rival his father. However, on their wedding day, she promised to love him through it all—but she had not. Like dandelion seeds, she let the wind take that promise. The end of their marriage was *all* on her.

With a cup of coffee and a caramel roll, Eddie joined Hank at the table. The dog's demanding eyes moved between Eddie's face and the sweet roll. After a few seconds, he bent forward and nosed his bowl toward Eddie. Laughing, Eddie tore off a chunk, dropped it into the dish, and pushed it back.

"You're a beggar, dog. Do you know that?"

Hank put his front feet on the table and helped himself to the treat. By the time he finished licking the dish, he was standing on the table, nose to nose with Eddie.

The door swung open after a quick knock. "Hey, Ed, you..." Deep lines grew across Buzz's forehead. "Why's Hank on the table?"

A shrug raised Eddie's shoulders. "Isn't that where you eat your breakfast?"

"Yes, but... Never mind." He scanned the kitchen. "You hire a maid?"

Eddie rubbed the back of his neck before looking at Buzz. "What do you want?"

"The guys are wondering if you plan to work anytime soon. With you and Ca..." Buzz shifted from one foot to the other. "Well, being short a couple of men, we've been putting in longer hours than usual."

The air felt like it had been sucked from the room. Eddie was unsure if he should be pissed or... No. He was pissed. "Are you really asking me that? My grandson just died. I'm grieving. There's no time limit on that."

Buzz nodded. "I get it, but you returned right after Melia's funeral, so I thought..."

Eddie slammed his empty cup on the table. "Hire some help if that's what you need." His eyes narrowed. "For the record, I have no idea when I'll be back. But since the farm's in my name, and *you* work for *me*, I'm pretty damn sure that entitles me to do whatever the hell I want."

Buzz was speechless. His mouth moved, but no words came out for several seconds. "Okay. I'll see who I can round up. Ain't a lot of guys willing to take a job for such a short time."

"That's not my problem. You're the farm manager—so manage and let me get back to grievin' my grandson."

Buzz sighed. "I'll see what I can do."

Hank jumped off the table and wandered to the door. He grabbed the lever of the heavy door in his mouth and tugged it down before pulling it open. When Buzz left, he nudged it shut.

Eddie rolled his eyes. "I wish people had their shit together as much as you do."

The dog jumped back onto his chair and shoved his bowl toward Eddie again.

"Alright." Eddie grinned. "You win."

After Hank's second caramel roll, the pair headed to their usual hangout.

20

Eddie

An eerie stillness washed over the hayfield. Eddie studied the woods for the better part of a minute before opening his chair and setting his thermos on the ground. His stomach flip-flopped. Adrenaline pumped through him, causing an agitation he had not felt since before his father's death. Was it the lack of alcohol in his bloodstream, or something else? Something more sinister?

The tractor was still attached to the old wagon. It had not been moved since the morning Cade died. Eddie gave strict orders—no one was to lay a finger on anything in the field unless they wanted to find their ass at the end of his boot, standing in the unemployment line. Gingerly, he ran his fingers along the first step of the tractor before hesitantly climbing the stairs. Eddie pulled the door open and stepped inside. Hank barked. Laying a hand to his chest, Eddie exhaled sharply.

"Dammit, dog! Go lie down," he growled. Dejected, the dog sauntered away and flopped next to the chair.

With the door still open, Eddie slouched, gingerly leaning against the deteriorating seat that was more duct tape than vinyl. This was where his grandson last sat, the view he saw before warning his grandfather of the gravity of the storm.

Eddie wrapped his arms around the big wheel, overly aware that the last hands to touch it belonged to Cade. He wanted to cry, wanted to feel something beyond weariness and detachment. Trying to force tears had always proven fruitless. He was 1930s Dust Bowl dry. His father saw to that. Besides rage, almost every emotion he felt disappeared between his fourth and fifteenth birthdays.

His eyes jumped toward the scrub on the outskirts of the field. Someone wearing royal blue ran to the left before being swallowed by the shadows of the towering trees. Eddie launched himself from the tractor, landing on his knees. His bad knee screamed. With an awkward run, he took off toward whoever was playing games.

"Hey!" he shouted. "Get the hell off my land."

Three steps into the thicket, Eddie tripped over a downed tree. Guardedly, he rolled onto his side and wrapped an arm across his ribs. He groaned. His labored breathing and a few random birds were the only sounds he heard as he closed his eyes and fought for air.

"Shut up," he wheezed, certain the birds were laughing at him.

Hank trotted into the brush. When Eddie rolled over, he was met with a wet tongue across the face.

Eddie shoved the dog away. "Stop it, Hank. Leave me alone." He dropped his head to the ground. "I just wanna die in peace."

Hank waited. It took several minutes and a few attempts for Eddie to sit. Between his blown-out knee and his aching ribs, he was unsure he could return to the lawn chair without assistance.

"Hey!" he shouted, hoping the intruder could hear. "If you're still in the woods, the least you could do is help me." Not a twig snapped, not a leaf rustled. "Fine, asshole," he muttered under his breath. "Have it your way."

Using a broken limb as a cane, Eddie grimaced as he hobbled toward his chair, stopping every few steps to rest, adjust his grip, and muster enough courage to keep going. Hank walked sideways, staying two steps ahead of him. With the chair a short burst away, Eddie almost smiled. Relief washed over him, and a long sigh escaped. Unable to bend his knee, Eddie uneasily turned in a half-circle and dropped into the chair. The webbing instantly gave way, and he fell through the aluminum frame. His backside landed on the ground, and his arms and his good leg flailed as he attempted to escape the jaws of aluminum.

"Son of a bitch!" he yelled. "Son of a bitch," he repeated through gritted teeth.

Eddie stopped moving and let the newest round of pain cut through him. Freeing himself from the chair would not be easy. Because his phone was lodged in his front pocket and he was folded in half, it was impossible to call for help. The only way out was to dump the chair on its side, but his center of gravity was low. It would take a lot more energy than Eddie had, but his stupidity left him with no choice. After several tries, the chair tipped, dumping Eddie on the shoulder he babied thanks to his dad's abuse. When he was seventeen, a shovel across the arm left him with permanent pain. It was something he never talked about.

Slowly, he slid out of the chair's grip. Finally free, he lay sideways on the ground. Pain shot through his knee, shoulder, ribs, and every inch of his body. He argued with himself about who to call. Jules was the only person he wanted, but he doubted she would even answer her phone after their falling out. Whether she would come or not remained to be seen.

Eddie groaned as he tried to reach for his cell. His shoulder ached, and until he could roll over, his phone was out of the question. *Would anyone even notice he was missing? Would his crew head home without checking on him? Was this where he would die—in the same place as his grandson?*

Staring into the woods, he again saw the flash of blue before his eyes fluttered shut.

21

Eddie & Jules – December 1981

A new moon hid the earth in darkness. It was the one night each month when the moon vanished, even on clear nights. But that night was not clear. Even a full moon was unable to penetrate the dense clouds. A storm was brewing. It would push into the area, dumping a foot and a half of snow over the next two days.

Eddie woke to find Jules missing. He got out of bed and stubbed his toe on the chair next to the bed. "Dammit!" he yelled, holding one foot and hopping on the other.

He clicked on the crystal and bronze bedside lamp and checked his toe—no blood and not broken. It felt a lot worse than it looked. As usual, the old farmhouse was freezing. He quickly pulled on the clothes he had abandoned the previous night and went to find Jules.

His wife of seven months was in the kitchen with her back against the sink. She pressed a hand into the small of her back and arched backward. Eddie froze. He was suddenly eight years old, and it was his mother standing in the kitchen on the day that left him an only child. Was it a premonition? Were they going to lose their baby too?

"Eddie," Jules moaned, clearly in distress. "It's time. We

need to go to the hospital."

Panic spread from Eddie's stomach to his chest. "For the baby? Isn't it too early?"

Jules's breathing was labored. She bent forward, one arm wrapped over the top and the other beneath her protruding stomach. Slowly, she stood up and took a deep breath.

"Okay," she whimpered. "I'll let the baby know it should wait." She frowned at him. "It doesn't work that way."

Sweat beaded on her face and chest. Her gray t-shirt was damp down the front. Grabbing a towel from the hook by the sink, she mopped the perspiration from her face and neck.

"We need to go now. I can't wait. I have to get to the car before the next contraction." She quickly moved toward the door and grabbed her coat. Shrugging into her jacket, she tugged at the front of it, but no matter how hard she pulled, the fabric would not cover her belly. Finally, giving up, she tied the wool belt over her stomach and beneath her breasts to keep it from falling open. Had it not been below zero, she would have skipped the coat altogether.

Eddie touched her cheek. "You're running a fever, Jules."

"I'm having contractions. I'm hot. It's not a fever."

Eddie set her clogs before her and held her arm as she slipped into them. Then he wrapped a black and tan scarf his wife had knit around his neck and buttoned his coat.

"How far apart are they?"

"Closer than they should be for being an hour from the hospital. You're going to have to drive fast." She shot him a warning look. "But be safe. Do you hear me? I don't want this baby to be born in a ditch between here and Ashton."

For the first time, Eddie smiled. "I got it. I'll get you there in plenty of time—and safely." He hooked an arm behind her back, placed the other under her elbow, and steered her down the stairs and toward the car. "Now, let's go meet our son."

"Or d-daughter," Jules wheezed as the beginning of another contraction took hold.

Suddenly, a gush of water hit the ground.

"Oh, my God! My water just broke. Eddie?" She doubled over and took several deep breaths.

Eddie rubbed her back as she breathed through the contraction. He beamed. "Davis Richard Greer," he said to the world.

Jules finally stood. She shivered as she crawled into the freezing car. In the short time they were outside, her wet sweatpants had begun to stiffen with frost. She closed her eyes and prayed the old car would even start in the freezing temps. Usually, the block heater would have been plugged in, but she was early—too early for a healthy baby. She read all the books. Something was not right, but she would never admit that to Eddie.

She rested her hand on Eddie's leg as he guided the rear-wheel-drive Dodge Dart along the icy driveway. "I hope you won't be disappointed if we have a girl."

Eddie smiled. "We aren't having a girl. You told me the doctor said the heart rate was slow." He grinned at her. "And the way you're carrying—well, that's definitely a boy." He set his hand on hers. "You'll see."

Within four hours, Melia Elizabeth Greer entered the world. Eddie felt like he had been punched in the gut when the doctor announced his baby was a girl. Doctor Willems cleared the baby's mouth and nose before a low-pitched cry filled the room.

Jules saw the pain on Eddie's face when the nurse set their baby on her stomach. She snuggled their daughter. "She's beautiful, Eddie. Look, she has your mouth." But Eddie said nothing. His face was a tangle of anger and disappointment.

After a few minutes, the nurse took their baby girl to the far side of the room to get her weighed, measured, and cleaned up. "She's perfect," the nurse said, holding their daughter.

"Oh my gosh," the doctor muttered. "Aileen, call for another crib, stat."

She set the baby in a small glass bassinet and extended the order to a nurse in the hallway.

Jules started breathing heavily again. She squeezed her husband's hand.

"What's happening?" Eddie asked. "What's going on?"

Doctor Willems tipped his head in surprise. "Looks like you're getting two babies for the price of one today."

"What?"

The second nurse patted his arm. "You're having twins, Dad. One for each of you."

Eddie's knees buckled. He collapsed onto the stool next to the bed. "Twins?"

"Nurse!" the doctor said. "Keep an eye on Dad."

The nurse handed him a glass of water and stood next to him.

"One more push, Jules. You've got this. I can see the head."

Jules grunted as she bore down. Moments later, the second baby came into the world. But instead of noise this time, there was silence. The doctor handed the baby to Nurse Aileen. She gently laid the baby in the cart and left the room with the bassinet.

"What's going on?" Jules asked. "Where's she taking my baby?"

Dr. Willem moved next to the bed. "I'm so sorry." He shook his head. "The second baby didn't make it. The umbilical cord was wrapped around his neck. Sometimes that happens."

Jules started crying. Eddie ignored her distress. He was too focused on what the doctor said.

"*His* neck? You said *his* neck. It was a boy?"

Dr. Willem nodded. "Yes, a little boy. I would say…"

Eddie suddenly grew very agitated. "You've got to save him. There's got to be something you can do." He began to pace. "Do your job, Doc. Save my son."

"I'm sorry, Mr. Greer. Unfortunately, there's nothing we can do." He returned to his stool and checked Jules. "I know this is hard, but you're luckier than most couples. You still have a beautiful baby girl. At least you aren't going home with empty arms."

Eddie's face fell. His eyes grew dark. "That's bullshit. Is that the only response you have for killing somebody's kid?"

"Eddie!" Jules sobbed. "He didn't do it. It just happened." She took Eddie's hand. "I'm so sorry," she whispered. "This isn't anybody's fault. We can try again." Eddie could not even look at his wife. "Talk to me, please. Tell me what you're thinking—what you're feeling."

"What I'm thinking?" He dropped onto the stool. "I'm wondering what the hell good a girl is on a farm?" he whispered. "I'd say she's pretty damn worthless."

"What?" Jules swiped at the tears on her cheeks. "She's your daughter—*your* little girl. I know you're hurting. I am too. But why can't she be enough? Are you telling me you can't love her?"

"I'm telling you, *she* should have been the one to die."

"You need to leave," Dr. Willems firmly instructed. "This isn't good for your wife, and until you get your head on straight, it isn't good for your daughter either." He pointed to the door. "Now go."

Eddie's jaw tightened as he stared at the doctor. Several seconds later, he stormed from the room and out of the hospital.

Within minutes, with a fake ID, at the beginning of the first massive snowfall of the season, Eddie sat at the counter at the

Gobbler Bar and Hotel with his first of many drinks. The self-destruction his father started came full circle the second the doctor told him his son was dead.

When he returned home a week later, wearing the same sweatshirt and jeans he had worn to the hospital, his mother rocked the baby while Jules napped.

His mom clicked her tongue. "Nice of you to join your family, Edward."

She had not called him *Edward* a day in his life. Her disappointed tone made him cringe. It had always been the two of them against the world.

"Where've you been, son?"

"Does it matter?" He looked down at his daughter.

With her eyes narrowed, she glared at him. "It does to your wife." She looked at the baby in her arms. "And to your daughter."

He flinched and dropped onto the couch near her chair.

"Eddie, I know you're hurting, but Jules is too. You aren't the only one who lost a baby. She needed you. And by the looks of you…" she tipped her head away from him, "and the smell, you have been drowning your sorrow in a vat of whiskey. Do you think that was fair to her?" She gently bounced her granddaughter. "Shame on you. I don't think I've ever said that to you, son. But shame on you. I'm embarrassed by your behavior, and you should be too. I didn't raise you this way."

Biting the inside of his cheek, Eddie kept himself from saying the one thing that would anger his mother more than anything else. *No, but you never stood up to Dad when he treated you like crap, so why are you riding my ass now?*

Because of Eddie's anger, Jules opted for no funeral. The undertaker dealt with the burial, laying their son to rest at the small log church with no one present except Jules, her mother-in-law, Melia, and the pastor. That day, Eddie sat in the barn nursing a pint of whiskey and a hell of a lot of anger.

22

Eddie

The longer Eddie lay on the field, the stiffer his body grew. The only person he longed for was Jules, but he knew he did not deserve her.

Groaning loudly, he rolled onto his back and painfully fished his phone out of his pocket to make the call.

"Hey," he moaned into the phone. "I, ah…"

"Eddie, what's going on? You sound like you're drunk. I don't have…"

"I'm not drunk." He winced. "I'm hurt. I fell."

"Where are you?"

He held his breath for a second before he could answer. "I'm on the hayfield. Can you…"

"I'll be right there."

Eddie dropped his hand and phone to the ground. Hank curled up next to him. "She's coming, boy. Maybe we still have a chance."

Thirty minutes later, she drove onto the hayfield.

Instead of opening her door, Jules rolled down her window and stared at him. "You look like hell, Greer," she teased.

"Don't judge. Just help me up."

Jules got out of her car and lowered herself to the ground.

"Now, what happened to you—besides the chair, I mean?"

Laying an arm across his forehead to block the sun, he sighed. "Someone was in the woods again. I thought I could catch them this time." He snorted. "But I tripped on a log and took a header before I got to them."

She nodded slowly. "Face it. You're old, Eddie Greer. You'll never catch whoever it is you think you see and hear over there. How old are you going to be before you learn that?"

"How old am I *today*?"

"Old enough to know better." Jules shook her head.

"Just help me up, will you? You'll have plenty of time to criticize me later. I have a feeling I'm not going anywhere for a while."

"Where do you hurt?"

"You mean specifically? I can't just say *everywhere*?"

"Well, it would be helpful if I knew where so I can figure out how to help you up."

Eddie tenderly raised each leg, testing them. "Right knee." He moved one arm and then the other. "Oh, crap. That hurts. Left shoulder." He touched his stomach and drew in a sharp breath. "And all my ribs." He lay flat. "And I may have blown out my back when the chair collapsed."

"Eddie," Jules chastised. "You should have called an ambulance."

"I know that now." He grimaced. "Just call Buzz and have him and one of the guys come and help."

Jules leaned sideways and pulled her phone from her back pocket. "And why didn't you call Buzz yourself?"

"We haven't exactly been on the best of terms. Honestly, I've been a little—difficult lately."

"Lately?" Jules laughed. "Eddie, the last time you were nice to anyone, Carter was president."

Buzz and Leo arrived minutes later. The pair helped Eddie

to his feet and settled him into the passenger's seat of Jules's Explorer.

"Might want to…" Buzz held his palms up and outward at his shoulders. "Never mind. I, ah, don't want to tell you what to do, boss."

Eddie grabbed his arm before Jules slammed the door. "I owe you an apology, Buzz."

His farm manager nodded. "Yeah, you do. More than one."

"Okay, I'll keep it until the next time I'm an asshole." He winked at Buzz. "For now, just put it on my tab."

Buzz grinned. "I figured." He carefully pushed the door shut and leaned on the open window. "But just so you know, your tab's getting mighty long. I ain't sure there are enough apologies in the world that are even gonna make a dent in the crap you've pulled over the years."

Jules started the car. Buzz stepped back and nodded to her.

Eddie sighed. "I deserve that." He shrugged his good shoulder. "Still, I'm gonna try."

By the time Jules got Eddie back to the farmhouse, he was sporting a leg brace and a sling. His bruised and battered ribs only *felt* broken. He had a prescription for pain, a breathing apparatus and exercises, and an appointment card for his return visit—that he was not likely to keep.

As much as he knew she wanted to leave him, Eddie knew she would not. It was nearly impossible to care for himself when he was healthy, and most of his appendages were working. Being injured would be a nightmare. Maybe this, like the *accident* that brought them together in high school, would finally make Jules recognize the man she fell in love with.

23

Eddie

Even with two extra bedrooms upstairs, Eddie insisted on sleeping on the couch, giving Jules their bedroom. His excuse was anything but the truth. *The sofa was firmer, and he needed that for his back.* But his back was not the issue. He wanted her to spend time in the one place where their relationship had not been so volatile—especially before everything went to hell. Before his grandson's death, he never wallowed in the past, but now he referred to memories as BA and AA—*before asshole* and *after asshole.* The first was nothing but a blip in his life.

Jules slid an end table in front of the arm of the sofa to house anything Eddie might need. She left only a glass of water, his cell phone and charger, and the television remote within his reach. She had taken his two bottles of whiskey upstairs, out of reach of bad decisions. His pain pills were also inaccessible. He watched her tuck them in her robe pocket. They were safe since he was no longer invited to touch her. They argued about his medication, but Eddie was not exactly in a position to win any fights. He needed her—and wanted her—so he gave in. Honestly, he would not have trusted himself, either. It would have been too easy to self-medicate.

"If you need anything, call my cell," Jules said. She gently plumped the pillow under his knee and the one beneath his shoulder. "And don't be so damn stubborn and try to do things yourself. With only half your body working, you aren't in any shape to play a sixty-year-old hero. Got it?" She gave him a warning look. "I'll be back when you're due for your next pill."

The one she gave him had not kicked in yet. Eddie grimaced as he adjusted his head. "You don't have to stay, you know. I can take care of myself."

Jules laughed. "You couldn't even get yourself off the field today, remember?" She walked toward him and frowned.

"Why are you looking at me?" He eyed her suspiciously.

"You know what, Eddie? I still love you. I think there's a part of me that always will." She pulled a quilt from the back of the couch and threw it over his legs. "But most of the time, you're the most infuriating man in the entire world. Sometimes, I have a hard time even *liking* you."

He wiggled his eyebrows and grinned before wagging a finger up and down his chest several times. "How could you not *like* this?"

Shaking her head, Jules turned away, but not before Eddie caught the faintest smile.

Hank trailed her to their bedroom.

"Traitor," Eddie called. Then he whispered, "Come on, Hank. Bring her back to us."

Eddie lay in the dark and thought about her admission, referring to the hundreds of times he had hurt her. Finally, he drifted off to sleep, memories flickering like old movies.

1984

Getting booted from bars was not exactly foreign to Eddie.

Most recently, he had been ousted from the Buckthorn and Matt's Bar. Since he could not step foot in *any* establishment in town, including the Firelight Inn, he took his drinking on the road, visiting the lake country bars: Brann's, the Palace, Brickhouse, and Round Lake Retreat. Sometimes, he stopped in for a meal; other times, it was only to forget for a while. Most of the time, it was the latter.

Twice, after brawls at Brann's, he was tossed out with burrito residue on his face and a tortilla plastered to his shirt. The second time was for good. The problem was, it was not just Brann's—or burrito. Almost everywhere he went ended with food on his face and a chorus of *Na, Na, Na, Na, Hey Hey-ey, Goodbye.*

With almost nowhere left in the community to support his habit, except at home in the presence of his fault-finding wife, Eddie landed at the Moose Lodge. Not willing to risk being ejected again, he always chose the darkest corner, keeping his back to the crowd. He interacted with no one. If anyone spoke to him, he kept his head down and his mouth closed.

By closing time each night, he was well past being able to drive. Occasionally, one of his crew would offer him a ride home, but he never accepted. He would rather take his chances behind the wheel than face his wife with a bellyful of booze. Often, he slept in the cab of his truck. In the dead of winter, he nearly froze to death a handful of times, but that had not stopped him from repeating the same behavior.

Everyone saw him as a drunk. But Eddie was not willing to admit that to himself or anyone else. As far as he was concerned—he drank. There was more than just a letter's difference between drink, drank, and drunk. He had a *drink*. He *drank* a few. But he was not a *drunk*—at least not a fall-down alkie like Larry Butterfield—soused no matter the time of day. Everyone in the community knew that guy was an expert elbow-bender. But that wasn't Eddie. No matter how much he drank the night before, by daybreak, he was always back on the farm overseeing his work crew, pitching in to keep the farm running smoothly.

His father, on the other hand, had been a drunk. He wasted every extra penny, disappearing into town under the lie of picking up *supplies*. That was a gross distortion of the truth. Every afternoon, he left the farm in search of the same supplies he had gone to get the day before. The only supplies he ever bought were consumed from a tall glass in the presence of a bartender.

Because of his dad's habit, there were weeks when Eddie and his mom only ate whatever she could scrounge up from the garden. Except for milk from the cows and every other day egg from the only chicken his father had not killed for *his* dinner, the refrigerator was almost always empty. One winter, Eddie ate canned peaches every meal for a week. Frequently, he went to bed so hungry, he cried himself to sleep. It was not until he was an adult that he realized his mom's claim of not wanting to eat was a cover to ensure there was enough food for him. Still, it was never enough. No matter how much they suffered, his father never seemed to experience the same trials. He often stumbled into the house smelling of booze and burger grease.

To make matters worse, his father refused to complete the paperwork for free school lunch. *No one else needed to know their damn business.* So, when Eddie sat at the lunch table without a tray, he fabricated tales about the massive breakfast his mom made him while he attempted to cover the noise from his grumbling stomach.

By age seven, he was nothing but skin and bones. The school nurse contacted his mother to ask if he suffered from tapeworm. After a short conversation, she sent him back to class but insisted he report to her office every morning to be weighed.

For the next two years, the school nurse, a gray curly-haired woman with a stern face and a rare smile, handed him a brown paper bag with a sandwich, a handful of vegetables, and a cookie on his way out the door. Had his father known, he would have put an end to it. So, Eddie told no one—not even his mother.

When Eddie turned ten, his mom had begun taking in laundry and mending to earn extra money. Customers never came to the farm. She made a deal with Marion to use Shaw's as a pickup and drop-off site. Marion, like everyone, knew about George's viciousness, so she agreed. It was the only way his mother could ensure his father would not stop her. That little extra money was the difference between life and death.

Unlike when his father owned the land, under Eddie's management, the farm was profitable. He had enough money in the bank to do whatever he and Jules wanted. The problem, however, was all Eddie wanted to do was drink, and all his wife wanted to do was nag.

What else did Eddie have? According to the doctor, more kids were out of the question. He saw that as a betrayal on his wife's part. After she let his son die, she promised they would have another. She had been the one to break that agreement, not him.

More than a handful of times, Jules got pregnant. That was the easy part. Each time Eddie believed he would finally get his son, but it never happened. Jules failed at bringing even one more child into the family. Time and again, she disappointed him—always getting his hopes up only to destroy them with her incompetence to carry a baby to term.

24

Jules

Eddie's clothes lay scattered across the bedroom. It was nearly impossible to tell what color the floor was beneath the mess. She began tossing anything with the tangy odor of sweat into the hamper. It would take several baskets to collect everything that needed washing.

Standing in the middle of the bedroom, she pulled her arms against her chest and slowly turned in a circle. The room was every bit as cozy as the day she walked away. It felt like home. She nursed their daughter, conceived six more children, and spent several months in the arms of her husband in this room—until their dreams imploded.

Jules slipped into a silky knee-length nightgown. It was one of the pieces of clothing she had not taken when she left. Hotel life was limited; it could not accommodate an entire wardrobe. She packed only two suitcases because she had not committed to leaving permanently. Leaving enough reminders to make Eddie miss her was part of her exit plan: lipstick on the dresser, a nightgown under her pillow, and a closet of her clothes. But the way the room looked, she doubted he noticed.

When they first started dating, she would not have believed it had someone warned her who Eddie would become. It was impossible to imagine. He was so kind, loving, and gentle with her—unlike the self-centered, indifferent drunk he became after the loss of their son.

Their first sixteen months together were amazing. In the beginning, she could see nothing that would drive them apart. Since they made it through the unplanned pregnancy, she believed they could face anything together. But she could not have been more wrong.

There was not a moment Jules did not long for the happiness of those early days. Perhaps she could have done something to change their trajectory. But that was a dream—or a nightmare. It was impossible to tell. Trying to change a person whose feet were mired in cement was hopeless. Over time, that was how she saw her husband.

Jules was also keenly aware their past could not be revisited except in regrets and sorrow. Even if, by some miracle, things changed, she could never trust Eddie not to backslide. They had faced too many steep hills and deep valleys in their marriage. The saddest part was that she had journeyed alone for most of that distance. A framed copy of their marriage certificate hung on the wall next to every other Greer who had owned the farm. It proved they were husband and wife, a partnership until death. But Jules never felt more alone. That was why she left. Everything that mattered to her was gone. At times, she found herself suffocating, drowning in loneliness. She deserved more, much more than Eddie was willing to give.

Once she conquered Eddie's clothes, she went after the bedside tables, double dresser, lamps, and windowsills. Scrubbing the bathroom was next on her list.

Thirty minutes later, she poked her head into the moonlit living room. The worries of the day washed away, and her body melted in relief. So much had happened in such a short time. Her heart ached for all she had lost. She glanced toward the sofa—and all she could still lose.

Returning to the bedroom, she snapped off the ceiling light. In the late 1950s, the once gas-powered chandelier was rewired for electricity. She turned what looked like a key on the bedside lamp. The bulb was dim but sufficient. Once in bed, she arranged the well-loved white and pink quilt over her legs and leaned against the marbled walnut headboard. Tears welled in her eyes. Home was a palace compared to her room at the Town and Country Motel. There was nothing wrong with the hotel, but it did not belong to her; she was only borrowing it. Jules breathed in the familiar smell of home. She ran her hand along the undisturbed side of the bed. It felt right to be back at the farm, even though she was still completely alone.

The 1940s pale wallpaper, covered in pink and white roses, had yellowed even more since her mother-in-law moved to the River House, and she and Eddie became the keepers of the farm. But Jules still adored it. This room was nothing like her 1970s bedroom décor, a rip-off of the *Dating Game*. Moving from that to this grown-up bedroom was a shock. At seventeen, she had stepped out of her childhood and into adulthood. But considering that she was expecting, it felt right.

The bedroom was classic and beautiful. To Eddie's annoyance, Jules had taken great care to preserve the past and the memories each item carried. She would not have traded her life for anything in those first several months. But after her daughter was born, she longed to return to her loud bedroom, her mother and father, and her life before Eddie. Even her miserable aunts, who saw her as nothing more than a stepping stone to their financial freedom, would have been a better alternative. And she *would have* returned with her daughter had they not sold the house and disappeared without a forwarding address. That would have been better than dealing with her selfish husband and his self-obsession.

Yet, she stayed. She promised to love, honor, and cherish Eddie until death parted them. But over the years, she discovered that death came in many forms. Marriage did not always end in a cemetery or with ashes scattered to the four winds. The death of theirs ended at the hands of her husband. He had killed it simply by being himself.

She glanced around the dimly lit room. It was not just the room that captured her love. If she were being honest with herself, she loved everything about the old farmhouse except the man her husband had turned into.

Jules removed a leather-bound notebook from the top drawer of her nightstand. On her wedding day, Elizabeth gifted her with a handful of journals. Her mother-in-law's words were still as fresh as they were that day. *Honey, sometimes the farm will get so lonely you'll need someone to talk to. If you can't find someone, these diaries will have to do.* Elizabeth could not have been more right. Her mother-in-law and Melia were her confidants because she could not turn to her husband. Eddie perfected ignoring her unless she said the wrong thing or used the wrong tone; then, it was like adding kindling to a fire. He was explosive.

Since they married, Jules had kept a dozen journals. There were sweet memories with Elizabeth, her daughter, and even her friends, but most of it was heartbreaking.

It was Elizabeth who taught her how to be a wife and a mother, teaching her to cook and clean, always to choose love, and to forgive and forget. She looked up, past the ceiling and into the heavens. "I'm sorry, Elizabeth. Some things are just too hard to forgive—and especially forget."

Flipping through the journal, Jules stopped on *July 12, 1986.* Laying her finger between the pages, she closed the book and brought the memory to life—in the hospital, alone, wondering what was wrong with her to have failed so many times. Eddie was not part of the memory until the very end. He had not cared enough to even go with her.

25

Jules—1986

Her fifth miscarriage in four years concerned Dr. Willems. He begged her to stop trying for another child. He handed her a pamphlet explaining that each miscarriage increased *her* risk of dying, but she needed to fulfill the promise she had made to her husband.

Eddie saw the toll it took on her: weight loss, depression, anxiety, sleepless nights, and deep black circles around her eyes. But he wanted a son more than he needed a wife. Regularly, he told her she looked like hell; he even told her to put on some make-up to cover *those raccoon eyes*. So, she did. She promised him a son, and if she was going to give it to him, making herself presentable enough to garner his attention in the bedroom was what she would do.

Jules became a calendar watcher; she took her temperature daily to know when she was ripe to conceive. On her most fertile night, while he sat at his desk completing bookwork, listening to the farm report on the local radio station, Jules put Melia to bed and went to him. She rubbed his back, took his hand, and led him to the bedroom. They no longer made love. They had *sex*—lasting no more than a couple minutes at best. There was no foreplay, no romance. He never stayed long enough to make sure she was satisfied. It was all done for the sole purpose of creating a baby.

When Eddie was done, he climbed off her, pulled on his shirt and pants, and headed toward the door. He leaned against the frame and buckled his belt. Feeling vulnerable against his judging stare, she raised the quilt to cover her nakedness. He scowled at her until she turned away. Pressure built behind her eyes, and tears threatened to fall.

"You know, *I* keep doing this over and over—and every single time, *you* let me down. If it doesn't work this time, if I don't get the son you promised, you and that girl of yours might as well pack up your crap and get the hell off my farm." Then, he turned and walked away.

Jules trembled. His words were callous. Their sharpness cut her deeper than anything he had ever said before—not because they were aimed at her, but because he saw his daughter as disposable.

It was rare Eddie ever returned to their bed after their time together. For that, she was grateful. The few times he returned, he did nothing but hurl insults at her. He called her a slut and referred to himself as her master.

Minutes after he left the bedroom, Jules heard the front door slam. She closed her eyes and wept. The truck sputtered before it started. She was unsure which was worse—Eddie leaving or staying. Jules wiped her face on her t-shirt before pulling it over her head. Then, she got down on her knees and prayed for a miracle.

Two months later, after several more cringeworthy rounds of *sex*, Jules was expecting. She breathed a tiny sigh of relief that the sixth time took. Still, she took great care in everything she did—from how she moved to what she ate.

Her worries eased just a bit when she passed the three-month mark, further along than she had gotten in any of her last five pregnancies. Eddie was positive he was getting his son. He said it aloud again and again, as if the more times he said it, the more likely it was to be true. *My son is going to take over the farm. My son is going to be strong and brave. My son will learn how to act like a man—and drink like a man.* Jules warned him not to get his hopes up, but he insisted God would not dare screw him over again. According to him, the man upstairs had already beaten him down too many times. He owed him.

Cautious but hopeful, Jules settled into the idea of becoming a mother for the second time. As her stomach grew, so did her relief. In her second trimester, she regained energy and began preparing the nursery for the newest Greer. Eddie seemed a bit more settled, happier even. It was rare he stayed away at night. She hoped it meant they were making a U-turn in their marriage—headed back to where they started.

During week eighteen, an ultrasound confirmed Eddie was right. That night, she cooked his favorite foods and baked a cake with blue frosting to let him know he was getting his son. For the first time in a *very* long time, he smiled. Five minutes later, he drove away, headed to a bar to celebrate—without her.

At her next appointment, she questioned why she had not felt the baby move yet. Dr. Willems assured her it would happen soon. While pregnancies were similar, they were also unique. Just like with children, pregnancy milestones were reached within a range.

The doctor smiled at her and warmed his stethoscope with the palm of his hand before pressing it under her belly, just above the pelvic bone. Repeatedly, he moved it, each time adding slightly more pressure. He helped her roll onto one side, and then the other. Jules watched his face. Panic set in. She bit the inside of her cheek to keep from screaming. Suddenly, Dr. Willems left the room, assuring her he would return with a better stethoscope. Instead, several minutes later, his nurse arrived and told her the hospital was waiting for her. They had better equipment to hear the baby's heartbeat.

The block to the hospital was a death march. She moved slowly, thought about everything except the baby: the brightly colored flowers, the brilliant blue of the sky, and the cracks in the sidewalk.

She finally took a deep breath and admitted to herself what no one else would. Better equipment was not going to bring back a dead baby. It was not going to give Eddie his son back either.

Days of Eddie's endless blaming and pointing fingers finally turned to deafening silence just before Jules left for the hospital. She delivered her stillborn son alone three days after she learned of his death. Eddie remained at the farm— translated: the bar, while his mother took care of Melia.

It was a déjà vu moment Jules could not shake. The memory of Melia's twin brother nearly suffocated her. Except for size, *Justin Wesley Greer* was a carbon copy of her first son. She cradled him in her arms and burned him into her mind: his smell, feel, and tiny face. He was as small as her childhood dolls, and just like her plastic babies, his eyes remained closed, and he never drew a breath. Tears blurred her vision and dripped onto his face. Gently, she wiped them off with the pad of her thumb. She cried for Justin, Davis, and every one of her babies who would never feel the sunshine on their skin. Tears fell for her marriage, for the loser Eddie told her she was, and for all she would never have. With a broken heart, she kissed her son before passing him to the nurse and locking away her emotions. Minutes later, they took her into surgery. Jules could not face loss again.

Justin was buried next to his brother without fanfare. Elizabeth and Melia flanked her. Her mother-in-law squeezed her hand. Melia bounced her back against her mother's leg. Just before they lowered the casket into the ground, Melia set a toy truck on top of it. She cupped her hands around her face and whispered something Jules could not hear. Then, she tipped one ear toward the casket for a few seconds before skipping back to her mom.

"Mommy, Justin said thanks for taking care of him in your tummy."

Jules dropped to her knees and held her daughter's arms. "Justin told you that?" The little girl's eyes grew wide, and she nodded. "Thank you, honey. I needed to hear that."

It was nearly dark by the time she left the cemetery. For hours, she sat between the two graves, silently praying for God to take her and Melia so they would no longer suffer at the hands of her husband. Before she left, she placed a small teddy bear on each grave. Then, she told her sons they were in a far better place. Had they stayed, their father would have destroyed their dreams.

Eddie learned Jules had her tubes tied from his mother rather than her. Too pained, she was unable to tell him. It cut her to the quick to know Melia, like her and Eddie, would be an only child.

Not having a boy meant the end of the Greer name, the end of the farm. Not a day passed that he did not throw that in her face. He chastised her for breaking her promise to give him a son, and he overreached in his criticism of her inability to succeed at *anything*—asserting she did not try hard enough. When he was not torturing her with reminders of her failure, he was sucking down whiskey. Jules did not like either of his habits, but she was unsure which she *hated* less.

Through the grapevine, she learned he had propositioned several young women, hoping to find a suitable carrier for a son—a descendant to carry on the Greer name and take over the farm. In his drunkenness, he flashed hundreds of dollars in front of women who could give him what Jules could not. But so far, her informants told her he had not left the bars with any of them. That meant he kept from inserting his *Part P* into every woman's *Part V*. For that, Jules was grateful.

Eddie's anger over not having a son made little sense to Jules. Running the farm was never his dream. In high school, he could have cared less if the ownership ended with his father, but now that he was in charge, he could not let it go. He told her there was no way he would let it fall to someone else. Other than having a child with someone else, Jules was at a loss as to how he planned to stop it.

He no longer attempted to hide his animosity for his daughter. His words were mean, and his actions were worse. Eddie saw Melia as nothing more than a carbon copy of the woman who repeatedly disappointed him. But that did not stop Melia from loving her father. After a challenging day, Eddie returned home to a little girl who wanted nothing more than approval and love from him. Jules watched Mel wind her arms around his waist and press her rosy cheek against his stomach.

"Daddy, Daddy, Daddy!" she sang.

Eddie untangled her arms and shoved her backward.

"Daddy," Melia whined, "I love you."

"Leave me alone," he grumbled, heading toward their bedroom.

"Edward Henry Greer!" Jules was two steps behind him. "That little girl is your daughter. How dare you treat her like she is nothing."

He spun around. "That's right, wife. She's my *daughter*—not my *son*. And that's on you. All I asked for was a boy to run the farm when I die. But that's not gonna happen now that you're… What?" He swirled a hand in front of her stomach. "*Closed for business? You* made that decision. I didn't." He slammed his fist into the wall, cracking the plaster and leaving a fine line in the striped wallpaper. "No one consulted me about it."

Jules sighed heavily. Deep lines gathered across her forehead. "When we got married, all you asked from me was to love you for the rest of my life. Remember? That was five years ago, Eddie. Four of those years have been the most miserable of my life. This marriage feels an awful lot like a life sentence."

Eddie spun around. He tightened his jaw and pulled his clenched fist across his chest.

"Go ahead, hit me," Jules taunted. "But if you do, it'll be the last time you ever lay a hand or eyes on me or your daughter. Neither one of us deserves this self-serving asshole you've become."

Slowly, Eddie lowered his hand and turned away. "As I recall, I told you to leave if you couldn't give me a son."

Jules circled him and poked a finger into his chest. "Don't. Tempt. Me. If I go, I'll ruin you. I'll take every penny you have and force you to sell the farm or buy my half. And I don't think there's any bank in Minnesota who'll loan money to a drunk." Eddie glared at her, but he said nothing. "Your mom put up with your dad's bull, but I won't—not anymore. I'm done. You don't want to mess with me. I don't have family to fall back on, but the people in this town would choose me a million times over you—and that includes the sheriff's department. You've burned too many bridges. I swear, your roads only lead to the bars."

He walked into the bathroom and slammed the door.

"You're a drunk, Eddie. And if things don't change, I'll sell my half of the farm to the—the Mayers."

The door flew open. Eddie's eyes were wild. "Don't

threaten me, Jules. You have no idea what I'm capable of."

She shrugged. "Oh, I know. You're evil." She stepped toward him. "But if you want me to play nice, don't treat me like one of your hired hands. I'm your wife, for crying out loud—the one you promised to love for the rest of your life." She pointed toward the door. "And that little girl is your daughter. Treat her like she matters, Eddie, because she does. And I won't let you hurt her anymore."

Their eyes locked, and neither would look away. Finally, Eddie quietly closed the door. Jules heard him collapse against it before sliding to the floor. She was done playing his game. If he wanted to treat her like crap, she would throw it back in his face.

26

Jules—1985

The start of kindergarten was less than a week away. Melia was ready; Jules was not. The program ran only two or three days each week, but those few days apart were enough to push Jules over the edge. She lost all her other children. Mel was all that remained, and the older her daughter got, the more distance she felt.

For the first two weeks of school, Jules drove Melia to town instead of allowing her to ride the bus. She walked her into the classroom, helped her find her seat, and stayed with her until Mrs. Stine gently escorted her out. By the third week, Jules was on a *parent plan*. She could drop Mel at the door but not enter the room. She was welcome to stand in the hallway for as long as needed but could not step through the doorway. In week four, she was only allowed to walk *to* the main door of the building, but not through it. Each week, Jules found it easier to let go of her daughter. Finally, on October first, Melia rode the bus for the first time—with Jules following. *Baby steps.*

Connie House convinced Jules to join a grief group in Ashton and even accompanied her to the first meeting. Each session, she learned something new that might get Eddie to express his grief rather than stuff it down. But it was two steps forward and three steps back. Finally convinced he would never *feel* anything, she gave up on him and focused on herself. Connecting with parents who suffered losses helped her realize she would survive.

Because Jules lost seven children, Diane Waller, her therapist, suggested she create a *small* memorial at home, a place she could visit whenever she needed to address her sorrow. Jules asked Elizabeth to help her design something beautiful. For weeks, her mother-in-law begged her to create something small, indoors, out of Eddie's sight. But Jules would not give in. To her, the more elaborate, the better.

Jules finally settled on a memorial garden. Seven stepping stones, each embedded with a different colored marble, would circle the flowerbed. The first two colors would represent her stillborn sons; the others would represent each child she lost through a miscarriage. Because Melia's favorite color was pink, a bleeding heart would take center stage—as the *watcher*. Jules knew she and Melia would one day reunite with these seven incredible little souls. As for Eddie, she was not so sure he would join them in the afterlife.

All winter, Jules worked on the stepping stones. Tears dropped into the cement as she mixed it. Somehow it seemed fitting. Buried in the center of each was a personalized note she had taken great pains to write. She included the name she would have given them—both boy and girl—just in case, their expected birth month and year, and a bible quote. On top, she laid a circle of stones in a color representing that child.

Most mornings, before Melia woke, Jules retreated to the garden to spend time with her heavenly children. Sometimes she read her bible. Other times she talked, whispering apologies into the wind.

She wondered if her memorial bordered on maniacal. It

obviously was more than what Diane intended when she said *small*. If it had not been, she would not have lied to her therapist about it. Did the garden keep her from healing? Or was it the only thing that kept her from going insane?

Eddie hated the garden. He did not try to hide his feelings about it. But Jules never said a word, even when he told her it was sick to memorialize children she failed to bring into the world—ones *she* let die. To Eddie, they never existed if they had not taken a breath. Repeatedly, Eddie reminded her the time she *wasted* in the garden could best be spent caring for *him*.

He also hated the hours she spent away from home and all the trips she made to Ashton because she was *sick in the head*. She was so tired of his judgment and condescending comments, but she held her tongue. Jules was too busy caring for herself to worry about what he thought.

Elizabeth helped Jules through her grief. Not only had they both lost a child, but they shared the misfortune of marrying Greer men. That alone called for a support group. Jules knew their closeness angered Eddie, but her mother-in-law and Mel were her only family. He was jealous of their relationship, and he aimed his spear of anger at them as he did toward everyone else in Holland Crossing. There was no way to convince him that no one was plotting against him.

By August, Eddie often disappeared in the late afternoons, leaving Jules and Mel to eat dinner alone or with Elizabeth. Truthfully, she did not mind. It was much easier to breathe when he was not drunkenly slurring sentences or criticizing her every move. And it was better for Melia not to constantly see her father three sheets to the wind.

Jules should have left long ago. But she could not. Elizabeth was the only person who understood why she stayed. The entire town wondered how she could live with a man who treated her like the manure he wiped from his boots. The easy answer was—she stayed for Melia. She wanted her to grow up on the farm near her grandmother. The honest answer was much more difficult to explain.

Until her parents died, Jules lived an idyllic childhood. After their deaths, she was thrown into a situation that left her longing for love. By default, she landed under the care of strangers who only saw her as dollar signs. The only person she really loved was Lottie. She trusted her best friend with her whole heart. So, when Lottie pointed her toward Eddie, she wanted nothing more than to believe she had found her soulmate, her happily ever after. In the beginning, she believed it. He was tender and loving and held her on a pedestal, high above her insecurities. But then came the death of their son, and everything fell apart. Eddie blamed her, and she believed his lie. In her head, she knew he drank too much because of his father. But in her heart, she thought it was her fault. So, she stayed to rectify the situation.

Nothing about their relationship was simple. From the start, there had been too many roadblocks and boulders dropped in front of them, separating them on this journey. If she waited long enough, the road was bound to clear, the potholes would be repaired, and Eddie would find his way back to her. But how long was *long enough*?

By the time Melia entered first grade, the flowers in the garden were fading. Once the snow fell, it would disappear into a world of white. Jules needed something she could see beneath the four feet of Minnesota snow. Finally, she settled on brick columns with colored concrete caps. Even in the deepest snow, she could see them from the house.

In late October, Eddie left for a *convention* in Fargo. Jules called Billy Dane, a high school friend who ran a masonry company. Since her marriage to Eddie, the two had not spoken. Billy became Eddie's nemesis when he broke the *bro code* by asking Jules to the Homecoming dance, shortly after Eddie, once again, broke off their relationship. Nearly a hundred students and a janitor, who tried to break up the fight with his mop handle, witnessed the two duke it out in the parking lot. If someone had kept score, Billy would have won by a landslide. But he was gracious enough to walk away before seriously hurting Eddie's ego more than he already had. Since then, Billy kept his distance out of respect for Jules.

Billy and his crew would bring her vision to fruition. On the first day, they poured footings. Two days later, the brick columns went in. The following day, her garden columns were ready for winter's snow.

Eddie returned after dark Friday evening. Without a word, he stumbled into the house, snatched a bottle of whiskey from the cupboard, headed to his office, and slammed the door.

Around 7:00 the following morning, the bathroom floor began to shake. Jules grabbed her robe, tightened the belt around her damp body, and raced out the front door. Eddie was headed toward the house in a bulldozer. A smirk crossed his face as he wagged his fingers. He was aimed directly toward her, and he was not slowing down. Had he snapped? Was he planning to kill her and his daughter? She raced into the house to save Mel. Jules shooed her to the barn and told her to hide in the loft until she came to get her. Then she raced to the front yard. Rounding the corner of the house, Jules saw Eddie turn sharply. He dropped the bucket and toppled the columns of her garden before he scooped up the stones and the bleeding heart. Dropping to her knees, she pounded the ground with her hands, sobbing hysterically. Eddie had not hurt her physically, but emotionally, he destroyed her. The intensity of losing her babies for a second time broke her.

27

Jules

Jules read her journal long into the night. Periodically, she stopped to relive events, poking the painful cavity of the past. Almost all the memories brought tears, but many drew anger. She stayed with Eddie for forty-two years, and in return, she received nothing but misery and heartache. There had been no compassion, tenderness, or love—not real love. After their first son's death, he built a wall, and she hated him because of it. Yet, she loved him; she always had. And for that reason, she hated herself.

By morning, her eyes were narrow slits from lack of sleep and the tears she allowed to fall. Jules was so exhausted, she could barely hold her head upright. Fatigue at sixty felt very different than it had even ten years before. Functioning on so little sleep was not pretty. But Eddie left her no choice; he needed her.

The farmhouse floor was cold on her bare feet as she limped across it. Eddie never turned the furnace on until the first snowfall. But because she was a guest, he owed it to her to ensure she was comfortable. She turned on the heat and cranked the thermostat to seventy-four degrees. Later, she would likely regret her decision, but September mornings were cold—no matter how warm the day became.

Waiting for the bathroom to warm up, Jules stared at herself in the mirror. The bruise on her forehead was still purple. A yellowish ring had begun to form on the edges. The thin strips that closed the gap on her forehead began to curl. She wanted to remove them but feared the gaping hole it might leave.

Finally warm enough to peel off her clothes, Jules stepped into the steamy shower. She turned on the water as hot as she could stand it and let it pelt her skin until it was red and wrinkled. But it did not help.

She slipped into her robe before finger-combing her damp hair into a high ponytail. Sunlight poured into the kitchen, making the ceiling light unnecessary. Her lack of sleep necessitated the need for the extra coffee she dumped into the filter basket. She checked the time before wandering into the living room.

28

Eddie

Eddie softly moaned. His eyelids fluttered open, and he jerked forward in surprise. Slamming his forehead into Jules, he saw stars. "What the hell?" he muttered, pressing his eyes tightly closed and grimacing.

Jules pressed the heel of her hand into her forehead and bit her lip. Sparks of light flashed when she closed her eyes. She dropped onto the arm of the couch and rocked back and forth until she could talk without screaming.

"What were you doing anyway?"

"Checking to see if you were awake." A breath vibrated her lips, releasing the last of the pain from the unexpected collision.

Eddie drew a deep breath. "Maybe, just ask next time."

Jules looked at Eddie and roared with laughter. "Oh, my gosh!" Her words were barely decipherable amidst her gasps of breath.

"What's so damn funny?"

She wagged a finger between them. "This." Jules shook her head and drew a deep breath. "Us." Pulling the amber medicine bottle from her robe pocket, she shook a tiny pill into her hand and handed it to Eddie. Gently, she worked a second pillow beneath his head before giving him the glass of water.

"Everything is just so hard. Even this was more complicated than it should have been. Life shouldn't be that difficult, Eddie. Don't you see that?"

Eddie slowly rolled onto his side and swung his feet off the couch. With Jules's help, he sat upright. He pressed an arm against his ribcage and held his breath for several seconds. The *fear* of a deep breath was worse than the real thing. After the third mouthful of air, his shoulders fell, and he relaxed.

"D-do you honestly think our marriage is over?"

Jules shrugged before sitting next to him. "I don't know." She sighed. "There have been so many times I should have left you. But for some reason, I couldn't."

He turned his body slightly, pressing one knee against hers. "So, why now?"

Light staked claim to a broad section of flooring, illuminating the threadbare braided rug. Jules studied the odd shape. "I don't know." She poked her hand into her robe pocket and squeezed the pill bottle. "I think I just got tired of being the only one in our marriage. I've put in a hundred percent, and you've put in…" Her shoulders fell. "Nothing. You've put in nothing, Eddie."

Eddie stared out the window. "Wow," he said softly. "I guess I didn't realize how much you hate me."

Jules shook her head. "I don't hate you, Eddie. I could never hate you." She snorted softly. "Believe me. If I were going to hate you for the things you've done, it would have happened long ago." She looked directly at him.

His face fell. "It's not like I haven't given you enough reasons to hate me over the years."

"True, but I don't. But you're not the same as when I fell in love with you. Everyone changes. I'm not that naïve." She raised an eyebrow. "But somehow, you took change to a whole new level." Jules rested her hand on his. "Once I realized you would never care about our family like a husband and a father should, I guess I stopped trying too." The lines around her eyes deepened. "Don't get me wrong; I tried for a long time. But not feeling loved wears on you." Her lips quivered. "I guess I finally left because I was tired of you writing my story in a light that always made me out to be the bad guy. I'm not the bad guy, Eddie. I never wanted there to be a bad guy in our marriage."

He shook his head. "I never thought you were the bad guy, Jules. Never."

"Yes, you did. From the moment we lost Melia's twin brother, you made it very clear I was to blame." She watched his face. "It was like you fell off a cliff that day, and you just kept falling. And since then, you've made me feel like the worst and least important person in your life. I understand being in line behind your mom. You two shared a history no one else could comprehend. You had to be there for her."

She let go of his hand and twisted a tissue she pulled from her other pocket. "Your mom rarely opposed anything your dad did or said. She weathered his outbursts rather than creating more waves. I did the same thing for years, but I can't do it anymore."

"Mom did that because she needed to keep the peace to protect me."

Jules laced her fingers through Eddie's. "I know. She told me. I did the same for Mel and our grandson—just not to the extent she did." She tipped her head closer to his. "But maybe she did it to a fault. If she hadn't let him walk all over her, you wouldn't be this angry man who finds his only happiness at the bottom of a bottle of whiskey. Maybe you wouldn't have become George Greer."

Eddie leaned into the cushions and closed his eyes. "I want to talk about this; I honestly do, but that pain pill is hitting hard. I need to sleep for a while."

Jules sighed softly. "Okay. Do you need anything?"

"No. I just want to sleep."

She adjusted his pillows. Soft snoring instantly filled the air. She pulled the covers over him. "Eddie, my heart aches for the amazing life we could have had."

Hank stood in the doorway between the two rooms. He looked from Eddie to Jules.

"Are you coming, Hank?" Jules asked. The dog whined softly before returning to the living room and dropping onto the floor in front of the couch.

When Jules was out of earshot, he opened his eyes and whispered, "I don't think she's coming back to us, Hank."

29

Eddie

By 9:00 a.m., Jules had washed and dried a load of Eddie's shirts. She took the warm clothes and headed toward the bedroom to fold them and put them away. Hearing her disappear down the hall, Eddie struggled to get himself off the couch and into the kitchen. With his good arm, he poured a cup of coffee and grappled with the discomfort of lowering himself into the chair.

As usual, Hank sat opposite him, awaiting his breakfast. Several times, he shoved his bowl toward Eddie. When he did not get what he wanted, he hopped down and nudged Eddie with his nose.

"You're gonna have to wait, Hank. I'm not in any condition to feed you this morning. Wait for Mom." Hank gave him a quick upward head nod, the equivalent of a human flip-off. Eddie laughed softly. "You don't hide your emotions very well, do you, boy?"

Whether from physical pain or the torment of their earlier talk, Eddie hurt everywhere. Pain radiated up and down his body—and across his chest. If he did not know better, he would think he was having a heart attack. His wife's words had caused him discomfort. He was unprepared for her brutal honesty. But then again, he had never been captive—or listened to her concerns. In the past, whenever she had started in on him, he always walked away. This time, he did not have a choice.

Eddie pressed a hand against his shoulder and moved it ever so slightly. He flinched. Pain was not something he was accustomed to—not this kind of pain. Usually, his tolerance level was off the charts. That was not true. In the past, emotional or physical discomfort had been his reason to self-medicate. If Jules had not confiscated every bottle he hid in the old farmhouse, he would lay a wager he would be hitting it hard this morning. He would most likely be three sheets to the wind.

Anger flooded Eddie, and he banged the table with his good hand. Instantly, he felt his mistake. Pain radiated up his arm and across his ribcage. "Son of a bitch," Eddie grumbled, holding his breath. He closed his eyes, squeezed his fist into a tight ball, and waited for the throbbing to stop.

"Good morning." Jules set a small pill on the table as she passed. "Sounds like you might need this." Eddie washed it down with a sip of coffee, praying for instant relief.

Jules did not speak as she fried a quarter pound of bacon and three eggs. A piece of toast popped up and she slathered it with butter and set it on Eddie's plate. By the time she set his plate before him, the words he had planned to say got stuck in his throat. In his head, he told her she had no right to be angry with him for their forty-two years of misery. She was just as much at fault. But more importantly, he wanted her to know she was wrong for taking away his alcohol. He would have said that if he had been courageous, but he was not. So, they ate in silence.

While Jules cleared the table, Eddie slowly chewed the last piece of bacon. "I need to go out to the hayfield this morning."

She spun around and stared at him as if he was mad. "Are you out of your freaking mind? You can barely walk, let alone drive. Why on God's green earth do you think you have to go out there today?"

Eddie stared into his empty coffee cup. "I can't explain it. I just have to."

"For what?" She turned her back to him and started running hot water into the sink. "You do recall yesterday, right?"

"You wouldn't understand even if I could explain it. I just need to be there for a couple of hours."

Jules grabbed his plate and added it to the dishwater. "Fine. I'll drive you out there and wait in the car."

"No." Eddie shook his head. "Just help me get into my chair and leave me, please? Hank'll be with me, and I have my phone. I promise I'll call you if I need anything."

Deep lines grew across his wife's forehead as she studied his face. "Fine."

Jules made a fresh pot of coffee and filled his thermos. She stuffed a handful of homemade cookies into a plastic container and snapped the lid closed before helping Eddie down the stairs and into the car. Soft moans escaped from him with each step.

Tightening her jaw, she watched him lie back against the headrest and finally let go of the struggle of the last few minutes. She leaned into the car until her forehead almost touched his. "So, going out there is worth all this pain?" Eddie nodded. Jules shrugged. "Okay then."

She reached across him and buckled his seatbelt, giving it an extra little tug. "Tight enough for you?" Jules smirked.

"Yeah. Thanks," he whispered through gritted teeth.

Hank jumped into the back while she went to the shed to search for a sturdy lawn chair. As they drove down the long driveway, each bump sent a flood of pain through Eddie, and he grimaced and whimpered.

Jules stopped in front of the River House. She stared at it.

"I was in there the other day," Eddie told her.

"Really? I haven't been in there since the week your mom died." She stopped in front of the house. Eddie was happy not to be moving. "It just never felt right being there without her. Still, I've always loved that house." She grinned. "Well, maybe not the house as much as the spot on the river. It's so peaceful. I get why your mom loved it."

Eddie nodded. "It's definitely the river—not the house. That place is a mess." Instead of looking at the lot, he watched his wife. "I've always wondered if you could live anywhere, where would you choose?"

Jules looked at him suspiciously. "I highly doubt you've *always* wondered that. As a matter of fact, I would guess this is the only time you've even thought about it." She turned toward the house. "I guess I would say—*here*. This is where I'd want to live."

"Seriously? You could live anywhere in the world, and you'd pick the River House?"

She nodded. "Yeah, I would."

"Why? I thought you hated the farm."

Turning toward him, she laid a hand on his arm. "I don't hate the farm, Eddie. I just don't like who we are when we're here together." She glanced at the lot again. "Besides, I could never leave Holland Crossing. The people here are my family. They've looked out for me since I came to this town. When my parents died, they took me in. When I lived with my miserable aunts, my house never felt like home—but everywhere else did: Lottie's, Shaw's Store, school, and almost everywhere else. That's where I felt at home." She watched an eagle through the sunroof. "And when I left you, I had no less than ten offers of a place to stay." She put the car in gear. "The people here have the biggest hearts I've ever seen." She pressed the gas pedal. "But you wouldn't know that because you won't let anyone in—including me."

Eddie did not believe that. He tried to connect with others. Granted, most of his attempts were at one of the bars in the area. And they almost always ended in a brawl, with him on his back in the middle of the parking lot. But at least he tried. Maybe people would have accepted him if it was not for the mayor's son. Perhaps he would feel differently had it not been for the accident. But there was no coming back after that.

30

Eddie – Winter 1995

The January wind left massive drifts across the driveway. Snow pillows blanketed the gravel road, making it nearly impossible to keep the truck between the ditches. As he approached each mound, Eddie picked up speed and plowed through it, praying the old truck would not lose traction or give up. At times, his wheels spun, and he had to shift between forward and backward to rock it out of his current plight. When he reached the River House to check on his mother, the snow was so deep, he struggled to get out of the truck.

The day was primarily gray. Occasionally, the sun tried to peek through the clouds, but the angry sky would not give in. Eddie grabbed the shovel from the back of his truck and dug a narrow path to the front door.

"Mom?" he called as he walked into the house. "Pack a bag, quick. You're coming back to the house with me." The smell of roast beef wafted through the small house, taking Eddie back to the days Elizabeth still cooked for him.

His mom tossed a dish towel over her shoulder. "Eddie, you're a worrywart. I'll be fine here. The wood stove will keep me warm, and I have several kerosene lanterns. I've already filled the tub with water so I can flush the toilet, and I have a bucket of drinking water on the kitchen counter." He felt her staring at him. "Anything I've forgotten?"

Eddie harrumphed as he looked around. "No. But I'd feel a lot better if you came back to the house."

"Son, you don't have to rescue me. I'm pretty good at taking care of myself. I've done it since before your dad died." She gave him that look. "I'm sure you remember." Slowly, she walked him toward the door. "Now, get yourself back home before someone has to rescue you. Jules and Mel need you, honey."

Eddie did not move. "Are you sure?" His mom nodded. "Okay, but if you need…"

"I'm fine, Eddie. Now go." She tugged the old door open a crack and froze. A high-pitched whine filled the snowy air. "What in the dickens is that?"

A pair of black snowmobiles with blue and purple markings tore across the field opposite the River House. Each held a lone figure, covered head to toe in black. The riders cut through the fresh snow, bouncing up and down through the deep drifts. They wove their way across the wide-open hayfield leaving little snow untouched. Eddie raced down the front steps, catching himself before he landed on his backside. He plowed snow with his shins as he ran toward the field, wildly waving his arms. Waving his hand toward the river, he signaled for them to move on. Snowmobiles put his crops at stake, but worse, these two jackasses were trespassing.

Eddie continued to wave, growing increasingly animated and angry each second they ignored him. The wind whipped against his face, and he folded up the collar of his jacket. Multiple times, the machines came close to him before turning around and racing back across the field. There was no doubt they were ignoring him—laughing at the grumpy old man.

"Get the hell off my fields!" Eddie knew he could not be

heard over the *brapping* sound of the machines. Again, he waved his arms and pointed. Finally, the pair sailed across what should have been the road, had it not been covered in a foot or more of snow, past the house and toward the shore before turning and heading west on the frozen river.

He stomped back into the small house. "Son of a bitchin' snowmobilers think they can ride wherever the hell they want. I don't want 'em ripping up the fields."

His mom reached up and placed her hand on his shoulder. "Eddie, you go home before you can't get there. I'll be fine here."

"You're sure?"

"I am. Now, get home, son."

The half-mile home was laden with snowmobile tracks. Imprints zigzagged across his cornfields on both sides of the driveway. Banks had been knocked onto the road, where they plowed through the powdery snow. Eddie clenched his jaw and maneuvered the old truck through the drifts and across the tamped-down snow.

When he got home, he dumped his coat on the bench and retreated to his den. The wind howled outside his office window, and the sky grew unnaturally dark. Earlier than normal, the security light came on, illuminating the swirling crystals and massive flakes as the wind launched them in every direction. Eddie watched the snow drift across the path between the house and the barn.

Like most days when he was not in the fields, Eddie holed up in his den, avoiding his family. At milking time, he plowed a narrow path to the barn with his quad, a used four-wheel ATV he had recently purchased. He questioned if it would still be visible in the morning. As the evening wore on, the intensity of the storm picked up, making it nearly impossible to see outside. The heavy snow captured the outside light, sending the yard into complete darkness.

Receipts and other papers were sorted and stacked in neat piles on his desk. He phoned his mom to check on her before returning to his task. Eddie continued to work as he spoke with her. If nothing else, the storm had allowed him to get a jump on his taxes.

Forty minutes later, the *trrring* of the phone cut through the house, but he refused to answer. The likelihood it was for him was slim to none. It rang a good twenty times a day, and it was almost always for Jules or Mel—friends with gossip, a complete waste of time. Many times, Eddie threatened to rip out the phone. He had once torn the cord from the wall, but because of his mom, he felt forced to have the phone company reinstall it.

"Eddie, the phone's for you," Jules hollered from the living room where she and Melia watched some God-awful show.

"Hello," he barked into the phone. He always assumed it was someone he did not want to talk to. More likely than not, it was a salesman hoping to cheat him out of money. Jules hung up the other phone. He heard the click before speaking again. "Hello."

"Ed, this is Mayor Thorp."

Eddie rolled his eyes and bobbed his head from side to side like a teenage girl. He had no time for the mayor. Even the fact the man referred to himself as *Mayor* Thorp made his blood boil. "What do you need, *Leo*?"

"Were you over at the River House around noon today?" The mayor's voice sounded husky, raw.

"What business is that of yours? Last time I checked, I can go anywhere I damn well please on my own property."

Eddie heard the mayor sigh. "Did you chase a couple of snowmobilers off your field?"

"Damn right, I did. They were ripping up my cornfield with

those stupid machines."

There was a pause on the other end. "One of those boys was mine."

"Good to know. I'm guessing you called to apologize, then. Maybe you should teach him to respect other people's property. At least now I know where to send the bill when spring rolls around, and I can see what kind of damage they did."

Again, there was a pause. "Listen, Greer. Those boys were so afraid of you, they took off toward the river."

Eddie laughed. "Bullshit, Leo. Those boys weren't afraid of me. They saw me waving them off the field and then turned around and raced across them again."

"Greer, I don't think you understand. My boy, Hunter, hit a dock trying to outrun you."

"Outrun me? What are you talking about? I was standing in a foot of snow. I wasn't chasing anybody anywhere."

"Don't lie to me, Ed. They said you were chasing them with your four-wheeler, and they barely got away."

"Whoa! Whoa!" Eddie was confused, bordering on pissed. "I don't know where you got that information, but I didn't even have my machine at the River House. I went to pick up my mom and bring her back to the farm. I sure as hell wouldn't have taken my quad to get her."

"Well, you can say that, but she isn't at your house, is she?"

Eddie scowled. "No. She didn't want to come."

"Well, that kind of makes your side of the story just a— story, then, doesn't it?"

"Ask her. I was there—*with my truck.*"

"The sheriff's already talked to your mom. He says she's not a reliable witness because she's likely covering for you."

"What? That's bullshit, Leo, and you know it."

"Regardless, when the storm's over, you're probably gonna find your ass sitting in jail."

"You're accusing me of something I didn't do, Thorp. I didn't even have my four-wheeler out there. Ask Jules."

"I'm not investigating this matter, Ed. That's the sheriff's job. All I know is that my son's likely coming home in a wheelchair because he broke his back. And I doubt he'll ever walk again."

Silence bubbled inside of Eddie. "I-I'm sorry, Leo. That's tough. But honest to God, you're barking up the wrong tree. I never chased those boys."

"Tell it to the cops, Ed." Then the phone went dead.

Two days later, the sheriff and his deputy braved the end of the storm and the poorly plowed driveway, arriving at the Greer farm just before noon. Eddie was out the door before they stepped foot on the front porch.

"Ed." Sheriff Porter tipped his head. "Doug and I have some questions for you."

Eddie nodded toward the barn and led the way over the freshly plowed path.

"I'm guessing you know why we're here. Mayor Thorp said he called you."

"Yeah, and he accused me of crap that never happened. I never chased those boys. My quad hasn't left the yard in months."

"So, suppose you tell us what happened, then." Deputy Almer took out a small pad of paper and a pencil. He licked the tip, pressed it to the blank page, and waited for Eddie to talk.

Eddie spent the better part of fifteen minutes replaying the events for the two men. He even told them what he and his mom talked about.

"Look, I feel bad for Thorp's kid, but doesn't it matter to you that those boys were out ripping up my fields? As I recall, that's trespassing, punishable by law." Eddie threw his hands out to his sides.

The sheriff took a deep breath. "The storm did a number on the roads and the fields, Ed. It blew so hard, there's no sign of snowmobile tracks anywhere." He twisted his mouth to one side. "That means there's no sign of your truck tires either."

Eddie glared at Porter. "Well, then, if there was any evidence of my quad being out there, those tracks are gone too, right?"

Sheriff Porter turned his head in question. "Are you saying there *were* tracks out there before the storm?"

"Of course, that's what he's saying." Deputy Almer stepped closer to Eddie. "Aren't you, Ed? I'd say that was an admission of guilt."

"No, it's not," Eddie hissed. "What I'm saying is that if you can't prove they were on my land, how can you prove I chased them?"

"Okay, for the record, I'm gonna ask you again. You're telling me you never chased those boys with your quad?" Porter asked.

"Like I said, I didn't even have my machine at the River House. Besides, I don't think my quad could have made it through that snow. So, how could I have chased them even if I *had* taken it." He poked a finger toward Almer. "But just to be clear, I didn't. I drove my old truck over to Mom's because I planned to bring her back here during the storm, but she wouldn't come."

The sheriff nodded. "We talked to Elizabeth the day it happened. Her story matches yours." He moved toward Eddie and placed a hand on his shoulder. "Maybe a little too closely. I have to wonder, Ed, if she isn't protecting you. Maybe you two coordinated tales."

Eddie's hands clenched. "You know I'm a lot of things,

Ray, but I'm sure as hell no liar. And you know that. I'm always gonna tell you the truth, even when you don't want to hear it. Ask Jules if you don't believe me. She's the one who suggested I bring Mom back to the house."

"We might just do that," Deputy Almer said, puffing out his chest. He took a threatening step toward the barn door. "Is she home?"

"She's in the house." He nodded in that general direction. "But if you won't trust my mom, aren't you worried Jules will lie for me too?"

"Your wife's respected in Holland Crossing." The deputy's eyes narrowed as he glared at Eddie. "Unlike some people around here."

Eddie shoved his hands into his jacket pockets to keep from punching Almer. "You…"

Sheriff Porter stepped between them. Almer grinned.

"I guess if she tells us the same story, we might believe it," The deputy tucked the notepad and pencil back into his front jacket pocket. "Only one way to find out."

Eddie's ears burned—not from the cold, but from anger. "What kind of crap is this?" His hands clenched into tight balls.

Deputy Almer was hated almost as much as Eddie in the community. The man's mouth should have been boarded shut. If he knew what was good for him, he would move on and take a job in a real town—where people did not know him enough to want to kill him.

"We just need to hear it from someone we trust." The deputy pushed the barn doors open and waited for Porter.

"She won't be able to tell you what happened at the River House because she wasn't there. But she can tell you I took the truck that day."

"That's all we need to hear, Ed." Sheriff Porter approached the house with Almer close enough to kiss his boss's ass.

31

Jules

Jules white-knuckled her way down the gullied driveway. The storms washed away much of the road, leaving potholes and deep trenches of mud that could pull her in. Periodically, she stopped before easing her car through a chasm spreading from one ditch to another.

Halfway to the highway, she met Buzz. He maneuvered the broken road in much the same way. Facing one another, she put her vehicle in *park* and climbed out. Buzz did the same.

He walked toward her. "Hey, Jules. I haven't really gotten to talk to you since..." Nervously, he stretched his neck. "How are you?"

Her head wagged gently from side to side. "Okay, I guess. It's just been so hard. Really hard."

"I'm so sorry." He harrumphed. "Eddie's put you through the wringer for a lot of years."

The sun peeked through the clouds. A ray of sunshine warmed her. She looked at Buzz and sadly smiled. "True." She stepped closer to the farm manager. "Can I ask you a question?"

"Of course."

"Do you think Eddie was to blame for what happened out on the hayfield?"

Buzz looked at his boots. "Well, I think…"

"Honestly," Jules said. "I want you to tell me the truth."

He shoved his hands into his back pockets. "No, I don't. That storm came out of nowhere. I mean, the sky was dark, but there was no indication of lightning until that first strike. If we had taken off across the field, it could have been bad. It was a crapshoot."

Jules slowly nodded. "That's what I needed to hear."

"I know it doesn't help any, but…"

"Thanks." Jules glanced in the direction of the River House. "What about Hunter Thorp? I know it was a long time ago, but does the community blame Eddie for his accident?"

Buzz's eyebrows pressed together. "Why are you askin' me? You're probably more connected to the town than most people."

"I think I'm too close. I'm not sure many people would tell me the truth."

He nodded. "Yeah, you're probably right. But, no, I don't think the town blames Ed. Porter didn't find him guilty. Not that that's any consolation. People judge, even when the facts are right in front of their noses." Buzz snorted. "Besides, Hunter Thorp's an awful lot like his dad—larger than life and a mouth to match. From the time that boy was born, he'd blame anybody he could for his mistakes. He learned that from Leo. There's a reason he ain't the mayor anymore." Jules nodded. "I don't even know if you know this, but Darren admitted to his dad that Ed didn't chase them. Of course, his old man took that info to his grave. But things in Holland Crossing have a way of coming out. I'm surprised you never heard about it."

"Like I said, no one really shares things with me. They try to protect me from…" Jules hooked a thumb in the direction of the house. She bent over and picked up a wayward scrap of paper that landed near her feet. "And Mel? Do you think Eddie was negligent?"

"I wondered when you'd ask me that. I figured maybe you didn't want to know."

"Honestly, I just wanted to believe Eddie's version. Everything else was too difficult to accept. But now I need to know."

"The accident wasn't his fault. I was there. I helped him hook up everything. Honestly, though, that old trailer shouldn't have been on the road to begin with." He raised his eyebrows. "However, I do fault Ed for lettin' Mel haul that machine. She had no business driving his truck with that trailer. But if you blame people for their stupid decisions, we'd all be found guilty ten times a day."

Jules smiled at Buzz. "Thanks. I needed to hear it from someone I trust."

Buzz touched her shoulder. "You've harbored those thoughts a long time."

"Too long."

"Are you okay? I mean, really okay. You look a little..." Buzz stretched his hand out in front of him and tipped it back and forth in question.

"I was thinking about what you said—about people making stupid decisions." She drew a deep breath. "Lately, I've been wondering if falling in love with Eddie was the worst thing I've ever done."

"Don't do that, Jules." He wrapped his arms around her. "I think everybody in town hopes you'll find your way back to one another. Now, that would be a love story the town could talk about."

Jules pulled back. "Maybe. But forgiveness is really hard. And even if I can forgive him, I can't forget the last forty-some years."

"No one's asking you to forget." He laid a hand on his chest.

"But we can't choose who we love, Jules. And I know you still love that asshole." Jules laughed, and Buzz grinned. "Just don't give up on him. I feel like he's coming around."

"We'll see. It's a little touch-and-go right now." She reached for his hand. "Thanks, Buzz. I really needed this talk."

With a quick nod, Buzz returned to his truck. He eased off the driveway just enough for her to sneak past. Any further, and he would have been axle deep in the muck. Unfortunately, that was exactly where Jules saw herself—in the mess of a life she built with a man who continued to rain on everything beautiful.

By the time Jules pulled onto the highway, the clouds had begun to dissipate. She drew a deep breath and headed toward town.

32

Eddie

When Eddie heard Jules's car approach the hayfield, he checked the time on his phone. Leave it to her to arrive on the dot. She was damn near perfect. Eddie knew she did not trust him not to get into trouble. But then again, what danger could he run into in a lawn chair—again? Besides, after his mishap the day before, he could barely move.

Eddie tried to hoist himself out of his chair, but Jules stopped him. "Wait." She popped her tailgate and grabbed a matching chair from the rear end. After placing it next to Eddie, she returned to her car for a wicker picnic basket.

"You brought lunch?"

Hank poked the basket with his nose, pointedly sending a message.

Jules rubbed his head. "Don't worry. I didn't forget you, Hank. How could I? You wouldn't let me." She raised the hamper for Eddie to see. "Do you remember this?"

Eddie shook his head. "Should I?"

"It was a wedding gift from Lottie and her folks." She raised an eyebrow and glanced at him. "Before we got married, you promised me we'd go on a picnic every week for the rest of our lives." Eddie looked down. "And I believed you." She set the basket on her chair. "Anyway, I thought maybe we should use it *once* while we're still married."

Eddie swallowed hard. "I promised you a lot of things. And I didn't keep any of them."

Jules nodded. She removed three Holland Crossing Baking Company sandwiches from the basket. Eddie took the full-size roast beef. The second, a plain turkey and ham with no condiments or vegetables, she unwrapped and tossed to Hank. She set the cooler on the ground and pulled her chair closer to Eddie's before opening her roasted turkey with cranberry cream cheese and avocado.

"So, what exactly do you do out here anyway?" Jules handed a bag of chips to Eddie.

"Mostly think. Today, I was remembering the snowmobile accident that paralyzed Hunter Thorp."

"Yeah, that one hurt."

Eddie tipped his head toward her. "How so? I mean, why do you say that?"

"I saw how much it hurt you, being accused of something you didn't do. The worst was they didn't believe you or your mom." She took a bite of her sandwich and chewed slowly. "I remember how angry you were."

He snorted silently. "Yeah, but they believed *you*. They *always* believe you."

"That was all Almer. I'm pretty sure Sheriff Potter would have taken your mom's word for it."

"I never wanted to celebrate more than when Almer took that job in Rochester. He was such a jerk."

Jules nodded. "I know you think people sided with the mayor, but that's not true."

"Bull. Ninety percent of the town blamed me."

Jules grabbed a chip from Eddie's bag and shoved it into her mouth. "No, they didn't, Eddie. After it happened, you were so angry with Leo and the Sheriff's Department that you refused to go anywhere except to the bars—where alcohol makes people's inhibitions disappear and their mouths flap." She took a swig from her water bottle before pouring some into a bowl she had brought for Hank. "Those were the people you were listening to—your fellow drunks. They got to you."

The two ate in silence while Hank watched for crumbs to fall.

Suddenly, Eddie's neck craned forward. "Did you hear that?"

"What?"

"Somebody's out there." He scanned the thicket. "Let me know if you see them."

"So, that's why you sit out here every day?"

"That's not why, but I swear someone's out here. Sometimes, I hear them call my name. Other times, I see flashes of them."

Jules ignored Eddie and threw the rest of her sandwich to Hank. "Thanks for batting clean-up, buddy."

She brushed the crumbs from her shirt before handing Eddie a brownie. "Are you almost ready to go? I need to get you home so I can make a grocery run."

Still scanning the woods, he nodded. "Yeah, I guess. But I need to know something before we go." He laid a hand on hers. "What would it take for you to move back into the farmhouse permanently?"

Jules zipped her sweatshirt. "I don't know. I guess I need you to become the person you were when I fell in love with you—or at least catch a glimpse of him occasionally." She frowned at him. "But I'm not sure that's even possible."

Eddie squeezed her hand. "Are you willing to give me a chance?"

She shook her head. "I've given you forty-two years of

chances. How's one more chance going to be any different?"

"Well, I'm talking to you, and I'm actually listening." One corner of his mouth hitched up slightly. "That has to be *different.*"

Jules stood up and started repacking the basket. "I suppose it is."

33

Eddie

Eddie showered while Jules finished the breakfast dishes. Without the knee brace or sling, he felt almost human. Until nightfall, his limp was nearly undetectable. Everything inside of him felt different—lighter, happier. He whistled while he showered, something he could not remember ever doing.

Completely out of character, he got his own cup of coffee and wiped the few drops that fell on the counter.

Jules pulled her head back in surprise. "Wow! When did you decide cleaning wasn't beneath you."

"Ha-ha. Very funny."

"You look nice. Is that the shirt I bought you a handful of Christmases ago—one of a dozen you've never worn?" Jules winked.

He looked down and ran a hand down the placket of the blue and white gingham checked shirt. "I've worn it before. You've just never noticed."

One eyebrow arched. "Well, it's rather odd that you'd wear it with the tags still on it." She watched his mouth open and shut. "That's what I thought."

Jules pulled the scissors from a cup on the counter, cut the tag, and held it for him to see. "I'd say this weathered pretty well for being washed." She grinned at him.

Hank landed on the kitchen chair Jules pulled from beneath the table. He almost knocked her to the floor. "You sure have made yourself at home since I've been gone, haven't you, Hank?" She wrapped an arm around his neck and laid her cheek against his boney head.

Eddie pointed with his chin. "That's *his* place now."

"Good to know." She sat between them in a chair badly in need of repair. "Eddie, I think we should talk. Since the picnic on the hayfield, I've spent a lot of time thinking. If you're really going to listen, I need you to hear what I'm going to say."

Eddie pushed his chair away from the table. "Did I do something?"

"Oh, you've done a lot of things." Her smile straight-lined, and she grew contemplative. "Listen, just because I've been taking care of you, and you put on a clean shirt…" Jules sniffed the air. "That doesn't mean I'm ready to move back in. Or that there's a future for us." She rested her folded arms along the table edge and sighed loudly. "There's a lot of hurt I need to come to terms with. A few days of you being on your best behavior doesn't erase the other four decades."

He reached across the table and cupped her hand. "I hear you. I know you don't believe I've changed—or that I can be the person I was before, but I'm trying. I really am." Eddie looked her in the eyes. "I know how hard this is for you."

She shook her head. "No, you don't. You have no idea." She pulled her hand away and leaned back in the wobbly chair. "But let me try to explain. You know the path to the barn—the worn one, the one where grass doesn't grow anymore?"

Eddie's eyes narrowed. "Yeah. What about it?"

"Well, that's how I feel. You've walked over me so many times, never seeing me, always just trudging your way to and from somewhere else." Her hands twisted in her lap. "I'm like that path. I just let you run over me time and time again. And like the grass, I haven't been able to grow, Eddie. Every time I feel like I'm finally getting my feet back on the ground, something happens that knocks them out again."

"Melia's death." Eddie swallowed hard. "Cade..."

Jules held her hands up to stop him. "It's everything. The farm, the kids, your mom, Hunter Thorp." She squared her shoulders and turned toward him. "And your damn drinking."

Eddie slumped against the back of his chair. "I don't..."

"Just so you know, *I don't* is never a good start to any sentence. It's a denial. You're denying things that everyone else sees. Eddie, my whole life has been this myriad of *maybe next times*—one right after the other. *Maybe next time he'll remember my birthday. Maybe next time he'll think before he gets drunk. Maybe next time we'll take that trip to Hawaii. Maybe next time Eddie'll put me first. Maybe next time...* Do you see where I'm going? Since the day our son died, I disappeared from your view." Jules released a long breath. "Since that day, I've never been more than...*here*."

"What?"

"Here," she repeated, pointing down. "From my perspective, you were always the headliner of this show. Even when bad things happened, you hogged the spotlight and made everything all about you. You used it as an excuse to drink and to justify your anger." She bit her lip. "I was always just the...the stage manager, I guess—the one who kept everything going no matter how much shit hit the fan."

Jules stood and leaned against the counter. "Yes, you had a crappy life growing up. No one is denying that. Your mom did the best she could, considering whom she was married to. But, Eddie, *you* didn't stop the misery. You were the understudy for your dad, and you just picked up where he left off." She turned and stared out the window. "But what I can't figure out is why you ever let George Greer be your role model."

Eddie slammed his fist against the table. Hank jumped. "My father wasn't anybody's role model—least of all mine. He was an asshole. No one would ever want to be like him."

Jules spun around and clenched her jaw. "You're right. Yet you keep following in his footsteps. You trail so closely, it's like you're the same person." She leaned in until their foreheads almost touched. "Whether you're willing to admit it or not, you became your father. You are George Greer Junior."

Eddie grabbed her arm and squeezed.

"You're hurting me, Eddie." Her nose wrinkled, and her eyes narrowed. "Let go," she growled.

He quickly pulled his hand back. "Jules, I can't believe…"

"I can." She glared at him. "Trauma runs deep. A car goes straight unless someone turns the wheel." She rubbed her forearm. "I turned the wheel, Eddie. By walking out on you, I gave you a different view. You think you can make this big change, but you can't. You're still moving in the wrong direction."

Eddie's eyes grew wide. "I'm so, so sorry, Jules."

"I know you are. But sorry doesn't change the past." She picked up her purse and headed toward the door. "And it only changes the future if you let it." The door creaked when she jerked it open. "I'm just not sure you're ready. And I can't be your stage manager for one more day. When you're ready to share the spotlight, give me a call. Until then, I need to find a show that lets me be the star once in a while." She scowled. "Just once, I'd like a little applause."

"Jules, please," Eddie begged, but she kept walking. "Please, don't go."

Angrily, Eddie tore open the front of his shirt. A few buttons let loose and pinged off the cupboards. Frustrated, he tried removing it without unbuttoning the sleeves. Finally, he wadded it up and whipped it to the floor. Nothing would bring his wife back until he learned to control his anger.

Silence hummed in his ears. The house felt emptier than it had weeks before. Maybe Jules was right. Yes, he suffered trauma as a child. But more importantly, he caused it for everyone else. He looked at the calendar hanging near the refrigerator. *For forty-two years, three months, and twelve days.* Was it even possible to change after that long?

34

Jules

Thoughts and threads of memories flooded Jules. Pulled inward, she let the car take the lead down gravel roads. She could not get out of her *own way* if she tried, let alone if she met another vehicle. Honestly, she should not be driving.

The most recent accident caused her to rethink her marriage—throwing it all away versus being miserable until their wedding vows expired. As she drove, scenes from four decades of their life together jockeyed for attention. She heard the theatrical ticking of reels and saw the flashing lights as they played.

The car turned down one unpaved road after another. Scenery she had not seen in years, if ever, appeared and faded like scenes of a movie. Yet, she barely noticed any of it. If anyone asked her where she had been that day, she would have been unable to tell them. Most of the landscape was buried in a blur of thoughts and memories. Each road coated her thoughts in a layer of dust, making it difficult to breathe, let alone untangle the past from the present.

With everything that happened in her marriage, did she still love Eddie? How could she know? Was it possible to separate the man she fell in love with from who he became? Did she love them both? How could she? But the bigger question was—did he love her? Had he ever been in love with her—or had she gotten caught up in his dream of escaping the farm and his father?

Her heart thudded so hard, Jules could see her blouse flutter with each beat. Slowing, she turned down a road that led to a camp. Hanging from the gateway was a sign notifying visitors they had found Holland Crossing Christian Camp. An oversized padlock held a pair of faded green steel gates closed, keeping trespassers off the property. Two small black and orange signs stated *Keep Out* and *Closed for the Season.* Jules snorted. How could God just close shop for the better part of every year? She needed Him. It was little wonder she was struggling.

She backed up and turned around, careful not to drop a wheel off the soft shoulders. As she passed through the narrows, the sun glinted off the lake on both sides. A tiny furball bolted across the road in front of her, and she slammed on the brakes, barely missing the black and white pup. A young woman raced after him, apologizing, but Jules could not hear through her closed windows. On the other side of the road, the woman grabbed the puppy and cuddled it. Unlike Jules, that dog knew love.

Jules waited for the pair to make their way back across the road. The woman held the dog tightly, waving as she drove past. New thoughts bombarded her as she watched them. *Knowing* one is loved and *feeling* it were very different. That lucky pup had both. Jules was not sure she experienced either—at least not with Eddie. It had been an exceptionally long time since she felt even the tiniest drop of affection.

Marriage was a two-way street. Both partners needed to give it their all. A half-assed attempt only led to two people clinging to the end of a rotten rope, holding on to something that would eventually break. Ultimately, they would both fall.

Since Eddie had not put an ounce of effort into their relationship, she would be the one to plummet first. And if past actions indicated future behavior, she knew he would likely push her off to save himself. Would he even notice she was gone—for any reasons other than cooking and cleaning? Not likely. She was barely hanging by a thread already. In all these years, he never noticed.

Eddie was more self-centered than anyone she knew. He wanted the limelight and center stage for himself. In high school, he earned it for baseball. Now, it was in a bar, on the receiving end of someone else's fist. For a man who never wanted anyone to know his business, he was all about flaunting his stupidity.

Jules's head and heart ached as thoughts continued to belabor her. Unable to spend one more minute defending herself—*to herself*—she pulled onto Lake Avenue and made her way to the log church. After driving on the washboard roads, the freshly paved parking lot felt like heaven. Slowly, she eased onto the rutted driveway and into the cemetery. Climbing out of the Explorer, she stood on the running board and checked the ground before stepping down.

She sneered at her best friend's headstone. "You were wrong, Lottie Jean. Eddie wasn't my soulmate." She pointed a finger upward. "One day, when we're together again, I'll tell you all about it. But for now, you just need to know how broken I am."

Jules patted the top of Lottie's gravestone. Careful not to step on someone else's resting place, she picked a path through the cemetery, stopping in front of a gray marker with black inlay. In script, the letters read *Melia Elizabeth Greer, January 13, 1981- June 27, 2009.* Mel's face was etched in the center of the stone. Beneath it were the words: *Life is but a moment. Eternity is forever. We can't wait to spend it with you.* When her daughter died, the only people she thought of as *we* were her and Cade. It was not likely Eddie was on the list to go *up*.

As the sole planner of her daughter's service, she chose the casket and headstone—from a catalog. It was like shopping for shoes or a new coat—only she did not need to worry about the size.

The memory of that room was still unforgettable: the smell of fresh paint and the thud against the old oak desk when she accidentally slammed her foot into it. Nothing said *dead* like gray, pictureless walls. There was no cross for fear of offending atheists or others who saw it as idolatry. Thick white sheers covered the picture window. Once a house, it had been converted into a funeral home. Periodically, she stopped turning the pages and stared through the translucent curtain, praying for her daughter to walk by, for her death to have been a mistake. But Jules knew God did not make mistakes.

The funeral director checked his watch multiple times while she studied each page. Most likely, he was closing in on a tee time or some other insignificant event, but she did not care. Was there a time limit on choosing a casket for one's only daughter?

Loneliness screamed inside of her. She wished she had brought someone with her—anyone *except Eddie*. Over the years, she learned they could be in the same room, yet she was still alone. Most of the time, she felt more isolated next to him than she did by herself. And unless he was angry, words rarely exited his mouth. He kept them tightly tethered.

Settling near Mel's headstone, Jules let her words catch up to her thoughts. She looked into the sky and wondered just how far heaven was. Was that something she could google? And if she truly wanted, could she be with her daughter by the end of the day? Finally, she drew a deep breath and rested her shoulder against the headstone.

"Hi, honey. It's Mom." She laughed softly. "But you

already know that." Jules wagged her fingers at the grave next to her daughter's. "Hi, Clarice. Thanks for watching over my baby girl." She never met Clarice Jensen, but based on the grave to her left, it was clear she had been a mother. Moms looked out for each other's children.

Tears tumbled down her cheeks. With the sleeve of her sweatshirt, she daubed at them.

"Can you believe this? I haven't even started talking, and I'm already a mess. It's been a rough couple of days, honey." She shook her head and rolled her eyes. "Who am I kidding? It's been a rough life." Picking up a pinecone, she twisted a single scale until it broke off in her hand. A tiny seed dropped from the cone. "You see it all, don't you? You know what it's like without me even telling you." Flicking the piece of pinecone between the graves, she drew a deep breath. "You and I tried so hard, but no matter what we did, we weren't enough."

Jules rested her head against the stone. "Do you remember when we used to sit on the porch and watch the sun set?" A sad smile tugged up the corners of her mouth. "I bet the sunsets in heaven are amazing." She sighed. "Someday, Mel. Someday we'll watch them together again."

The wind suddenly picked up, and the ponderosa pines swirled in big circles along the edges of the cemetery. Zipping her sweatshirt, Jules crossed her arms to protect herself from the stiff breeze.

"You were always so precocious, Mel. When you were four, you asked if the time between sunset and dark was day or night." Jules straightened her legs, wincing as she crossed her ankles. She considered her words. "Sometimes I feel stuck in that space—between daylight and darkness. I'm trapped between walking away and staying with your dad." A violent shudder cut through her. "Yet somehow, it feels wrong to give up on him. But he's buried in the past, and I don't know how to dig him out."

Jules glanced up and watched the trees. "Please tell me it's going to get better, honey. You must have some pull with God or at least some inside information, don't you?" Tears poured down her still bruised cheek. She could not stop them had she tried.

The cuff of her sweatshirt was damp by the time she got her waterworks stopped. She rolled up her sleeve, corralling the tears and the mucus from her nose inside the fold. "I'm so sorry, Mel. Just when I think I'm finally getting my shit together, I fall apart. I miss you so much. Other than Grandma, you were the only one I could really talk to about your dad."

A female cardinal landed on Clarice's headstone. The two-part whistle with the slow trill made her smile.

"Is that you—trying to tell me something?" Suddenly, the bird flew over Jules and into the pine tree on the far side of the cemetery. "Well played. I take it you want me to leave your dad and fly away like that bird? That's..." She rolled her neck in a circle. "I'm sixty. Starting over isn't going to be easy. No man wants to see stretchmarks, cellulite, boobs encroaching on the belly button, or batwings on their new woman." Jules laughed. Her smile quickly fell. "But I'd put up with it all again just to have you in my arms—even for the short time you were here."

"Honey, you have no idea how often I wish God allowed *do-overs*. The day you died would be the first I'd choose. I wouldn't have given in to your dad. I would have been stronger." She closed her eyes. "Instead, I spend every day wrestling with the knowledge that my weakness killed you. I should have stood up to your father long ago. Then maybe you and I could be sitting on the couch talking about life—rather than how I want to end mine."

35

Jules – 2000

Jules held her daughter's face between her palms. "What's your heart telling you, honey?" She watched Melia's eyes. Jules's mother asked her that question many times when she was young. It gave voice to her feelings, her innermost thoughts. From the time Mel first started speaking, Jules asked that question. It fit every situation: *boys, friendships, teachers, and choices.* It was how she taught her daughter to problem-solve situations in her life. She hoped Melia would use it with her children.

"M-my h-heart is broken *and* f-full." Mel sniffed.

Jules nodded. "Okay, let's focus on the latter. We'll have to deal with the other at some point, but for now..." She kissed Melia's cheek. "Right now, you don't have to give it space in your heart or your head."

The women simultaneously drew a deep breath. Jules pressed her cheek against Mel's, mistaking her daughter's tears for her own.

"Oh, for God's sake. What the hell's going on in here?" Eddie stormed into the house and crossed to the kitchen sink. Bits of mud and freshly cut grass scattered across the floor. The water splashed onto the counter and window as he washed his hands. "If this is that monthly crap, I don't want to hear about it. Go somewhere else. Or better yet, just shut up about it."

Jules aimed her daughter toward the table. She pulled out a chair and nodded for Melia to sit.

"Eddie, Mel has some wonderful news."

He plucked the dish towel from the hook next to the sink, dried his hands, and threw it on the counter. Jules rolled her eyes, grabbed the towel, and tossed it into a laundry basket at the end of the counter.

"About damn time we had some good news around here today. Lost a cow this morning, and the seeder decided it was a good time to take a damn vacation. I've about had it."

He wiggled the cork from a whiskey bottle and poured himself a drink. On the way to the table with the bottle in one hand and the start of a bender in the other, he stopped dead. "Out. Get out of my chair," he barked. Eddie shook his head. "I can't believe you're that stupid, girl."

Melia quickly switched seats. Eddie set his cache on the table and collapsed onto his chair. He emptied his glass and poured a second.

Mel reached for Jules's hand and pulled her closer.

"So, what the hell's this good news?" Eddie looked from his wife to his daughter.

Melia pressed her face into her mom's side and shook her head. Jules slung an arm over her shoulder.

"Eddie, we're going to be grandparents." There was no response, but then again, she had not expected one—at least not one she wanted to hear. "I don't know about you, but I'm excited to have a baby in the house again—someone to call me Grandma." She smiled and squeezed Mel's shoulder.

The muscles in Eddie's jaw tightened, and he glared at his daughter.

"Eddie, did you hear what I said?" Jules stared at him.

"You're going to be a grandpa."

His mouth twisted, and he shook his head in disgust. "So, you got yourself knocked up, did ya?" His eyes narrowed. "I thought I'd raised you better than that." He angrily poked a finger in Jules's direction. "This is *your* fault. The apple doesn't fall far from the tree, does it? Neither one of you know how to keep your legs shut."

"Stop it, Eddie! I didn't get pregnant by myself. As I recall, you had something to do with it."

Infuriated, he jumped up, slamming the chair into the cupboard. He pressed his nose against hers. "And as I recall, you never did one damn thing to make sure we didn't have a kid. You left that all to me."

"Eddie, stop," she whispered. "This isn't the place for this discussion." She tipped her head toward Mel. She was face down on the table, sobbing.

"I don't give a rat's ass." He stepped back. "Like mother, like daughter. You're both a couple of whores."

Jules took a deep breath and bit her tongue. She reminded herself that a zebra could not change its stripes. Eddie was a zebra. He would never change.

He took a long draw from his glass and grabbed Mel's ponytail, yanking her head off the table. "What's the plan, girl? Marriage? Abortion? 'Cause I sure as hell don't want another mouth to feed or another kid to raise. I've already done that."

"Edward!" Jules was livid. "Leave her alone. What's done is done. We'll deal with it."

He emptied his glass and slammed it on the table. "So, where's the father?" Melia stared at him but said nothing. "Huh! That's what I thought." He pressed his hands to the table and leaned close to his daughter. "You've just made a name for yourself in this town, girl—*slut*. That's how people will always see you."

"I told you to stop!" Jules wedged herself between Eddie and Melia. "Stop being a bully. This is your daughter and your grandchild you're talking about. Show some compassion."

"She's not *my* daughter. You deal with this mess." He slammed a hand on the table. "But if I hear one word about this kid from either of you, I'll toss you out of here so fast, it'll make your head spin."

Jules pressed closer to him. "Really? Do you think your mother would approve of how you're treating her granddaughter and great-grandchild?"

"Don't! Don't ever mention my mother again."

His eyes grew dark, but Jules did not stop. "If she knew any of this, she'd kill you herself. Elizabeth would be embarrassed by your behavior—and rightly so. I sure as hell am."

In a huff, Eddie grabbed the bottle and stormed from the house. The old truck sputtered before revving up.

"W-what did Dad mean w-when he said I wasn't his daughter?"

"You *are* his daughter—no matter how much we both wish it weren't true." Jules pulled Mel from her chair. "Your dad's a Greer male. They blame everything that happens on everybody else."

Melia planted her head in her hands. "S-should I have an abortion?"

"Is that what you want? What's your heart telling you?"

Silence swelled. Melia laid a hand on her stomach. "I want this baby," she whimpered. "But I don't want to lose Dad." A ragged breath ripped through her. "I'm afraid if I keep the baby, he won't have anything to do with me ever again."

Jules hugged her daughter tightly. "You can't do anything to please your father, honey. I learned that a long time ago. He's an angry man who spends every waking moment fighting ghosts of his past. Unfortunately, we just happened to walk into the middle of his war." She stood and gently rubbed Melia's back. "Your dad, well, he's a mystery. He always has been, even when we were dating." She shook her head. "Believe me, there were red flags, but I chose to overlook them. It wasn't until Grandma told me about his dad that I understood him a little better." Jules sighed. "I know you never knew your grandfather, but they are an awful lot alike. I'm not sure your father has the capacity to love either of us. But regardless, no matter what you choose to do, *I* will support you. *I* will always be here."

Melia closed her eyes and whispered, "I want to keep this baby, Mom."

Jules shrugged. "Okay. Then that's what you'll do." A wide smile spread across her face, and she brushed Mel's bangs out of her eyes. "I can't believe my baby is going to be a momma with a little one of her own." She raised her eyebrows in disbelief. "And I can't believe I'm going to be a grandma."

Melia rested a finger against her bottom lip. "Is Dad ever going to forgive me?"

"It doesn't really matter, honey. This baby isn't going to wait for him to decide not to be an asshole."

36

Jules

It was early afternoon when Jules drove out of the cemetery. She made a quick stop for coffee at the Perk Up. Darcey came around the counter as soon as Jules entered. She laid a hand on her back and steered her toward a corner table, away from a group of gossips.

"Sit. Let me grab you…"

Jules caught Darcey's arm. "I just need a coffee to go, Darce. I have to be in Ashton by three."

Darcey signaled to one of the servers to bring a cup of coffee to go. She pulled out the chair next to Jules and sat down.

"How are you?" She gave her *the look*. "I mean, really? 'Cause, honestly, you look a little like you were attacked by an angry squirrel."

Jules chuckled. "That's how I feel." She set her purse in her lap. "I'm okay. I'm doing about as well as can be expected. None of this has been easy."

"You mean since high school?" Darcey winked. "I'm kidding. I can't even imagine what you're going through. I don't know how you stay upright."

Jules nodded. "Sometimes I don't," she said softly. "Lately, I've shed enough tears to fill a lake."

Darcey laid her hand on Jules's arm. "I'm always here if you want to talk." She tipped her head toward the gossips. "And I don't have a big mouth like some people."

Chloe set a disposable cup of coffee in front of Jules. She reached for her purse.

"It's on the house," Darcey told her.

Jules's shoulders dropped. "Thank you. You have no idea how kind that is—especially today."

"We all need a little help from time to time."

She took a sip. "Can I ask you a question?"

"Yes, of course."

"I need you to be honest." Darcey nodded. "Back in high school, was Eddie as screwed up as he is now?"

Darcey twisted her mouth and looked at Jules. "You want the truth?" She shook her head. "Okay. It's funny. Clark asked me the same question a few days ago." She slid her chair closer to Jules and folded her hands. "Honey, Eddie is a Greer. The Greer men have been messed up since the beginning of time. Our parents told us stories. And I'm sure their parents had tales as well."

Jules nodded. "So, you saw it?"

"I did. We all did. But I wouldn't say he was more messed up than anyone else in the seventies and eighties."

"Why did no one tell me? Why did Lottie push me toward him?"

"I don't think Lottie *pushed* as much as you *ran*." She looked at Jules. "Honey, you were so lost after your parents died. I'm pretty sure you would have fallen in love with a broom if it had shown you a little attention. Eddie just happened to be the first by your side when you finally hit bottom."

She nodded. "You're probably right. Looking back, I can see how broken I was." Jules twisted the sleeve of her cup. "But was he really that bad back then? I mean, the guy I fell in love with was sweet and caring. At least that's how I remember him."

"He was as sweet and caring as any self-centered high school boy can be, I suppose. What we didn't realize is they all change. Some for the better and others for the worse." She frowned. "But I'm pretty sure you already knew which direction Eddie was headed." Darcey folded her hands and laughed softly. "Clark has had his moments—believe me." Thought lines bunched across her forehead. "But as for Eddie, I think we all saw the biggest change after Mel was born. He was different somehow."

"That's when we lost our son."

Darcey leaned back. "What're you talking about?"

"We never told anyone, but Melia had a twin brother who was stillborn."

"What? Really?"

Jules nodded. "That's when the man I fell in love with became a real a-hole."

"Why didn't you ever say anything?"

"Because it was easier to face it alone. I didn't want people feeling sorry for me or to focus on my loss when I still had a beautiful little girl to raise." Her shoulders raised and dropped. "I also lost six other children."

"Well, you're full of news today. I mean, I knew about the one little boy—your last pregnancy, I guess it must have been."

"Five miscarriages." She held up one hand. "Five."

"I'm so sorry, Jules. I had no idea you suffered like that." Darcey shook her head. "Is that why Eddie went... well, off the rails, so to speak?"

Sunlight streamed through the large window. "It was a lot of things: being forced to take over the farm, feeling like he had to stay in Holland Crossing to watch over his mom, and dealing with his dad's anger. Eddie also felt he let the entire town down when he didn't become this shining baseball star. And then there was my failing—not being able to give him the son he always wanted."

"You didn't fail. It wasn't your fault. Everything happens for a reason." She patted Jules's hand. "I didn't know any of this. I don't think anybody does." Darcey called over her shoulder, "Seems like a town this small would have a better gossip mill."

"You would, wouldn't you?" Jules smiled at the women Darcey referred to as the gossipers. "We kept everything quiet. Eddie wanted no one knowing our business—good or bad."

"I understand that. But people would have rallied around you—made you meals, helped on the farm, watched Melia."

"I know. But my husband doesn't exactly know how to handle kindness. He thinks people are only nice if they want something." Her nose wrinkled, and she scowled. "Right now, I'm so angry he's been such a jerk for so long. But more than that, I'm mad at myself for staying with him—for letting him destroy our family."

"I'd be the last one to judge you for your choices. I've done some pretty questionable things in my day. We all have." She laid her hand on Jules's arm. "When the time is right, I hope you tell him what a jerk he's been."

Jules nodded. "I hope I get that chance."

37

Eddie

Hank set a paw on Eddie's thigh and waited to be noticed. When Eddie did not acknowledge him, he impatiently poked him in the knee with his nose. When that garnered no attention, he barked loudly.

"What?" Eddie snapped. The harshness of his voice made Hank back away. "I don't have time to deal with you right now. What I need is for everybody to leave me the hell alone for a while." He glowered at the dog. "And that means you too. Go lay down."

Hank turned his back to Eddie and dropped beside the lawn chair. Dejected, he rested his chin on the back of his front legs. Eddie watched him. He knew exactly what the dog was thinking. *Asshole!* It was the same as everyone else. Why should Hank think any differently?

The cracks in the red thermos cup had deepened. Since he started coming to the hayfield, they expanded almost to the bottom of the plastic container. Eddie squeezed the sides together before pouring coffee inside, but the liquid dribbled out, leaving dark spots on his jeans.

"Son of a bitch!" With the back of his hand, he swiped at his pants before the heat seeped through the fabric.

He dumped it out and muttered a string of inaudible cuss words. Eddie did not let anyone or anything better him, so he tried again. First, he spread his knees. Then he filled the cup only to the bottom of the deepest crack. Glancing into the cup, he twisted his mouth into a frown. At this rate, it would be like spoon-feeding caffeine into him.

Furiously, he pitched the thermos cap to the ground and drop-kicked the chair. It tumbled a few unsatisfying feet before folding flat. Hank turned his head and glanced at Eddie, but he never rose. Even when Eddie headed for the truck, the dog did not budge.

Minutes later, Eddie returned with a roll of duct tape. Snatching the chair from the ground, he flipped it open and moved it closer to Hank. He scooped up the cup and fell into the chair.

"Everything is crap nowadays. Nobody makes anything decent. You'd think companies could get their shit together and make things that last—but nooooo." He continued to mutter as he stared into the distance and reflectively created a list to support his assertion. "A fifth of whiskey. Money. Marriages. None of it lasts." Eddie turned toward Hank. His face wrinkled as he slowly lifted his arm and sniffed. "Deodorant." He smelled the other side and made a face.

"Even your damn food dish is falling apart." With the toe of his boot, Eddie poked Hank in the hindquarters. "Did you hear me, boy? Before long, you're gonna be eating off the floor." The dog continued to ignore him. Eddie snorted. "What the hell? You spend a friggin' week with your mother, and you start acting like a girl—all moody and shit." Hank rose slightly, crept out of Eddie's reach, and lay down. Eddie shrugged. He rocked his head back and forth, mocking Hank. "I guess you told me."

Ignoring the dog's snubbing, Eddie set about patching the cup. At one time or another, nearly everything on the farm had been repaired with duct tape. It was the fastest and cheapest way to rectify anything broken. If only it worked on Jules.

The first piece he tore from the roll became a wadded tangle that stuck to his hand. "Dammit!" Eddie fought with another hunk, but it did not play nice either. "Oh, for cryin' out loud. What the hell's wrong with this crap?"

Exasperated, he pulled the sticky mess from his thumb, rolled it into a ball, and flung it to the ground near the first. The next two strips made their way around the cup—in a rudimentary way. Smoothing out the wrinkles proved fruitless. Eddie tore one additional section and wrapped it over the top of the knobby mess. The result resembled a preschool art project gone wrong. From the outside, the only red that could be seen was around the lip of the cup. Satisfied, he raised it into the air—a flip-off to the universe—and grunted his success before filling it with coffee.

The sun glinted off the silver flask he pulled from his jacket pocket. Eddie grinned as he twisted the cap off. He held it over the steaming cup but did not tip it enough to combine the two. Thanks to Jules's constant hovering after his accident, he had been sober for nearly a week. Not a drop of liquor passed through his lips. It had not been easy. At times, it almost killed him. So, throwing away a week of sobriety gave him pause.

The minute the whiskey entered his stomach, it would all be over; he would want more. He knew that the longing would hound him endlessly, and it would be harder the next time he tried to break the cycle.

He stared into the sky. "Dammit, God! You owe me. With all the shit I've put up with in my life, the least you could do is let me have one drink without slamming me with these damn cravings. Give me a sign, will you?"

Eddie listened but heard nothing. He tipped his head from side to side and considered his dilemma. Did it honestly matter if he liked a drink here and there? Or how much he drank? There was not a living soul who cared what he did anymore, including his wife. After their last go-round, the likelihood of Jules returning was virtually nil.

Eddie looked at his dog, still pouting several feet away. Hank did not need him to be sober. All he wanted was food. Even on Eddie's worst days, he remembered to feed him. It might not always be kibble, but what dog did not like bacon and eggs, a liverwurst sandwich, or a rotten apple occasionally? So, why was he even considering anyone else in this choice? It was his alone to make.

In one hand, he clenched the flask tightly against his thigh, anxiously bouncing it. In the other, he held the mangled duct-taped cup against the arm of the chair. If he were in AA, he would receive his one-week pin tomorrow. Any alcoholic knew that was a significant accomplishment. But then again, Eddie was not a drunk. He repeated that over and over, but no one ever listened. They doubted him and gave him that look—like he was crazy. He was not; he knew he was not. Sure, he liked to indulge and periodically *overindulge*, but he was not hurting anyone. And there wasn't an accident on his driving record.

Eddie spat onto the field. The bouncing slowed, and then it stopped. A week without a drink *was* a big deal. He understood that. He had been there twice before. And it was hard work—emotionally and physically.

God, grant me the serenity to accept the things I cannot change, the courage to change the things I can, and the wisdom to know the difference. That was the AA motto. Both times he had given up drinking, he rambled that prayer several times a day.

Suddenly, the message became crystal clear. He didn't need the courage to change. Everyone else needed the wisdom to know he didn't need to change. And by God, they needed to make peace with that.

38

Eddie – 2009

The office door flew open and banged against the wall. Eddie jumped, knocking an empty whiskey bottle to the floor. His eyes were half-mast, and he could see the shadow of his eyelashes through his narrowed eyes.

Jules scooped the bottle from the floor and slammed it on the desktop. Again, he jumped.

"What the hell, w-woman? I was working in here." His words slurred together.

"Working on this bottle of whiskey, you mean?" She pointed to the container. "Eddie, I swear to God, if you don't get your drinking under control, Cade and I will walk out of here, and you'll never see either of us again."

Eddie chuckled. "I-Is that s-supposed to be a threat? 'Cause it's not."

Jules picked up the empty and newly opened bottles and left the room.

"Hey, b-bring that back. I got w-work to do," Eddie yelled.

Jules reappeared in the doorway. "You go back to AA, or I'm leaving. And I'm not kidding."

Eddie toggled his head from side to side and flapped his lips mockingly. "AA's for d-drunks. I'm no drunk."

"I'm sure that's what every person at those meetings thinks too." She glared at him. "I expect you to be at that meeting tomorrow night. Do you understand me?" Silence echoed through the room. "Did you hear me, Eddie?"

"Yes, I heard you."

"Good." Jules walked away.

Eddie crossed his arms on his desk and laid his head against them. There was no one he hated more than his wife.

He would not sleep next to *little Miss Perfect* without more whiskey. Instead, he fell asleep on the couch in his office. The sofa was too short and the armrest too steep, but it was a million times better than being scrutinized for blowing off a little steam.

Just before midnight, Eddie woke. He sat up and cocked his ear toward his office door. *Silence.* With the moonlight as his guide, he made his way into the kitchen to retrieve his whiskey. But in the light, he saw how Jules spent her evening. A row of empty and rinsed bottles lined the kitchen counter next to the sink. He clenched his jaw. This was his wife's passive-aggressive way of letting him know she was not kidding.

Clumsily tiptoeing across the kitchen, Eddie opened the front door just enough to keep the hinges from squeaking. He squeezed through, leaving it open for his return. Soundlessly, he staggered to his truck, grinning at outsmarting Jules. But his smile quickly disappeared when he pulled an empty vodka bottle from beneath the seat. Either she outwitted him, or he was an idiot.

He wildly swung his arms. Stepping backward up a slight incline, he lost his footing and crashed to the ground, landing on his back. Dew clung to the tall blades of the overgrown lawn. It soaked through his shirt, but he was too angry and drunk to get off the ground. Within minutes, exhaustion and alcohol rendered him unconscious.

At dawn, he awoke to his wife standing over him, holding a

feisty chicken. "I found this in the house this morning. Do you know anything about that?" She looked toward the porch. "Then, I came outside and saw you lying out here." Her eyebrows pressed together. "Still think you're not a drunk?" She flung the chicken at him and stormed back to the house.

That was three months after Melia's death. That night, Eddie returned to AA for Round Two.

Clearly, Holland Crossing harbored its share of drunks because the VFW held daily meetings. Eddie knew what to expect once he stepped inside those doors, but it felt different this time. Maybe it was because he failed before, or perhaps it was the uneasiness of people knowing why he came back. The entire town hated him for the death of his daughter. They didn't believe it had been an unfortunate accident. When it came to Eddie Greer, the town followed gossip rather than truth.

He arrived at the meeting at ten minutes to five. His heart thudded in his chest. For a brief moment, he was convinced he was having a heart attack. Eddie wished he would die. That would serve his nagging wife right. More than a handful of times, he got in and out of his truck before finally approaching the door. People walked into the building. Locals ignored him. Those who did not know his past offered to accompany him inside. But he couldn't go with them.

By the time he mustered enough courage to enter, the meeting was already in progress and had been for a good ten minutes. Standing in the entryway behind a gray metal door, he listened for another ten before finding the nerve to enter the room. Once seated, he heard nothing but his heart pounding in his ears. He kept his eyes low and did not utter a word.

A few attendees came from other communities to keep from admitting they were addicts to their neighbors and friends. He should have considered that. Based on the locals in attendance, he figured they were given an ultimatum too: *change or lose everything*. But the difference between them and Eddie was they all had something to fight for. His marriage was a lost cause. Even though he kept his end of the bargain, Jules had every reason to leave him—and not a single one to stay.

For almost an entire year, Eddie was sober. During that time, he kept his head low and mouth tightly closed. Except for his crew, wife, and grandson, he stayed away from individuals who might set him off. He avoided bars and even went out of his way to keep from driving past his favorites. But then something inside him snapped.

Two weeks shy of his one-year chip, Eddie fell off the wagon—or rather, he jumped. During a week in Fargo at a conference, he let loose. The first two nights, he drank soda—passing it off as whiskey and Coke in the presence of the other attendees. By the third night, he hooked up with a wayward group from the Iron Range in Northern Minnesota. They did not know about Eddie's last year of abstinence or the death of his daughter. And they were unaware of his wife's warning. So, they ordered him the real deal—and Eddie did not refuse.

Once that first drink entered his system, he was not able to stop. He did not *want* to stop. The following morning, he woke in an unfamiliar hotel room with a strange woman asleep beside him. She was scantily clad, but he was fully dressed, so he assumed he passed out before anything happened. At least, he hoped that was so.

For two years, Eddie hid his headlong stumble back into the bottle. A container of vodka hung in the sling beneath the seat of his truck. He made a show of regularly attending meetings but never made it through the door; rarely did he make it as far as town. Instead, he always found himself down some long-ago used logging road, drinking enough to face his wife. His perfectly timed returns caused no suspicion.

His wife was oblivious to his drinking. He covered his bottle-clutching exceptionally well. But that secret meant learning to control some of his other issues too—namely, anger. Periodically, it reared its ugly head. But he was careful. To continue drinking, he had to strangle that monster and keep it tied up.

The end of Eddie's two-year clandestine affair with alcohol started as the last seven hundred or so previous nights—down a rutted road. But the night ended with a DUI and a stint in jail. He was not driving erratically. It was a broken taillight that betrayed him. His heart skipped a beat when the blue and red lights flashed behind him before he reclaimed control. If anybody could hide their drunkenness, Eddie could. For three years now, his sobriety was the talk of the town—even without his attendance at meetings. People believed Eddie finally earned a win. So, when Scott Hendrick, the town cop, knocked on Eddie's truck window, he thought he would find a sober Ed Greer—and that was who Eddie gave him—until he let his mouth get the better of him.

Before Jules picked him up the following day, she scoured the house and the farm for his hiding places. She even discovered the one in his truck that the cop impounded. From then on, he no longer tried to hide his drinking *or rage*. His mouth spewed hate toward everyone—especially his wife.

Eddie shook the memory away. His shoulders fell as he admitted to himself: *a week without alcohol was a big deal.* One drink could send him into a tailspin. It would not be the first time. He drew a deep breath and held it. Finally, he upended the metal flask and watched the contents soak into the ground. A guttural howl of emotional pain tore across the field as he whipped the container. Hank raced toward him. The dog's eyes told Eddie all was forgiven.

Suddenly drained, Eddie shivered. Whether from the cold or dumping his faithful friend on the ground was unclear. He adjusted his jacket and buttoned it to his neck. Every day, autumn made its appearance known a little bit more. A degree or two colder, less light on both ends of the day, and a crispness to the air signaled an end to summer. The leaves had begun their transformation, giving a nod to the beginning of three weeks of stunning views before six months of dormancy.

Two deer bounded out of the woods, and Eddie slid to the edge of his chair in search of more. Hank barked but did not give in to the chase. A month from now, the pair would likely be hanging from someone's oak tree. He hoped they stayed long enough for it to be his.

Suddenly, Eddie froze. Just as before, he heard someone call his name. He waited. A flash of royal blue cut through the woods—standing out among the brilliantly-colored leaves. *Was that why the deer ran? Was someone out there?*

Eddie wrapped his hands around his mouth and hollered, "Who's there?" He heard his name again, louder. This time, the sound came from his left. When he stood, the chair folded in half. "What do you want? Why are you here?"

He searched the thicket and beyond. *Who was trying to make him think he was losing his mind? Or was he actually losing it? Was he drunk? Had he been drinking and not remembered? What the hell was happening to him?* Standing perfectly still, he scanned the brush with only his eyes. Finally, after several moments, he picked up his chair and cautiously resettled.

His heart banged against his chest. Eddie was sure it was Ben Mayer. Was he trying to scare him into selling? The man was not to be trusted. None of the Mayers were. Every meeting between the families had gone sideways faster than a coyote after a jackrabbit.

Again, he scanned the open land. Hay bales peppered the field. Anyone could be hiding behind them. He limped along the edge of the woods, searching for Mayer. Hank walked next to him.

"I swear to God, Mayer, if you're on my land, I have every right to kill you. Trespassers be damned." But he saw nothing.

Eddie scanned the field one more time before returning to his chair. Another month and Holland Crossing would likely see its first snowfall. The hay needed to be put up in the barn or wrapped before then, or it would be useless. But Eddie refused to allow anyone on the field since Cade's death.

Eddie's ears rang—one more downside of growing old. Was it from a lifetime of drinking or his habit of rage-charged jaw-clenching? Both were equal suspects. Aches and pains were a constant lately. A new malady presented itself daily. He could hurt himself sleeping or breathing. Like most things on the farm, he fell into the category of *beyond repair*. His knee ached worse than the day before. Getting old was definitely not for sissies.

He rubbed his knee as he watched the woods. Finally, he let go of the feeling someone was still out there. He ran a hand down Hank's back, leaned back, and closed his eyes. A troubling thought pecked at him. If his grandson had not met with fate here on the hayfield, Eddie would most likely be drunk on another part of the farm. But he was not. He was sober and feeling the pain of his life's decisions. That made him wish he had not emptied his flask.

39

Eddie – 2001

Eddie was almost finished with the milking when Jules walked into the barn wearing the same blouse and jeans from two nights earlier. Her hair was pulled into a messy ponytail, and a faint shadow of black mascara had settled into the fine lines beneath her lower lashes.

After pressing a couple of buttons, she shoved the back of a digital camera toward him.

"Meet your first grandchild, Grandpa." Jules's voice was buoyant and blissful. The sound grated on Eddie, and he cringed.

He shoved her hand away, knocking the camera into the hay. "I got chores to get done," he snarled. "I don't have time for other crap."

Jules scooped up the camera and wiped the viewer on her jeans. "Eddie, look at him." His back straightened. "How could you not love him? He has your eyes."

"Him? It's a boy?"

"Yes. You have a grandson. *Cade Weston Greer.*" Once again, she held the small screen in front of him. "Look how adorable he is."

Eddie glanced at the screen briefly before knocking the

camera from her hand a second time. "Well, if we gotta have another mouth to feed, at least it's a boy—somebody who can help out around here—eventually."

"Edward Henry Greer, you are the most insufferable man on earth. How dare you think of him as a burden. He's your *grandson*." After snatching the camera from the floor again, she headed toward the door but stopped. "Oh, and Mel's doing fine—*now*. I know you don't care about your daughter, but she almost died. She lost a lot of blood after Cade's birth. It was touch-and-go for a while." Eddie felt her eyes burn into the side of his face. "Thanks for asking, by the way." She kicked the barn door open and stomped toward the house.

The cow mooed, waiting for Eddie to finish. He released a loud breath. So, he was finally getting the boy Jules could not give him—the one she swore she would give him. Only this kid was not *his* son. In anger, he kicked the milk bucket. The foamy white liquid sloshed inside before narrow rivers trickled down the outside of the metal pail.

"Son of a bitch," he whispered. "Why does this crap always happen to me?"

From the time Cade was born, he was small—fifth percentile small. Flaxen-haired and pale-complected, he was not only sickly looking, but he acted the same. Due to his asthma, Mel or Jules spent many nights in the bathroom with the shower running, walking the creaky floor. The noise angered Eddie because it interfered with his sleep. Eddie saw the boy as a liability. *Why had God even created such a weak link?*

By the first of March, Cade was stricken with his first of a dozen cases of croup. Doctor and drug store bills accumulated. Eddie paid the debts, but not without complaint. It did not take long for him to realize his grandson would be as worthless on the farm as his daughter.

When Cade started school, he could already read and write. He had read his way through most of Melia's childhood books. From his first day of kindergarten, he was at the top of his class. Not only could he read well above grade level, but he was also math-smart and could solve any problem in seconds. His first word was not Mom; it was *automatically*. Within a matter of weeks, he grew from simple to complex sentences. He used words Eddie had not heard since high school—ones he only ever used on tests. But words and numbers were useless to Eddie. Unless the boy could drive a tractor, toss hay, or mow the lawn, what good was he?

Cade celebrated his eighth birthday seven days before his mother was killed. After that day, he turned inward, becoming a recluse—a select mute who spoke only to Jules. Days turned to weeks and weeks to years. All that time, he holed up in his room with an MP3 player and earbuds, blocking out reminders of life outside himself. Outraged, Eddie removed his grandson's bedroom door. And when Cade created a hiding place inside his closet, Eddie took that door off too.

Eddie accused Jules of coddling their grandson. In his mind, allowing him to eat in his room and catering to his every need made him soft—*and weird*. Eddie fought with her about buying things he could do alone in his room: a TV, books, and video games. She took him to a therapist every week to talk about his *feelings*. It was hogwash as far as Eddie was concerned. It made the boy weak. More than once, he had screamed, "*Suck it up! Everybody has crap to deal with. Grow up and stop acting like a wuss.*" Eddie's outbursts were followed by reprimands from Jules—which led to him getting drunk. If it were up to him, he would have that kid's ass glued to the kitchen chair until he could straighten up and fly right.

Then one day, about three years after his mother's death, Cade ventured downstairs at dinnertime. He pulled out his chair, sat down, and ate his meal without a word. Eddie did not look at the boy, but Jules fawned over her grandson. Five minutes into dinner, Eddie could not take it anymore. He stormed out of the house and headed to town to *breathe.*

Just as he had always referred to Melia as *girl* or *kid*, he did the same to his grandson. He never called him by name. It was always *boy.* In his head, he called him names that would make Jules's skin crawl, but the boy deserved it. Eddie hated it when his dad refused to use his name. But this was different—he was not his father.

In middle school, Cade's physical education teacher introduced him to weightlifting. Even though he never broke five foot seven, he bulked up enough for his grandfather to notice. By high school, he learned to control his asthma enough to join track. He ran short sprints—the *hundred* or *two hundred*—and was a fierce competitor in the long jump. Jules sat in the stands and cheered for her grandson during every track meet while Eddie marinated in alcohol at one bar or another.

The stack of college catalogs on Cade's desk grew. Eddie overheard multiple conversations between his grandson and Jules regarding universities, scholarships, and his future away from the farm. By January of his senior year, he had been accepted to his top pick: Carlson School of Management. He planned to major in Business Law. Cade received a partial scholarship that would pay nearly half his tuition. With their heads pressed together, he and Jules completed financial aid forms to borrow the rest of the money. Since shortly after his mother's death, Cade knew law school was where he was headed. But Eddie hated lawyers.

After a particularly harrowing day on the farm, Eddie snapped. He tromped upstairs, grabbed every school catalog he could find, and hauled them out to the burning barrel, where he doused them with lighter fluid and set them ablaze. When Eddie turned around, his grandson stood behind him, shivering. He wore no coat and only a pair of Nike slides on his sockless feet. His arms were crossed inside his t-shirt as he watched it all burn—including his acceptance letter to Carlson. The anger and hurt in his grandson's eyes should have destroyed Eddie, but they did not. He felt nothing.

Cade could still attend college without those catalogs or the letter, but the moment Eddie lit that match, the boy's dreams went up in flames. The light that had relit three years after his mother's death was gone again. It never flickered; it just went dark.

For nearly five years, Cade never mentioned college or that he aspired for anything other than farming. Day after day, he kept his head low. He made no eye contact with his grandfather. Eddie did not know if his eyes were green or brown or blue; he never saw them. And, until the morning of Cade's death, he never heard his grandson speak one word to him.

40

Eddie

The inside of the house was eerily still. Even the remnants of the storm did not calm Eddie's nerves. He flipped on his mother's old radio. The white plastic was now yellow, and the dial had turned from clear to an unsightly dark gold. Eddie rotated the knob slightly left and then back again but could not tune it perfectly. KKOQ, an AM oldies station, crackled in the storm. Even staticky voices were better than the silence that echoed inside him.

It had been several days since Jules walked out again, but he could still feel her presence. In his head, she was everywhere: paging through a magazine in the sunroom, drinking coffee at the kitchen table, and watching a movie with Hank curled up beside her. She was everywhere, yet nowhere. He felt a deep ache. In their four decades together, he could not recall ever missing her. But then again, it was hard to forget someone who busted your balls about every little thing. Eddie's shoulders fell. *Was there any truth in that? Was she the battle-ax he remembered? Or had the alcohol made him paranoid and angry?*

Eddie stared out the kitchen window. Unexpectedly, lightning zipped across the sky, followed by a deafening clap of thunder. He jerked the red and white gingham curtains closed and pressed his hands against the edge of the sink. The flash took him back to that morning on the hayfield. He did not want to remember. But how could he forget?

The aroma of coffee wafted through the kitchen. Removing Jules's favorite cup from the cupboard, he filled it to the brim before melting into his chair. Hank sat next to Eddie and repeatedly jerked his head toward his spot at the table.

"What?" Eddie stared at Hank. His jowls drooped, and he looked dejected. "Don't give me that look. This is just how it's gotta be from now on." Eddie sighed. "You can't sit at the table anymore. In case you've forgotten, you're a dog. Remember? In a week, your mom taught you to act like a dog." He snorted. "That's something I haven't been able to do in three years."

Hank turned around and faced the door. He let out a loud huff and dropped onto his belly, his backside aimed toward Eddie. After several seconds, he shoved the dog's chair away from the table. "Alright, I give. Your mom's not here. One of us might as well be happy."

Hank walked to his chair but did not climb onto it. Instead, he rested his chin on the seat.

"Oh, for God's sake. This is a man's house. And you're a man. Get up in your chair." Eddie held the cup below his lips and blew on his coffee before taking a sip. "Besides, right now, you're the only one who'll put up with me."

Hank stayed perfectly still for a few seconds before slowly climbing onto his chair. Eddie grinned at him across the table. "See? Back to normal."

After filling the dog's bowl with a smorgasbord of items from the refrigerator, he set it on the table in front of Hank. "Bon appetit!" Hank enthusiastically dug in. "Only you would get that excited about a hunk of cheese, dried-out salami, and a few rotten bananas."

A loud buzz from the AM station coincided with a flash of lightning. Between the crackling of the radio and the thunder, Eddie could barely make out the lyrics.

He heard his name in the rain against the windows. *Ed. Ed. Ed.* As the wind picked up, the pitch changed. *Boy. Boy. Boy.* In the downpour, he heard his dad's voice. *Puss-y. Puss-y. Puss-y.* He turned up the volume of the radio. The last person he needed inside his head was his dad.

Sizable storms pushed through during the night. By daybreak, they circled back, taking a second and third shot at the farm. Every depression was hidden beneath a pool of water. Some were mud-puddle size. From the window, others appeared to be *bury-your-truck* size.

The wind upended the rickety metal swing set. As a child, Eddie spent hours lying on his stomach across the rotting wooden seat, pretending he could fly. Before he turned four, his imagination took him on trips around the farm. But after his father became violent, his daydreams took him and his mother and grandmother far, far away. Now, he saw the equipment as a worthless piece of junk.

If the weather report were accurate, the sun would pop out within the hour. Until then, he and Hank were confined to the house. Eddie retreated to his office and turned on a small TV. The kitchen radio fought for attention with the television, but he was listening to neither.

By 10:30 a.m., the fog that followed the storms gave way to mid-morning sunshine. *Foggy at seven, clear by eleven,* floated through his brain as he filled his thermos. It was one of the old wives' tales his mom often uttered. This one he counted on to be true because he needed to get out of the house.

Thanks to Jules and her insistence on keeping the cupboards and fridge full in case of snow, no matter the time of year, he could slap together a few ham sandwiches with thick slabs of cheddar cheese and tomato. When he pressed a slice of multigrain bread on top, mustard oozed down the side. It was not his favorite, but the bread was his only choice. Studying it, he swore there were enough seeds to feed a flock of birds for an entire month.

Honestly, he didn't see it as bread. It was a brick—heavy and firm. But this was all there was unless he made a trip to Shaw's, which was not happening. So, he made do with *chicken feed bread.*

Eddie shoved the sandwiches into three plastic containers and snapped the lids on each. He put the boxes, his thermos, a couple water bottles, and a bowl inside a canvas bag. As always, Hank waited by the door.

"Alright, buddy, in the truck." The dog bounded down the steps and through the soaked grass. He jumped over some puddles and plowed through others. While Eddie picked his way through the yard, Hank waited next to the rusty vehicle. Opening the truck door was the one thing his dog had never mastered.

When Eddie did not head toward the hayfield, Hank barked. He pawed the window and whined.

"Not today, buddy." He rubbed Hank's head. "We're going somewhere else."

For the better part of an hour, Hank watched the road. Finally, he turned around several times and collapsed onto the seat. His head rested on the bag between them. Impatiently, he poked Eddie with his paw.

"Not yet, boy. But soon."

Just east of St. Cloud, Eddie eased the old truck onto a road needing serious repairs. The storm had not helped the pothole situation. Eddie weaved his way over the gravel, easing through unavoidable divots. Several farms and a cemetery appeared on the right side, while the left was dotted with dwellings in various stages of collapse. A strong wind could put most of them out of their misery.

A couple of miles down the road, he turned left, bouncing along what amounted to nothing more than a grassy trail. Above them, enormous trees leaned inward, meeting over the path to form a canopy. They were clustered so tightly together that even the sun could not muscle through.

Hank sat up and stared out the window. Repeatedly, he adjusted his paws to keep from falling onto the floor. Another mile passed before Eddie pulled into a clearing adjacent to a small body of water. Lake Sheridan was a little-known treasure George Greer inadvertently introduced Eddie to on one of his many benders. As a child, he had been there only oncc. As an adult, he visited more often than he cared to admit. His father's frequent visits to the lake made sense. People were rare, and police sightings were virtually nil. It was too far off the beaten path. So Eddie spent a lot of time looking at the lake and burying his difficulties in booze.

He swung the strap of his bag over his shoulder and fished the lawn chair out of the back of his truck. Even after ninety minutes on the road, the bed held rainwater. The webbing of the chair was soaked. Water dripped from the aluminum frame as he walked toward the lake. Hank slowly wove his way down the dark narrow path, sniffing messages other animals left.

Twenty feet from the shore, Eddie stepped into another world—darkness to light. The sun suddenly burst forth in all its glory. The crystal-clear water reflected the dazzling blue sky. Eddie's shoulders fell, and a feeling of peace eased in. Closing his eyes, he drew a deep breath of damp earth and fresh air. Standing in paradise, the cares of the world fell away.

After giving the chair a final shake, he flipped it open and dropped onto the seat. Water soaked into the back of his jeans. He shivered at the coolness, but he knew it would warm quickly. Hank lapped the water near the shore before returning to Eddie. The dog widened his eyes and opened and closed his mouth several times, letting Eddie know he was ready for lunch.

"You're really something, boy. Can't I just sit for a while before we eat?" Hank's mouth opened wider this time. "Fine. You win."

Eddie tossed Hank a plain ham and cheese sandwich before unboxing his own. He slowly chewed as he thought about his many trips to Lake Sheridan. More times than he could count, he had slept—or passed out—on these shores. He often woke with sand glued to his cheek or inside his clothing. Over the years, he found himself in a faceoff with a skunk, coyote, and bear—none of which stopped him from returning.

Eddie squirmed in his chair. *Why had he come to a place with so many memories he wanted to forget?* But he already knew the answer. This was one more step in deleting his father from his life.

41

Eddie – 1973

It was a beautiful fall day. George Greer set the newspaper on the table and glanced at his son.

"Headed to St. Cloud to pick up some supplies this afternoon. Wanna come?"

Eddie froze. The words made sense, but the question did not. His dad had never willingly invited him anywhere. Eddie finished chewing. "How far is St. Cloud?"

"It don't matter, boy. Do ya wanna come or don't ya?"

Eddie did not trust his dad. Worse, he hated him. But he could not waste it if there was even the slimmest chance of encountering the father he used to know, the one who existed before his fourth birthday. His mom nodded when he looked at her. The mother-approved trip gave him hope.

"Okay." He wolfed down his lunch, dumped his plate in the sink, and ran to grab a jacket. Five minutes later, he stood by the door with a blue hooded sweatshirt and a few dollars his mom tucked into his front pocket.

"I made you boys some dinner." She handed the bag to George before kissing her son on the cheek. "Be a good boy, Eddie. Do as he says, and things'll be fine," she whispered.

Eddie nodded slowly, unsure about his decision.

Multiple times that day, Eddie opened his mouth to ask a

question but closed it again, letting the words dissipate. He wanted to ask his dad so many things while he had a captive audience, but he was afraid to ignite his anger. So, he spoke only when necessary.

The day played out exactly as his father described. In each store, Eddie trailed closely, afraid of being left in the big city. He fingered the three bills in his pocket, longing to buy a candy bar or a book, but he was too afraid his dad would not wait or he would confiscate his cash if he knew of its existence.

On their return trip, not far from St. Cloud, his father turned down a gravel road.

"W-Where are we going?" Eddie asked.

His father scowled at him. "Boy, you ask too many damn questions. Just keep quiet."

Eddie felt his panic rise when his father turned down a second road. The sky was locked away on the other side of the enormous trees. Horrible thoughts raced through his mind as it grew darker and darker. *Was his father going to kill him? No one would ever find him back here. Who would protect his mother?*

When they pulled into the parking lot, Eddie felt the grip on his chest loosen slightly. The sign read *Lake Sheridan*. Holland Crossing was surrounded by lakes, but Eddie had never been to one. He only knew they were blue because of the pulldown map at school. The River House was as close as he had ever gotten to a body of water, and depending on how fast the water was running, sometimes it looked more brown than blue.

"Grab the bag your mom packed." George plucked a pair of chairs from the back of the truck and started down the path toward the lake. Eddie followed, careful not to trip or draw attention to himself.

Just before the water, he stepped from the dark into the light. He chuckled softly and walked back and forth several times.

Mary Perrine

Dark—light. Dark—light.

"What the hell are you doing, boy?"

Eddie instantly headed toward his dad. He waited until George was seated before taking the chair his father did not claim. The last thing he wanted to do was upset his dad again.

Suddenly, his father got up and headed toward the trail. Eddie raced behind him.

"Get back there." George pointed toward the chairs. "What? Is the little baby too afraid to stay alone?" He laughed as he turned and walked away.

Eddie swallowed hard. Was it possible his father would leave him stranded? Tears filled his eyes, but he swiped at them so they would not leave damp spots on his t-shirt, evidence of his wussiness. He walked toward the lake and studied the shore. If his dad did not return, which way would he go? The few houses were so far away. It would take hours to reach them.

Suddenly, his father stepped out of the shadows with a six-pack of beer in one hand and another tucked under his arm. Eddie's stomach sank. The day had been tolerable, but things would fall apart quickly once his father started drinking. Abandonment might have been better.

Moving slowly, Eddie returned to his chair. Saying and doing nothing was the only way to survive his dad's lapse into the dark side.

George dropped the dinner bag into Eddie's lap. "Eat, boy." He side-eyed Eddie. "Besides, you're way the hell too scrawny to be a kid of mine. You got some height, but a decent breeze could blow you away."

Eddie ignored his father and unboxed the first sandwich. He held it in front of his dad.

His father shoved his hand away. "I don't want that damn thing." He pulled the tab from a can of Grain Belt and flicked it toward the lake. Holding the beer into the air between the two of them, he grinned. "I got the only dinner I need right here."

The lower the sun moved into the sky, the more nervous Eddie grew. He watched it carefully, praying his dad would want to leave soon. Once the sun fell below the trees on the other side of the lake, the thick grayish-blue sky had not taken more than a few minutes to swallow the daylight. *How long did his father plan to stay?* He squirmed. *They should be getting home. His mom would be worried.*

"Dad, I have to pee."

"So, go pee." George swung his beer hand toward the woods. Foam shot from the can and landed on his tan pants. Rage burned in his eyes. "Did you see what you made me do?" He turned toward Eddie. "Did. You. See. What. You. Made. Me. Do?"

Eddie nodded, but he knew better than to speak. He tipped his head down and closed his eyes. His father's unexpected backhand sent him and the chair tumbling. Blood gushed from Eddie's nose. He wiped it on the front of his shirt and pinched the bridge like his mom showed him the last several times he connected with his dad's hand. A metallic taste filled his mouth, indicating a split lip or a sliced tongue. He wanted to scream. But no matter how badly it hurt, Eddie refused to cry. Tears were what his dad wanted. They would prove his son was indeed a baby.

George tilted his head back and emptied the rest of the can. "Get your ass off the ground, you little dick."

Eddie righted his chair a little farther away from his father. Too frightened to draw attention to himself, he did not spit. So, he swallowed the blood and wiped his nose on his shirt again. His actions were small and slow. Startling his dad was not something he was willing to chance again.

George looked at him. "I thought you had to pee, boy? So, go pee?"

"W-where?"

"For God's sake. The whole world's your toilet. Ain't nothing or nobody too good to be pissed on from time to time." He raised an eyebrow. "Except me."

The remaining light was quickly fading. If Eddie was going to go, it had to be right away. Clenching his jaw, he warily walked toward the woods. A large owl flew toward the lake, directly over Eddie's head. The steely eyes panicked him, and he dropped to the ground.

"Chicken-shit. Are you afraid of an itty-bitty owl?"

The owl scared the piss out of him. The front of his jeans darkened, but he could not let his dad find out. He unzipped his pants and pretended to pee into the grass not more than ten feet from their chairs.

"Good God, boy. Pee in the woods. Ain't nobody wants to see or hear you, you little nitwit. And nobody wants to smell what you're putting out."

Eddie pulled his t-shirt down over the front of his pants and raced back to his chair. The moon laid a wide beam of light across the lake. The wind picked up. Eddie's sweatshirt was back in the truck. He looked toward the trail entrance. Instantly, he decided against getting it—at least, not alone. And he knew there was no way his dad would go with him.

He pulled his feet onto the chair, tucked his arms inside his t-shirt, and tugged the stretchy material over his knees. His father continued to ignore everything but his beer.

Pressing his face against his knees, Eddie closed his eyes and prayed. If he stayed there all night, he would freeze to death.

"Dad?" When he did not answer, he poked him in the arm. "Dad?"

A can fell from his father's hand. "W-What the hell, boy?"

"Can we go home?"

His dad snorted. "D-Don't you see I ain't in no c-condition to drive?"

Eddie got up and looked toward the path. "I'll drive then."

George grabbed the front of Eddie's shirt and jerked his son toward him. The chair tipped sideways. "You'll d-drive? W-What are you, like seven?"

"I'm eleven," he whispered.

His dad let go and stared at his son. "Well, then, e-eleven is a fine age to d-drive." George stumbled as he stood. "Let's go."

His dad started toward the trail without him. Eddie glanced at the chairs. The ground was littered with cans and garbage. He knew he should pick it up but was petrified of losing his father in the dark.

George nearly fell a handful of times before reaching the truck. After slamming his father's door, Eddie raced to the driver's seat and climbed in. He was happy to be anywhere that was not outside. As he studied the dashboard, he shoved his arms through the sleeves of his sweatshirt. A lawnmower was the most powerful machine he had ever driven. This would be a challenge.

"Well, w-what the hell are w-we waiting for?"

Eddie turned the key. The truck sprang to life. He glanced at his dad, who had already passed out in those few seconds. The muffled sound of liquid hitting denim told Eddie his dad had wet himself. He could smell the stench of urine. He was unsure if it was his or his dad's.

His heart raced inside his chest as he replayed everything he knew about driving. Eddie's memory was amazing; he forgot nothing. The road home was a piece of cake: a right onto the second gravel road before a left onto the highway. From there, it was a straight shot to Holland Crossing. Eddie just needed to find the courage to put it all together.

Finally, he shifted into gear. The truck lurched forward. His dad's head banged against the side window, but he did not wake. Eddie wanted to make it happen again, but he did not want to waste a minute getting home. After several near off-road mishaps on the gravel, he finally got the hang of steering.

He took a deep breath and turned onto the highway, praying for guidance. Then, slow and steady, he headed toward Holland Crossing. Deer were abundant, but there was little traffic. For that, he was grateful. Only once did a driver lay on his horn and zip around him as he drove nearly thirty miles an hour under the speed limit.

Four hours later, he pulled up to the house. His mother was waiting on the porch. Anger and relief etched her face as she raced toward the driver's side. Eddie knew she was roaring to give his dad an earful. A bloody-faced Eddie looked back at her when she jerked the door open. He gave her an exhausted smile before collapsing into her arms. She kissed the top of his head and led him into the house.

"What about Dad?"

"He's not going anywhere. He can spend the rest of the night out there for all I care." Sucking in a deep breath, she released it through her pursed lips as she studied her son's blackening eye. "Did he do this to you?" She shook her head. "Of course he did."

Guilt welled on Eddie's face, and he looked down. "It was my fault. I made him mad."

"It doesn't matter, Eddie. He had no right to hit you." She held his face in her hands. "Are you sure you're okay?" He nodded. "All right then. Go upstairs and get cleaned up. I want you in bed." He was almost to the top of the staircase when she called to him. "You did good tonight, honey, real good. I'm proud of you. But in the future, remember, your father isn't your concern. If he ever puts you in a situation like this again, leave him. He's not worth it."

Eddie nodded. "Love you, Mom."

"I love you too, son." Then she turned toward her bedroom.

It was nearly 3:00 a.m. by the time Eddie crawled into bed. He studied the same moon that hung over the lake. "I never want to be like him," he whispered. "Never."

Around 10:30 a.m., his father staggered into the house. Eddie grabbed the last piece of bacon and shoved it into his mouth. A small part of him expected a thank you for getting them home safely last night. But, instead, his father walloped him across the top of the head.

"For God's sake, boy. Ain't ya ever heard of a gas station? The least you coulda done was put fuel in the truck. Now I gotta siphon some outta one of the machines just to get to the store." He shoved Eddie's shoulder. "What the hell's wrong with you?"

"Leave him alone, George."

Eddie said nothing. He had learned long ago that answering questions only brought more trouble.

The lake sparkled in the noonday sun. Hank poked Eddie's hand. He opened and closed his mouth, demanding more. Eddie tossed him the last sandwich, mustard and all.

In the dozens of times Eddie made his way to the lake, he had never come to feel closer to his dad. No, he hated the bastard. Instead, just like his old man, he came to hide—from the world, Jules, and the people of Holland Crossing. He was always in their crosshairs. If they were not gossiping about his wrongdoings, they were waiting for the next shoe to drop. There was no mistake about it.

Eddie was mortified to have become such a loser in a town that deserved better—to people who thought he was their best chance of getting their town on the map. But he let them down.

No *Home of Edward Greer* sign ever appeared on the *Welcome to Holland Crossing* sign because he had quit. His father had destroyed the town's dreams, not just his own. It was no wonder they stared and talked about him behind his back.

So, what was he doing here? That was easy. He needed to show Lake Sheridan he was no longer the drunk who repeatedly passed out on the shore. And he needed to prove to himself he could change—that he *was* changing. Being there was a commitment to himself and Jules.

With Hank asleep beside him, Eddie poured the last of the coffee into the duct-taped cup. He took a sip of the lukewarm caffeine. Suddenly, he straightened his back and slid to the front of his chair.

"Edward." The voice was clear and very distinct. "Edward."

His arm rocketed upward, and his cup burped from his hand. The chair tipped sideways when he jumped out of it and spun around.

Someone called his name. It was as plain as day. It was not in his imagination, and it sure as hell had not come from the lone boat on the far side of the lake. This time, Eddie recognized the voice. It was his father, George Greer—a dead man. *Or was he?*

His heart raced as he stuffed everything back into the bag, grabbed the chair, and raced along the path. He crawled into the truck and slammed the door. Hank stood on his hind legs at Eddie's window and barked. Eddie flung his door open and let the dog climb over him. Before Hank settled, Eddie slammed the truck into gear and raced from the lot, through the trees, down the gravel road, and onto the highway, headed for home.

His father was alive. Because if he was not, then Eddie was going crazy.

42

Eddie

Eddie's mind raced. Images of his possibly alive father flashed in and out. Questions badgered him, pulling his attention from the road. *Did his dad fake his death? If so, where had he been all this time? Why did he not show himself? Why was he playing these mind games?* And the biggest question of all: *Was it even true?* Eddie was more convinced than ever he was losing his marbles.

The trip home from St. Cloud was a blur. He could not remember turning in town, passing Matt's Bar, or the Firelight. The red and blue of a police squad, siren blaring, zipped around Eddie, but he did not pull over. Even when the cruiser passed and the lights were in front of him, he still did not notice.

A large SUV swerved to avoid t-boning him as he turned into his driveway in front of the oncoming vehicle. Washboard ridges and muck alternately commandeered his truck, throwing it sideways and then sucking it into the mud repeatedly. He was driving so fast, the ninety-degree corner toward the house became a *General Lee* moment.

"Ahhhhh, shit!" Eddie hollered. Pressing the pedal to the floor, he steered through the shallow waterlogged ditch before jerking it back onto the road. Eddie's long exhale hit the windshield and returned to him, but he did not slow. Had he done so, the hands of sludge would have pulled the truck into the bowels of mud so deeply, it would have been held hostage for days. The road was too soft for farm equipment to extricate him, so he would have been walking. He did not have time for that.

Mud flew from his tires as he raced up to the house. He dove out of his truck, left the door hanging open, and took the stairs two at a time. His office was a disaster like the rest of his life since Jules left. Still, he knew exactly where to find what he was looking for—a death certificate. The handle of the wooden filing cabinet let loose when he yanked it. It bounced across the floor, followed by a few choice words. After prying the drawer open with his knife, he ran one finger along the tabs until he came to the file marked *George Greer*. He fell into his desk chair, shoved the mess to one side, and laid the folder in the open space.

If Eddie was anything, he was organized—at least until his wife jumped ship. His dad's birth certificate was in the front of the file: *July 17, 1937*. Unlike his demise—if he really *was* dead—his birth had been unremarkable. He had been born on the farm with the help of a woman named Elsa Wiitala. Flipping the folder over, he lifted the back cover and removed the last sheet: his father's death certificate. Scanning the document, he relaxed when he saw the date and cause of death: *June 3, 1980. Impaled. Accident.*

Eddie let go of a chasmic sigh, freeing the anxiety of the last two hours. After closing the folder, he planted his feet on his desk, leaned back in the squeaky chair, and folded his hands behind his head. George Greer was dead. *End of story.* The certificate clarified what he had always known. But an uneasiness stirred again. Because of the gravity of the accident, his mother opted for the casket to be closed. He had not seen his father's body in the casket. A ragged breath cut through him, reviving every emotion he had released seconds earlier. Anyone could have been inside—or no one at all.

Again, he scanned the death certificate. There was no way his father could have survived. Eddie had seen his body lying in the hay—facedown, unmoving. And there was blood, so much blood. But could it have been staged? Could it have been animal blood?

A flash of memory swirled in Eddie's mind. When he sorted through the farm accounts, there were numerous checks of significant size to *cash*. He had written them off as money for booze or perhaps gambling. Now he wondered if his father paid someone to help him escape his life. *Could George Greer still be alive?* He would be eighty-five, so it was not out of the question. But if he was, he must have had someone help him with every detail.

Eddie's feet dropped to the floor. Again, he opened the file and perused the death certificate. It looked authentic. But was it? Back then, it would have been much easier to fake a death, disappear, and assume a new identity—especially if someone helped him.

If he was alive, had he watched Eddie struggle through life for the past forty-two years—laughing at him, silently criticizing his every move? If his dad forced him into this miserable existence so he could live a better one, Eddie would kill the son of a bitch. He did not care if he lived out his remaining years behind bars. He had nothing left. Eddie spun a toy roulette wheel. Killing his old man with the possibility of going to prison was a chance he would take.

Pressing his elbows onto the desk, he leaned his head into his hands and grabbed handfuls of hair. His dad must be alive. Because if not, how could he continually call his name? Or was his imagination haunting him with the voice of the man he despised more than anyone else? Had that hatred manifested an invisible chokehold so strong, he actually heard it? His body shook violently, and he wrapped his arms around himself and moaned in agony.

Hank raced into the den. Eddie had abandoned the dog outside, but Hank was a survivor. Except for the truck, Hank could manipulate every handle on the farm.

The dog hopped onto his lap and rested his head on his shoulder. Eddie wrapped his arms around Hank and buried his face in his fur. "Something's wrong, boy." Running a hand up and down the dog's back, he whispered, "I think I'm going crazy."

The grandfather clock was a drum in the silent room. Eddie watched the hands move in tiny, rhythmic beats. His heart ached as he tried to untangle memories. Finally, he set Hank on the floor and headed toward the backdoor.

The sun dipped low in the western sky. Within an hour, daylight would fade, and dusk would settle across the farm. One memory burned deeper than the others. Eddie hobbled across the field and into the woods. The tall trees cast dramatic shadows, blocking much of the remaining sunlight. Fishing his phone from his pocket, Eddie turned on the flashlight and searched the ground. Hank trailed him, nearly colliding with his leg when he stopped suddenly.

Eddie awkwardly dropped onto his good knee. The dog sat on his haunches for a few seconds before lying flat. Hank remained silent, clearly aware of the importance of the place.

What was once undergrowth was now a dense forest filled with tall trees and layers of dead vegetation so thick, the rock marking Zeppelin's grave was barely visible. Eddie leaned forward and brushed away everything from around the stone. His hand touched a small board entangled in the weeds. He unearthed it. With his fingernails, he scraped the dirt from the front. An intense memory smothered him, sending him back to that agonizing day when his father killed Zeppelin.

A week after Eddie buried Zep, he pried a piece of siding from the barn wall. It had not taken much effort. Like most things on the farm, the building was in shambles. Unable to locate a paintbrush, he dipped the wood into an old bucket of house paint and tipped the board back and forth until it was coated in white. When it dried, he used a crosshead screwdriver to carve Zeppelin's name across the front. That was nearly fifty years ago. The board had weathered and swelled, and Zep's name looked like nothing more than a few scratches. It was a rotted hunk of lumber to everyone else, but to Eddie, it was one more way his father destroyed who he should have been.

Eddie leaned onto one hip and rested against Hank. The air rushed from him. Tears burned his eyes but did not fall. His words slipped into the air as he spoke to a *dead* man—which was still questionable.

"I hate you, Dad," he hissed. "You took everything from me—including Zep. You had no right to kill him. No right!" Eddie punched the air. "You thought you were such a big man, taking away something that I loved. You did the same to Mom." He knelt again. "The only person you ever cared about was George Greer. The rest of us were just collateral damage."

Angrily, Eddie threw the old sign toward the grave. He rose and headed toward home, neither flipping on a light nor slowing for the uneven ground. Hank tugged at his pant leg. "Dammit, Hank! Let go." But the dog pulled harder. He dug all four feet in and growled. "Stop it!" Eddie slammed the heel of his other foot into the dog's underside. Hank yelped loudly and let go. Staying low, he crawled toward the grave and collapsed near the rock.

Eddie's heart jumped into his throat. What had he done? Hank was his best friend—his *only* friend. He had not killed

Hank, but the pain he caused was unacceptable. Eddie was not so unlike his father after all.

He dropped onto the ground beside the dog and pressed his face against his head. "I'm so sorry, Hank. I don't know what I was thinking." He ran his hand along the dog's side, feeling for broken ribs. "Please, please forgive me."

Hank lay next to Eddie. Rubbing the dog's side stirred the memory of lying on Zep's lifeless body. Eddie turned on the phone's flashlight and carefully stepped over the roots and weeds. Picking up the sign, he set it in front of the stone and pulled the rest of the weeds away. His hand dropped into a slight depression. Eddie pointed his flashlight toward the hole, silently questioning whether the animal that dug it might still be present.

Gingerly, he poked a small branch into the depression to check its deepness. It was shallow, not more than a few inches deep. Again, he tapped the stick into the hole. The clunking sound signaled a rock or something metal. He enlarged the opening with the branch. Warily, he reached in and removed a small metal can. How did it get there? He would have seen it when he dug Zep's grave.

Eddie looked toward Hank. He was lying on his side, panting.

"Hey, buddy. How're you doin'?" He needed to get Hank back to the house. With such limited light, it was going to be a challenge.

"We gotta go, Hank." His voice was soft.

The dog slowly rose, took a tentative step, and whined. Eddie shoved the small can into his pocket and lifted Hank into his arms. The dog hooked his head over Eddie's shoulder. Careful not to touch his side, Eddie locked his hands beneath Hank's haunches. He held his phone flashlight between his thumb and one finger. The beam bobbed slightly in front of them as they made their way out of the woods. Periodically, Eddie stopped to readjust.

"I'm so sorry, buddy," Eddie whispered. "I'm such an ass." He was his father's son in so many ways. It killed him to admit it, but kicking Hank proved he was George Greer's son.

By the time they reached the house, Eddie's arms ached. He shoved the door open and slammed it with his foot. Gently, he laid Hank on the couch before settling next to him. Hank slid toward Eddie and rested his chin on his leg. Eddie's shoulders plunged downward. *Unlike people, dogs loved unconditionally. There was no reason for Hank to forgive him, yet he had.*

Eddie removed the can from his pocket and threw his coat on the floor. In the light, he recognized it as a Spam container. His father wolfed down cans of the cold meat whenever he went on a bender. The old burn pile was filled with charred once-blue and yellow cans.

But this one was different than the others found around the farm. Each corner was sliced and bent inward to create a makeshift cover. Eddie went to the garage and returned with pliers and leather gloves. Dirt fell from the can as he pried the top back and looked inside.

Immediately, he recognized the red plastic egg. Running a finger across the raised lettering, Eddie recalled an Easter long ago. The container of Silly Putty had been the only thing in his basket that morning. They were poor; he knew that. Expecting what his classmates got as gifts was something he could not afford to do. The comparisons were too painful.

Long before the rooster crowed that Easter morning, Eddie sat in bed, reading a comic book. Suddenly, his dad pushed his door open and dropped his nearly empty basket on his bed.

"Ain't no money for candy this year, boy. Besides, I think you're too old to be told lies about some fake rabbit, but your mom feels bad. So, if you know what's good for you, you won't say nothin' to her." He grabbed Eddie's face in one hand and squeezed hard. Eddie's teeth dug into his cheek, but he was afraid to make a sound. "If you do, you'll be cutting your own willow switch." He gave Eddie that look that said everything. "Now, hide this damn basket and say nothin' to her. Understand?"

Eddie tried to nod, but he could not move his head. Finally, he managed to eke out agreement enough to satisfy his dad. His father shoved his head backward, slamming it into the wall. The thud echoed inside his brain, but he refused to cry. Wrapping both hands over his head, Eddie curled into a ball, expecting a second attack. By the time he dared peek, his father was gone.

Fearing the sight of the red plastic egg would anger his father, he hid it in the back of his closet and never took it out.

A week later, Eddie discovered a dollar bill near the barn. He was sure it belonged to one of the farmhands. His dad would never be so careless with money; he pinched it too tightly. Nevertheless, Eddie remained tightlipped about his good fortune. If he told his mother, she would make him find the rightful owner. If his father found out, he would keep it. So, while both of his parents were out of the house, he snuck into his dad's office for an envelope and a stamp. His eyes were set on a pair of X-ray glasses advertised in the back of his comic book.

To keep the top drawer from squeaking and signaling his defiance, Eddie slowly inched it open. When he saw what was inside, his mouth almost hit the floor. Chocolate eggs, jellybeans, sugar-coated marshmallow chicks, and a half-eaten chocolate rabbit were surrounded by wadded pieces of brightly colored foil wrappers. His dad lied. He had stolen Eddie's Easter candy. Quickly glancing over his shoulder, Eddie snatched a handful of eggs and hid them in his pocket in case he got caught. At that moment, he abandoned the idea of the glasses. Instead, that dollar became the start of his *runaway fund.*

Eddie squeezed the red egg in his hand. The brittle plastic crumbled when he tried to pry it apart. The only thing inside was a yellowed sheet of notebook paper folded tightly.

His heart raced as he carefully unfolded the paper, afraid it would disintegrate in his hands as the egg had. Eddie's breath caught in his throat. It had been forty-four years since George's assumed death, but he would never forget his father's barely legible scribbling. Sensing Eddie's angst, Hank scooted closer.

Torn between reading the letter or burning whatever lies his father spewed, Eddie watched his reflection in the dark picture window before opting for the first. Tilting the page toward the lamp, Eddie deciphered his father's note.

Ed, I'm so damn mad. Something evil's got a hold of me and it ain't letting go. Today is the worst it's been in a while. And if I don't disappear, I'm gonna kill somebody. If I had to wager a bet, it's gonna be you or your ma. Somehow I became the one person I never wanted to be—my old man. He had a disease he spread to damn near everybody. I carry that same sickness. Even if you don't wanna admit it, you do too. I didn't fight it and now I'm stuck in the muck of hate. I lash out at everybody. I ain't sober no more 'cause I don't wanna feel nothing. My dad ruined me, and I'm doing the same to you. I can't do it no more. It stops here— tonight—one way or the other. I can't let the Greer poison screw up one more person. I'll see you and your ma again if God sees fit to forgive me. If he don't, then I'll rot in hell with my father and the rest of the Greer men. I deserve that. Dad

Like a child's toy top, Eddie's brain spun. Each time he felt it slow, someone pulled the string again. Pressing his face into his hands, he silently begged for mercy.

Was this his father's suicide note? Or had his old man just disappeared into the night? There was no way he could have. He saw his father's bloodied body in the barn. But had it been a setup? Was it possible his parents conspired with the police to rid the world of George Greer—the man everyone in Holland Crossing hated? Had he slipped into the night with a new identity?

Two questions still plagued Eddie, so much so, he could barely breathe. Hank inched closer. It was a question he would never have an answer to: *Of all the places his father could have left the note, why next to Zep's grave? And had his mother been part of the plan?*

The only riddle that constantly badgered Eddie was whether his mother had killed his father. Deep in his bones, Eddie believed it. That notion sparked when he saw her face that long-ago night. Immediately, he buried it, protected it deep inside so no one would suspect anything. Still, he was afraid it would resurface like bad chicken. Silently, he gave her accolades for saving them from their miserable existence.

The events of that night had been neatly compartmentalized—*before George Greer's death and after*. There was no during. Those images were tucked away in a box marked *Do not open*. Finding this letter blew up everything. He questioned the *neatness* of how everything was put to rest. Not the crime scene itself but the ease with which the police accepted his mother's story. *Accident—case closed* within minutes. Nothing added up. The pitchfork he supposedly impaled himself on was lying next to him, yet he was still on his stomach. How was that piece of evidence overlooked?

Eddie snapped the lamp off and stood at the window. The security light cast shadows across the farm. Had his father stood in those shadows and watched them for forty-some years? In the dark, he paced the room. Just like his father, all Eddie ever felt was rage. And drinking dampened his feelings. The Greer men were angry drunks. Based on the letter, it was in their genes. His anger, alcoholism, self-loathing, and the need to destroy everyone around him were inherited traits. Before his death, Cade was headed down the same path. Maybe his grandson was the lucky one.

Eddie dropped onto the couch and squeezed his eyes shut. Emotions kneaded his stomach until he ejected his lunch into an antique pottery bowl. The tightness around his chest burgeoned. It was the same feeling his dad described. Finally, the storm inside him let loose in a torrent of tears. And for the first time since his father killed Zeppelin, Eddie cried—deep, gut-wrenching, and soul-cleansing tears.

43

Eddie

Red, green, and gold splashed across Eddie's face. The sun melted the colors into shapes that barely resembled the stained glass hanging. Hank nosed his hand, prodding him to wake. Eddie shielded his eyes and grumbled. For a moment, he wondered if he was in the throes of a massive hangover. But unlike the other mornings, there was no whiskey bottle in sight. Still, whatever went down last night had left him with a pounding headache and eyes he could barely pry open.

He ached—not the pain of hard work, but of passing out on the couch in an awkward position. He would have barely noticed ten years ago, but today, his body screamed at him. Moans filled the room as he stretched. His neck popped as he bent it one way and then the other. And he tested each leg before standing.

"What in the hell happened last night, Hank?"

He pressed his hands into his lower back and bent backward before twisting from one side to the other. His heart jumped into his throat as the memory hit him in full force.

"Oh, God." The barely audible words held powerful meaning.

Picking up his father's letter, he read it for what must have been the tenth time since he found it. Each time, the message walloped him, sending him into an internal battle with what he believed to be true and what could be a lifetime of lies.

Eddie folded the paper in half and shoved it into the nearest book—an old Swedish bible that once belonged to his great, great-grandmother. The leather cover was worn—undoubtedly from searching for words of wisdom about dealing with the Greer men.

Facing this new truth was more than he could bear. Those words could have been written by him and left for his son, daughter, or grandson—had any of them survived. The pain of loss deeply cut him. He could have been the raging drunk his father spoke of in the letter, the one to disappear. Truthfully, he still could run.

It was impossible to bring back his daughter or grandson, but was it too late to become a better person? To love Jules as he promised? To be the man he aspired to be over forty years ago?

Highlights of the previous night replayed. His shoulders fell, and he collapsed onto the floor. Eye level with Hank, Eddie pressed his forehead against the dog's cheek. "I'm so sorry, buddy. I didn't mean to hurt you."

A tongue mopped Eddie's face, and he smiled. "It looks like all is forgiven, huh?" He rubbed the dog's head and stared toward the bible. "I'm not sure I deserve to be forgiven by anybody else, though."

Hank dropped his front feet off the couch and stretched before climbing down. Eddie watched him saunter into the kitchen, grateful for no limp. When he walked in, Hank was on his chair waiting for breakfast. Eddie filled his bowl and set it on the table. Hank attacked the kibble while Eddie started a pot of coffee. In a dirty pan, he fried four eggs and dumped half into the dog's bowl.

There were only two things Eddie knew for sure. He never wanted to feel desperate enough to write a suicide note or disappear from his life—whichever his father had done. And he wanted his wife back. How he would make that happen was anyone's guess.

After showering, Eddie slipped on another shirt Jules gifted him years before. For the first time since Cade's death, he texted Buzz to tell him he planned to be gone for a while. He was sure his farm manager expected nothing less since he had not done a day's work since his grandson died. His phone vibrated. The message read *OK*. Eddie knew *So what?* would have been a more truthful response.

Five minutes later, Eddie and Hank passed the crew. All he got was a hand from Buzz as he walked away from the road. He passed Shaw's Store and headed toward the log church. It had only been a few weeks since he set foot out back. His stomach stirred when he turned into the parking lot and drove around to the cemetery.

Buried in the same graveyard, but scattered like seeds in the wind, seemed fitting for the Greers. They barely tolerated one another in life. Why would they wish to spend eternity together? Although Eddie was reasonably confident the Greer men would reunite in hell.

He slowed as he drove along the gravel trail, reading each headstone he passed. Melia was buried inside the circle. That was as much as he knew. Eddie stood at her grave only once— on the day of her service. His heart crumbled when he spotted her headstone. A loss he had never felt before gripped his chest; it hurt to breathe. The truck sputtered when he killed the engine. He and Hank climbed out, but he did not move. Finally, Hank poked him in the back of the knee, nearly knocking him to the ground.

Nervously, Eddie moved toward the headstone. He lowered

himself to the ground and leaned against the marker. Hank sat on the opposite side, keeping a watchful eye on Eddie.

Words churned in his head, but he could not link them together in anything that made sense. Did his daughter know he was here? Was he supposed to talk to her—out loud? He knew two things about dead people: they stopped breathing, and you buried them. That was it. What happened after that? Did anybody really know? He believed in heaven and hell and that people were separated based on their actions or inability to admit wrongdoing or ask for forgiveness. Eddie also knew he was facing the down escalator unless he made a U-turn.

"Hey, ah, kiddo." He was unsure what to call her. She was his daughter, but he was the person to destroy their relationship. Did he even have the right to call her that? Did he even dare say her name? The word had never passed through his lips. He repeated her name in his head, but when he tried to say it, the letters disappeared. His mouth felt like the Sahara—dry and barren. He drew a deep breath and tried again.

"Melia." The word came out like barbed spikes on a cactus, not like a blend of beautiful letters. "This is D-Dad." Could he call himself that? For the twenty-eight years she was alive, not once had he acted like her father. "Mel?" Silence. He was not naïve enough to expect an answer, but somehow, he hoped to feel her presence.

He should not have come. The breeze rustled the trees above him as he debated whether to stay or run. Would it get easier the longer he sat here? Jules would know exactly what to say. He had been a failure when his daughter was alive, and things had not changed in her absence.

A small vase attached to her headstone held a bouquet of waning flowers—pink carnations, white daisies, and variegated pittosporum. A single red rose was tucked into the center. Except for that flower, Eddie could name none. Did that make him a bad person?

"Looks like your mom's been here." He shrugged. "She was always good with…ah, these kinds of things. She remembered birthdays, delivered flowers to everyone, and helped anyone who needed a little extra." He sighed. "Your mom picked up where I fell short." He stared at the picture of his daughter. "Which was everywhere. I failed you. I failed our family."

He shifted his weight. "Now I know it was the circumstances I was angry with—not the people. But I think it's too late."

Eddie snatched an acorn from Melia's grave and side-armed it across the cemetery. He swallowed hard. "My father ignored and belittled me; he made my life a living hell. And I did the same to you and Cade." He touched the image of his daughter's face. "Turns out I'm exactly like him."

Another vehicle entered the graveyard, but Eddie did not look up. "I'd give anything to go back and change the past…" He snorted. "But life doesn't work that way, does it? Wishing for the impossible doesn't change a damn thing." His eyes grew wide, and he looked into the sky. "Sorry."

"Eddie?" Jules put her hand on his shoulder. "Are you okay?"

He jumped. "Jules? Oh, my God! You scared the living crap out of me." He grinned at her. "I'm not drunk if that's what you're thinking." He glanced toward the church. "Did someone call you and tell you I was out here kicking down headstones?"

"They're just concerned about you, Eddie."

He shook his head slightly. "Concerned enough to call *you* but not worried enough to check on me themselves? I suppose that's fair after all I've done."

She lowered herself to the ground next to him. "Well, I guess you can't blame them."

"No. I can't blame anybody but me." He pointed toward the

dark window upstairs. "I'd bet anything they're up there watching us—making sure I don't spiral out of control."

"Stop. They don't hate you, Eddie. They're just worried about you." Jules plucked the rose from the center of the bouquet and held it to her nose. "Can you believe our little girl would be forty-four?"

Eddie sighed. "*Both* of them would be forty-four."

"Yes. But, Eddie, we only knew Mel. We didn't even know we were having twins until they were born." She touched his arm. "And until Cade was born, Mel was our whole world."

"She was *your* world." He watched an ant climb across his hand. "I failed her as a father."

Jules's phone buzzed. She typed a few words and slipped it into her back pocket.

"What? Are they making sure I don't have a gun? Checking that I don't kill myself here in the cemetery?" Eddie asked.

"You always think the worst of people. Karol just wanted to make sure you were okay."

Eddie waved toward the church. "I think she wants to make sure *you're* alright."

The hum of tires on Lake Avenue floated around the church and across the cemetery. A set of brakes squealed in the distance.

"It's so weird to sit back here where it's so peaceful and still be able to hear the commotion on the other side of the church." She squeezed his hand. "As for failing as a father? You did. I'm not going to pretend it's not true. But honestly, you weren't much of a husband either."

Eddie tapped his chest twice. "That hurt."

"I'm not going to sugarcoat it. You only thought of yourself. Whatever Eddie wanted, Eddie got. You were self-centered, ornery, and angry almost every single day—not to mention drunk. I don't recall ever getting a Christmas, birthday, or anniversary gift the entire time we were married."

Eddie raised a hand in protest, but she shot him down.

"None. When Melia got old enough to understand gift giving, I bought gifts for myself and signed your name to them." She scowled at him. "Those are the gifts you remember."

The corners of Eddie's mouth drooped. "Why'd you stay?"

Jules looked at her daughter's headstone. "Because I loved you. Because we had a daughter—and a grandson." She twisted her wedding ring—a narrow silver band. "Because I always thought it would get better—that *you* would do better." She looked at Eddie. "I left when I finally realized it wasn't going to happen. You were never going to change."

He locked his fingers with hers. "But I want to."

A soft laugh escaped Jules. "Wanting to and working on it are very different. You can want something with your whole heart, but if you do nothing to get it, if you don't change your behavior, it was never that important to you."

"I'm working on it, Jules. I really want to fix us."

"Eddie, you can't fix *us*. You have to fix *you*." She bit her lip. "After that, we can see if there's anything still left of *us*."

"I hope there is." Bending one knee, he slid sideways until he faced his wife. He recalled falling in love with her. "I asked you if you could live anywhere, where it would be, and you told me the River House. Are you sure?"

Her eyes narrowed in confusion. "Why are you asking again?"

"Humor me."

Jules pulled a weed that sprang up through the lush green grass of their daughter's grave. "Okay. Yes, I'd choose the River House."

"Seriously? On the farm? Why?"

"Your mom and I spent a lot of time there. The house is too small, but the view is gorgeous." She looked at Eddie. "And

Holland Crossing is my home. But unfortunately, the farmhouse doesn't feel like home anymore. There's too much baggage, too many bad memories."

"And the River House doesn't have that?"

"No. I would love to travel in the winter and tend to the gardens in the summer." She tore the weed in two. "What about you? Where would you live?"

Eddie touched her cheek. "Wherever you are is home. I just never understood that until now."

Jules laid her hand over his and held it there for a few seconds. Finally, she set it back in his lap. "I have to go. Are you sure you're going to be okay?"

Eddie nodded. "Thanks for checking on me." Jules headed toward her car. "I love you," he called behind her.

She stopped for a second before climbing in and driving away.

Eddie leaned against his daughter's headstone. "I need your help, Mel. You owe me nothing, but if there's any chance you could make your mom fall in love with me again, I'd be forever grateful."

44

Eddie – 2009

Eddie stormed into the kitchen, holding one arm above his head. His good hand clutched his elbow for support. Blood pulsed from a slash on his forearm, leaving a trail on the linoleum floor. The pain was excruciating, but he was too stubborn to admit it.

"Jules!" he screamed. "Jules! Dammit! Where the hell are you?"

His wife raced through the front door with a basket of vegetables. "Oh, my God, Eddie. What happened?" She dropped the container on the table and washed her hands.

Folding back his blood-soaked sleeve, she examined his arm. "It's deep. You're going to need stitches."

"Bullshit. Just clean it up and stick a band-aid on it. 'Cause I'm not paying for something you can do for free."

Jules shook her head. "Eddie, you're going to need a tetanus shot too."

"I don't need no damn shot." He closed his eyes for a moment and exhaled. "Besides, I already had one."

"That was in high school."

"What's your point?" he growled.

Jules removed the first aid kit from the cupboard and

rummaged through it. She set a bottle of peroxide, petroleum jelly, several narrow strips of medical tape, and gauze on the counter. This was not the first time she was called to doctor a wound for her husband, nor would it be the last.

"Sit before you pass out."

Eddie dropped onto the chair. His legs were rubbery, but he would never admit that to her.

She pressed a clean dish towel against the cut and applied pressure. "It's way too long and deep. You need to go in and have them…"

Eddie jerked his arm away. "You can help me, or I'll do it myself." He grabbed a bottle of whiskey from the table and poured a shot over his arm. "Jesus, Mary, and Martha! That son of a bitch burns." His eyes squinted into lines. He gritted his teeth so hard, he could have snapped a log in half. The muscles in his neck and face tightened, and he let rip a string of garbled cuss words. It took a full minute to regain his composure.

Finally, he released a deep breath and opened his eyes. Arms crossed, Jules stood before him and grinned.

"Are you ready to do it my way?"

"If it involves a doctor—no!"

"Fine. I'll do my best, but it won't be pretty."

"I'm not entering any beauty pageants here, for cryin' out loud."

She wiped the whiskey from the table, recorked the bottle, and set his elbow on a towel.

"Hi, Mom. We're home," Mel called from the entry. She rounded the corner. The trail of blood stopped her in her tracks. Melia looked at her dad before intercepting her son in the hallway.

"Cade, I need you to go upstairs. Grandpa hurt himself, and I need to help Grandma."

That was all Cade needed to hear. He tried to outmaneuver

his mother to get a peek.

"Go now, please. I'll come to talk to you in a while."

Finally, giving in, her eight-year-old son disappeared up the stairs.

Mel dropped her purse on the floor. "What happened, Daddy?"

Eddie rolled his eyes and mocked her with a high-pitched baby voice. "What happened, Daddy?" He jerked when Jules poured peroxide into the cut. "How old are you anyway?"

Mel closed her eyes and took a deep breath. "Mom, what do you need me to do?"

"Can you grab an old white sheet and tear it into strips about four inches wide? We're also going to need the bottle of ibuprofen."

"Got it." Mel headed for the linen closet. Minutes later, she returned with a handful of long strips. The edges were frayed and slightly puckered.

Jules daubed the cut with a clean dish towel before dousing it again.

Eddie wailed on the leg of the table. "Dammit, Jules! That stings like hell. Are you trying to kill me?"

"Sorry. If you'd rather have a doctor..."

"Just hurry up. This whole thing has put me behind schedule."

Melia stood watch, awaiting her next order. Finally clean and dry, Jules held the cut closed while Mel placed butterfly strips across the wound. She daubed petroleum jelly over it and wrapped Eddie's arm with gauze before covering it with a layer of sheeting. The medical tape held the ends in place.

"I'll run get some wound film at Shaw's after lunch. For now, you need to lie down for a while. Mel, will you grab an ice pack from the freezer?"

Melia did as she was told. Eddie chose the recliner instead

of the couch. "I think you're supposed to keep a wound above your heart to help it heal. If you…"

Eddie's eyes grew dark. "So, when the hell did you become a doctor? Last I remember, you barely graduated high school." He tipped his head. "Then you went and got yourself knocked up. I guess that earned you an A in *sex*." He raised an eyebrow. "You're not really someone I'd take advice from."

"Stop it, Eddie. Leave her alone." Jules tucked a pillow under his arm and gently laid the ice pack on top. "You do remember I was pregnant before we were married, right? Or have you forgotten?"

Deep lines gathered across his forehead. "Must run in the family then—easy Greer women."

Jules's jaw tightened. Melia stood near the picture window, trying to hold back her tears. "Sometimes you are a horrible person. Do you know that? You need to learn when to keep your mouth shut."

She picked up the glass of water and four tiny pills and held them toward Eddie. He shoved her hand aside, sending the tablets flying.

"I don't want those. Just bring me some whiskey."

Without a moment's hesitation, Mel answered his demand. "Here," she said, shoving the bottle and glass toward him.

"I don't need no f-ing glass. I only got one hand. Or are you so stupid you forgot?" Holding the bottle between his thighs, Eddie fought with the cork. Finally, Mel grabbed the bottle and removed it for him. "I could have done it."

Two hours later, Eddie stumbled into the kitchen and toward the front door.

"Where are you going?" Jules grabbed his arm to steady him.

"That b-bobcat isn't gonna fix itself," he muttered. "I g-gotta get it to Finlayson before they close."

"Dad, you can't drive. You're drunk."

Eddie jerked his arm from Jules's grip and lunged at his daughter. "I may or may not be d-drunk. But you, girl, will always be a piss-poor excuse for a d-daughter. You're nothing but a leech—you and that wimpy-ass kid of yours."

"Eddie, shut up!" Jules shoved him into a kitchen chair. "You leave her alone. All she's done for the past two hours is help you."

"About d-damn time she earned her keep."

Tears rolled down Mel's cheeks as she closed in on her father. She held her hand toward him, palm up. "I'll go. I'll take the machine to Finlayson. Give me the truck keys."

Eddie laughed. His words slurred together. "Y-you're a girl. You d-don't know nothin' 'bout pullin' a machine. Hell, you've never even d-driven my truck before."

Jules shook her head. "You're not going, and neither is your father. Maybe I can get one of the crew to run it over there this afternoon."

"Yeah, good luck with that. They're not even h-here." A loud belch reverberated across the kitchen. "They're out at B-Beller's rebuilding their barn."

"Give me the keys." Mel impatiently wiggled her fingers. "You've already got it loaded and ready to go. So, give me the keys."

Eddie pulled them from his pocket and dropped them on the floor. Then, he kicked them under the counter. "This'll just b-be one more thing you fail at."

Jules pulled her aside and whispered, "Honey, you don't have to prove anything. Your dad's just being his usual asshole self."

"D-Don't you be talking shit 'bout me."

Mel turned her back toward her dad. "I know I don't have to prove anything. But if he's ever going to respect me, I have to show him I'm better than he gives me credit for."

"Like hell that's g-gonna happen." Eddie's cheek was pressed to the table.

Jules pulled her daughter into a hug. "Please be careful. Drive slowly. Hennen's is open until nine, so there's no rush."

Mel nodded. "I will."

"Call me as soon as you get there." She held her daughter at arm's length. "I love you."

"I will. I love you too."

Eddie's eyes were open, but his breathing was heavy.

Two hours later, the sheriff pulled into the driveway. Jules was in the garden collecting the cucumbers to pickle. Eddie was on the front porch, his feet propped up on a wicker stool. A nearly empty bottle of whiskey was tucked between his leg and the chair.

Sheriff Tate climbed out of his cruiser. He nodded toward the porch but turned toward the garden. Eddie stumbled down the stairs.

"What the hell, M-Mick? D-did I do something, or are you just here to piss me off?"

Jules's eyes were wide. She dropped the basket and headed toward Mick. "What happened? Is it Mel? Did the truck break down? Is she okay?"

Mick somberly shook his head. "Let's talk on the porch."

"Is that s-son of a bitch M-Mayer tellin' lies 'bout me again?" Eddie staggered toward the porch. "This oughta be good."

Eddie tripped on the bottom step. Mick caught him by the back of the shirt and helped him up the stairs. Jules slowly followed.

"Can I get you something, Mick?"

The sheriff shook his head. "Mel was driving Eddie's truck today. Where was she headed?"

Eddie slapped his thigh. "I knew that d-dumb-ass girl would fail. She can't do a d-damn thing right."

"She was headed over to Hennen's in Finlayson." Jules knit her fingers together. "Why?"

"There was an accident between here and town." Mick looked down before making eye contact with Jules again. "I'm afraid Mel didn't make it."

"What do you mean she didn't make it? To Hennen's?" Tears erupted from Jules's eyes. "Or are you saying she's— she's dead?"

"It looks like the hitch ball broke off the truck just before the intersection of six and seventy-five. The trailer let loose and flew into the ditch. The safety chains took the truck with it." He shook his head. "Mel was ejected because it had no seatbelts."

Jules dropped to her knees on the porch. A strangled sob assaulted the air. Mick helped her up. She glared at her husband, but his eyes were at half-mast. "Do you understand, Eddie? Did you hear what Mick said? Mel's dead. She died trying to make you love her."

Eddie raised his eyebrows. "Well, sounds like she d-didn't do a very good job. I told you s-she fails…"

"Shut up, Eddie. Just shut up. I hate you," Jules sobbed. "I hate you so much."

Mick held Jules while she cried.

Eddie wobbled when he stood. "Get your d-damn hands off my wife."

Sheriff Tate ignored him. Stepping back, he looked at Jules. "What can I do?"

Eddie stumbled toward them. "I'll tell you what you can d-do. First, I told you to take your d-damn hands off my wife. Then, you can take that m-motherless son of hers out of here."

"Edward!" Jules warned. "How dare you? Cade's going to need us now more than ever."

"We're not gonna raise another kid. His mother's d-dead, so he's gotta go too."

Cade's head pressed against the screen door. He looked from his grandmother to his grandfather. "Mom's dead?"

Those were the last words Cade spoke to Eddie until the storm that took his life.

45

Eddie

The sun had barely broken the horizon when Eddie stepped onto the porch. Before Hank realized he was missing, he loaded a dozen cardboard boxes and two tool bags into the truck. The dog had been up much of the night, growling at something—*or someone*. Around 1:00 a.m., Eddie crept onto the porch, but nothing indicated an intruder. Still inside, Hank moved toward the back of the house. He stood on his hind legs and snarled. With a long-handled flashlight, Eddie slowly circled the farmhouse. Rounding the corner on the east side of the house, he froze. A shadow moved across the lawn near the front porch. In the security light, it lengthened and changed shape. Eddie's heart jumped into his throat. He snapped his flashlight off and backed against the house. Inching along the wall, the flashlight as protection, Eddie watched the dark shape continue to move. He was almost to the corner when Hank jumped in front of him.

Eddie dropped the light, leaned forward, and clasped his knees. "Dammit, dog! You scared the crap out of me." Hank slurped Eddie's face, but he pushed the dog away and stormed toward the house. He was not ready for Hank's apology.

Minutes later, he shut Hank in Cade's room, where he could grumble to his heart's content without driving Eddie insane. But

Hank's uneasiness was hard to forget. Whatever had riled him sank its claws deeply into Eddie as well. Even though there were no signs of anyone outside, he locked all the doors and the downstairs windows. That was a first. Honestly, he did not know locks existed.

He tried to sleep, but his brain would not shut off. Old films of his father replayed until he could not stand it one minute longer. To avoid facing the past, he rose early to get some work done.

Eddie sat on the porch with a cup of coffee and scanned the farm. A dense layer of fog hung low, making the tops of the buildings appear as if they were floating. It was not an uncommon occurrence in September, but after the previous night, not being able to see what was hiding feet away disturbed him. So, he waited it out—hoping to find the culprit of Hank's upset.

The farming season was nearing an end. The cornfields had been harvested, and the stover sold to Keith Kelley for his cattle. By the first snowfall, Buzz would be the only crew member on his payroll. The rest would be plowing snow for Joe Kerbler. It was a win-win for everyone. It kept them off unemployment and fed their families until spring.

After breakfast, Hank sniffed his way around the house. Eddie laid on the horn. The dog looked up and raced toward the truck at a dead run. He leapt over Eddie and landed in a heap on the floor. Without missing a beat, he jumped onto the seat and stared out the passenger's side window. Eddie shook his head in disbelief.

"Swift move there, buddy." He rubbed the dog's head, but Hank refused to acknowledge him. "Come on, Hank. You can't pretend you didn't just wipe out. I saw it." The dog turned away from Eddie and hung his head out the window.

Eddie cut through the yard and headed down the gravel

road. The crew was parked along the edge of the driveway about a quarter-mile before the turn. A 1996 Toyota Camry led the group. He tried to connect people to vehicles as he drove past, but he saw no one he did not recognize. His agitation grew as he turned right and headed toward the hayfield. At the River House, he pulled off the road and instructed his phone to text Buzz.

"Who's driving the Camry?" he said into his phone. Fifteen seconds later, his cell phone hummed with a response. *Old man. Lost.*

Old man, my ass. Hank spun his truck around and headed toward the cornfield. By the time he returned, the car was gone, leaving nothing in its wake but a cloud of dust.

"Who the hell was that?" Eddie yelled as he stormed toward Buzz.

"I already told you—some old guy looking for Ashton Lake Resort."

A handful of thoughts needled Eddie. "I doubt that." He turned and headed toward his truck.

Buzz shrugged. "Oooo-kay." He knew better than to keep the conversation going.

Eddie sped toward the highway but saw neither the car nor an old man. He waited at the end of the driveway, hoping the guy would make another pass. Finally, he made a U-turn and headed toward the farm.

At the ninety-degree corner, he continued straight. He eased the truck off the road and onto the overgrown driveway of the River House. His brain still raced with questions. Had the old geezer—*who may or may not be his father*—been what upset Hank? He shook his head. It had to have been a coincidence. His dad was dead, at least to Eddie. If he did not stop thinking about it, he would drive himself right back into the arms of a whiskey bottle, and that was the last thing he wanted.

For the second time in a handful of days, Eddie found himself in front of the tiny house, facing his past. His father had never spent a night inside. He could not understand it, but Jules would choose it as her dream home—or dream location rather. But if he wanted his wife back, Eddie needed to make it happen.

He walked around the house, taking note of the backyard. A rabbit hightailed it out of the woods, freezing when Hank approached. The dog was not a killer. All he wanted was to play, but the cottontail responded as if he were prey. Slowly, Hank approached the animal, poked him with his nose, and ran a handful of steps in the other direction, hoping for a game of chase. Instead, when Hank ran, the rabbit raced into the brush on the far side. Disappointed, Hank dropped heavily onto the ground. Seconds later, Eddie watched the hare hop out of the thicket and toward Hank. After a couple more episodes of trancing, the rabbit finally decided to play. The two tore around the yard, playing a pseudo game of tag. For the first time in what felt like forever, Eddie smiled widely.

Grabbing a bag of tools from the truck, Eddie headed inside to appraise the house. This time, he saw it through his wife's eyes. The original designer kept it simple: basic and economical. It was small, too small for two people. If they lived there together, they would be sardines in a can. But if Jules refused to take him back... Eddie shook his head. He would not let that happen.

On a small notepad, he scribbled ideas. A two-story was out of the question. Bowlegged with a deteriorating body screamed for a one-level. Eddie slowly turned in a circle. It would be best to gut the house or, better yet, tear it down and rebuild, but that would never fly with his wife. So instead, he decided on a large addition with a wraparound porch. The new bedroom and the living room would overlook the river.

After sketching what he believed would make his wife

happy, he spent the next two hours packing everything in the house. He sorted things into three piles: keep, donate, and toss. Jules would have kept it all, but that was not the point of this change. She had already lived in old. It was time for something new, something better. Eddie worried she would take *anyone* better than him.

Seven boxes were already folded closed and stacked near the front door. When Eddie entered the bedroom, a deep feeling of loss settled in the pit of his stomach. Memories pulsed through him with each item he boxed. He could feel his mother's presence— how she held him, protected him, and made him think things would be all right.

Eddie picked up her photo. "It's time, Mom. I'm finally becoming the person you wanted me to be." He snorted softly. "It took me long enough. Better late than never, I suppose."

The curtain fluttered, and Eddie's heart jumped. "Mom?" When he approached the wall, his shoulders fell in relief to realize it was only an open window. A gentle breeze blew into the room. He took a deep breath and laughed softly. But slowly, his smile faded.

Eddie looked at the photo again. "Is Dad with you?" His eyes narrowed as he touched her face. "After everything he put us through, I'd like to think he's suffering in hell. But lately, I have this creepy feeling he's still here." He glanced toward the window. "Is the bastard still alive? Has he been watching us for the past forty-some years?" He sighed. "Please, Mom, I need to know."

Eddie waited, but no sign appeared. Finally, he wrapped the frame in a large doily and placed it into a box. Hatred for his father surged as he moved from one end of the room to the other, sorting items into keep and donate boxes. Tossing anything of his mom's seemed wrong.

The few items in the closet came off the hangers and joined

the others in the donation box. Shoes, purses, and a pair of fur-collared black rubber boots that had been placed on the top shelf joined the other items. A round fabric-covered tan tweed box with three navy stripes across the top was pushed into the corner. Eddie would wager a bet it was older than his mother.

He removed the delicate box and set it on the sagging bed. The lid stuck. It squeaked as he gently pried it apart. An inscription on the inside read *To Hazel Ann Winchester—on the day of her birth, March 5, 1919. Love, Mam and Pap.*

It was a time capsule, a piece of his family's history he had been too young or too self-centered to appreciate until now. Like Jules, the women of his family undoubtedly cherished the past. Never wanting to be reminded of his failings, Eddie pitched everything—set fire to it in the burn barrel. But this—this was like finding a treasure in the midst of all that was imperfect.

Peering inside, he shivered. An ivory hairbrush and matching mirror with copper inlay were at the top. His grandmother always wore her hair in long braids wrapped tightly around her head. Eddie tried to imagine her hair loose and flowing down her back. But it was impossible.

He set them on the bed and claimed the next item: a small black leather clamshell box with several tarnished brooches. One was a cameo surrounded in gold; another sported deep red gems. The third was a butterfly pin with pearls on its wings. He could not recall seeing her wear anything other than a dress. Her hair was always perfect, and her lips were colored the palest shade of pink. Whether working in the garden or going to the store, one of the three pins was attached to her dress.

A handful of yellowed letters were bound together with a red ribbon. Eddie fanned through the stack. Most were sent by Mrs. August Winchester of Cloverlly, England. August and Effie Winchester were his great-grandparents. They had been the parents of three children. His Grandma Hazel was the only one to leave England *for something better*. Fate would drive her into the arms of Walter Greer. And everyone knew he was *not* better. No Greer man was.

Eddie set the envelopes aside and scooped a handful of loose buttons from the bottom of the box. Some were made of wood or ivory. Others were from bones or pearlized shells. A simple gold band and several loose pearls lived among the buttons.

A black leather bible was the last of the treasures. Unlike the one at the end of the couch in the farmhouse—written entirely in Swedish—this one was in flowery English. Eddie had not seen so many *thus, thee,* and *thines* since he had Shakespeare shoved down his throat in high school. He would not have despised it so much had the substitute English teacher not been a hundred-year-old woman with a mind like a steel trap—that was missing teeth and was broken. Eddie was not a man of culture. His world consisted of nothing more than grunts and profanity-laden messages.

The inside front cover claimed Hazel's mother, Effie, as its owner. Paging through, he discovered several old clippings and photos from the past: obituaries, wedding announcements, and handwritten notes. Corinthians was home to a black-and-white photo torn in two pieces. He carried the pieces to the window and read the back before tilting the picture toward the light. It was his parents' wedding photo. As odd as it seemed, he had never seen a photo of them together. Thumbing through the book, Eddie came across a second image. This one was ripped into a dozen pieces or more. He reassembled them on the cover of the bible. Pressing his hand against the picture of the couple, he turned the book over and removed it. In tiny script, the back of the photo read *Walter and Hazel Greer*. No Greer woman wanted a reminder of the day they made the worst mistake of their life. He wondered if Jules had destroyed *their* wedding picture also.

Eddie continued to search through the bible. A five-page letter, folded in half, had been left inside the back cover. The first sheets were farm history. He knew much of that information. But the third held information that was new to him.

February 29, 1972

My name is Hazel Ann Winchester. I was born in Cloverlly, England to August Luther Winchester and Effie Martha (Johnson) Winchester. At 16, I left England for the land of golden opportunities—America. My aunt and uncle settled in Holland Crossing, Minnesota, years before. They invited me to stay with them.

A year after my arrival, I married Walter Bennett Greer. His parents were Hugh and Mamie Greer. They owned a large farm north of town. The original owners were Hugh's father and mother, Karl and Henni.

My father-in-law drank like a fish. Even during prohibition, he never lacked for alcohol. Mamie suffered in silence because a wife never questioned her husband's choices. When we married, Walter promised he would never be like his father. For three years, he stayed true to his word.

Our son, Bertram Walter Greer, joined our family a year after we married—1922. The following year, we had twin boys, Will and Erich. But the Lord called them home before they were a month old. Fourteen months passed before we were blessed with a beautiful daughter, Nettie Mae. It was after Nettie's birth that everything changed. Our family was second to his love for whiskey. I continued to slip down the ladder until he no longer saw me as his wife. I was his maid. He saw Nettie as a burden rather than a gift.

After a barn-raising for the Sandas', I and many other wives came down with smallpox. I moved into the extra bedroom to protect Walter, Bert, and Nettie from the deadly disease. After nearly two weeks of delirium from my high fever, I was given the news that two-year-old Nettie had fallen down the stairs and met her maker. There was no funeral. Walter put her tiny body in the wooden crate my parents shipped my belongings in. He dug a hole in the backyard and buried her beneath the willow tree. I later gave her a proper burial. But to this day, I don't believe Walter's account of the accident. I never trusted him with Bert. I couldn't. I wanted to leave Walter, but it was impossible to return to England, and my aunt told me I had made my bed, so I needed to lie in it. Where else was I to go?

When Bert turned twelve, I gave birth to another son, George. It was a wonderful surprise. I was overjoyed. Walter was not. He had a son. He didn't want or need another. When Bert enlisted in the army, Walter was thrilled. But when Bert didn't return, his father hit the bottle harder than ever. He became a mean and ruthless drunk. Walter drank away his days and slept it off at night. I feared George would inherit this trait. It turns out I was right to be worried.

In 1959, George married Elizabeth Sundberg. Three years later, she gave birth to my grandson, Edward Henry Greer. I watched George like a hawk. I prayed for Elizabeth and little Eddie. Those prayers seemed to work—until Eddie was four. That was when George turned toward the bottle. I have warned Elizabeth to keep an eye on Eddie, but I'm afraid the devil has a tight hold on the Greer men.

I fear that each generation of Greers will suffer the same fate unless someone challenges Satan. I pray someone is strong enough. After everything that has happened, I can honestly say I am ashamed to call myself a Greer. Love to future children, Hazel

Eddie reread the letter. If his grandmother had lived to see him into adulthood, she could have written *Edward Henry Greer—ditto. Same story, different name.*

He refolded the paper and tucked it back inside the bible. His grandmother had been ashamed to call herself a Greer. Those words assaulted him. Alcohol was the thread that tied every generation together—his Great-Grandfather Hugh, his Grandfather Walter, his dad George, and him. As far as he knew, his daughter never touched alcohol. Maybe it was because she saw what it did to him, or perhaps the gene did not affect Greer women like it did men. Eddie saw what it did to Cade. While Eddie sat drinking in the dark, his grandson stumbled into the house many nights.

What was it that turned Eddie to alcohol? Was it staying on the farm? Having his dream of baseball destroyed by his father? Was it finding out he would be a father at the tender age of 18? Was it having the responsibility of the farm dumped on him just before he married the person he should have cherished? Or was it everything? Had it been a perfect storm that destroyed his life?

Over the years, Eddie woke up with a hangover more times than he did not. Yet he always denied being a drunk. He lied to himself and everyone else. How long was the line of drunken Greer men? How many generations before his great-grandfather had it permeated?

His grandmother's letter was clear. The Greer men were a selfish bunch who found joy in alcohol. It was the reason his dad treated him like dirt and why he had treated Melia the same. Eddie tilted his chin upward and closed his eyes. He sighed deeply. Understanding why did not excuse it. Eddie needed to take responsibility for himself if he hoped to earn his wife's trust and love.

Eddie returned the bible to the box. As far as he could tell, there was only one good thing to come from his miserable existence. There would be no future Greer men to carry on this nightmarish trait. No woman would have to suffer the way his grandmother and his mother, and Jules had. But right now, his wife was the only one who mattered.

This was the end. He had no intention of going to his grave being ashamed of being Eddie Greer. Not anymore.

46

Eddie

Nearly every day, shortly before sunrise, Eddie and Hank arrived at the River House. While Eddie built Jules's dream home, Hank played with the animals that frequented the yard or sat by the fireplace. The floors and the cabinets had been removed, and the wall between the kitchen and the living room was no more. The addition was taking shape, and he could imagine the completed structure. It felt good to be working again, to develop blisters and calluses on the palms of his hands. Since his grandson's death, the most he had accomplished was throwing a pity party and chasing tan Camrys, trying to locate the old man who cornered Buzz at Shaw's a few days after their initial conversation—this time asking about the old farm.

Under strict secrecy, Eddie hired Jeff Canter and his crew to work with him, putting on the addition and remodeling the existing structure. Because winters were slow, Buzz jumped in whenever he did not have other work.

As the house came together, Eddie smiled. He whistled even. Instead of walking on eggshells around Eddie, Jeff's crew included him in their jokes and break time-banter. Not since his high school baseball years had he felt part of something bigger than himself.

At night, Eddie and Hank returned to an empty house. He was both exhausted and invigorated. Yet, in the evening, the silence and loneliness became overwhelming. It rang in his ears and punched him in the gut. So often, he wanted to unburden himself with a drink, but he remained stronger than the bottle. Instead, he would shower and call it a night earlier than ever before.

It was rare to find him without a book in his hands. An excess of reading material lined the shelves in a small alcove. Both Jules and his mother were voracious readers. As a child, he had also been, but since taking over the farm, he exclusively read repair manuals. If only there was a manual that told him how to undo what he so effortlessly obliterated with his wife. He needed it to explain how to go from *creep to sixty* in a week. But it was impossible to fix a broken marriage in seven days. He had done the crime, so he needed to put in the time to rebuild the life he managed to implode.

Eddie's first attempt at fixing his marriage came in texts. His fingers were too fat, and he did not have the dexterity for a verbose message, but he was committed to sending something daily. Two weeks later, he built up the nerve to call her. He paced the kitchen floor for nearly ten minutes, testing phrases aloud. Since the invention of the cell phone, their calls almost always started and ended with him being disagreeable and obnoxious.

Before his third call, he practiced ending with *Love You*, but he could not release the words until Jules hung up. The phrase felt foreign. The last time he said those words was lost somewhere in their first year of marriage. That alone did not bode well for forgiveness.

On Jules's birthday, he sent sixty red roses—one for each

year of her life. The month, he knew, but he had to dig through their old tax returns to find the specific date of her birthday. And for no reason, he sent her a pair of diamond earrings. Giving was something new for him.

Sunday, a few days after a lonely Thanksgiving dinner of frozen pizza, his phone rang. Eddie was pacing, practicing for his next call to her. Without preparing, he was afraid to answer, afraid he would say the wrong thing.

"Hi." Her voice was whisper soft. "I haven't heard from you today. I thought I'd check in."

"I'm okay. The farm's been keeping me busy," he lied. "Otherwise, I'm good."

Silence spanned the line as he tried to conjure up a response.

His wife sighed softly. "Well, okay, then. I just wanted to make sure you were alright. Bye."

"Wait! Jules?"

"Yes?"

"Would you like to have dinner with me Friday night?" Eddie moved his phone to his other ear. Her quietness made him nervous. "I understand if you don't want to." His shoulders fell. "Maybe it's too soon."

"No, it's not." Eddie listened to her breathing. "I'd like that. Were you thinking we'd go out, or did you want me to cook?"

"Definitely out. I owe you that much."

"Are you okay if we go someplace where we aren't giving the locals fodder for gossip?"

"Of course. Does Grand Ridge work? We could eat at Everwood."

Jules laughed. "There's no way you could know that's my favorite restaurant. We've never been there—together, I mean."

"You'd be surprised by what I know. Is 7:30 okay?"

"Perfect. Do you want me to make a reservation?"

"No, I will. I'll pick you up at quarter to seven."

"Is this a date? Like a real date?"

"Well, I gue… Yes, it's a date."

"Sounds like a reason to buy a new outfit." He could hear the smile in her voice. "See you Friday."

"Love you." But again, the words fell on a dead line.

Eddie immediately called for reservations. There was so much he wanted to tell his wife—beginning with, he had finally decided she was more important than booze and ending with a goodnight kiss. He could hope. Could he not?

The last time Eddie wore cologne was before he got married. Anything he found in the bathroom would be rancid, but he still checked. In the linen closet, he found a white bottle with a silver plug in a shoebox. It once belonged to his father. Memories of sailor commercials flooded back, the ones where the whistling seafarer always got the girl. That was Eddie's goal. Jules was his girl, and he intended to reclaim her love.

Did men's cologne go bad, like women's did? Pulling off the gray plastic cork, he took a whiff. His eyes watered, and his nose wrinkled. Did it always smell that way? After a half-century, it had definitely gone rotten. Opting for the natural smell rather than rotten eggs, Eddie pitched the bottle into the trash.

After trying on nearly everything in his closet, Eddie finally settled on a pair of gray slacks he had not worn in at least a decade and a half and a white shirt. In the back of his closet, he found an old sports coat with suede patches on the elbows. Dust clung to the shoulders. He brushed it off, sending the specks into the air. Pressing the fabric to his nose, he sneezed. Fabric softener and the dryer were his best hope. Standing in front of the full-length mirror a half hour later, he wondered how out of date his clothes were. Was he a walking time capsule from the year 2000, or was vintage cool? He mentally added *shop for clothes* to the list of how to please his wife.

Hank followed Eddie to the door. "Not tonight, Hank. Your mom and I have a date." He rubbed the dog's head. "Did you hear that? A date." He chuckled. "I'll be back later." The dog dropped heavily to the floor. "Don't make me feel guilty. I'm nervous as hell already."

Grabbing his keys from the bench, he gave them a little toss and caught them. He whistled a Peaches and Herb song from their dating days: *Reunited.*

"Wow!" Jules circled Eddie. "Did someone dress you?"

Eddie looked down. "Oh, this old thing?" He grinned. "I just grabbed the first thing I saw out of the closet." His smile widened. "You don't look so bad yourself." Jules frowned. "I mean, you look *really* nice."

"That's better." She laughed.

Her hair hung in loose curls. She wore a black pantsuit with a freshly ironed white blouse. Eddie ran his hand down the front of his shirt, extremely aware of the few wrinkles he had not taken the time to remove.

He removed her coat from the hook by the door and held it for her to slip into.

Jules shook her head in disbelief. "I can only recall one other time you held my coat for me."

"I'm turning over a new leaf. I have it in me, you know."

She pulled the door open and nodded. "It's nice to see it periodically."

"Would you be okay if we take your car rather than my truck? Your black pants covered in Hank's fur probably isn't the look you're going for."

She dangled her keys in front of him. "Good call."

297

Benign conversation filled the forty-five minutes to Grand Ridge. Jules told him about volunteering at the church and a shopping trip with a friend. Eddie talked about Hank, the farm, the weather, and his follow-up visit to their daughter's grave. Not once did he mention his work on the River House. That was news he was saving for the perfect moment. It was the final scene in a romantic movie. The gesture would seal his fate—one way or the other.

At the restaurant, he took her coat, checked it, and held her chair. He ordered a soda for himself and a glass of red wine for Jules. She balked at drinking wine when he was not, but he would not take no for an answer. Eddie had worked hard on his sobriety. Alcohol had destroyed their life. He would not let his problem take away his wife's joy—at least not anymore. They shared a decadent chocolate lasagna for dessert: five layers of brownie and raspberry cheesecake, topped with powdered sugar and a mound of berries. The top was drizzled with ganache.

Eddie wiped his mouth and returned his napkin to his lap. He offered coffee to Jules before pouring his own. "So, I think we need to talk."

"Here? Eddie, are you sure? Maybe we should talk in the car in case…"

"Are you afraid I'm going to make a scene? I'm not." He took a sip of coffee. "This isn't even about us."

"Ooo-kay," she said slowly, clearly confused.

For the better part of a half-hour, Eddie told her about his dad's note. He admitted having dreamt of writing a similar message, wanting to die rather than living his life in reruns of rage. Jules held his hand.

"I have this nagging thought that keeps me awake at night, though." Eddie laid his napkin on the table.

"What is it?"

"In the note, my dad used the word *disappear*. I keep

wondering if he faked his death and just left Holland Crossing."
Eddie shared about the tan car and the old man fishing for
information from Buzz. He told her about the night Hank would
not settle down.

"Oh, Eddie. I think that man's appearance after you found
the letter is just a coincidence. You chose to focus on the
possibility rather than the likely. I think saying he planned to
disappear was the nicest way he could let you know he was
about to…" Jules shrugged and collected her thoughts. "He had
no idea how old you would be when you found that note—or *if*
you would find it at all. I would guess he was protecting you.
Besides, your mom and I talked about everything. I can't
imagine her taking a secret like that to her grave."

Eddie stared at his wife. "But the voices I hear, what about
those?" Jules nodded. "I swear it's my father."

She poured another cup of coffee. "Our brains play all kinds
of tricks on us. Sometimes I hear my mom's voice. It happens
when I really need her." She held her hand up, interrupting his
protest. "I know you don't need *him*, but here's what I think.
Because you've been to the River House, your mom's been on
your mind lately. And, for better or worse, your dad was a huge
part of her life. So, you hear his voice. Regardless, I think it's
safe to believe he's gone."

Lines deepened across his forehead, and his eyebrows drew
closer together. "So, then, I *am* crazy."

"You're not crazy. You've never been crazy." The corners
of her mouth curved slowly upward. "Annoying? Hell, yes. But
not crazy."

Eddie laughed softly. "Well, that's good to know—because
there's more."

He shared about finding his grandmother's letter,
confirming what Jules told him. Alcohol was the devil, and he
was under his thumb. All the Greer men had been. They were a

dysfunctional, mean family of drunks. He apologized until there was no breath left in him, no more words to say. His chest heaved one final time, and relief washed over him. Finally, Eddie said what he needed to say.

"Wow," she finally whispered. "That's a lot of information to process. I can't even imagine how you're dealing with it." She rested her chin on the back of one hand. "Are you okay?"

He nodded. "I am. For the first time in a very long time, I feel good. I've been sober since you rescued me on the hayfield. I finally realized there's more to life than booze." He reached for her hand and took a quick breath. "I love you, Jules. But I understand if you don't feel the same way anymore." Eddie stared into her eyes. "I won't push you, but I want you to know that I am rediscovering the boy you fell in love with years ago." He cleared his throat. "I can't make up for the past, but I can give you the future you deserve."

Jules looked down and gently shook her head. Finally, she made eye contact again. "Those are beautiful words, Eddie. They're the words I've wanted to hear for so long." She pulled her hand away. "But how do I know they aren't just—*words*? How do I know I can trust you again?" Drawing a deep breath, she continued. "You hurt me. I can't go through that again."

Eddie's shoulders fell. "I never want to hurt you. I won't. I promise."

"Then I need to see *that* Eddie for longer than a couple of months." She checked her watch. "We should probably get back. I'm meeting with Barbie at the realty tomorrow morning."

Eddie's eyebrows raised. "A realtor? Does that mean you've already made up your mind?" He wagged a finger between them. "About us?"

Jules drank the last of her coffee. "Until tonight, I had no reason to believe your changes would be permanent. You've never given me any indication of that in the past. Sure, you've been attentive with calls and texts. And yes, you sent me flowers and earrings, but…" She set her cup down and leaned toward him. "But anyone can make a nice gesture from time to time. It's the day-to-day actions that count. The laughter, the romance, dinners out, snuggling on the couch, a kiss." She took his hand. "I can't remember the last time you kissed me—or told me you love me—not counting a few minutes ago. You broke me, Eddie. You broke *us*. I don't know what it will take to put our life back together." A long sigh assaulted him. "Or if it's even possible."

Eddie crossed his arms and rested them along the edge of the table. "It is. Let me show you. Give me a chance, Jules. Give me until spring. Please don't make up your mind until then."

With her jaw clenched, Jules studied his face. "Okay. I'll give you until June first to become the man I fell in love with."

His shoulders dropped, and he exhaled deeply. It was the most he could hope for. "I won't let you down. By then, you'll fall in love with me. You'll see."

"Eddie, I've always loved you—even when you haven't loved yourself."

47

Eddie

By the first January snowfall, Jeff's crew had closed in the addition of the River House. The dark wooden beam and exposed tresses magnified the beauty of the Great Room. Except for the gas fireplace surrounded by flagstone, floor-to-ceiling windows offered unobstructed river views. Eddie opted for a matching fireplace on the outside wall—offering warmth on crisp autumn evenings. The dining room extended from the side of the house onto the wraparound deck, allowing a view of the water also. Jules's studio and the owner's suite opened to the back porch. Eddie designed it so she could sit outside with a cup of coffee, gathering inspiration in the early morning, and put it on canvas when the light was right.

As each day passed, Eddie felt his nerves fray. Questions nudged him constantly. *Would it be enough to make her stay? Or was it too much? Worse—would she see it as a desperate attempt to buy her love?*

Since their *first* date, Eddie texted her every morning and fell asleep to the sound of her voice in his head after their nightly call. They ate dinner together several times a week, often traveling to Duluth or another larger city. Periodically, they tested local restaurants and the rumor mill. A handful of times, Eddie cooked dinner. Those events usually involved a combination of restaurant-purchased meals, warmed bread, and a salad Jules helped prepare. Not once had she complained or called him out for the takeout packages she found buried in the garbage can.

Jules had canceled her appointment with the realtor the day after their dinner. She had moved from the hotel to a rental in Holland Crossing—a one-bedroom in town. It gave her room to begin painting again.

Every time their night together neared an end, nerves swelled inside him. He still had not kissed her. He promised he would not push, and he had not. Near the beginning of February, Eddie stood on her porch after an afternoon date to the zoo. He zipped his jacket and shoved his hands deep inside his pockets.

"I had a really nice time today," Jules said. "I can't remember laughing that much in a very long time."

Suddenly, she moved toward him, raised onto her tiptoes, and kissed his cheek. "Thank you."

It was not what he wanted, nor what he envisioned of their first kiss in four decades, but it was more than he had gotten since trying to win her heart again. He returned to his car feeling like a schoolboy falling in love for the first time.

By March, Jules kissed his lips. By April, they spent nights snuggled together on the couch. Eddie knew his life was about to change. He could feel it.

By mid-April, Jeff's crew finished the house, and Buzz returned to managing the farm. The interior designer he hired from Duluth understood his vision. The pieces came together into something grander than he could ever have imagined.

A warmer-than-usual spring gave him additional time to landscape the yard. He drew plans and hired a local nursery to help with the layout of the plants. The design incorporated Jules's favorites: lilacs, daisies, and red roses. Near one corner of the back porch, he planted a memory garden. It held nine miniature bushes surrounding an engraved stone in remembrance of the family they lost. Near the river, Eddie built a pergola complete with a table and chairs. A stone walkway led to the structure and the firepit. White Adirondack chairs circled the pit.

By the beginning of May, Eddie began clearing brush from beneath the trees at the edges of the yard. One overcast morning, when he returned to his truck for a new blade for the brush cutter, a lone figure stood in the road near Hank. It was a child, probably no more than a dozen years old and as skinny as a string bean, not so unlike Cade at that age.

"You need something?" Eddie scanned the area for a vehicle or an adult.

"Is this your dog?" the boy asked.

"Yeah. That's Hank. And clearly, he's taken a liking to you. What's your name?"

"Ethan. Ethan Mayer."

Eddie froze. "Mayer, you said?"

The boy nodded once. He pointed in the direction of the hayfield. "I live on the other side of those trees." He pulled off his royal blue sweatshirt and tied it around his waist.

"I know where you live." Eddie glanced in that direction. "Does your dad know you're here?"

Ethan shook his head. "He and my mom are out of town for a few days. My grandma's staying with us."

Eddie relaxed. "So, why are you here?" His face twisted in question. "Don't you have school today?"

"My mom homeschools me and my brothers. She says it'll keep us from *falling in with the wrong crowd*." He looked directly at Eddie. "Those were her words."

Eddie tipped his head. "Smart woman. I'm guessing I'd be lumped in with the group she'd rather you avoid." He dug through the bed of his truck until he found the new blade. "Your old man and I haven't exactly seen eye to eye over the years."

"My dad doesn't hate you, Mr. Greer."

"Eddie. Call me Eddie."

"Okay, Eddie. He just wishes you were…" Ethan shrugged, "friendlier, I guess."

"How old are you?"

"Fourteen."

"Do you always hang out in the woods, spying on people?" The *royal blue* sweatshirt was not lost on him.

Ethan drew a line in the dirt with the tip of his black tennis shoe. "I'm kind of shy. I don't have many friends." He frowned. "My dad says farming'll be good for me because I don't have to deal with a lot of people. Since I'm the oldest, I'll take over the farm."

"You don't say?"

"My brothers don't want to be farmers. They want to leave Holland Crossing. Well, I don't know what the baby wants." He shrugged. "But I want to stay 'cause I like it here."

Eddie nodded before starting back toward the woods. "Well, if you don't mind, I've got work to do."

The teen followed. "Can I help?"

Eddie stopped. "Why?"

"Because I like to work. I help my dad all the time."

He shrugged. "Suit yourself."

Eddie cut the brush, and Ethan stacked it near the firepit. By dinner time, they had cleared one side of the yard.

"Can I help again tomorrow?" Ethan's eyes were wide with hope.

"Seriously? There's nothing else you'd rather do—watch TV, play video games, throw rocks in the river? Nothing?"

Ethan shook his head. "I had fun today."

"Whatever you want, k... I mean, Ethan. I'll be out here at 10:00 tomorrow."

"I'll be here." He took off toward the woods.

"Wait! Come here a minute."

Ethan returned. "Yeah?"

Eddie pulled a twenty-dollar bill from his wallet and held it toward the boy. "I appreciate your help today. Take this in case you don't make it back tomorrow."

Ethan smiled as he reached for the bill. "Oh, I'll be back. Thanks, Eddie."

The boy took off at a dead run. Eddie watched him until he disappeared into the shadows. Royal blue sweatshirt—it all made sense. He was being stalked by a fourteen-year-old kid.

Eddie walked into the newly remodeled River House. He washed up in the mudroom, grabbed a soda from the fridge, and headed onto the porch. Sitting on the top step of the deck, he stared at the river.

That young boy gave Eddie something he had not known he was missing—Cade. He had wasted so much time hating everyone that he missed out on a life with his grandson and his daughter. For the second time in a handful of months, Eddie cried until there was nothing left inside.

Ethan showed up at 10:00 on the dot for the next several days. He brought his own lunches and drinks and even offered to share with Eddie. Hank took up residency in the hammock while the pair worked side by side, clearing the way for a better view of the future.

48

Eddie

June first had finally arrived. The day could not have been more perfect. The sky's brilliance was indescribable, yet, somehow, Jules captured it in one of her paintings. In the last few months, she not only shared them with Eddie but offered them for sale at Bush's Woods Gallery in town. As a surprise for his wife, Eddie convinced the interior designer to purchase one of her paintings to hang on the living room wall in the River House.

Decision Day—the day Eddie waited for and feared for months. His stomach churned, and his hands shook as he packed a picnic lunch. He paced the kitchen, then enlarged his path, taking on the rest of the farmhouse. Finally, when the house became too tiresome, he moved outside and walked the yard.

His brain was a rollercoaster—replaying memories. At the end of each, he experienced those few seconds of hang-time before he plunged downward into a panic. Jules had given him until June to become the Eddie Greer of decades before. That was six months ago. Had he met the challenge? He hoped so, but he was uncertain if Jules would agree.

They were definitely closer, but Eddie could not take

anything for granted. He had spent forty-two years fighting his demons—not caring about anyone but himself. That was difficult to live down. Ultimately, it might be too much for Jules to forgive. When they first started dating in high school, he was content and happy—as long as he kept enough distance between him and the farm. Now, he had the farm but no life. He knew it was unfair, but his happiness rested in his wife's hands.

A trail of dust followed the Explorer up the driveway. Eddie felt his knees tremble. In the back of his mind, he feared she would not show. At least now that she was here, he had one final chance to state his case. Eddie lifted the cooler and picnic basket into the bed of his truck as he watched her approach.

When she stepped from her vehicle, her pale blue blouse, tied at the waist, fluttered in the gentle breeze. The flip-flop of her sandals and her knee-length tan shorts made his heart skip a beat. How did he never notice how beautiful she was? Sixty looked stunning on her. Eddie glanced down at his jeans and polo shirt. Compared to her, he looked like a slouch. Shorts were not his thing. He could not recall ever owning a pair of shorts.

Wrapping one arm around her waist, he pulled her close. He gently kissed her forehead before opening the passenger side door of his truck. Hank leapt onto the seat. Eye level, the dog watched them. Somehow, Hank knew this was his big day too. Jules laughed out loud.

Eddie threw his free hand to one side. "You gotta help me out here, Hank. I'm trying to woo your mom."

Jules poked Eddie in the ribs. "Woo? Really? What is this—the fifties?" She climbed into the truck and slung an arm over the dog's neck. She kissed the side of Hank's face and pressed her face against his. "There's always been something between us," she chuckled. "Today, it's Hank."

Eddie smiled at his wife as he started down the driveway.

At the T, he turned right.

Jules's brows pinched together. "Are we eating on the hayfield? As I recall, you could barely move the last time we did that."

A wide grin slowly spread across his face. "You'll see. You ask too…"

Suddenly a whooshing sound fogged Eddie's thoughts. Sweat beaded on his forehead, and he could barely breathe. He grabbed his chest and moaned. The truck rolled to a stop in the ditch, and he collapsed against the seat.

"Eddie? Eddie? Talk to me."

Something touched his cheek, and he felt a warmth like none other. His eyes fluttered as he tried to open them. Through the slits, he saw a light—so bright and so beautiful. Music played softly, and a feeling of peace washed over him.

He opened his eyes but quickly closed them. He opened them again. This time, the light was gone, and there was only darkness. Beeping and humming replaced the music that had played moments earlier.

When he turned his head, the first face he saw was Jules's. She flashed him a weak smile.

"What happened?" he whispered.

"You don't remember?"

He gently shook his head. "We were going on a picnic, and…"

Jules's eyes narrowed. "A pic…"

Suddenly, he reached up and touched the cut on her forehead. "Did we have an accident? Are you okay? Did I cause that?"

"I'm fine." She touched her bruised cheek. "I fell at the…"

"Can you tell me your name?" The doctor cut her off mid-sentence.

"Eddie. Edward Greer."

"Good. Do you know what day it is?"

"June first." He gently squeezed his wife's hand.

The doctor tipped his head and glanced at Jules. "Can you tell me the year?"

"Twenty-twenty-three." He coughed. "Can I have some water?"

Jules filled a glass and held the straw to Eddie's lips.

The doctor scribbled something on his clipboard. "Eddie, do you know what happened to you—why you're in the hospital?"

One corner of his mouth hitched upward slightly as he looked at Jules. "Yeah. I was taking Jules on a picnic. It was a surprise." He swallowed hard.

Jules's shoulders lifted in confusion.

Eddie's smile broadened. "The picnic wasn't a surprise. I was taking you to the River House. I remodeled it for you. I'm sorry you didn't see it before I ended up here."

Jules gasped softly. She wedged herself between the doctor and the bed. "Eddie, the River House burned down in the storm. Do you remember the storm?"

Eddie's eyes fumbled across the room, touching everything but focusing on nothing. He tried to make sense of Jules's words. The beeping of the machines sped up. His breathing grew labored, and his heart raced. The doctor slipped a mask over his mouth and nose, but it was confining. He fought to pull it off, but the staff was more determined.

Finally, he successfully pulled it down and whispered, "What storm?"

Jules looked at the doctor. "Go ahead." He nodded. "Nurse, I need two and a half milligrams of Haldol."

Jules sat on the edge of the bed. She spoke softly. "Eddie, today isn't June first. It's September fifteenth, twenty-twenty-two. Four days ago, you and Cade…"

Eddie drew a sharp breath and mouthed *Cade*.

"Yes. You and Cade and the crew were on the hayfield when the storm rolled in. You were on the wagon. Do you remember?"

Again, Eddie scanned the room, trying to recall the events she was referring to. "Cade?" he whispered.

Jules nodded. "Yes. Cade was there. But you were hit by lightning. Do you remember that?" She stared at him. "It knocked you off the wagon. The crew got you into the truck, and Buzz met the ambulance halfway to town."

He shook his head. "Cade?"

"Cade helped save you."

"No. Cade was hit by lightning."

"Cade's fine, Eddie. *You* were the one who was hit. That's why you're in the hospital."

Eddie's head ached. His ears rang with anger. Why was everyone lying to him? He had been there. He saw it happen.

The nurse reappeared with a syringe. The doctor touched Jules's shoulder. "He needs to rest so he can process what you told him. I'm going to give him a mild sedative to help him relax."

"No. Wait, please?" Eddie touched his arm before turning toward Jules. "Cade's dead. I saw the lightning hit him."

"Eddie, Cade's fine. He got knocked to the ground, but he wasn't hurt."

Suddenly, a high-pitched noise filled the room. Covering his ears, he pleaded with God to make it stop. He had no idea the noise was coming from him.

49

Eddie

Jules was asleep in the chair next to Eddie's bed. Her tangled hair looked like it had not seen a comb in days, yet he knew she came and went from the hospital nightly. She had even spent a couple of nights at the farm. But it was unlikely she slept much. Eddie could not take his eyes off her. A palm was pressed against her cheek to hold her head upright. Tiny puffs of air parted her lips with each exhale. Yet, even with saliva trickling down her wrist, the yellowed bruise on her cheek, and a cut on her forehead, she was beautiful.

Eddie finally accepted the events of the past week. *He* had been the victim of the storm, not his grandson. Cade was still very much alive. Much to his disappointment, making Jules fall in love with him again happened only in his subconscious, while he was in the coma. The River House had never been remodeled because it no longer existed. Much of what he believed happened were lies his mind conjured up. The letter from his grandmother and the note from his dad were also part of his brain's deception. Yet, both missives held too much truth for them not to exist—if only in his thoughts. Nothing explained the Greer men more.

Unlike the events his mind twisted into falsehoods, most

memories from the coma had actually happened. The stories were part of his past. They were raw and honest. He had done those things—ruined people's lives. Remembering felt like salt in the wounds he had worked so hard to forget, drawing the venom to the surface. The mayor's son was paralyzed. His dad shot Zeppelin when he was fifteen and attacked him with a baseball bat during the conference game when he was seventeen. And the truth about his father's death, whether by accident or at the hands of his mother, had gone to the grave with her. Without his support or understanding, Jules gave birth to two stillborn sons: *David and Justin*, and she suffered five miscarriages. His daughter, Melia, spent her entire life longing for him to show her even the tiniest morsel of affection. But he had been too self-absorbed and hateful. The poor girl died without ever hearing him say *I love you*. And because of everything he did to her, his wife of forty-two years left him six weeks before the lightning storm. Yet here she was, at his side when he needed her the most.

Eddie closed his eyes. His chest heaved with sorrow for all he had lost and all he rebuilt in his subconscious that had slipped through his fingers like sand. A shudder rocked him.

"Eddie? Are you okay?" Jules sat at the edge of the recliner, attempting to unsnarl her hair and pull it into a ponytail.

"I want to see the bo..." He squeezed his fists and swallowed the word. Old habits die hard. "I want to see Cade."

"You will. He and Amber are planning to stop later today." She grinned. "They've been a little busy lately."

Eddie stared out the window. The sky was angry. Rain fell in torrents. Had a storm not landed him here, Eddie would have enjoyed the magnificent lightning show. Because of the thick glass, it was like watching TV with the sound turned off. He needed to see it, to understand the power of electricity surging through his body—to know it had somehow changed him.

Jules pulled the curtains across the window. "You don't need any reminders…"

"No. It's okay. Leave 'em open."

"Are you sure?" She held the pull rod in her hand, awaiting his final decision.

"Yes." He shook his head and blinked several times. "I just feel so confused. All these memories of my life—*our life*—have gotten twisted up with things that didn't really happen. Yet it all seemed so real. All of it." He rolled onto his side.

"In my…*dream*. I don't even know what to call it. Anyway, while I was unconscious, I kept hearing these voices."

"Voices?"

"I heard people calling my name. Most of the time, it happened when I was on the hayfield, but once it happened in a place I went with my dad." He was quiet for a moment. "And there was often this flash of bright blue—like someone was watching me."

Jules took his hand. "That was probably us. We talked to you, trying to bring you back to us."

A breath left Eddie in a rush. "That makes sense. I heard your voice. But I thought I heard my dad too."

"That could have been Cade. He was quite worried about you."

Eddie let that knowledge wash over him. He had not heard his grandson's voice in so long, he did not even know what it sounded like. Was it possible they sounded similar? He reached out and took Jules's hand. "I have to ask you something."

"Anything."

"If you could live anywhere in the world, where would you choose?"

A tiny smile curled her lips. "You're in the hospital recovering from a lightning strike, and you want to know where I'd live if given the choice?" She laughed softly. "Seriously?"

Eddie nodded. "I do."

"Well," she stared at the door, "I would have chosen the River House, but the storm took care of that."

Eddie rolled onto his back. He could still save his marriage.

With the help of some young nursing assistant who appeared more embarrassed than Eddie, he got a shower for the first time in several days. She avoided eye contact. And when he dropped the soap, he saw her mortification at having to retrieve it.

After breakfast, he took a short stroll with a walker. Randy, a physical therapist twice his size, held on to his gait belt. It was like being on a leash. Hank would have hated... His heart sank. Hank never existed. The perfect dog was just another of his illusions. Randy mistook the tears in his eyes for pain. It *was* discomfort—not from walking, but from waking up to a life he thought he had left behind and no one else deserved.

Eddie finally convinced Jules to go home for some much-needed sleep. She fought him but eventually gave in, promising to return before dinner. He was grateful for some time alone. There were pieces of his new life he needed to set in motion. Exhaustion covered him like a hundred-pound blanket, but he fought it off.

When Jules returned, he was in the vinyl recliner beside his bed. She brought a bouquet and hot coffee that had not been brewed in a two-hundred-cup urn in the hospital cafeteria.

"Oh, thank God. I was beginning to think I had only imagined good coffee existed."

Jules laughed. "You have some visitors in the hallway if you're up for company."

"Yeah," he answered hesitantly.

"You don't sound so sure."

Eddie raised an eyebrow. "Well, if you were sitting here in a gown that played peekaboo with your family jewels, you wouldn't be so anxious to have company either." He rearranged the white blanket over his lap. "I don't know why they can't give you pajamas with a crotch."

"You're fine." She turned around before she got to the door. "Just don't stand up."

Cade cautiously stepped into the room. He never took his eyes off his grandfather.

Eddie's eyes filled with tears. Cade tried to fade into the wall. Jules crouched next to her husband. "Are you okay? We don't have to do this now. We can wait until you're up to it."

He let go of a deep breath and wiped his face on his sleeve. "Cade." He looked at his grandson. "I-I can't believe you're ali—here," he corrected.

Eddie had twenty-two years of misery to make up for with his grandson. *Where would he even begin?*

"Cade knows about your…*dreams*, Eddie."

He nodded. "I don't know what to say." He swallowed hard. "I'm just so sorry—for everything."

A young woman stepped into the room.

Jules touched his arm. "Eddie, do you remember Cade's girlfriend, Amber? And this little bundle is their baby. He was born two days ago."

"He?" Tears rolled down Eddie's cheeks, dropping onto his gown. He no longer tried to stop them or even wanted to.

Cade took the baby from Amber and walked toward his grandfather. He cautiously set him in Eddie's arms. "Grandpa. This is my son."

Eddie stared at his grandson. An overwhelming warmth surged as he cradled the baby in his arms. He glanced back and forth between the two of them. They were his flesh and blood.

"Do you want me to take him?" Cade asked.

"Can I hold him a little longer?"

Cade looked at his grandmother before nodding.

His grandson's voice was lower than he remembered, more mature. Except for the day of the storm, Cade had not spoken to him in years. Eddie studied his face. Cade's eyes were blue. He would never forget.

"We named him Noah. Noah Edward Greer."

Eddie's shoulders shook, and his breathing fragmented as he sobbed with his great-grandson in his arms. "Noah, you will want for nothing." He pressed his face against the little boy's.

"Are you sharing?" Jules finally asked. "I'd like to hold our grandson too."

Reluctantly, Eddie lifted the baby toward her. Once free, he mopped his face with the blanket in his lap.

"Cade, I need to talk to you." He pointed to the edge of the bed, signaling for his grandson to join him. His girlfriend leaned against the doorframe. "Amber, join us. This concerns you too." He waited until they were both seated. "I know you didn't plan to have a baby this young, but life happens." Eddie slowly shook his head. "And, Cade, I screwed your life up in so many ways. If I were you, I'd never forgive me."

Jules narrowed her eyes and looked at her grandson. She shrugged slightly.

"Like me, you had bigger dreams than taking over the farm." Eddie played with the edge of the thin blanket. "I was wrong to take them from you. I'd like to think those aspirations are still inside of you." He reached up and held his great-grandson's tiny hand before returning his attention to Cade. "I want to give those dreams back to you. I don't want to be the asshole my father was."

"Maybe a little late, huh?" Jules jokingly elbowed Eddie's shoulder.

"Maybe *a lot* too late." He drew a deep breath. "I want you all to know I've decided to sell the farm."

Jules gasped. "Eddie! What are you talking about? That's crazy! The farm's been in your family since the eighteen hundreds."

"Grandpa?" Cade looked from his grandmother to Eddie.

He shook his head. "It doesn't matter. That entire time, it's caused nothing but unhappiness. Besides, the decision's already been made. I never found happiness at the end of a pitchfork, and neither will Cade." He looked at his grandson. "I'll pay for college on two conditions."

Cade nodded. "Anything."

Eddie folded his hands and leaned forward. "You support your son no matter what career choice he makes." He reached for Cade's hand. "And you stop drinking." He stared into his grandson's blue eyes. "The Greer men are drunks. And you're one of us." He bit his lip. "I've seen you come home barely able to walk."

Cade smiled. It was the first time Eddie ever saw joy in the boy. "I already quit, Grandpa. I've been sober for six months."

Eddie released a grateful sigh. "Good. Because the Greer curse stops right here, right now."

Jules kissed the top of her husband's head. "Eddie, I think you should rethink selling the farm. We have the money to pay for Cade's schooling without selling."

"Jules, you're not happy there, and I'm certainly not. So why would we keep it?"

A knock on the doorframe garnered their attention. "Don't mean to interrupt." A man and teenage boy stepped into the room.

Jules looked sharply at Eddie. "What did you do?"

Eddie held up a hand to the man in the doorway. "Cade, you and Amber should go home and enjoy your son. Be the happy family your grandma and I never were."

Cade hugged Eddie tightly. "Thank you, Grandpa," he whispered.

No one spoke until the young family left.

"Ed, this is my son…"

"Ethan," Eddie nodded. "I've seen him in the woods near the hayfield." He looked at Jules, suddenly unsure which life that had happened in—*the real one or his dream*.

Ben Mayer looked at his son. "Have you been bothering Mr. Greer?"

Ethan shook his head, confused. "I've never been on his land."

Ben tipped his head. "Okay, let's keep it that way. We respect property, son."

He looked back at Eddie. "If you're serious about selling, we wanna buy. I talked to my lawyer this morning. He'll draw up the paperwork while you're out of commission. I'll hire an appraiser to give us a fair price."

Eddie shook his head. "Not necessary. I know what the land's worth. I'll sell it to you for less than that." He grabbed a piece of paper from the nightstand and handed it to Ben. "The top number's what I could get from anyone else. The bottom's what I'm asking from you."

Ben's eyes widened. "That's quite generous, Ed."

"But you need to understand something." He locked fingers with Jules. "I'm keeping ten acres along the river where the River House was. I'm gonna build my wife the house of her dreams." Jules's mouth dropped open.

"That's fair." Ben shook Ed's hand. "Are you okay with my lawyer drawing up the paperwork?"

"I trust you to do what's right for both of us."

Eddie looked at Ethan. "I have a feeling you'll be at the helm of the farm one day."

"I will. I love farming." The young boy grinned.

"Good. Then I'm leaving the farm in the right hands." He looked at Ben Mayer. "As for my crew…"

"Not to worry, Ed. With that much more land, I'll keep 'em on. You're a highly respected farmer around Holland Crossing. If you think they're good, they all have jobs."

The words *highly respected farmer* echoed inside Eddie. He never thought of himself in that regard. He spent his entire life believing the townspeople saw him as a drunk and a failure. Perhaps Jules was right. Maybe he was wrong about the small town all along.

With a second handshake, Ben and his son left to take care of the details. Seconds after they stepped from the room, the doctor stepped in. He wore royal blue scrubs. Eddie froze. If the voices he heard calling his name belonged to Jules and the staff, had he also seen flashes of things happening around him while he was unconscious? Had he *seen* the doctor? There was no other explanation.

Once again, Eddie and Jules were alone. He was lying in bed, feeling like a schoolboy about to ask the cutest girl in school to the prom.

He took her hand. "Jules, I won't ask you to come home."

She looked confused. "O-kay?" she questioned.

"After all that's happened, you deserve to be romanced." He winked. "I want to make you fall in love with me all over again."

"Eddie, I've always loved you." She sat on the edge of the bed.

"I know, but I haven't always loved myself. And I definitely haven't loved you the way you deserve." He grinned as he squeezed her hand. "So, prepare to be wooed."

"Wooed? Really?" She laughed. "I don't even know what

that means."

"It means for the next seven months, I am going to spend every day making up for being an ass."

Jules grinned. "Well, that's going to take some doing."

He snorted. "Don't I know it?"

EPILOGUE

June 1, 2023

Rows of white chairs to the right of the newly rebuilt house faced the river. Curtains of tiny white lights hung from the pergola walls. The front of the structure was decorated in white and pink flowers attached to greenery sprays. Rose petals lined the walkway between the chairs. A string quartet played soft music as guests mingled.

Pastor Grace tapped Eddie's shoulder and pointed to her watch. He whispered to Cade, and the two men made their way toward the pergola. Guests scrambled to their seats just before Ethan Mayer came down the aisle, pulling eight-month-old Noah in a shiny red wagon. The boys were dressed in white shirts and tan pants. Each wore a pair of brown suspenders and matching bow ties. A pair of rings, attached to the ends of white ribbons, flew upward when Noah tossed the silk pillow into the air. Ethan stopped several times to brush it off and return it to the little ring bearer. Noah giggled so hard, no one else could hold their laughter.

Suddenly, the music changed, and two women stepped out from behind the house. Eddie's breath caught in his throat. Jules had never looked more beautiful. She was beaming. The spray of white and pink flowers cascaded down the front of her dress.

The pink matched the color of her cheeks. Eddie's breath caught in his throat. He knew he was the luckiest man in the world.

The crowd grew still as the music faded. Grace smiled at the couple and welcomed the congregation. Eddie scanned the crowd. The people he once believed hated him had come to celebrate with them. He belonged in Holland Crossing. He was finally sure of it.

Thousands of white lights strung through the trees lit the night as daylight dimmed. Rows of long tables lined one side of the yard, each decorated with vases of pink and white flowers. Waitstaff placed plates of tenderloin, asparagus, and roasted red potatoes before each person. At sunset, a row of ten small food carts lit up. Each was filled with a different treat: pizza bites, chocolate chip cookies, soft pretzels with dipping sauces, donut holes, popcorn, bruschetta, mini cheesecakes, veggies and dip, chocolate, and fruit kabobs. Mocktails were free-flowing, but alcohol had no place at a Greer wedding.

After dinner, the babysitter took Noah home. A DJ kept the crowd dancing long into the night. Eddie commandeered the microphone multiple times, toasting everyone— especially his wife.

By midnight, the crowd disbanded, leaving Eddie and Jules alone for the first time since the rooster crowed. Eddie wrapped an arm around Jules and walked her to the far end of the lighted dock.

"Well, Mrs. Greer, was today everything you imagined?"

"More." She leaned her head against Eddie's chest and stared into the water. "I never thought our lives could be like this. You're a different person than you were before the accident."

"Thank God." He tilted his chin downward and kissed her gently. "I often wonder whether it was the lightning strike or you walking out on me made me realize everything I was losing."

Jules shrugged. "I suppose both. Dr. Shay said being struck by lightning can change a person's entire personality." She kissed him again. "I'd prefer to think you were ready. I've never seen you this happy. And I've never been more in love with you."

He pressed his forehead against hers. "I wasted a lifetime, Jules. I don't want to lose one more minute."

The dock wobbled as three people approached.

"Looks like it's time, Mr. Greer." Jules winked as she looked toward their visitors. "Amber, honey, you changed."

Amber smoothed the front of her blue dress. "I did. It's *your* turn now." She hugged Jules.

Pastor Grace smiled. "Dearly beloved. We are gathered together to renew the vows of Edward Henry Greer and Juliette Ellen Greer."

Eddie stared into his wife's eyes. She outshone the moon and stars, and she could stop any storm that tried to destroy them—again.

ACKNOWLEDGMENTS

To my husband, Mitch: Thank you for being my biggest cheerleader, alpha reader, and sounding board. You keep my water glass and stomach full. I especially appreciate the encouragement and motivation you periodically deliver in the form of Godiva dark chocolates. You seem to know just when I need them. I couldn't live this dream without your support. I love you very much.

To my beta readers: Laura Chevalier, Bridget Christianson, DeeAnn Eickhoff, Barb McMahon, Cheryl Meld, Ruth Novack, and Linda O'Neil. You read the rough draft with a critical eye, making *The Storms of Eddie Greer* so much better. Your time and attention to detail is immeasurable. A simple thank you is not enough for all you do.

To Beth at BZ Hercules: You started as my editor and became my friend. I am so grateful for everything. I wouldn't want anyone else in my corner when it comes to the *next round* of editing and revising. You are truly amazing!

To the people of McGregor: Thank you for sharing stories and answering my many questions about the town's history. Even growing up there, there were many things I never knew.

To my readers: I appreciate your messages of support, encouragement, and love. Your words live in me.

Mary Perrine

NOTES FROM MARY

For as long as I can remember, I have written stories. There hasn't been a day that I haven't authored something—either on paper or in my head. (Some things are never meant to see the light of day.)

The idea for The Storms of Eddie Greer has circled inside me for a long time. I wanted to pay tribute to the small Minnesota town where I grew up. McGregor was the perfect setting for this book. No matter where I have roamed, it has always been home. Until the end, Eddie never understood the town. He was too blinded by his family's history to see what Jules saw: a loving community who looks out for everyone.

We are the only ones who can change our pathway. So, the next time you see a roadblock, make a turn. Find a path that leads to love.

Always move toward love.

Mary Perrine

BOOKS BY MARY

Hidden

The Lies They Told

Life Without Air

Outside the Lines

The Storms of Eddie Greer

I encourage you to write a review—

especially if you loved the book.

Made in the USA
Monee, IL
17 August 2023

41098838R00184